PRAISE FOR STINA LINDENBLATT

"A feel good, sensual, intoxicating and sexy love story; if you love contemporary romance you do not want to miss *Decidedly Off Limits*." —Slick, Guilty Pleasures

"Sweet, sexy and invigorating, *Decidedly off Limits* is a friends to lovers story that is truly a breath of fresh air!"—Read & Share Book Reviews

"Oh my goodness this book was so much fun!!!"—For the Love of Books (*Decidedly With Baby*)

"There are steamy moments but you are just left with feel good melty moments more."—Books Are Love (*Decidedly With Baby*)

"Be warned dear reader, this book will have you giggling and blushing as you devour it."—The Subclub Books (*Decidedly With Love*)

"...a truly unique and utterly swoon-worthy romance." —Mary Dubé at Frolic/USA Today's HEA (*Decidedly by Chance*)

"This is a great read, fresh, funny, sweet and romantic, with amazing characters and lots of surprises." – Blog on the Run (*Decidedly by Chance*)

"Stina Lindenblatt writes an emotional, heartfelt story about single parenthood, friendship, and love. Add to that great chemistry and tons of feels and this is a great book for anyone who enjoys this trope." – Ari at Red Hatter Book Blog (*Decidedly by Chance*)

"...you'll laugh, you'll cry, you'll swoon and you'll fall in love"—Book Addict Reviews (*Decidedly with Luck*)

"This book needs more than 5 stars, heck, it needs all the stars."—Happy Ending Always (*Decidedly with Luck*)

"I can't wait for more Daniels brothers."—Mary at USA Today HEA (*Cowboy Most Wanted*)

"Are you in the mood for a fun, hot, sweet, romantic read that will have you blushing, laughing and glued to the pages then look no further than *Cowboy Most Wanted*."—The Subclub Books

"HOLY HOTNESS!! Not only this book was a fun read, but it was so sexy as well!"—Blog on the Run (*Cowboy Most Wanted*)

"I'm loving this series!"—Red Hot Blue Reads (*Once Upon a Cowboy*)

"Filled with emotion, intensity, a lot of sexual tension and the perfect amount of heat."—About That Story (*This One Moment*)

"Romantic angst powers this fast-paced novel, and readers will return to the series to learn more about the enigmatic side characters whose own stories are waiting to be told."—Publishers Weekly (*My Song for You*)

"A just-right balance of comedy, tragedy, heat, and ice."—Publishers Weekly (*Heat It Up*)

ALSO BY STINA LINDENBLATT

Contemporary Romances

Carson Brothers Series

One More Chance

One More Secret

One More Betrayal

One More Truth

Spicy Romantic Comedy Novels

By The Bay Series

Decidedly Off Limits

Decidedly with Baby

Decidedly with Love

Decidedly with Mistletoe

Decidedly by Chance

Decidedly with Luck

Decidedly with Wishes

Copper Creek Series

Cowboy Most Wanted

Once Upon a Cowboy

Fix Me Up Cowboy

Visit stinalindenblattauthor.com for more books

FIX ME UP COWBOY

STINA LINDENBLATT

*To the caring individuals who help kids fall
in love with reading and become stronger readers.
You were the inspiration for my heroine.*

FIX ME UP COWBOY

1

KATE

"Toto, looks like we aren't in Kansas anymore," I say to Charlie, my Cavalier King Charles spaniel, as I drive the rental Cadillac through downtown Copper Creek. On Main Street, quaint brick buildings with ground-level stores catch my eye.

It looks like something straight out of a postcard.

Truth? I've never been to Kansas. Or even a small town.

Unless a five-star resort counts as one.

Charlie barks from the passenger seat, accompanied by ABBA's "Dancing Queen" piping through the car speakers. I've been singing and bopping along to the movie soundtrack ever since we left Billings Airport.

"What do you think?" I ask him. "It's not quite Beverly Hills, is it?" No expensive boutiques, no posh spas, no restaurants boasting world-renowned chefs.

No dance clubs with exclusive guest lists.

From what I've seen so far, the closest thing the town has to a dance club is a building with a neon sign proclaiming that it's Joe's Bar.

It looks like something straight out of a movie.

My phone rings and I accept the call.

Drew's voice streams through the car's speaker. "Kate, what's this craziness about you going to Montana?"

That would be brother #1: Andrew. And no, you aren't allowed to call him Drew.

"Hi to you too, Drew," I say, and I swear Charlie chuckles.

Even though I can't see him, I can guarantee my brother is rolling his eyes. He does that a lot around me.

"Why on earth would you go to Montana?"

"The real question is, why wouldn't I come here? The air is clean and the mountains are majestic." Yes, I read that in a brochure about the area.

I haven't been out of the car yet to judge if the part about the air quality is true, but the brochure got it right about the mountains.

"You shouldn't be there on your own."

"I'm not on my own. Right, Charlie?"

Charlie barks in reply.

"That dog won't be able to keep an eye on you and help you when you get yourself into trouble."

"Yes, because I'm such a rebel, always getting into trouble," I say with a laugh. "News flash, Drew—I'm a big girl now."

"You're a woman with a permanent limp."

"What does that have to do with anything?" It's the same argument I've had to deal with from my family since the accident eleven months ago. They seem to think I'm no longer capable of doing anything on my own.

When the limp strategy doesn't work to get me on the plane back to LA, my brother tries Plan B. "You should be here, attending charity events with Lucinda." Our stepmother. "It's a golden opportunity to find the man who will one day take care of you."

"Oh, I'm sorry, I have to let you go, Drew. I have an incoming call from Chauvinists Unite. They want to interview me about your membership application."

"I'm serious, Kate."

"Me, too." Plus, I've long since realized that men aren't interested in me, because of my limp. It's a dark mark against me: I'm flawed. Broken. No longer perfect.

Oh, well. What's a girl to do?

Other than hang up on her brother—which is what I do after saying a quick "Good-bye."

A minute has barely passed before the phone rings again. I quickly glance at the screen, accept the call, and turn off Main Street. "Hi, Tiffany." My best friend.

"Please tell me it's not true?" Her tone drips with feigned horror.

"What's not true?"

"That you're in a hick town somewhere in Montana, packing up your crazy great-aunt's house."

"Yep, that pretty much sums it up—except my great-aunt wasn't crazy." Charlotte is my *deceased* great-aunt from my mother's side of the family. "She just didn't share our families' sentiments about living in Beverly Hills."

Story has it that she moved here in her twenties because she craved adventure.

That, and because she wasn't interested in marrying the man her parents had picked out for her.

Have I met her?

Once, when I was nine years old. She visited us but hadn't been back since. And Copper Creek isn't exactly on the family-approved list of vacation spots.

Not even close.

"But why do *you* have to do it?" Tiffany asks. "Couldn't you just hire someone?"

That's a definite no. My family can't afford to risk a stranger stumbling across some buried family secret that we'd rather remain buried.

And who knows what I'll find in Charlotte's house.

But I'm not admitting this to Tiffany.

A man's voice can be heard in the background on Tiffany's end. At the familiar low rumble of his voice, the equally familiar sensation of porcupine quills prickles deep in my chest and my gut.

Tiffany replies to whatever he asked her, but this time her voice is muffled.

She's your best friend. She couldn't help who she fell in love with. The words keep repeating themselves in my head, with the enthusiasm of a cheerleader hyped up on too much sugar and caffeine.

Granted, it would have been better if Mathew had at least been honest with me and ended our relationship first...and if Tiffany had waited until *after* he and I broke up before having sex with him.

You know what else would have been a fantastic idea? If I had listened to his housekeeper when she warned me he was too busy to talk to me. Instead, I raced upstairs, eager to share my good news with him, found him in bed with Tiffany, and then fled like a criminal caught at a candy-store crime scene.

And while we're adding to the list of great ideas, grief-stricken me shouldn't have hightailed it out of Beverly Hills in my cute Mustang convertible, so I could lick my wounds in private. Then I wouldn't have been in the wrong place at the wrong time when the delivery truck lost control on the highway. It wouldn't have totaled my poor baby, and my leg wouldn't be badly damaged.

Yes, in retrospect, I should have listened to my great-aunt Margie that morning when she warned me that, according to my horoscope, my luck was about to change.

She might have had a point there.

"Darling," Tiffany says, her voice like maple syrup on grilled salmon. "I have to go now. Mathew and I have one of those horribly boring charity events tonight. We promised his mother that we would attend. She's going to introduce me to some important people in the art world." Tiffany fake air-kisses me through the phone and hangs up.

The charity event she's talking about? It's the Reach for the Stars Fundraiser to help kids in low-income families achieve their full potential. I was involved with the planning, but since it was a romantic couples-only event and I had no one to go with, I opted for an early departure to Copper Creek.

"Hey, don't look at me that way," I say to Charlie. "She and I have been friends forever. She made a mistake, which is why I chose to take the high road and forgive her."

Twenty minutes later, I travel along the neglected driveway leading to my great-aunt's house. It's not so much the road that's neglected as the grass. It's at least thigh-high.

My gaze moves from the overgrown grass to the house that appears just as ill-kept—and my stomach free-falls. "It looks haunted."

Charlie barks in agreement.

"I wonder how easy it is to sell a haunted house. Do you think there's a big demand for them?"

Do you think the ghost will have a problem with me living here for the next few days?

And the biggest question of all: how easy will it be to sell a house that clearly needs work done? I don't know about the inside, but the outside is a mess. The large wooden structure is begging for a new coat of paint, the shutters have to be replaced, and the roof has seen better days.

"Maybe the interior looks better." Optimism plays bedfellow with my tone.

Charlie doesn't respond.

I park the Cadillac behind a small, older-model blue

vehicle and climb out. A painful cramp from being cooped up for so long seizes my left thigh—but it's nothing compared to when I take a step.

My leg buckles under my weight, and I grab the door to keep myself upright.

Charlie scrambles onto the driver's seat and whimpers at me.

"I'll be fine," I say, doing my best to reassure him. Charlie isn't a fan of me being in pain. "My leg is just a little grumpy right now, but it'll be a happy camper in a few minutes."

All right—happy might be pushing it, but a girl can hope.

Charlie cocks his head to the side as if trying to decide if he believes me. Then he hops down from the seat, sniffs the ground, and wanders off to find somewhere to relieve himself.

"Don't go on the grass," I tell him. "Otherwise I'll never find you again."

I smooth down the silk organza skirt of my pleated pink floral sundress, which I've paired with my raspberry ballet flats. Dolce & Gabbana meets Tory Burch.

I'll admit that I look better suited for a garden party with royalty than...than this place. But it's one of my favorite outfits.

The sound of creaking wood pulls my attention to the house. Two women my great-aunt's age are now standing on the porch that extends along the front of the building. Both are wearing jeans and T-shirts. Both are smiling at me.

I smile back at them. They're nothing like my grandmothers. These two look like they could be a lot of fun. My grandmothers? Not so much.

And in case you're wondering, sliding down the banister is not considered ladylike. *Wow. Who knew?*

Of course to my grandmothers, partying with your friends at the latest IT dance club is also considered unladylike.

"You must be Kate," the taller, slightly heavier woman says. "I'm Meg, and this is Tilly."

I take several steps forward, my gait slow and robot-like. "It's nice to meet you. I hope you haven't been waiting too long for me." The stiffness in my leg lessens with each step, and I climb up the stairs without too much grumbling from my muscles and bones. Charlie joins me.

"Not at all. Anyway, here are the keys to the house." Tilly passes me said keys.

A phone rings from Meg's oversized, faux-leather purse by some unknown label. She answers it. "Oh. Is everything all right...? Okay...I'll let her know."

She ends the call. "That was Sophie West, Pine Meadow Ranch's brilliant horse trainer. Or as the Daniels brothers like to call her, their horse whisperer. She's unable to show you how to tend to Lady and Scoundrel, but one of the Daniels brothers is coming in her place—"

I put my hand up to stop her flow of words. "Lady and Scoundrel?"

"Yes, Charlotte's horses."

I can feel a slight frown form between my eyes. "Horses? No one said anything about horses."

"Yes, Charlotte loved to ride, and she taught riding lessons. But now that she's no longer with us, someone needs to take care of them. Anyway, as I was saying, Noah is the youngest and is still single. But I'm working on that." She winks at me, and Tilly chuckles.

I'm not paying much attention to what she's saying. My mind is still stuck on the previous part of the conversation. "What do you mean, someone needs to take care of them?"

I retreat a step, ready to flee home, but my flat heel catches on the raised piece of the wooden porch.

Sending me tumbling backward.

Oh, crap.

2

NOAH

I slam shut the hood of the black 1955 Ford Thunderbird that I've been restoring for the past eight months.

"It's looking good," Jake says, standing next to the driver's door.

"Where the hell did you come from?" I glance up at the ceiling of the old barn, searching for signs of the rope he must've rappelled down, James-Bond style.

"It's amazing how you can be so oblivious to your surroundings when you're working on your car. It's about the only time your concentration is on super mode."

He's right about that. "Maybe if school had been about restoring vintage vehicles instead of reading books I didn't care about, or solving math equations I'd never use in real life, my grades might've been better."

"What difference does it make now? It's not like you were interested in attending college."

"But at least then the old man wouldn't have kept asking me why I wasn't more like you." The old man being our grandfather.

"You mean a space nerd?"

I laugh. "Yeah, something like that."

"If it makes you feel any better, I wanted to get a degree in astrophysics. It was Granddad who sat me down for the talk—and I don't mean the kind that involves birds and bees and condoms. He talked me out of pursuing my dream of working for NASA and convinced me to get a business degree so I could run the ranch. He was hoping that would catapult it to a new level of greatness."

What the old man hadn't expected was that TJ—my oldest brother—and I would convince Jake to switch from cattle to horses after Granddad died. It was a risky endeavor because cattle generate more income than horses and because there was already a successful horse ranch in Copper Creek. But Scottdale's focus is on breeding Thoroughbreds. We focus on quarter horses. Future rodeo champions.

Jake's gaze travels over the convertible. "It's looking great. How much longer till it's finished?"

"Maybe another month." Or less. "Then I can start work on Charlotte Wilson's old Chevrolet Bel Air." Once I've moved it here and once I've saved enough money for the parts I'll need.

"But first I have to determine if I can even restore it," I add. I'm good at what I do. Frank—my old mentor in Seattle—trained me well. But I'm no Frank, and I'm no miracle worker. "I'll need to do a cost analysis to estimate how much the repairs will set me back." Frank taught me how to do the calculations. It was the only time math made sense to me.

The look in Jake's eyes at what I just said makes me laugh. "Did the cost-analysis part give you a hard-on?" I've never met anyone else who gets more excited about business talk than Jake. There's a reason he's taken on that part of running the ranch while TJ and I stick with the grunt work.

"Maybe."

"Well, count me out when it comes to relieving it."

He grins. "That's what I have a gorgeous fiancée for.

Speaking of which, she was supposed to go over to Charlotte's and show the new owner how to take care of Scoundrel and Lady. But she got hung up and I volunteered you for the job."

"First—what new owner? Second—why me?"

"Because you're the youngest."

"Dumbass, that line might have worked when I was a kid, but not anymore. You go do it." I have better things to do.

"How about we do rock, paper, scissors?"

"What are we, like eight years old?"

He chuckles. "I was kidding. About rock, paper, scissors, that is. TJ and I are about to see if Thor can knock up one of the mares. But if you'd rather do that..."

I grunt. "Fine, I'll go deal with the new horse owner." Given how long it's been since I last got laid, I'm hardly interested in watching TJ's horse get more action than me. "Please tell me the person at least knows what to do with horses."

Jake shrugs. "I have no idea. Sophie never said anything about that."

With another grunt, I return to the house, cut up an apple, which I put in a Ziploc bag, then head to the old Wilson property.

I don't bother to park in front of Charlotte's house. Instead, I drive along the dirt road to the rear gate that has long since been forgotten. This is the best way to get there; the ground is too rutted for a car, but my truck handles it just fine.

When I was a kid, she and I would hang out at the natural pond at the back of her property. It's the spot where she would bring me cookies and her favorite book: a compilation of fairy tales.

I park near the gate and climb over it. It's easier to do that than to try to open the gate when the hinges have long since rusted.

I head toward the old barn where Charlotte kept the Chevy Bel Air. Unlike the house, the wooded area I have to pass through hasn't changed much. It's where we used to have our adventures together—back when I still believed in pirates and fairies and dragons.

In no particular rush to meet the new homeowner, I pause at the pasture where Lady and Scoundrel are eating grass near the fence. The gray mare spots me and ambles over like she does every time I visit. I remove the apple slices from the Ziploc bag and feed her one. Not wanting to be left out, Scoundrel—the black gelding—joins us a minute later.

"So have you met your new owner yet?" I ask them.

Lady nickers. Scoundrel snorts.

Once they've finished eating the snack I brought them, I head to the barn where the rusty Bel Air is still parked. I can almost imagine Charlotte driving around in the convertible, with the top down, a scarf covering her hair. She has a photo on her mantel of her sitting in the car, looking like Marilyn Monroe, her idol.

The 1954 Bel Air might be rusty, but you can still see bits of its original Neptune-green color here and there. I offered several times last year to buy it from Charlotte. She refused each time, saying the car meant a lot to her. Even though she knew what I was capable of, she wasn't ready to part with it.

She did bequeath it to me, though.

From the looks of things, the restoration won't be quick. Nor will it be cheap.

I lie down to inspect the undercarriage.

3

———

KATE

I windmill my arms, fighting to regain my balance, then grab hold of the porch railing, saving myself from an embarrassing tumble.

"Are you okay, dear?" Meg asks, taking a step forward to help me.

"Yes, thank you."

As soon as the words leave my mouth, Meg is back to excitedly telling me about the mysterious Noah. All I can do is gape at her, still digesting the part about the horses.

So far I've caught, while in my daze, Noah's age: twenty-eight.

His astrology sign: Scorpio.

He has two older brothers.

The rest is a blur.

"So let me see if I've got this right," I say, finally finding my voice. "I'm now the owner of two horses, and there is no stable hand?"

"That's right."

Oh, darn it. I was really hoping I had misunderstood her.

14

"Do I want to know why Charlotte named her horses Lady and Scoundrel?"

"Your great-aunt had a thing for historical romances."

Tilly laughs. "That's a bit of an understatement."

Okay, that makes sense—even if it doesn't solve my current dilemma. "Do you know anyone who's looking to buy a horse or two? Preferably sooner rather than later. I'm only here to pack up the house before putting it on the market, and I don't expect that will take too long."

Not that I've had much experience packing up belongings. When I moved into a guesthouse on my parents' property, the house staff did the actual packing.

But I did supervise—so that must count for something. Right?

Why didn't I just pay someone to pack up Charlotte's place? If I had done that, then I could have stayed in Beverly Hills and continued with the parties and the red-carpet lifestyle I'm used to. Paying someone to do the work for me would have made more sense—to most people.

But that's exactly why I decided to come here. Ever since the accident, the invites to the parties and the dates to hang out have dried up like a prune in the Sahara. I can't dance like I used to. I can't party like I used to.

And, as Tiffany carefully explained to me, I've become a bit of a drag because of my leg.

She's right though, even if the truth does hurt. I can't keep up with my friends anymore. While they were out having fun, shopping, clubbing, vacationing, I was working hard on my physical therapy, just so I could walk again.

So why did I come to this tiny town?

I need to figure out what to do next with my life—a person can't spend their entire existence partying, despite what some of my friends might think.

I also need a break from the reminders that I wasn't pretty

enough or good enough in bed to keep my boyfriend from wandering. And I need a break from the reminders that guys are turned-off by my limp.

Granted, a break at a five-star resort would have been more preferable, but I'm all for a little adventure...even if it means slumming it for a bit.

As long as I'm not expected to camp in a tent with bugs crawling all over the place, I've got this.

And the other reason I'm here? The reason none of my relatives know about?

"You know there's more to life than living in a mansion and having staff wait on you so you don't have to clean the house, do the laundry, or cook," Aunt Charlotte had told me. I was nine years old the summer she had visited my family in LA. Everyone else was too busy with their activities to spend time with her, although I suspected when it came to my stepmother and stepbrothers, it was because Aunt Charlotte wasn't their relative. She had been my mom's aunt.

"Like what?" I asked, my eyes wide with awe, eager to hear everything she had to tell me. From the moment she walked through the front door, I instantly liked her. She was interesting, she didn't try to suck up to anyone, and she loved to tell me funny stories about her life back home.

About some of the adventures she'd had in places my parents would never dream of visiting.

About how she volunteered at the local library, helping kids learn to read.

About how she entertained the kids at the library with her puppet shows.

"Like making puppets out of old socks and scrap fabric," she said. We then spent the afternoon having fun creating sock puppets...and making a big mess.

A few days after Aunt Charlotte left Beverly Hills, my step-mother discovered them and threw them away because people in our position didn't make puppets out of discarded junk. We bought the finest puppets money could buy.

And she did exactly that.

Three days later, I found several expensive new puppets on my bed, but I never loved them the way I had loved the ones Aunt Charlotte and I made.

The other reason—the biggest reason—I'm here is because I want to see the place that my great-aunt had loved so much and to learn more about her. Because deep down, I've always regretted that she and I never got the chance to spend additional time together after that summer.

"You're selling the house?" Tilly asks, sounding a little surprised at my news. She and Meg exchange looks. Maybe it's my imagination, but they both seem disappointed.

"Mr. Oliver didn't tell you?" I ask, stating the obvious. Maybe his lack of comment on the topic is part of attorney-client privilege.

They shake their heads.

I repeat my earlier question. "So, do you know anyone who is looking to buy a horse or two?"

"Can't say offhand that I do," Meg says. "Not older horses, anyway. But we can get the word out that Lady and Scoundrel are looking for a new home."

I smile. "Thank you. That would be great. I don't suppose you know anyone who would be interested in working as a stable hand?"

Both shake their heads. "But we can ask around, if you'd like." Tilly gestures to the front door. "Would you like a tour of the house?"

I nod and mentally cross my fingers—and my toes—that the interior isn't as bad as the outside.

She opens the front door and waves me inside. I step into the main foyer and I do my best not to openly cringe. *Oh, Lord Almighty, there really is a hell.*

The faded mint wallpaper—covered with stripes of jungle green, flamingo pink, and white diamonds—is straight from the 1950s. On the wall opposite the front door, a large golden sunburst mirror hangs above a pale green, wrought-iron hall table. "Oh. My. I can seriously say I've never seen anything like this."

Tilly and Meg don't even blink at my reaction. They continue their tour, and it quickly becomes clear that Charlotte's two favorite colors were mint green and muted pink. Even the toilets and bathroom sinks are pink.

What was she thinking?

Another thing I soon discover as we walk through the house is that my great-aunt liked to collect things. By things, I mean newspapers, horse figurines, old records, magazines.

I pick up the March 1954 issue of Vogue from the top of the pile in what was once Charlotte's bedroom. "Was my great-aunt collecting these, or did she just forget to throw them away?"

"Charlotte loved reading historical romances set in the eighteen hundreds," Meg says, "but her heart was still in the nineteen-fifties. She even has a vintage car from back then. But it's now rusty and doesn't work. She refused to sell it or have the dump pick it up."

I mentally add that to the list of things I'll need to take care of while I'm here.

Or maybe Antonio would like it. He's an artist-slash-horti-culturist who loves turning yesterday's trash into today's plant pot. The guy is absolutely amazing...if not a little odd.

I walk over to the dresser against the far wall. Lying on top of it is a white bunny puppet made from one of Drew's very old athletic socks. My heart does a little happy squeeze. "Bugsy?"

I'd made the funny-looking puppet that summer when Charlotte visited LA and gave it to her before she returned home. I'd stolen one of my brother's new socks and stayed up late to glue the ears and eyes and nose on it.

"I can't believe she kept it all these years," I mutter to myself, smiling, and return it to the dresser.

In the living room, after our tour is complete, I turn around, absorbing everything. "This will definitely take time to clear out," I say on a sigh.

It's a good thing my schedule is free for the next few weeks. I have a feeling this mess will take more than the week I'd originally set aside for it.

"Is anyone joining you to help with this place?" Meg asks.

I shake my head. "I'm a one-woman show."

"Well, let us know if you need any strong men to help you. We have quite a few around these parts who fit the bill."

"And they're single and good-looking, too," Tilly quickly adds—as if that will change my mind.

"I'm sure she has a boyfriend back home," Meg tells her. "Which means it won't matter if they're single or not."

Both women look at me expectantly, waiting for me to confirm this, which is funny, given that Meg was just telling me all about Noah—like she was trying to set us up on a blind date.

At that thought, a shudder races through me faster than a stolen Ferrari chased by a cop.

The likes of which is exactly what happened during my first and only blind date five years ago.

I can't even begin to describe how much fun it was explaining what happened to my father. Fortunately, no nunneries were interested in locking me up and throwing away the key, so all was good. Eventually.

"I don't have a boyfriend." *I'm still dealing with the humiliation of the last one cheating on me.* "And you're right, it doesn't matter if the men are single or not."

Charlie barks at Meg and Tilly, his way of saying he wants to be fussed over. Luckily for him, they speak Charlie. Both women give him the attention he craves.

"Aren't you just a sweetheart?" Meg says.

I grin at the threesome, shifting slightly to take the weight off my leg. "The kids at the library where we volunteer certainly think so."

Tilly straightens. "Charlie volunteers at the library?"

I puff my chest out on his behalf. "He's a reading dog."

"What's a reading dog?"

"He helps kids who struggle with reading. Often they feel self-conscious because they believe they're being judged when they read to an adult. With reading dogs, the kids read the book to the dog. Sometimes they pet the dog to help relieve anxiety. Charlie loves it, and the kids love it."

"I happen to know the librarian in town," Tilly says. "Would you and Charlie be interested in volunteering there while you're here? I can think of a few youngsters who would benefit from that."

"What do you think, Charlie?" I ask him. "Would you like to visit the library?"

He barks his reply.

"Splendid. I'll ask Sarah tomorrow," Tilly replies, deciphering his reply to mean yes.

After the tour of the house, Meg and Tilly leave me to my new, exciting task.

"So what do you say we go check out the yard and the horses that I have no idea what to do about?" I say to Charlie.

We walk through the kitchen...which has less pink than the rest of the house but is still heavy on mint, including the linoleum flooring. The cupboards are hunter green.

I open the back door and follow Charlie onto the patio.

"Oh. My." It would seem that Charlotte wasn't much of a gardener.

Half the square patio stones are split into several pieces, with weeds growing in between. Numerous planters, created from wooden barrels, sit on the perimeter. From the looks of it, nothing has bloomed in them for a while.

In the center of the patio is what was once a pond. I peer into the vast space. At some point it was emptied, keeping it from resembling a swamp.

Taking care not to trip on the uneven stones or catch my heel in another crack, I continue beyond the patio, down a path that is in equally bad shape. But at least the grass isn't thigh-deep here. Someone has mowed it in the past month.

Charlie walks ahead of me, eager to explore the rest of the property. I slowly limp along. The stiffness has finally receded. Now the limp is solely the result of the injury and not because of the long car ride.

Breathing in the fresh country air, I turn my face skyward to the warm sun that kisses my skin.

Okay, maybe fresh is a bit of an exaggeration with the strong whiff of manure lingering in the air. I wrinkle my nose.

"What do you think Roberto would say if he saw the state of this place?" I ask Charlie. Roberto is the head gardener at my parents' mansion. The man has been featured in several prestigious magazines. Which means my parents' property has been featured in several prestigious magazines. "I'm not sure if he would enjoy the challenge of taming this mess or if he would have a heart attack at seeing it."

Or maybe a little of both.

We arrive at what looks like a pasture. Two horses—one gray, the other black—chomp away on grass a couple of yards from where Charlie and I are standing.

"They must be Lady and Scoundrel."

The two horses continue to ignore me, so Charlie and I head toward the closest of the two large wooden buildings at the end of the pasture.

At the sight of the barn, I release a long *What-did-I-get-myself-into?* sigh. "That doesn't look any better than the house."

Nor does the rusty car partially hidden in the grass next to the old building.

This time when I look skyward, it's to ask my great-aunt what the heck she was thinking when she left me the house and the land and the horses and the falling-apart barn.

"Did I wrong you in a lifetime that I'm not aware of?" I call up to the sky.

A muffled noise comes from the other side of the car. A raccoon, maybe?

Before I can step forward to investigate, a man wearing a black cowboy hat stands up.

My heart slams on the brakes, Charlie barks, and I gasp.

4

NOAH

"Sit, Charlie. Is there any particular reason you're on my property?" a female voice says from the other side of the Chevy Bel Air.

I glance up. "Your property?"

There are two things I know about the woman in front of me. One, I've never fucked her, because there's no way I'd forget her if I had. And two, *holy shit*. She's gorgeous...and definitely not my type.

Not unless she's naked.

My type is like the women around town. They dress in western clothing, often flaunting their bodies. They're fun. Looking for a good time. Casual. But they also know how to get dirty.

Everything this woman isn't.

Her pink, flowery sundress reveals curves and makes her legs seem never-ending. It brings to mind designer labels, with a price tag higher than most people's monthly salaries. She probably sleeps in silk sheets and the bed is the only place she fucks. And I bet the idea of being entered from behind while bent over a bale of hay would disgust her.

So pretty much just like my ex-girlfriend.

The only difference is, Samantha was tall, blonde, tanned, and lived in stilettos. This woman has pale skin that has rarely seen sunlight, and her dark hair has a wave to it, like a '60s pinup girl.

She also has a small scar cutting across the outer edge of her eyebrow, and a thick, jagged scar on her shoulder. Both are still pink, so they can't be all that old.

"That's right," she says. Her small dog gazes at me, sizing me up as either friend or foe. Or a juicy steak. "My property. So do you have any particular reason for being on the ground next to my car?"

"I was worshiping it." I run my hand along the vehicle's rusty hood the way I'd caress a woman's naked body.

The corners of her mouth twitch. "Is that so? Do you usually lie on the ground while worshiping cars that don't belong to you?"

"Can't say that I usually do, but I'm always up for an exception." I wink at her.

"Okay, well, I'll just leave you to your worshiping while I contact the police about you trespassing on my property."

I laugh. "I don't think the sheriff will be too concerned about me being here."

"Why not? Oh, you're not by any chance him? The Sheriff?"

"No, but he is a friend of mine. Well, more like family now. He's the brother-in-law of my oldest brother." He's also TJ's best friend.

"And does he not believe in upholding the law when the brother of his brother-in-law breaks it?"

"Well, given that I've spent more time on this property over the past twenty years than you have, he might not see it as trespassing. And how do I know you're not the one who's trespassing?"

"You have me there, Mister...?"

"You can call me Noah." I wipe my dirty palms against my jeans and hold out my hand to her. "And just so you know, the car actually belongs to me. I just haven't had a chance to move it to my ranch yet."

The woman's gaze drops to my hand. It doesn't share the look of disdain that Samantha's would have adopted, but it does hold an edge of uncertainty.

It only lasts for a second before the woman shakes my hand, her grip surprisingly strong, her skin soft. "Charmed I'm sure, Mister Daniels."

"Ah, my reputation precedes me." Which is definitely not a good thing. Not that it matters either way, since I can't see her dropping her standards to roll around in the hay with me.

Not unless she's looking for a distraction...much like Samantha was. I was nothing more than a mindless pastime while she was busy getting engaged.

"And what reputation is that?" A warm, teasing smile plays at the corners of her mouth.

I can't help but smile back. "Take your pick. I'm sure you'll come up with something good."

"I daresay that I will. But right now, all I know is that you're supposed to teach me about two horses that until an hour ago I had no idea I apparently own. And you're telling me that's *your* car"—she points to the vehicle in question—"but my great-aunt bequeathed me her property and everything on it. So I don't see how the car can possibly be yours."

"She left you everything but the car. That, she left to me in her will. You can ask her lawyer if you don't believe me, Miss...? Do you have a name?"

"It's Kate. And this is Charlie." She points to the small dog sitting next to her. "And yes, I'll be double-checking your claim with her lawyer."

I crouch and offer Charlie my hand to sniff. He does, then

happily lets me stroke him. "How is it, Kate, that I've never heard of you before?"

"Why would you?"

"Because I've known Charlotte almost my entire life, and I don't remember her mentioning you. And the last time I was in her house, I don't remember seeing any photos of you either."

"She's my great-aunt. Or was my great-aunt."

I straighten. "I'm sorry for your loss. She was a great person." Kate thanks me with a small smile. "So, what are you? The black sheep of the family? Someone she dared not talk about?" My mouth slides up to one side.

"Unfortunately, I only met her once. She wasn't close to my family. She preferred to live in this town. She didn't like visiting LA, and my family only vacations in exotic locales." She points at Scoundrel and Lady. "Meg said you're going to show me how to look after them."

"My brother Jake might have mentioned that to me, too. Do you know anything about horses?"

She shakes her head. "You mean other than they're big and they poop like any other mammal?"

"That shit is the stuff you'll be cleaning out of their stable every day." A job that I'm sure this princess will never do—much like Samantha would never do it either. The task is beneath them.

If the screwing up of Kate's nose is an indication, she agrees one hundred percent with my assessment.

"You have a dog who I'm sure craps," I say. "Are you telling me you don't pick up after him when you're walking him?"

That was Samantha's number one reason for not getting a dog. The idea of putting her hands anywhere near its shit freaked her out.

Kate lifts her chin. "Of course I pick up after Charlie. But in case you haven't noticed, he's a small dog. Small dogs make small poop. Horses make—"

"A big pile of steaming horseshit." I laugh. "But unlike dogs, you don't put your hand near the crap. You use a shovel and a pitchfork to scoop it into the wheelbarrow." I make a show of checking out what she's wearing. "I don't suppose you have any clothes and footwear you don't mind getting messy?"

She looks down at her outfit—the expensive dress and the expensive shoes—and her skin pales.

Which is quite the accomplishment, given how pale it already is.

"I brought my yoga pants and a pair of sneakers so I'd have something to wear when I pack up the house. But they aren't suitable for cleaning out a dirty stable."

"Maybe Charlotte has something you can wear."

Kate wrinkles her nose in that adorable way of hers. "I'm not wearing clothes that belonged to a dead person."

"It's not like she died in them."

"That's not the point."

"What is the point, then? It's not like she's going to haunt you because you're wearing them."

She rolls her eyes. "Can't I just hire you to clean the stable and take care of the horses?"

"I already have my own chores to do at *my* ranch. I don't have time to drive here twice a day to feed and take care of *your* horses."

"They're not *my* horses." She adds a little extra huff to "my."

"Technically, Princess, they are. According to Charlotte's will, I got the Bel Air." I point at the rusty vintage car. "And you got the horses."

Her lush lips transform into a pout, making her look even more like a sexy pinup girl. A pinup girl who wants to be kissed.

Although I'm pretty sure, given our conversation, kissing is the last thing on her mind. I'd say stomping her foot against the ground—or possibly on top of my foot—is a more likely outcome.

"Fine, I'll hire someone else to take care of them," she says.

"You could try that. But in the meantime, someone will have to look after them. So what will it be? Do you want me to show you what you'll need to do to keep them happy and healthy...or are you going to let them suffer because you're too high and mighty to look after them yourself?" My words contain an equal dose of challenge and mockery. Mockery because she reminds me so much of my ex-girlfriend. Challenge because I know Kate loves animals—or at least she loves dogs.

Charlie stands up, gives a little bark, and wags his tail as if to encourage her to pick the first option.

Kate chews on her lip for a second, her gaze directed at Charlie and then at the two horses, who are busy chomping grass.

After another moment of deliberation, she nods. "Fine, show me what I need to do. But first I have to find something more suitable to wear."

"Is that going to take long? I don't have all day." It used to take Samantha what felt like hours to make up her mind when it came to her clothes.

"It's not like I've inspected Charlotte's clothes yet. I have no idea what she owns."

Which definitely doesn't bode well for me when it comes to how long this could take. "Well, in that case, I'll help you find something."

Translation: the first thing I put my hands on is the outfit she's wearing.

"I don't need your help finding something to wear." The huffiness is in her tone once again.

"I know your type, Princess. I can guarantee you need my help if I don't want this to take all day."

"Would you stop calling me Princess? The last I looked, I'm not a member of royalty."

I shrug—because what do I care if she is or not? I just love the way her eyes flare with her pissed-off attitude whenever I call her that.

Did I ever use the nickname on Samantha? Never. While I'm sure she would've loved to align herself with royalty, the nickname didn't suit her.

Not in the way it suits Kate.

I tap a finger against the back of my wrist and wave for her to get moving. "I don't have all day."

"Fine ," she utters on an I-really-hate-you sigh—which makes me grin.

She starts limping toward the house.

"Are you injured? You're limping."

"It's nothing you have to worry about." She doesn't even turn back to me when she says it. She just keeps walking, head held high. Charlie gives me one long, curious glance, then follows after her.

I chuckle at Kate's sassy attitude and join them. The path is too narrow to walk side by side, so I follow behind them.

I grunt at the thought.

"You sure you're okay?" I ask. "I could carry you if you want."

Or maybe this is her way of getting out of taking care of the horses. A damsel-in-distress move to gain my sympathy.

I bristle at the thought that she's possibly playing me.

"What?" Kate says. "So you can toss me over your shoulder like some kind of Neanderthal? I'll pass on your kind offer, thank you."

"You don't think very highly of me, do you?"

Do I care what she thinks of me? Not at all. From what I can tell, she's nothing like her great-aunt. Charlotte was kind and generous and a force to be reckoned with, especially when it came to my grandfather.

Kate? She comes off as entitled.

And much like Samantha, she has no doubt left a trail of broken hearts over the years.

"You don't come off as the sort who cares what others think of you," she says. "Am I right?" She glances over her shoulder.

Which is an unfortunate thing to do when you're walking on uneven paving stones and not paying attention to where you're going. Kate trips on a stone.

On instinct, I wrap my arms around her waist to keep her from toppling over.

In my attempt to keep her from going down, I yank her against me. Her soft body temporarily yields against me and my own goes on high alert. Her light floral scent is nothing like what Samantha used to wear. It's both sweet and sensual, and not at all in-your-face.

"Careful, Princess," I growl huskily in her ear.

She pulls away from me. Instead of the pissed-off attitude I was expecting, her cheeks are highly flushed, and she murmurs an embarrassed thank-you.

"Anytime, sweetheart," I reply.

We make it to the house without any additional stone-tripping catastrophes. Then after some more protesting from Kate about my offer to help her find something to wear from Charlotte's closet, we go upstairs to her great-aunt's room.

"Are you staying here or at the hotel?" I ask. Yes, our town of three thousand has a hotel. Well, more like a small inn.

"Here." Her gaze travels across the room and she cringes.

"Where's your luggage?" I didn't notice any downstairs, and if Kate is anything like Samantha, she doesn't pack light...even for only a few days.

"It's still in the car. I don't suppose you could help me with it?" The earlier blush returns to her cheeks.

"Sure. I'll do that while you're getting changed." I walk into Charlotte's closet and pull out the first pair of jeans I find and a T-shirt, which I hand to Kate. "These will probably fit you. You look like you're about the same size as Charlotte. You might want to grab some socks from her dresser drawers."

Because there's no way in hell that I'm going riffling through Charlotte's underwear drawer to search for them.

I start walking toward the door, then pause. "I'll need your vehicle key so I can bring up your luggage. Where is it?"

She narrows her eyes at me. "You're not going to steal it, are you? Or go for a joyride?"

I shake my head in exasperation and not in answer to her question. "I'm a cowboy, not a criminal. They might start with the same letter, but I can assure you they aren't the same thing."

She cringes again, but this time out of embarrassment. "I know they aren't the same thing. The key is on the wrought-iron table near the front door."

"Okay, you put those on"—I nod at the pile of clothing in her hands—"while I get your stuff."

"Don't forget the bags in the back seat, too," she hurriedly says as I walk out the door.

Outside, I open the trunk of her rental Cadillac. Yep, just as I expected. It's filled with luggage, each piece fitting perfectly together like a giant puzzle.

And what didn't fit in the trunk was placed in the back seat.

One by one, I remove them from the car and stack them on the porch. Then I take them into the house and carry the largest suitcase up the stairs to Charlotte's room.

The door is open, so figuring it's okay to do so, I enter the room...at the same time Kate steps out of what I'm guessing is the master bathroom.

The moment I see her frown and recognize Charlotte's T-shirt, I burst out laughing.

The slightly big-for-Kate, bright-pink T-shirt proclaims in

large white print, "Yes, I smell like a horse. No, I don't consider that a problem."

Her hair is no longer loose around her shoulders. It's been pulled up into a high ponytail.

"Nice T-shirt."

She glares at me. "I can't go out wearing this."

"Why? Because you think it will offend Scoundrel and Lady?" I grin. "I really don't think they'll care."

To keep her from returning to the closet to find something else, I step in front of it. "Now, I suggest you get your ass downstairs, or else you'll have to figure out for yourself how to look after the horses."

"What about my luggage?"

"I'll bring it upstairs once we're finished. But if you don't get going now, you'll have to bring it upstairs yourself."

She gives me a curt nod. "All right. Lead the way." Her gaze shifts to the closet, and I recognize that look.

"Not a chance, Princess." I nod toward the bedroom door. "You lead the way." Because the moment my back is turned, she'll be in that closet, searching for something else to wear.

At least the jeans aren't too bad on her. They're baggier than what she's probably used to—and not exactly flattering for her body. But the horses and the horse shit aren't going to give a damn, and that's all that matters.

"I don't have anything to wear on my feet...other than these." She holds up a pair of dingy white athletic socks.

"I'm sure we'll find you something downstairs."

Several minutes later, we're walking along the path toward the stable. Kate has on a pair of rubber boots that are too big for her, but they were the only things she would agree to wear.

And by agree, I mean the look of disgust was marginally less than the one Charlotte's cowboy boots resulted in.

"We'll start with the stable first," I tell Kate.

She groans. Loudly.

I laugh. "Don't worry, you'll get used to it."

"Oh, I have no intention of getting used to it. I'm just here for a week or two to pack up Charlotte's things. Then I'm putting the house on the market and selling the horses."

A week or two? She has enough luggage to last her a few months.

"Which means I need to get to work on finding new owners for the horses and hiring someone to look after them until I do," she says.

I have nothing to say about that—because hell if I'm helping her there—so I keep quiet.

Inside the stable, I grab the wheelbarrow, pitchfork, broom, shovel, and wheel them over to Lady's stall.

"The horses are already outside," I explain, "but normally you'll need to release them into the pasture for the day before you clean the stable, then bring them in for the night. That's the routine they were used to with Charlotte."

Kate stares at me as if I've just spoken in Russian. "Bring them in? Do you mean you just open the pasture gate and they return to the stable?"

"Not exactly. You'll have to put a halter on them to lead them in."

Her expression is a tug-o-war of horror and confusion, with horror on the winning side.

"And how exactly do I do that?"

Christ, this is going to be harder than I was expecting.

5

KATE

The next morning, I'm awoken by two sounds I'd rather not hear. Especially not at...

I push up the fuzzy white sleep mask covering my eyes and pick up my phone. Six a.m.

Rain hammers the bedroom window and my phone is playing "Good Morning."

Except I've never programmed it to play that song.

I check who's calling, groan, and accept the call.

"Good morning, Princess." Noah's voice is too cheerful for this time of day, and I mentally curse him.

Yesterday, at his request, I gave him my phone so he could program his number, in case I had questions about Lady and Scoundrel.

"Why are you calling me so early? It's still the middle of the night." Okay, that might be an exaggeration. I haven't considered six in the morning to be the middle of the night in over a year. But either way, it's still earlier than I normally get up.

Noah chuckles. "I just want to remind you that even though it's raining, you still need to clean the stable."

"You couldn't have waited to tell me that in, say, oh I don't

34

know, another two hours?" It's not as if I'd planned to clean the stable before that.

Of course if I had my way, I wouldn't be cleaning it at all.

And I won't be for much longer—once I hire someone to do it for me.

"No, it worked better for my schedule to call you now." Laughter sits squarely in his tone.

Jerk.

"I'm sure it did." Especially if he could irritate me so early in the morning. "Well, thank you for the wake-up call, Noah. I'll let you return to...well, whatever it is that cowboys do at this hour."

"Does this mean you're going back to sleep, Princess?" The mocking is still in his voice, only it's been dialed up a notch.

I wish I could. But one of the side effects of the rain is that the pain in my leg increases. Falling asleep again is now impossible.

I release a slow breath as I visualize blowing the pain molecules out of my body. *Nope.* Still haven't mastered that skill yet. My leg is grumpier than a toddler who has skipped nap time.

"No, I'm getting up. I have lots to do today. This isn't a vacation for me, in case you're forgetting."

The sooner I pack up the house, the sooner I can put it on the market and return to Beverly Hills.

I tell Noah good-bye and end the call. Then I get up, swallow an over-the-counter painkiller, and do my morning yoga practice and physical therapy exercises.

By the time I'm finished, the rain isn't coming down as hard as it was when Noah called. Now it's more like a light spring shower.

That isn't so bad. I can live with that.

I pull on Charlotte's rubber boots and the yellow rain jacket that Noah also found in her hall closet yesterday. "Thank God no one back home can see me now," I say to Charlie.

And thank God I'm not a celebrity who has paparazzi stalking her, eager to take a photo to be published alongside the headline, "What was she thinking?" in reference to the celebrity's clothing choice.

My uncle, who stars in a popular home renovation and design show, has had his share of paparazzi snapping his photo. But no one ever criticizes his style choice.

Men don't realize how easy they have it.

"Okay, Charlie. Let's get this over with." I open the back door, and we walk down the path leading to the stable. I take my time, paying attention to the uneven stones. We make it to the stable with no catastrophes.

It's only then that I realize I'm shaking. "Do you think horses sense fear?" I ask Charlie.

And more importantly, are they going to attack me because of it?

They're not wolves, I remind myself. Now if only my inner voice was a little more convincing.

According to Noah, the two horses are actually very sweet and accommodating. But that's easy for him to say; he knows what the heck he's doing.

I enter the small room attached to the stable, prepare two buckets of food, remove Lady's halter from the wall, and head to her stall.

The top half of her door is open, and I show her the halter. "Hi. Do you remember me? My name is Kate and I'm Charlotte's great-niece. Plus, I'm a friend of Noah's."

All right, the last part might not be true, but she seemed to like him yesterday, so I figured name-dropping couldn't hurt.

"I'm just going to put this halter on you and then feed you. Then you and Scoundrel can play in the field while I start clearing out Charlotte's house. I mean unless you want to help me. Because between you and me, I don't know what I'm doing there either. Sure I have an art history degree with a minor in art and design, but that's not too helpful when it comes to packing up the home of a deceased person.

"Heck, it's not too helpful when it comes to cleaning out stables either."

Lady makes a small sound. I have no idea what it means. Maybe she's laughing at me. Can't say that I blame her.

I carefully open the door wide enough so I can slip through the opening. Then I shut it. Charlie waits for me outside the stall.

I wrinkle my nose at the smell of fresh horse poop and cautiously tiptoe the short distance to where Lady is standing watching me. "Please don't take offense, but this is really disgusting."

I repeat the steps that Noah showed me yesterday for putting the halter on the horse. She patiently lets me do it without any complaint.

"Thank you," I whisper, voice a little shaky. I tentatively stroke her neck to show her my gratitude. "How about some breakfast now?"

I lead her outside, to the metal bar in front of the stable, where I tie her halter rope. It takes me three attempts to get the knot right. "I guess that serves me right for never being a Girl Guide," I tell her.

She bops her head in agreement.

I grab her bucket of food from the tack room and place it in front of her. "All right. Don't go anywhere. I need to get your boyfriend." Or husband. Or whatever they are to each other. "Hopefully he's as sweet as you are."

Lady makes the gentle sound she made earlier in the stall. I hope that's a confirmation that Scoundrel is indeed as sweet and obliging as she is.

You're Charlotte's great-niece. That must count for something. Just channel your inner Charlotte.

Yep, easier said than done.

I fetch Scoundrel's halter and approach his stall. My phone rings from my back jeans pocket. It's not playing "Good Morning," so I know it's not Noah.

I remove the phone, check the screen, and accept the call. "Hey, Troy." My cousin.

"So how are you surviving small-town life so far?"

"I haven't seen too much of the town yet." Not that there seems to be a lot to it, judging from what I saw yesterday when I drove through on the way to Charlotte's house. "But so far I'm surviving it."

Troy laughs. "That bad huh?"

"You don't know the half of it." I explain how I'm now the owner of not one but two horses. "And now I'm about to clean their stable. So not only do I have to clear out Charlotte's house, I have to clean the stable every day. But that's not the worst part."

Troy laughs harder. "There's something worse than cleaning a stable? Especially for the girl who gets a rash if she sleeps on anything but Egyptian sheets?"

That's not true about the rash. And yes, I did bring my sheets with me. How could I not? I had no idea what kind of primitive conditions I'd be living under while staying here.

"You haven't seen the state of Charlotte's house. It could be on your father's show." If the house were in LA. "The interior alone should be considered illegal. As soon as I'm finished here, I'll send you photos. But be prepared to look at them with a strong drink in hand." Troy works with my uncle and is super talented. That's because he has practically grown up on Uncle Jacob's renovation sites and is a licensed contractor.

"I can't wait to see them. I think. But now I have a question for you, Kate."

"Ask away."

"Since when do you know how to clean a stable? Hell, since when have you even been within a mile of a horse?"

Scoundrel neighs, which I interpret to mean I need to get moving because he's getting hungry.

"Some cowboy that Charlotte knew came over yesterday to show me what to do," I explain.

"What cowboy?"

I shrug even though Troy can't see me. "His name is Noah Daniels." *Tall. Strong. Sexy. But you don't need to know any of that.* "He and his brothers own a horse ranch outside of Copper Creek." And apparently he likes rusty old cars, if what he's claiming about Charlotte's old car is true. I haven't been able to contact her lawyer yet to confirm Noah's claim.

"We're talking about some crusty old cowboy, right?" There's a shudder in Troy's tone—out of sympathy more than anything.

I chuckle. "Not exactly. He's probably about my age. And good-looking. Especially for a cowboy."

An image of Noah dressed in an Armani suit flashes in my mind, and my body unexpectedly hums. Much like it did yesterday when he prevented me from doing a face-plant after I tripped on the paving stone.

And when he said "Careful, Princess" with his husky voice, well, let's just say I can't remember the last time my body responded that way.

Which just proves my body is more broken from the car accident than originally believed. It's somehow short-circuited.

Yep, that must be it.

"Are you telling me that some cowboy is sniffing around you?" Troy asks, tone wary.

Now it's my turn to laugh. "He's a man, not a dog. And don't worry, I'm positive I won't see him again. I'm not his type."

"What type is that?"

Broken. Imperfect. "The type who favors designer labels." I glance down at Charlotte's old jeans, boots, and rain jacket.

"You mean high-maintenance?" Troy says on a chuckle.

"Hey, I'm not high-maintenance. Now, Lucinda"—my step-mother—"is high-maintenance."

"I won't argue with you on the last part."

Scoundrel neighs again.

"Sorry, I have to go," I tell Troy. "The other horse is getting impatient to be fed."

"Okay, but be careful."

Why do I have a feeling he's not just talking about the horses?

I end the call and cautiously open the door to Scoundrel's stall. "All right, boy. You be nice to me, and I'll give you an extra treat. How about that?"

He makes a noise and shakes his head. I don't know if that's a good thing or not.

I step around his big pile of poop. "Charlotte must have really hated me to do this to me," I mutter to myself. To Scoundrel, I say, "You only have to put up with me for a day or two. Three at the very most. And then you'll have someone better to look after you. What do you say? Do we have a deal?"

I take a step closer to him.

He moves toward me. *Oh, God. He's going to kill me.*

I take a step back...right into the pile of yucky, smelly horse poop.

"Ewww!" I remove my boot from it and frantically wipe the sole and heel against the straw, desperate to scrape away the disgusting mess. "Seriously, what did I do to deserve this? I'm a nice person. I donate time and money to charities. I even forgave my best friend after what she did. What do the karma gods have against me?"

I swear Scoundrel snickers.

"It's easy for you to laugh. You're not the one who's currently trapped in a 1950s time warp. I notice your stall doesn't have tacky wallpaper."

I continue scraping the bottom of the boot against the straw. "That's it. I'll have to burn these boots after I'm finished here."

Get a grip, a voice in the back of my head says. It's the same voice that helped me during the early days after the accident, when I felt like giving up during physical therapy.

If you could survive that, it reminds me, *you can survive stepping in horse shit. You've been through hell and survived. You've got this.*

I let out a long huff. It's right. This is nothing compared to what I've been through. It's just horse poop. It's not an alien that's planning to annihilate me.

"I'm sorry," I say to Scoundrel. "I'm better now. How about we get going with this? I'm sure you're dying to hang out in the pasture." I put the lead rope over his neck, then slip his halter onto his head and over his ears. "Good boy," I coo.

Once I'm finished, I take him out of the stable to join Lady. A few minutes later, he's tied to the metal bar and eating his breakfast.

"I'm just going to work on your stalls now," I tell the two horses. "Then I'll take you out to the pasture to do whatever it is you do out there."

My phone vibrates in my back pocket and I check to see who's texting.

Noah: Have you cleaned their stalls yet?

Me: No. I'm about to do it. But I did survive putting their halters on. They're eating breakfast now.

Noah: Congratulations. Glad to see you're still alive, Princess.

Me: Ha, ha. You're funny.

Noah: Have fun cleaning their stalls.

Ass.

"Okay, Kate," I say to myself. "You've got this." I've already done the hard part—with the halters.

And I've lived to tell the tale.

I mentally high-five myself. I wanted an adventure. What could be more adventurous than cleaning a stable?

At least it's safer than skydiving off the Eiffel Tower.

Which, by the way, isn't on my bucket list.

I gather up the shovel, pitchfork, and broom, and put them in the wheelbarrow. Charlie supervises.

I wheel everything over to Lady's stall. Thank God no one back home can see me. *Good-bye, manicure. It was nice knowing you.*

Eager to get out of there and start work on Charlotte's house, I quickly clean the stall. The floor has to be completely dry before I can spread out the clean straw, but I'll do that later, before I bring in the horses for the night.

At one point, I pause long enough to shrug off the raincoat and hang it over the stall door. Between the physical labor and the raincoat, it's like working out in a sauna.

The cool air pleasantly greets me and I return to my task.

By the time I'm finished cleaning their stalls, one of my French tips has definitely seen better days. But it's nothing that a trip to the local spa won't cure.

Or at least I'm hoping there's a local spa.

I didn't exactly spot one while driving through downtown Copper Creek yesterday.

I untie Lady's lead rope from the metal rail and walk her to the pasture. I remove her halter, close the gate, and return for Scoundrel.

"Try not to get too muddy," I tell the pair after I've removed Scoundrel's halter.

I back away slowly...until suddenly my left foot starts sinking quickly into the mud.

Oh, damnit. I attempt to lift my foot but the boot is solidly stuck. And my right foot is sinking into the mud, too.

Lovely. So this is how it ends.

I survived putting halters on Lady and Scoundrel and I survived cleaning their stable, and now I'm going to die a slow and painful death in the mud version of quicksand.

My insides tighten and swoon, wondering if it's too late to write a will.

Since I'm not eager to die this way, I use my foot as leverage, yanking it up hard.

The good news? My foot is no longer stuck.

The bad news? My boot is still stuck in the mud, and I'm sailing backward.

Shrieking, I land on my butt with a splat, mud flying everywhere. It's in my hair, covering my skin, soaking through my jeans and my T-shirt and my sock.

Double-damnit.

Charlie barks his concern.

I scramble onto my knees and try to push myself to my feet. But they slip out from under me and I fall face-forward into the mud.

Giving up the goal of getting to my feet, I crawl through the mud to dry land.

This time when I attempt to stand, my feet stay planted firmly on the ground. I pull my phone from my pocket. Just like the rest of me, it's covered in mud.

"That can't be good." I rub the screen against Charlotte's T-shirt. All I succeed in doing is smearing the mud and making things worse.

I let out a hard breath. "I really miss Beverly Hills, Charlie."

He barks a more upbeat sound.

"You're right. I just need to make some apple strudel and everything will be better."

Do I know how to make strudel?

Not at all.

But how hard can it be?

6

KATE

As soon as I return to the house, I head upstairs to shower. The bathroom is thick with steam by the time I'm finished, but not a molecule of mud remains.

On me anyway.

The same can't be said about the pink tile floor or Charlotte's clothes.

"I guess before I can start making the strudel, I need to do some laundry and clean the bathroom," I tell Charlie.

I change into a light-pink sundress, and then with the muddy clothes held well in front of me, I carry them downstairs to the laundry room and dump them into the washing machine.

Studying the control panel, I frown. "Any idea what I'm supposed to do now?" I ask my trusted sidekick.

The advantage of living in one of my parents' guesthouses is that housekeeping does my laundry.

But how hard can it be?

I scan the array of laundry supplies, select a bottle of bright-pink liquid soap, and dump a healthy dose into the machine.

Then dump in some more.

You can never have too much soap—especially when it smells like apple blossoms.

Next, I grab a bottle of bleach. Who knows what disgusting germs were lurking in the mud? Since I don't want to catch any equally disgusting diseases while I'm here, I unscrew the lid and pour some of the contents into the washing machine.

My nose is instantly assaulted by a nasty smell, and I quickly shut the lid. "That should do it," I tell Charlie.

And that's when I spot a bottle of fabric softener with a cute teddy bear on the front. According to the label, it will make my clothes smell like lilacs. It certainly couldn't hurt. I add it to the load, select the hot water setting and the heavy-duty wash cycle, and hit start. "That seems easy enough."

Next up? Cleaning the bathroom floor.

Fortunately, I don't have to hunt too hard to locate the cleaning supplies. They're stored in a laundry-room cupboard.

By the time I'm finished with the floor, it's already after ten a.m., and I haven't even begun packing away Charlotte's house.

Never mind my original estimate of it taking a week or two to pack up everything. At the rate I'm going, it will take me a couple of months to finish.

Things won't be so bad once I've hired someone to look after the horses, I remind myself. Then I'll have more time.

With a damp paper towel, I do my best to clean the mud off my phone. It takes several minutes for me to properly see the screen again. I push the button to bring up the home screen; it remains black.

Oh, no. That's not good at all.

I killed my phone.

Maybe there's a shop in town that can resuscitate it. I have to drive into town anyway to check out the local spa. I can hunt down a phone repair store at the same time.

God, between cleaning the stable, the mud, and the dead phone, the apple strudel has become a matter of life and death.

It's my #1 way of dealing with whatever life hurls at you. Nothing soothes the soul better than apple strudel.

At least that's what Olga always tells me.

I spend the next few minutes searching online with my iPad for a recipe. "What do you think?" I show Charlie the image on the device. "Doesn't it look yummy? And it doesn't look that difficult to make."

All right, I have no idea if that's true or not. I'm a twenty-eight-year-old woman who doesn't know how to cook.

But in my defense, it's not like I've ever needed to, thanks to my parents' cook. Who wants to cook when you have Olga?

I scour through the kitchen for the ingredients. The only things Charlotte doesn't have are the apples. Luckily, I'd bought some yesterday before leaving Billings because of my apple obsession. So I'm good to go.

"All right, Charlie. Let's do this!"

I slip on one of Charlotte's aprons with frills on it, study the recipe, then do the same to the three apples sitting on the counter. "How exactly does one peel an apple?" Not a problem. I search for a video to show me how to do it.

Except the video makes it look easy when in reality, the opposite is true. It takes me several attempts to pierce the skin and remove even a small amount. And forget about the impressively long piece the woman unfurled in one go. Mine comes off in tiny chunks.

Forty minutes later, the apples are peeled and unevenly sliced. I mix them with the flour, almonds, and raisins, and then I put them aside.

Next up is the puff pastry. But if I thought peeling the apples was tough, that's nothing compared to making the dough.

"Why does it keep sticking to the counter?" I ask Charlie. "It looked so easy when Olga made it." Maybe I should have actually *watched* her make her infamous strudel.

The extent of my watching her amounted to me telling her that she was the best, kissing her cheek, and skipping out the door.

None of that is helping me here.

I reach for a knife from the counter and accidentally bump into the bag of flour. Before I can yelp out my warning, it lands on the floor next to my poor, unsuspecting dog.

The bag explodes on contact, and flour covers Charlie—from head to tail.

"Oh, I'm so sorry!" I crouch next to him and brush the flour off him. Unsuccessfully. "Looks like I'll have to give you a bath."

But at least it's not mud. How hard can it be to clean flour from dog fur?

With the apple strudel temporarily abandoned, I carry Charlie upstairs to the master bathroom. I place him on the tile floor next to the bathtub. "Sorry, I wasn't expecting to give you a bath while we're here. I don't have your grooming supplies." Other than his brush.

I fold a towel, set it on the floor, and fill the bathtub with a few inches of water. Then I lower Charlie into it. He barks his happy sound, and I attempt to wash the flour from his long fur.

"Oh, *sugar*," I say at my lack of success. Apparently, flour combined with water creates a goopy paste.

Which is now tangled in Charlie's fur.

Wow, who knew?

In my defense, high school chemistry wasn't my strong point. I swear, my junior year science teacher aged ten years every time we did a lab experiment. All right, I'll admit I wasn't paying attention to the recipe that day when I accidentally created the wrong chemical reaction. No humans or animals were hurt in the making of it.

But the smell? That was something else.

It takes a while, but I eventually get the paste out of Charlie's fur. I remove my soggy dog from the bathtub and wrap him in a pink towel.

He gives me an indignant look as if to say, *Really? Pink?*

"Sorry, this is the best I can do for now." All of Charlotte's towels are that color.

I dry him off and carry him downstairs. My apron and dress are wet and covered in flour, but since I still have to finish the strudel, there's no point changing my dress just yet. I switch the apron to a clean one.

With a lot of effort, a few frustrated sighs, and a string of *I can do this, I can do this, I can do this*, I finally manage to lift the pastry with the filling onto the baking sheet. Some of it is still stuck to the counter, but there's not much I can do about that.

I put the strudel in the preheated oven and start cleaning up my mess.

"I don't remember Olga making this much mess when she cooks." But then Olga wouldn't have accidentally dumped flour on Charlie or the kitchen floor either.

By the time I'm finished cleaning, the yummy smell of baking pastry and apples fills the room. *That's always a good sign.* My stomach growls in anticipation.

On the way to Charlotte's home office, to sort through her desk drawers, I make a detour to the laundry room to put the clothes in the dryer.

The room now smells strongly of bleach. Is that a good thing? I don't know. Hopefully it is.

I open the washing machine and pull out the clothes, one by one, to put in the dryer. "Oh, my," I say, holding up Charlotte's old bright-pink T-shirt. It now has some interesting white blotches and streaks on it. "That doesn't seem right."

I look skyward. "I'm really sorry. I obviously have no idea how to do laundry. Just like I don't know how to clean stables and take care of horses. My skill sets lie more in the realm of shopping and clubbing and having fun."

Once upon a time, they used to give my life meaning. But since the accident, I feel like I'm wandering around without any real direction—other than the volunteering I do with Charlie.

Maybe deep, deep, *deep* down, that's why I decided to come to Copper Creek—I need to throw myself into a project and determine my next steps.

Great idea…in theory. Now I just need to figure out a project to pursue.

And no, cleaning stables is not it.

I toss the clothes into the dryer—bleach stains and all— and start it. With luck, I'll dry the clothes without burning down the house. I'm sure aunt Bertha will be happy to include that Fun Fact in her upcoming family newsletter.

Fun Fact: Kate is now domesticated.

Since the strudel still needs to bake for another twenty minutes, I sort through the desk drawers in the office. According to my great-aunt's lawyer, he set up her estate so that all her bills, like the utilities and Internet, are automatically paid via her bank account. The same thing for the horse supplies.

The drawers don't contain anything of interest. Most of the papers are outdated and can be thrown away as far as I can tell. I dump them into the box marked Recycling.

I remove the last of the papers from the drawer, revealing an old-fashioned-looking key. It's not the house key—that much I know.

"What do you suppose this is for?" I ask Charlie. I haven't found anything in the house so far where it might fit.

The timer on my iPad dings. I turn it off, but as I return to the kitchen, an alarm starts shrieking from there. I stride into the room, half prepared to find flames engulfing the place. Instead, smoke is pouring from around the closed oven door.

Unsure what to do first, I stand motionless, a deer caught in the headlights of a fire truck. It's Charlie's bark that snaps me out of my stupor. I grab the oversized, padded mittens and cautiously open the oven door. Dark smoke unfurls in a big gust.

Oops.

I grab the hot baking sheet and set it on the cooling rack. The strudel doesn't look burnt on top, but juice leaked from holes in the pasty and is burnt onto the metal sheet.

The alarm continues screeching like a chicken that's been sat on. I open the kitchen door to the patio, snatch the tea towel from the counter, and wave it at the alarm. Charlie howls at it, but alas, the alarm doesn't turn off.

After some frantic arm actions on my part, the kitchen becomes less smoky and the alarm decides enough is enough. It finally goes silent—as does Charlie.

"Well, it's about time," I tell it, my tone a little snootier than planned. To Charlie I say, "Okay, so I need a little more practice when it comes to cooking. It just means I won't be throwing any parties while I'm here."

I turn my attention to the strudel. "Other than the gaping holes in it and all the burned juice, it doesn't look too bad." I locate a knife and cut a piece.

Or attempt to.

"Must be the recipe," I tell Charlie. "If I had used Olga's, it wouldn't be so hard. Hers is puff pastry. The recipe I used must be for something else. But it should still be good. It's just a little crunchy."

Charlie eyes me with a doubtful expression.

It takes a little effort, but eventually a tattered slice sits proudly on my plate. With a fork, I break off a piece and pop it into my mouth.

Nodding thoughtfully, I chew on it for several seconds,

make a face, then spit the half-chewed mouthful into the trash. "Oh, that's not good at all," I say around the bitter taste.

I hastily grab a glass from the cupboard, fill it with tap water, and chug down the contents. Normally tap water is a big no-no for me, but desperate times call for very desperate measures.

Surprisingly, the water tastes good. A definite improvement over the apple strudel.

Note to self: once I return home, sign up for cooking lessons.

It definitely can't hurt.

For all I know, I have a master chef inside me, waiting to be released. I just need to find the key to unlock her.

After the less-than-delightful experience with my attempt at cooking, you would expect my apple craving to run away screaming. But unfortunately, that's not the case. Now I crave a sweet apple dessert even more.

We can blame my stressful morning for that.

"How about we go into town for a bit?" I ask Charlie. "I can try out the bakery"—where I should have gone to begin with—"and then we can visit the library."

Tilly had phoned me yesterday after Noah left, to tell me that Sarah the librarian was excited to have Charlie and me volunteer with their program. She'd asked if I could drop by to discuss our availability while we're in Copper Creek.

Charlie barks his reply. I change into a red-and-white strapless sundress with a hem that twirls when I spin around. On my way out the door, I slip on a strappy pair of ballet flats and drive us to the park near the town hall.

Like yesterday, the sidewalk along Main Street isn't busy. Nothing compared to what I'm used to back home. We stroll toward the bakery I saw when I drove through town yesterday. Several heads turn my way as if I'm an alien from another planet.

As always, I'm limping. But I suspect that's not why people are staring. In my designer dress and shoes, I stick out like the Queen of England at a rock concert.

The atmosphere inside the bakery is bright and cheery. I join the line and check out the desserts in the display case while Charlie waits for me outside.

I'm practically drooling at the array of treats. Apple strudel is sadly missing, but the other apple desserts look equally yummy.

While I wait my turn, I watch the woman behind the counter serve the customers. She's tall. Very tall. Maybe six foot. And she has an Adam's apple. She's also smiling and chatting with the customers, asking about their day so far. Asking about the grandkids. Normally when a cashier or salesperson asks you how your day is, it's mechanical, insincere. Not so with this woman. It's warm and welcoming—like the delicious-smelling air.

The lady in front of me leaves, and I approach the counter. The smile from the woman behind it is infectious, and I can't help but grin back.

"Welcome to Copper Creek," she says. "I'm Roxy, and you must be Kate, Charlotte's great-niece."

I feel my eyes widen. "How did you know?"

Roxy laughs, the sound deep and soothing. "Tilly manages the town's Facebook page. Which means everyone in town now knows you're here while you deal with Charlotte's estate. So which dessert would you like?"

It's my turn to laugh. "What makes you so sure I'm getting a dessert? I might be getting a meat pie or a sandwich."

"You had a certain sparkle in your eye while you were checking out the desserts. It told me everything I need to know. I bet I can even guess which one you're going to order."

"All right, which one?"

"The French apple tart. An excellent choice, by the way."

Wow, she's good.

I order that and a cream puff—because who can say no to all that creamy goodness? And after the morning I've had so far, I deserve them both.

"I'm looking for a place in town where I can get my iPhone fixed," I say. "It had a nasty run-in with some mud and doesn't seem to be working."

"Have you tried putting it in uncooked rice?"

I shake my head. "And that will help?"

"It might. It won't get the dirt out of the charging port or the speaker. You'll need to Google how to do that. But the rice will help absorb the moisture. Otherwise, your best bet is to drive to Golden Falls to get a replacement phone."

"What about a spa?" I ask. "My manicure is in desperate need of a repair job."

Roxy chuckles. "I wish we had spa around here. That would be fabulous. But I'm sorry to say that the only spa in Beaver Ridge County is located in Golden Falls, and it's closed for renovations."

"What about a dry cleaner? Is there one here?" After the disaster with Charlotte's clothes, it's clear that I'll need professional help when it comes to washing my own clothing.

She shakes her head. "That would also be located in Golden Falls."

Seriously, how did Aunt Charlotte survive here? How does anyone survive here?

"How about someone who works with horses?" I ask, hoping to at least strike gold with this question. "Do you know anyone who can clean Charlotte's stable and look after her horses on a daily basis? I'm sure Lady and Scoundrel would prefer someone more qualified than me."

Which really wouldn't take much.

"Not off the top of my head, but I can certainly ask around for you if you'd like."

I nod. "I would like that very much. Thank you."

Outside, I untie Charlie's leash from the empty bike rack and we walk to the library. The paper bag with my desserts is in one hand, the leash in the other.

"And maybe while we're in there," I say to him, "I can find a cookbook."

As if answering that question, a rumble of thunder echoes in the valley. Then the sky opens up, drowning poor Charlie and me.

Shish kebab, I'm really starting to dislike this place.

7

NOAH

"So, Deacon," I say to the three-year-old sitting on my shoulders as we walk down Main Street. "Where would you like to go next?"

We've just come from the vet clinic, where we visited with some kittens. It was raining when we first arrived there, but the rain has since stopped.

TJ and Violet—my sister-in-law—have a doctor's appointment this afternoon. And Grandma Meg? Who knows what my pseudo-grandmother is up to with her friends? Usually when they get together, trouble is involved.

"Library," Deacon replies.

"All right, one library coming up." I continue carrying him on my shoulders until we get to our destination. Then I lower him to the ground and help him pull the red wooden door open.

He rushes inside and heads straight to his favorite section with the toddler-friendly shelves. I follow after him, my stomach clenching like it normally does whenever I come in here.

My gaze falls on the old puppet theatre in the corner.

"What are you doing here?" my grandfather's booming voice said behind me. I was seated on the floor with my friends, watching the puppet show.

I turned around and looked up at him. "Watching the show. Grandma said it would be okay."

"Your grandmother doesn't run the ranch, I do. You were supposed to go there after school to do your daily chores." I didn't live at the ranch. I lived with my brothers and parents closer to town. But they had all agreed that it would be good for my brothers and me to help out around the ranch—and earn some money.

"You have no right being here." His voice was huffy like the big bad wolf before blowing down the three little pigs' homes. "Only kids who can read belong in the library."

I had no answer for that, so I mumbled bye to my friends and stood. He was right. I couldn't read. I tried, but the words kept getting jumbled on the page.

With his hand on my shoulder, we walked toward the door, my head forward so no one could see the shame from his cutting words.

"Thomas. Adam. Davison," Miss Wilson said. Her tone was soft, but her words were a bullet shot from a gun. "How dare you treat the boy that way!"

My grandfather turned to face her, and I braced for a bloody showdown.

"He can't read very well, so he's better off on my ranch learning the skills he'll need for when he's working there full-time."

I'd never been asked if I wanted to make the ranch my career. My grandfather just assumed it. My father, a thriller author, had a different opinion, but he was careful about the battles he chose to fight.

Apparently, Miss Wilson wasn't of the same mind. "He's better off in the library where I can help him learn to read." She looked down at me. "If you're interested, that is."

My eyes widened and I swore hope sat up and took notice.

"Well, he's not." My grandfather guided me out of the library without another word to me or Miss Wilson.

I feel a tug on my hand.

"I wanna hear this book." Deacon waves it at me, then leads me toward the colorful reading mat in the corner.

But we don't get that far. I'm stopped by the sight of a damp-looking Kate on a chair there. Logan McKenzie is lying on his stomach in front of her, his casted leg behind him. She's looking over his shoulder as he reads the book while at the same time petting an equally damp Charlie.

The six-year-old looks over at Charlie and continues talking as if he's reading the book to the dog. I step closer. None of them pay attention to me.

He pauses for a moment, sounding out a word. He doesn't get it quite right, and Kate gently corrects him. Logan repeats the word, and she smiles at him. It's a warm and encouraging smile that instantly brightens the room.

Deacon tugs on my hand again, but I'm too mesmerized by Kate to move.

"Come on, Uncle Noah." Deacon gives my hand a harder tug.

At hearing my name, Kate looks up and frowns. Then she returns her attention to Logan.

Deacon leads me to where he wants to sit, hands me the book, and plunks himself onto a large turtle cushion.

I drop down next to him and start reading the story. I ask him questions with each page like Charlotte did with me. He bounces on his butt as he excitedly replies.

"Did you break your leg?" Logan asks Kate loudly.

"Why do you ask?" Her voice is hushed but not enough to keep me from hearing her reply.

"I saw you limping. Will I limp after they take off my cast?"

"I was in a very bad car accident, and my leg required lots of surgeries to help it heal. That's why I limp."

"It didn't heal?"

"It did, but not fully. It had…complications. But your situation is different, so I'm sure you'll be fine." She smiles that warm, reassuring smile again, and nods toward the library doors. "It looks like your mom is ready to leave now. You want to say bye to Charlie first?"

"Thank you, Charlie, for being the best reading dog in the whole wide world." He hugs the dog, who gives a happy doggy grin.

Logan's mom approaches the threesome and spots me with Deacon. She smiles at us. "Hey, Deacon. Hey, Noah."

Deacon waves at her, then looks in Charlie's direction.

I return her greeting, after which, she walks over to collect her son. "Do you want to meet the dog?" I ask Deacon.

He nods with supersonic speed.

I push myself to my feet. "All right."

Deacon scrambles off the pillow and we head over to Kate and Charlie. Logan and his mom are already walking away from the pair.

Kate stands from her chair and nods at me.

"Kate, this is my rambunctious nephew, Deacon. Deacon, this is Kate and Charlie."

"Can I pet him?" Deacon asks her. His parents have an Australian shepherd, and Jake and Sophie have a one-year-old black Lab who practically grew up with Deacon. But even though he's familiar with dogs, Violet taught him to always ask strangers first if it's okay to pet *their* dog.

"Yes, you may. In fact, he'll be disappointed if you don't."

Deacon crouches next Charlie and gently strokes him.

"I texted you earlier to see how things went this morning," I tell Kate. "Since you never responded, I take it things didn't go too well?" There might be a twinge of smugness in my tone, which I guess isn't totally fair. Kate might be cut from the same designer cloth as my ex-girlfriend, but she's not the one who sucker-punched me.

That would be all Samantha.

Kate shrugs her delicate pale shoulders, the scar there more noticeable than it was yesterday. "Sorry, I didn't see it. My phone isn't currently working."

"What's wrong with it?"

"It had an altercation with a muddy puddle this morning. The puddle came out the winner. I'm just waiting to see if my phone can be brought back to life." The corner of her mouth twitches briefly to one side.

"You dropped it in a puddle?"

A slight scowl appears on her face. "Not on purpose. If I had my way, neither myself nor the phone would have ended up in the puddle."

This is getting better and better.

"You ended up in the puddle, too?"

"Well, it wasn't so much a puddle as it was mud. And yes, I ended up in it because my boot got stuck and when I tried to pull it free, my foot came out but the boot didn't go anywhere. As a result, I went flying backward and landed in the mud. So I guess you can save yourself a phone call tomorrow morning." Now she's grinning at the realization that I won't be able to bug her at six a.m. like I did today.

"That's too bad, Princess. I was really looking forward to that. Now my day won't be complete." I wink at her. "So is there any particular reason why you and Charlie are in the library?"

The grin from earlier, the one that lit up the room, is back. "Charlie is a reading-therapy dog. He helps kids who struggle with reading. Instead of getting stressed by reading to an adult, they read to the dog instead."

Well, that's different. "Does he do that often?"

She nods. "Yes. We volunteer weekly at an elementary

school in LA. The kids love reading to him, and it helps improve their skill level."

So Kate's not only beautiful and sexy, she's sweet and giving, too. Which means, she's earned another two check marks in the Why-she's-nothing-like-Samantha column.

But that still doesn't mean I want to get mixed up with her sort again.

"How did Charlie end up being a therapy dog?"

"After my accident, I struggled with depression. One of my cousins thought a puppy might cheer me up, so he gave me Charlie. And he was right. Looking after an energetic puppy helped me forget..." Her gaze drops to Charlie and Deacon. "Anyway, I was bored one day and decided to read to him. He lay down and listened to me as I stroked his fur. I remembered an article about reading-therapy dogs, and I searched online for more information."

Her warm brown eyes returned to mine. "I guess you can say Charlie saved me."

"I'm glad he did." For some unknown reason, a sudden urge to kiss her lunges through me. Without meaning to, I lean in.

"Uncle Noah." Deacon's voice snaps me from my daze, and I step away from Kate, acting as though kissing her is the furthest thing from my mind.

"Yes?"

"Can you get a dog like Charlie?"

"He's a Cavalier King Charles spaniel," Kate tells him. This gets her an If-you-say-so blank look from Deacon.

I laugh. "I'm not sure his breed would make a good ranch dog. If I got one, it would be big and—"

"Manly?" Kate supplies.

Charlie gives me a look that can be loosely translated to, *Who are you calling "not manly"?*

"So, is this going to be a regular thing?" I ask her. "You and Charlie volunteering at the library?"

"For now, yes. I figure it's going to take me about two weeks to sort out Charlotte's house before I can put it on the market. So in the meantime, Charlie and I can spend a few hours while we're in Copper Creek, helping the library with their reading program."

"Noah," a woman says, approaching us. Her face is familiar, but I'm drawing a blank on the name.

She steps closer to me without acknowledging Kate's presence. "Hi, Noah. How are things going?" Her face breaks out into a smile. It's nothing like the one Kate wore a moment ago. This one has a shy yet seductive edge to it.

Yes, I do remember the night she and I hooked up at Joe's, and yes, it was good. But even if she had been the best fuck of my life—which she wasn't—I'm still not interested in a repeat performance. I find things less messy that way.

"I'd better get going," Kate says. "I have a house to clean. It was nice meeting you, Deacon." She nods at me. There's nothing shy or seductive about it. "Noah."

She smiles at the woman—who doesn't even notice—and walks away. Charlie follows her.

"I was wondering if you want to maybe get a coffee?" the mystery woman says, drawing my attention back to her. "I don't have to be anywhere for a few hours." The way she says it tells me it's not coffee she has in mind.

Deacon tugs on my hand. "Uncle Noah. I have to go potty."

"Sorry," I say to the blonde. "Duty calls."

"I can wait."

"I'm sorry, but I'm just not interested. And I do remember saying when we hooked up that it was a one-time thing. And that includes coffee or anything else you're thinking of. I'm sorry, but I just don't date. No exceptions."

Having someone else stomp on my heart isn't on my to-do list. Once was enough with Samantha. Plus, I'm too busy to have a girlfriend.

I don't wait for her reaction. I know from experience that when Deacon has to pee, you don't have a long grace period.

I take his hand and lead him to the men's room at the back of the library.

"Uncle Noah?"

"Yes?"

"What does 'hooked up' mean?"

"Nothing you have to worry about." *For a very long time.*

He nods as if that makes perfect sense.

8

KATE

The next day, my hair is pulled back in a ponytail, and I'm wearing yoga pants and a tank top when I climb the attic stairs. The stable and horses have been taken care of. And after a slight delay, due to two of my brothers and my best friend checking up on me, it's now time to focus on Charlotte's house.

No, my phone still isn't working, but Charlotte's landline is.

And no, I never told Tiffany about the horses and how I have to clean the stable. She was horrified as it was that I was coming here to pack up my great-aunt's house. I thought I'd ease her into the part about the stable...after I hire someone to do it for me.

I also haven't told my stepmother for the same reason. She's already stressed out due to a huge charity event that she's organizing. The news about me cleaning the stable might push her over the edge.

My limp is more pronounced than normal as I climb the stairs, but not enough to slow me down.

I enter the space, and my mouth drops open in dismay. The

64

floor and contents are covered with a thick layer of dust, and an abundance of cobwebs call the attic home. "Oh, my."

The musty smell warns me it's been a while since the enclosed space last felt the brush of fresh air.

I weave past the old wooden chests, cardboard boxes, and a wardrobe straight from the movie *The Lion, the Witch, and the Wardrobe*. "I don't suppose I'll get lucky and find the entrance to Narnia in there," I mutter to myself. Maybe I could find a nice Narnian to help me out here.

I set the broom I'm carrying against a pile of boxes and attempt to open the small window on the wall opposite the door.

It doesn't budge. "Darn it." I try again. Nothing. I release a defeated breath. Yoga and physical therapy haven't prepared me for something like this.

"Oh, well. The sooner I get started in here, the sooner I can finish." And then I can hang out with Charlie downstairs while I take a break. He's currently napping in the living room.

I spend the next half hour clearing the cobwebs with the broom and sweeping the dusty floor. Fortunately, I don't find any spiders. So that's a positive.

Once the task is finished, I comb through the attic's contents.

The wardrobe has an old-fashioned lock that might possibly match the key I found downstairs in Charlotte's desk. I twist the doorknob, half expecting to find it locked. It easily turns, and I open the door.

"Well, hello. What's this?" I'm not sure what I'm expecting to find inside, but it definitely isn't period dresses. I remove the hanger with a dark-red ball gown that resembles one from the 1800s. The bodice is low-cut, the sleeves short and puffy, and an intricate design has been embroidered in black thread above the hem.

When Meg said Charlotte had a thing for historical

romances, she wasn't kidding. The rest of the dresses and accessories look like they came straight out of a novel.

Not all the dresses are from the 1800s. Several resemble fancy dresses from the 1950s.

Wow, these are amazing. I wonder where she got them. They look handcrafted, not something she might have bought from a store.

I can't remember if the Charlotte I met sewed, other than to make sock puppets, but I wouldn't be surprised if she did make these dresses. It seems like something she would have done. The Aunt Charlotte I met was creative.

I close the wardrobe door to protect them from the dust. Then I remove a box from the top of the closest stack and search through it.

And now I know where Charlotte kept her historical romances. Some of them date back to the 1970s. I read the blurbs as I work, setting aside any that look good. The sexy ones. With lots of suspense.

This includes a dozen books from the authors whose stories used to leave my girlie parts tingling every time I read them. It's been awhile since my girlie parts—or any other part of me—has tingled that way.

For a moment my mind drifts to Noah, and my core wonders what it would feel like to have his light beard rub against it. It sighs in anticipation even though there won't be any beard rubbing—or any other kind of rubbing—going on.

I'm not interested in being someone's one-night stand.

Especially not with someone as aggravating as him.

Having made that quite clear to my body, I return to sorting through the attic. My yoga pants are looking less black and more gray from the dust, and my red tank top isn't faring much better.

I slide the almost-empty cardboard box to the side,

revealing a dark wooden chest with intricate flower carvings in it. The chest isn't much bigger than a breadbox.

I attempt to open the lid, but it's locked. The keyhole looks to be the same size as the key I found downstairs. I move the chest to the door and ignore the strong itch to take it downstairs to see if the key does fit. My curiosity will have to be patient a little longer.

My curiosity snorts mockingly at that. As a kid, it used to get me into a lot of trouble. They say that curiosity killed the cat. I'm not sure if that's true, but it did result in a lot of lectures while I was growing up.

Charlotte had been the only person who had embraced it. *"Remember, Kate, everything around us exists because of curiosity. Innovators push the limits of their curiosity to discover something new and wonderful. Never quit trying to get answers and exploring the boundaries of your imagination."*

I had no idea what she meant at the time, but like everything she told me back then, it sounded like cool advice.

Over time my curiosity toned down, mostly due to my stepmother's influence. Apparently, it was eager to play again.

Pushing the curiosity aside, I shift a tall, ornate screen away from the wall—disturbing something big and black with wings from its hiding spot. I scream and duck as it flies toward me.

The creature circles back for another attack, and I scream once more. This time louder and longer—like a girl being chased by a man with a chainsaw. My heart pounds fast in my chest, rattling the cage to make its great escape. When that doesn't work, it aims for my throat and gets stuck.

I flail my arms around, doing my best to protect my head from the fanged creature's claws.

As the bat swoops in for another attempt to turn me into a vampire, I vaguely register the sounds of heavy footsteps on wooden stairs.

I scream again, not that it helps my situation any.

"What the hell? I thought you were being murdered or something," the deep male voice says.

I whirl around to find Noah in the doorway, frowning.

"There's a bat in here—and he's looking to turn me into a creature of the night."

Noah chuckles. "I doubt that, Princess. Vampires are nothing more than a myth."

I grunt. "Are you seriously planning to argue the merits of his existence right now?" I gesture in the bat's general direction.

It swoops across the room, barely missing the top of my head. I duck while at the same time shuffling toward the window. "The darn thing's attracted to my red top."

Forget chuckling. This time, Noah full-out cracks up. "He's a bat, not a bull."

By now I'm closer to where I left the broom, and I lunge for it.

"Before you hurt yourself and that poor defenseless creature, how about I open the window and see if it'll escape?"

"The window won't open."

Noah doesn't believe me. He walks to it and, after a moment, pushes it open.

Go figure.

It doesn't take the bat long to realize freedom is within easy reach. He hurls his icky body through the open window.

It's only then that I realize my heart is still beating fast, and my breath sounds like I'm participating in a spin class.

I lean my hand against the wall and work on slowing them both down.

"Are you okay?" Noah asks.

I nod, still breathing hard. "Yes. Thanks. What are you doing here?"

"I came to check on you and the horses because your phone isn't working, and I heard you screaming."

"And you broke down my front door to rescue me?" That

might be the sweetest thing a man has ever done for me—ignoring the part where I now have a broken door to fix.

"The front door wasn't locked."

"Oh. Right. What time is it?"

"Just before noon."

"Already? I was having so much fun, I lost track of time. Would you like to join me for lunch?"

His gaze travels down my body. "You're not a vegan, are you?"

"Are you asking me because I'm wearing yoga pants?" My very dusty yoga pants.

Right, because he never gets messy working the range—or whatever it is cowboys do.

"Possibly."

"You're safe. I'm not a vegan. I like to eat ice cream and cheese too much to be one. So the invite still stands. I'm not much of a cook"—understatement of the year—"so it won't be anything fancy."

"That's fine by me."

Now that my breath and heart have had a chance to calm down from the bat attack, I take a quick moment to appreciate what Noah is wearing: The green plaid shirt rolled up at the sleeves, revealing taut muscles. Muscles from a hard day's work. The worn-in jeans that fit his body just so. The standard cowboy-approved belt buckle. The scuffed cowboy boots. The black cowboy hat.

Yum!

The men back home pay a fortune to obtain a body like his, thanks to the personal trainers to the stars. The only difference between them and Noah is their choice of clothing—with the men in Beverly Hills favoring designer labels.

Surprisingly, what Noah is wearing is kind of a turn-on.

Not that I'm turned-on or anything.

Doing my best to push the image of Noah's body from my

mind, I walk to the ornate wooden chest near the door and make a move to pick it up.

Before I have a chance to touch it, Noah's strong and capable hands are on it. "I've got it," he says.

"You do realize I can lift that, right?"

"I'm sure you can, but you're making me lunch, so the least I can do is be helpful. That's assuming you want this downstairs."

"I do. Thanks."

His gaze scans the room. "Anything else you need me to bring downstairs?"

"Eventually I could use some help. But I'll pay you of course."

He nods, indicating for me to go first. I turn off the attic light and walk down the steps. My leg aches, but it's mild enough that it doesn't bother me too much. I'm used to it when I walk downstairs.

Noah follows me.

"Where would you like this?" he asks once we're on the main level.

"On the coffee table in the living room would be good. Thank you."

"It looks like a treasure chest."

"With floral designs on it? Not very pirate-y. I daresay I won't find any gold doubloons inside." Although it would be cool if I did. I used to fantasize as a kid of being a kickass female pirate back in the old days, sailing the Caribbean and doing pirate-y things.

I even tried to convince my father to buy me a fancy sword, so I could start practicing for my future career. Mom signed me up for gymnastics lessons instead.

Noah chuckles. "You might be right. Charlotte didn't seem the 'doubloon' type."

We enter the living room, and he carefully places the box on the glass coffee table.

"I take it you knew Charlotte?" I ask, leading him into the kitchen.

"I knew your great-aunt since I was eight years old."

At the fondness in his voice, guilt skittles through me like a tipsy spider.

"You're lucky. I only met her once, when I was nine, and I thought she was amazing. Unfortunately, she wasn't a fan of LA and never visited us again. My family is allergic to small towns, so we never visited her either. I kept in contact with her at first, but like for most kids, the writing thing got boring and I eventually stopped." We tried talking on the phone too, but I was always so busy, and then life moved on.

Recently, I discovered that she had asked my parents several times over the years if I would like to spend the summer in Copper Creek. Without even asking me first, they always told her I wasn't interested.

"That's too bad. And you're right. She was an amazing woman."

"How about you tell me more about her? All I know now is that she liked vintage pink and mint green, had a thing for historical romances, loved the nineteen fifties, and she was a collector. Oh, and she apparently loved playing dress-up. She has several historic costumes in the attic."

"Well, I'll admit the dress-up and the thing for historical romances are news to me. The rest I knew about, but it's kind of hard to miss the color part." He gestures at the green flooring and kitchen cabinets, and I laugh.

I remove the artisan bread from the paper bag on the counter and start slicing it. At least that I can do without any major catastrophes.

"I first met Charlotte when she volunteered at the library," Noah says.

I look up from the wooden cutting board. "She mentioned that when she visited my family. I think that might be why I ended up following in her footsteps years later. She also said that she used to do puppet shows for the kids. "

He nods. "That's right. Every Friday afternoon. They were funny as hell. She got right into character."

"I haven't found any puppets yet." Other than the one I made for her. "But I did notice the puppet theatre at the library."

"She made the puppets but donated them to the library when she could no longer perform."

"How come you never took over her job of puppeteer? Or maybe you did." I grin at him, head tilted to the side.

"I'm not an actor, and I'm pretty sure the kids would throw books at me if I tried."

"I don't know about that. You might have a hidden talent you're not aware of."

I open the cupboard with the plates in it. The door is barely hanging on by a hinge. Whoever buys the house will need to do some serious renovations and home repairs, as well as a complete interior design do-over—starting with removing the wallpaper, retiling the bathrooms and kitchen, and replacing the appliances.

Not that I've given it much thought or anything.

"When it comes to acting," Noah says, "I can guarantee that's not the case."

"So you only knew Charlotte for her puppeteering?"

Shaking his head, he leans against the counter. Another item that could stand being replaced with something more modern—like black marble granite. "No, she was the one who taught me how to read. I hated reading mostly because I couldn't do it. You're a lot like her."

"Because I help kids learn to read?"

"Partly that. And partly because you have the same eyes and

hair that she had. Or at least the same hair she had when she was younger. I've seen photos of her from back when it was black, and her waves were similar to yours."

This I know to be true because I've seen some of her old framed photos around the living room—to fill in my vague recollection of what I remember of her. She looked similar to my mom, before the cancer sucked my mom's life out of her.

"Did she also have my vampire skin-coloring?"

That makes him laugh. "I wouldn't say you look like a vampire. And no, she wasn't pale-skinned. She worked outside on her land, and she rode her horses."

At the thought of her working on her land like a farmhand, my skin tightens three sizes. She gave up the glamour of Beverly Hills and for what? To be stuck in the middle of nowhere, with no Neiman Marcus, Saks Fifth Avenue, Chanel Boutique, or Prada?

"What else did she do?" I ask. "Was she married at one point?" My family never mentioned a spouse, but maybe they didn't know. Maybe he and Charlotte eloped.

"Can't say it ever came up. She wasn't married when I got to know her. I have no idea if she was before that."

I nod, taking in everything he's telling me, starving for more. "So other than looking after her property and volunteering at the library, what else did she do?"

"She used to teach until she retired. She also gave riding lessons. She was always busy with one activity or another."

That sounds about right.

I finish arranging the lunch on plates while Noah tells me more about her. He takes a plate from me, his calloused fingers brushing against mine—and my girlie parts release a dreamy sigh.

I jerk my hand away. *Down, girls.*

The last person in the world I need to get involved with is a cowboy.

Especially one who likes to irritate me half the time.

He's only here having lunch because I'm being a good hostess and because he chased that icky bat out of the attic, I remind my body. Don't get used to him being around.

We sit at the table. Noah hangs his hat off the back of the chair next to him.

"Have you lived in Copper Creek your entire life?" I take a nibble of my bread and cheese.

"No, I left for a while after high school. I returned a few years ago, after my grandfather died, to help my brothers with the ranch."

"Tilly mentioned your ranch has horses."

"That's right. My grandfather used to breed cattle, but my brothers and I switched to quarter horses. Do you ride, Princess?" His mouth twists into a cocky smile.

Because he already knows the answer to that.

"Of course not."

I wouldn't mind riding him, a voice in my head says—and my body thoroughly agrees.

Focus, Kate. Don't think about what it would feel like to ride him.

"Would you like to?" he asks and my face heats up.

No, no, no, he's not talking about riding him. *He's talking about the horses.*

"No, that's okay." I scramble out of my seat, face still hot. "You know what? I really should get going. I need to drive to Golden Falls to replace my phone. But don't hurry on my account."

And with that, I hightail it upstairs.

9

____

KATE

Later the next morning, I'm back in the attic, making up for lost time after I spent yesterday afternoon replacing my phone.

But at least now I've rejoined the twenty-first century.

A bead of sweat rolls down between my shoulder blades, and I wipe my hand across my damp brow. Even with the window open, the room is heavy with dust and heat.

A large part of me wants to ignore the attic, to go downstairs and see if the key I found fits the lock for the box I discovered up here. Cleaning out the attic isn't fun.

Solving a mystery? Now that sounds exciting.

But I can't do that. I have a responsibility to pack up the house—because Charlotte willed me the place and because no one else in my family has time to do it. My brothers and stepbrothers have careers. As does my father.

So the quicker I'm finished here, the sooner I can put the house on the market and return home.

The sooner I can go to a spa and have lunch with friends.

The sooner I can shop in my favorite stores.

The sooner I can block the unpleasant memories of cleaning the stable.

With my curiosity temporarily held back, I continue my task as I sing songs from old movies like Mary Poppins. There's something cathartic about singing "Chim Chim Cher-ee" while dancing around the attic.

Charlie watches me work, every so often barking his opinion on one thing or another. Luckily, this time I don't accidentally uncover any sleeping bats.

By the time my leg is ready to call a strike, I've done a fair amount of work.

"So what do you think?" I ask Charlie. "I'll have to hire some men to help me move the furniture and the heavier boxes downstairs. But otherwise, I'm done up here." *Thank God.* "Once everything is downstairs, I can take photos and contact Florence."

Florence owns an antique store in Beverly Hills. My stepmother's interior designer introduced me to her two years ago. I also have several other contacts who might be interested in some of the items.

I shut the window and go downstairs. Charlie follows me.

In the master bathroom, I gather the essential oils I brought with me from home and run water into the claw-foot tub. Once it's full, I strip down and climb in.

The tension in my muscles dissolves in the heat. I lean back and close my eyes, allowing my nature soundtrack to engulf me. I imagine the feel of the warm breeze brushing against my face. I imagine the woodsy scent of whatever it is that makes Noah smell so good.

All right, the last part was unexpected. But instead of pushing away the thought of him like I should, I imagine his lips against my jaw, his light beard against my skin, his calloused fingers sliding along my inner thighs.

Only it's not Noah's fingers gliding up my legs—they are my own.

They continue to the apex of my thighs, to the one place a man hasn't touched me in a very long time.

I spread my legs a little wider, and gasp slightly at the sensation of Noah's fingers brushing my clit. A spark ignites in my lower belly. He continues teasing me, causing me to moan. I writhe under his touch, my lips parted, eager for a kiss that will never come. The flame in my lower belly grows bigger, wilder... until it consumes me like an out-of-control forest fire. My inner muscles clench hard and I groan out his name.

Is this the first time I've touched myself? Not at all. A woman has needs, and it's not like I have a boyfriend to meet them. But this is the first time it's felt this intense.

Would it feel the same with the real deal touching me versus my Noah-induced imagination?

I mentally shake the thought from my head and finish soaking in the tub—doing my best not to think of Noah.

But every time I redirect my thoughts to my great-aunt, they keep sliding back to Noah. To what he told me about how she'd helped him with his reading.

I finish my bath, change into a sundress, and go downstairs. Even though I've been in the house for three days, the sight of the mint wallpaper—with the pink, white, and green diamonds —still makes me cringe.

At this rate, the only way I'll be able to permanently block it from my mind is to go on a week-long spa retreat once I return to LA.

After pouring myself a glass of wine, I head to the living room with the mysterious key from Charlotte's desk. I settle onto the couch and try the key in the lock. It fits perfectly. Inwardly, I do a happy dance.

The box is filled with several stacks of opened envelopes. One stack in particular has a thin, pink ribbon tied around it. I remove that pile first, my mind racing with all the possibilities of what could be inside.

"Do you think these are love letters?" I ask Charlie, even though I'm quite sure he has no idea what that means.

The envelopes are all addressed to either Charlotte or a man named John Turnbull. The same names are listed on the return addresses. I remove the letter from the first envelope in the pile and read it. It's dated May 3, 1953.

> *My Dearest Charlotte,*
>
> *I wish I could count down the days until I can be with you again. I wish I knew the exact date this war will end. I can't wait to hold you in my arms and make love to you. It's been such a long time.*
>
> *I can't wait to see our new home and to start our life in Montana. I can't wait for you to be my wife.*

He then writes about his time in Korea and some of the men in his unit. He tells of one adventure that has me laughing. The letter concludes with his declaration of love and his hopes that the war will end soon.

I remove the letter from the next envelope. This one is addressed to John from Charlotte.

> *My dearest John,*
>
> *I can't wait for you to see the house and the lands of our new home. You'll love it here. The people in Copper Creek are friendly and the area is breathtaking. Bitterroot Valley is just as we imagined*

it would be. It's nothing like Beverly Hills and it's nothing like LA. It's fresh air and majestic mountains. It's freedom.

She then talks about the town and the people living here and her friends.

I still have your baby with me. That gets my attention. She's parked in the garage, waiting for your return. Like me, she's hoping that will be one day very soon.

The letter ends with an *I love you* and a *Please stay safe.*

I'm reading another letter when my phone announces that my stepmother wants to Skype with me.

"Hi, Lucinda," I say, smiling. "Is that a new dress? It's gorgeous."

"Thank you, sweetheart. I saw it at Chanel and knew I had to have it. It will be perfect for the upcoming tea party that I'm hosting." It's the annual event that leaves the society pages in quite a buzz every time. It's usually a lot of fun, and I always look forward to it.

She glances around her, as if to make sure no one is within hearing range, then leans closer to the screen. "I can't tell you who, because it's a big secret, but there's going to be an engagement announcement at the event."

My insides squish like an accordion with a hole in it. When I was dating Mathew, Lucinda kept telling me that she hoped to one day announce our engagement at the tea party. Now it looks like that honor will go to someone else.

Especially since I'm as close to falling in love as I am flying to the moon. But after Mathew cheated on me, he stole a large chunk of my ability to trust—and I haven't yet found where he hid it.

Add the scars and the limp, and I'm wondering if it's too early to apply for spinsterhood.

Maybe the membership comes with a nice welcome pack from Saks Fifth Avenue. A consolation prize, if you will.

"Are you not getting enough sleep?" Lucinda asks. "You look tired. Let me talk to Rosalita." Her favorite esthetician. "She'll know exactly what you'll need. Then I can send everything to you in a care package."

This is why my stepmother is the best. She's always looking out for me.

"I'll also need something for my hands," I say. "They're kind of a mess, and there are no beauty spas out here." Other than the one in Golden Falls, which closed for renovations.

"Oh, heavens. Let me book you an appointment for your return. And in the meantime, I'll find out from Rosalita what she recommends for your hands while you're in that little hick town."

"Thank you."

"You're a beautiful woman, Kate. I just want to make sure things stay that way. Looks are everything."

Unfortunately, in the world I live in, that is so true. That's probably why there are so many plastic surgeons per capita there. Beauty is everything, especially if you're a female. That doesn't mean I like it, but it's just the way it is—like ice cream in the summer and leaf colors changing in the fall.

"Did you hear the big news about Wilfred Vandenberg?" Lucinda asks, shifting to her gossip tone. It's the one she uses whenever she's got some exciting news she wants to share. "He's getting married."

Married? He's about two hundred years old, give or take a decade.

The last I heard, he was looking for trophy wife number

five. Ex-wife number four recently turned thirty—which will make me over-the-hill by those standards in less than two years.

"Who is he marrying?" Thank God, not me.

"Victoria Gluttenstein."

I blink. "As in my friend, Victoria?" I must have misheard her. That's the only explanation.

"Yes, that's the one."

Holy cow. "Does she know that she's engaged to him?"

I can see her with Wilfred (Will) Vandenberg the third. The two of them had a fling five years ago.

But Wilfred Vandenberg the first? There's no way she would marry him.

"She's the one who told me the news when I saw her in Neiman Marcus two days ago," Lucinda says. "She was positively glowing."

Lucinda continues to gush about the news, but I don't hear a single word. Victoria is one of my closest friends, and yet she never told me that she's engaged.

I guess she was afraid I would try to talk her out of it.

And she's right.

I would have.

But then I would have supported her decision.

Because that's what friends do.

"When's the wedding?" I can't imagine it's going to be a long engagement, given his age.

She tells me the date. It's in three months.

Lucinda and I talk for a few more minutes before she has to leave for her massage appointment.

I send Tiffany a text.

Me: I just heard that Victoria is getting married. Wow.

Tiffany responds a moment later.

I know!

My phone rings as I sit there processing everything. I accept the call.

"Wait until you see her dress," Tiffany immediately gushes. "It's gorgeous. And wait until you see mine. It's just perfect. She asked me to be her maid of honor. And we've been talking to the different venues..."

They have? But I've only been in Copper Creek for three days. When exactly did Vandenberg propose to Victoria?

Tiffany tells me all the wedding details that have been confirmed so far. She also gives her own insight as to how she would do things differently. It's not that she's being mean. If Tiffany had been born under different circumstances, I swear she would be a wedding coordinator.

But alas, it isn't a dignified career as far as her family is concerned. It's a career better suited for a commoner (their words, not mine).

So instead of pursuing her dream career, Tiffany has been planning her dream wedding. All I can say is that it's a good thing her family is wealthy. Like the rest of us, her tastes don't run cheap.

Eventually, she has to end our conversation and get ready for a pre-gala party.

And I still have to prepare Lady's and Scoundrel's beds and bring the horses in for the night.

I put my phone on the coffee table and stand. I only make it a couple of feet before my phone pings. I check the screen.

Troy: When are you going to send me those photos you promised? I want to see if the place is as bad as you say.

I laugh.

Me: It's worse.

I walk around the house, taking photos and sending them to Troy, giving him a taste of how out-of-date everything is. Every so often, I tell him how I would lay out the room or how I would make the most of the space. Mostly because he asks for my opinion.

He texts after the photo tour is completed.

Troy: That is bad.

Troy: And you're planning to sell the house like that?

Me: That's the plan. Why? Don't you think I'll be able to?

Troy: Depends on the asking price. But based on what I've seen from the photos, you won't be able to sell it for much. Although I'm sure if there is an enterprising individual in the area, they'll buy the house and flip it.

Me: But at least it won't be my problem anymore.

Troy: That's true.

Me: And then I can go home and find another project to keep me busy.

Troy: That's true, too.

Troy: Any idea what that's going to be?

I sigh.

Me: Not a clue.

Unwilling to risk yet another phone's life while in Copper Creek, I place my new one on the kitchen table and head out the back door to the stable.

Maybe Lady and Scoundrel will have some suggestions for what I can do once I return to Beverly Hills.

Just as long as it has nothing to do with horse poop—or any other poop—I'm all for it.

10

———

KATE

Meg and Tilly—the two women who were at Charlotte's house when I arrived in Copper Creek —are in line at the bakery when I enter to pick up my new favorite treats. Both are wearing jeans and matching white T-shirts. Meg's top states that she's Trouble Maker #1. Tilly is Trouble Maker #2.

"Hi, Kate," Meg says, smiling. Tilly also grins at me.

"I love the T-shirts."

I couldn't imagine my grandmothers wearing T-shirts like that. But I also couldn't imagine them wearing clothes that aren't from one of their favorite high-end designers.

"That would be my grandson's doing," Meg says. "He's the town sheriff and has one heck of a sense of humor. He's also an ex-Navy SEAL and is still as good-looking and as fit as the day he enlisted."

"And he's single," Tilly eagerly adds. "So, what do you think of Copper Creek so far?"

"I really like it here." But that doesn't mean I can imagine living here permanently—especially given the lack of high-end shops.

85

"What would you like, Meg?" Roxy asks. The customer in front of the two older ladies has already walked away from the counter.

"A nice, tall, handsome man to keep me warm at night." She sighs, then giggles.

"I think Roxy was referring to what you would like to order," Tilly says with a laugh.

"Well, if Roxy is now offering a nice, tall, handsome man on the menu, I'll take that. But otherwise I'll have a banana nut muffin and a peppermint tea."

"I can help you with the latter two," Roxy says. "Not so much with the first request."

"Would you like to join us?" Meg asks me and gestures to the small, round cafe-style tables. There's no one here except for a group of either young mothers or nannies, who are talking and cuddling sleeping babies.

"I would like that very much," I say. "I'd love to know more about my great-aunt, if that's okay with you." I figure they will have a different perspective of what she was like than Noah did. And maybe they will know something about the mysterious John.

Once we've all placed our orders and paid for them, we carry the food and drinks to a table close to the window.

"How long did you know Charlotte?" I ask them.

"For most of the time that she lived in Copper Creek," Tilly replies.

"I met her once I moved here," Meg says. "She'd already been living in town for a few years by then."

"When did her husband die...or did they get divorced?" Neither my father nor my stepmother had mentioned that she was married or divorced, but because she was from my biological mother's side of the family, they didn't talk about her. And neither did my grandparents.

I take a sip of my ice water.

The two women exchange looks. "She wasn't married," Tilly says.

"She wasn't?" The letters to John said she was living in Copper Creek when she wrote them. "Was she engaged?"

"At one point. Yes. It was an arranged marriage. Her family thought it was an advantageous match. Charlotte disagreed. The way she explained it, she left LA and eventually ended up in Copper Creek."

"What are you looking for in a man?" Meg asks me, leaving me dizzy from the abrupt change of topic.

The image of Noah pops into my head. My face heats as the memory of last night in the bathtub also visits. "A man who is sweet and loyal."

"That sounds more like a golden retriever," Tilly says. "But as nice as the breed is, it's not a man."

Can't say I disagree with her there.

I take a bite of my apple fritter.

"You must have more requirements than that," Meg prompts, giving me a hopeful expression.

"I want a man who will respect me, who will never let me down, a man who is there for me and who will appreciate me for who I am." And as soon as I figure out the last part, I'll be sure to tell him.

When I think about it, Mathew was none of that. Only I didn't realize it until after I caught him in bed with Tiffany.

Oh well. Live and learn.

"Do you like snow?" Tilly asks me.

"I can't say I've had much experience with it." My family has always been more about hot vacation spots than swishing down ski runs. The only exception is Troy, my cousin. He loves to vacation in Lake Tahoe during the winter.

"What about cold weather?"

"How cold are we talking about?"

"Minus twenty degrees."

I shudder at the mere mention of it.

"Must admit that I agree with you there," Meg says, grinning. "Hence my request for a hot-blooded man to share my bed with. Especially in the winter."

"So Charlotte left LA because of the arranged marriage?" I ask. "There wasn't any other reason for leaving her family?"

I can't say that I blame her for that. If my parents tried to marry me off to some guy I wasn't interested in, I would have left home, too.

"She once told me that she felt like a prisoner back in LA. Charlotte was very much a free spirit, an adventurer. Her family had so many expectations of who she was supposed to be. I guess she had enough of it and left."

"Did she ever mention a John Turnbull?"

Both exchange looks again, then shrug.

"The name sounds familiar," Tilly says. "But I don't know why. Maybe he visited once and that's why I know the name. I can't be sure. My memory isn't what it used to be."

Maybe the letters between Charlotte and John hold the answers. I never finished reading them yesterday. I became distracted after sending Troy pictures of the house, and then I went onto Pinterest for some decorating inspirations...just because I could.

"Have you heard of the game where you have to name the person you would marry, make love to, or murder?" Meg asks.

I nod.

"I have a new version. You have a hot cowboy, a hot sheriff, and a hot veterinarian with you on an island. Who would you marry, make love to, or murder?"

Tilly laughs.

"Are these three the only other people on the island?"

They nod.

"Well, murder is easy. The sheriff. Because if anyone can solve a murder, it would be the sheriff. So if he's the one who's killed, then it will be tough to solve his own murder."

"Wow, I didn't think of it that way," Tilly says.

Meg pouts. "All right, who would you make love to?"

Except she says it the same moment the door opens and my bathtub fantasy walks into the bakery.

"Noah," I say, forgetting about the game.

This has both women laughing.

"That's not what I meant," I quickly say.

"Oh, so you would marry him?" Tilly asks in a hushed voice. Thankfully.

"No, I wouldn't marry him. He's a player. Players are designed to break hearts."

"Not if he finds the right woman."

"Are we talking Noah specifically or players in general?" I don't wait for their reply. "Can you give me a second? I need to talk to Roxy and Noah." More like I need to escape the current line of questioning. Now that Meg has me tripping over what I'm saying, I doubt it will be easy to reroute the train back onto the tracks. Not when she seems so eager to promote Noah as my future date or husband.

I practically sprint to the counter, leaving the chuckling women behind.

"Hi, what can I get you?" Roxy asks him.

"I came to see if you had any bat muffins. Or maybe cupcakes with bats on them." He winks at me.

"Ha ha, you're very funny. But you have to admit it was a scary bat. And you have no idea if it had ambitions to turn me into a vampire or not."

"Something tells me you were safe from being transformed into a mythological creature." Noah's mouth slides cockily to one side, and my girlie parts tingle.

Roxy laughs, the sound deep and smoky. She then looks him over, making a *Well-isn't-he-yummy?* sound. Or maybe that's just me making it in my head. "By the way, Noah. No flirting with my customers, please."

"And where's the fun in that? My day wouldn't be complete without one of your donuts and a little harmless flirting with your customers." He nods at me. "Kate specifically."

"Just don't go breaking her heart. The last thing I need is for you to chase Kate off while she's in town. And I promise you this, Noah Anthony Daniels, if you do either of those things, you'll be banished from the bakery for the next year."

I glance over at Meg's table. Both women are watching us with great interest. The young moms—or nannies, I'm still not sure—who are much closer to us, continue chatting as though we don't exist. They're not hanging onto our every word like some people are.

They're not leaning closer to us, trying to catch everything we're saying.

Noah snorts a laugh. "You really play hardball, don't you?"

This earns another deep laugh from Roxy. "What can I say? I know your reputation, and it's my job to protect Kate's virtue." She inspects the display case. "I'll be right back with some more donuts."

"Wow, you've really got her wrapped around your finger, don't you?" Noah says. "You're the only woman I know who's put me at risk of being banished from here."

My gaze darts to the two older women. Both are tilted so far to the side, they're at risk of falling off their chairs.

"What did he say?" Tilly asks, a lot louder than she'd probably realized.

Meg hushes her. "I can't hear anything if you keep talking."

Noah looks over his shoulder at them. "Do I want to know what they're up to?" He jerks his head in their direction.

Smiling, I shake my head. "Probably not."

"Now you have me even more curious."

I lean closer to him. If I move my head slightly to the left, my mouth will be brushing against his cheek. "They want to know who I would marry, fuck, or murder: a cowboy, a sheriff, or a veterinarian."

At the f-word, Noah sucks in a hard breath and then chuckles.

"What did you tell them?" His warm breath fans against my cheek, and the tingling in my girlie parts from earlier increases.

"Wouldn't you like to know?" I laugh and step away.

In time for Roxy to appear with a tray of chocolate-glazed donuts.

Noah steps back, attempting to look innocent.

"Have either of you found anyone yet who can help me with the horses?" I ask.

Roxy shakes her head. "No, but I do know someone who might be interested when he returns to Copper Creek in two weeks. So if you're still looking..."

My insides feel like a balloon that has been untied, and the air is slowly released. I was hoping to have found Lady and Scoundrel a new home well before then.

Which means I'm still stuck cleaning the stable. Unless...

"I'll definitely keep him in mind if I still need someone in two weeks." I look at Noah.

He shrugs. "Sorry, I don't know anyone who would be interested." *Right—except that spark of mischief in his eyes suggests otherwise.* "But I was able to arrange for someone to remove the Bel Air off your property. He'll be there Tuesday."

"So what are you planning to do with it anyway? Sell it for scrap metal?"

"Are you almost finished here?" He nods toward where I was sitting a few minutes ago.

"Almost. I was just asking Meg and Tilly questions about Charlotte."

"All right, I'll meet you out front in ten minutes." He winks at me again and leaves the bakery. A trail of whispering from *all* the women in the store follows him.

Tilly is grinning at me. Meg rubs her hands together, an identical expression on her face.

Why do I have a feeling that's not a good thing?

11

NOAH

Kate emerges from the bakery. She's wearing body-hugging jeans, a red tank top, and matching red shoes.

Shit, she's gorgeous.

Gorgeous, but too much like Samantha.

Money is the center of her world—and her world will never fit in Copper Creek.

My truck is parked in front of the store and I wave at her. She spots me and waves back.

She climbs into the vehicle and fastens her seat belt. "So where are we going?"

"To my ranch."

"Do you live there?"

I put the truck in drive and pull away from the curve. "Yes, with my brothers, my sister-in-law, my nephew, Deacon, and my future sister-in-law."

"You all live in the same house?"

"Fortunately, it's a big house. But yes, and it will be more crowded once Violet and Sophie start popping out lots of

93

babies. It's a good thing I'm planning to remain single and kid-free, or else the place won't be big enough for all of us."

"How come you don't want kids?" she asks.

"Don't get me wrong, I love kids. Deacon is a blast. But love takes trust. And trust isn't something I easily give." Not anymore. Not after Samantha.

Which means I'll just have to enjoy being Uncle Noah to TJ's and Jake's kids.

"I agree with you there," Kate says. "Some people treat trust like it's something they don't have to earn or nurture. If they break it, it's not a big deal. Only it is...."

A strange feeling gnaws inside me that there is more to those words than she's saying, but since I don't want to discuss Samantha, I leave it alone.

We're quiet for a few more minutes. Country music plays on the speakers. It's a comfortable silence. Kate doesn't seem to be the kind of woman who chatters nonstop because she can't handle the quiet.

The main part of town has thinned out, with houses now spaced farther apart, as we drive along the main road to the ranch.

"So have you lived in Copper Creek your entire life?" Kate asks.

"No. I left when I was nineteen."

"You did? Where did you go?"

"All over the place at first. Doing odd jobs. Whatever I could. Eventually, I ended up in Seattle."

"So you're a big city boy, too." It's not a question, but at the same time it feels as though it is.

"I'm not sure if you could say I'm a big city boy. I've been to LA. It doesn't hold any appeal to me. I prefer living in Copper Creek. Seattle is smaller—but not small enough that everyone is in your business."

She laughs. "Unlike here?"

"Yes, that is the one downside to living in a small town, as you know from meeting Grandma Meg and Tilly."

"Grandma Meg? She said the town's sheriff is her grandson. But if he's the brother-in-law of your brother, how does that make her your grandmother?"

"Meg isn't my biological grandmother. She and my real grandmother were best friends. Grandma Meg and her husband, Bert, were like grandparents to my brothers and me. So when my grandmother died, Grandma Meg naturally took over her role and none of us thought anything of it."

"You're lucky."

"How so?"

"I really like Meg. She seems like she'd be a lot of fun as a grandmother. Which means your own biological grandmother was a lot of fun, too."

"Yes, she was." She was the opposite of my grandfather.

"Fun isn't in the dictionary when it comes to *my* grandmothers," Kate says. "They're all about being a proper young lady. No running in the house. No fidgeting. No climbing trees. No wearing short skirts. No cussing. That doesn't mean I didn't do those things—other than the cussing. I just did my best not to get caught, so I didn't have to stick around for a lecture."

I laugh at the image now in my head. "I'm sure Grandma Meg had the no-cursing rule for Austin and Violet. Austin just chose to ignore it. But she definitely didn't have those other rules for Violet. The girl could climb a tree like nobody's business. And I wouldn't be surprised if Grandma Meg has climbed a tree or two in her day."

Kate giggles. "I can see that. It didn't help that I was born into money. My family has a reputation to uphold that has been with us for many generations."

My head briefly turns to her. "So how wealthy are you? Are we talking Rose-on-the-Titanic, old-money wealthy?" My eyes return to the road.

I knew she had money, but I just assumed it was a more recent thing. Like maybe her father is the CEO of some high-tech company.

"I'm not sure what I think of that analogy. She let the love of her life die in the end. I can tell you if a man loved me that way, I wouldn't let him freeze to death in the ocean."

"You're avoiding the question."

"Clearly I learn from the best."

I turn back to her in time to see the smirk on her face directed at me, and I laugh. "Apparently you do."

"Yes, I come from old money. Fortunately, times have changed and I don't need a man in order to survive. There are still expectations placed on me, like there were for Rose, but they aren't the same."

"So no slumming with a guy from the wrong side of the tracks?"

"If we're talking about my grandmothers' view on things, then you're right. That would be strictly forbidden. But strictly forbidden doesn't hold much weight. I still do what I want, which drives my grandmothers crazy."

We pull past the wooded area along one side of the drive-way, revealing the huge ranch house.

"Wow. The place is gorgeous," Kate says. "It's nothing like I was expecting."

"What were you expecting, Princess? A small shack in the wilderness where we all share the same bed?"

She chuckles. "Some of my friends refer to the guest house I live in on my parents' property as a shack. *This* house makes my home look like a shack."

"Well, it's good to know that you're okay with slumming it," I joke. "I'll keep that in mind."

I park the truck in front of the house. Before Kate has a chance to open the passenger door, I beat her to it and help her down.

"This is where you live?" she asks.

"That's right. But I didn't bring you here to see the house. I want to show you something else."

"Really? What?"

"You'll find out when we get there."

"Where are we going?"

"You're not good with surprises, are you?"

She shakes her head. "I'm the worst at them. It's not that I don't like them. I'm just too eager to find out what they are."

"I take it when you were a kid, you were a pain the ass at Christmas when it came to presents."

She grins. "You might be right about that."

"Good to know. Anyway, the thing I want to show you isn't far from here. It's just down that path." I point to the one I'm referring to.

She walks alongside me, limping a little more than the other day.

"Are you going to be okay?" I ask.

For a second she seems confused; then the slight frown on her face vanishes. "Oh, you mean my leg? I'm fine. It is what it is."

Her gaze takes in our surroundings: The freshly mowed grass along the path leading from the house. The training ring where Sophie is currently working with a mare. The stable beyond that. The pasture where the mares and colts graze during the day. The hut where TJ creates the wooden rocking horses he donates to kids dealing with cancer.

"That's really sweet," Kate says after I tell her about the rocking horses. "My only female cousin died of leukemia when we were kids. She always wanted to ride a horse. Unfortunately, she never got the chance."

We arrive at the old small barn where my 1955 Ford Thunderbird is located. "This is why Charlotte willed me her Bel Air.

I restore vintage vehicles. This is what I love to do in my free time."

Kate stares at the car, mouth open.

It's a few seconds before she recovers and lightly traces her hand along the car's hood.

An unexpected twinge of jealousy pumps through my veins, and I briefly wonder what it would feel like to have her touch my body the same way.

"This is gorgeous, Noah. Where did you learn to do this?"

"Seattle. After I left Copper Creek, I eventually ended up there. I helped a guy who was being mugged. He offered me a job and taught me everything I know about restoring old cars. He died over a year ago and willed his equipment to me. I was the son he never had."

She smiles. "You're a man of surprising talents."

"So I've heard." My voice comes out husky, and she blushes.

Kate walks alongside the Thunderbird, her fingers skimming across the recently painted metal. I step closer to her, her subtle floral perfume pulling me in like a fish at the end of a hook.

Driven purely by the craving to test if her skin is as soft as it looks, I brush my thumb against her cheek.

Is it as soft as I thought? Softer.

She tilts her head up, lips slightly parted. My pulse kicks up a notch, my body humming, and I lean down, waiting for her to let me know if I should stop or keep going.

"Uncle Noah!"

Deacon's out-of-breath voice breaks me from the trance Kate has me under, and I jerk away from her. He's running toward us, his little legs covering less distance than his father behind him. Asgard, their Aussie shepherd, is jogging alongside Deacon.

Deacon flings himself at me, and I lift him up into my arms.

"Hey, little buddy. What are you doing here?" Other than preventing me from kissing Kate.

"Where's your doggie?" Deacon asks Kate.

"Charlie's at home. I had to run into town to do a quick errand, and he wanted to keep snoozing."

I eye my brother before returning my attention to his son. "You came all this way to ask about Kate's dog?"

He vigorously shakes his head. "Auntie Sophie wants to know if Kate wants dinner?"

"It was more like Sophie asked if you would like to stay for dinner," TJ tells Kate.

"That's sweet of her, but I just came here to see Noah's car. I have to get back to my great-aunt's house and do some more cleaning. I still have lots of work to do before I can put it on the market."

"How about afterward?" he asks. "You've got to eat at some point today. And you can bring Charlie if you want. Asgard here is good with other dogs. Right, boy?"

Asgard woofs his reply.

"Jake and Sophie's dog is good around other dogs, too."

"It's just TJ's evil cat who might be a problem." I feel my mouth curve to one side.

"Hey, would you quit hating on my sweet and adorable cat?"

I crack up laughing. Deacon laughs, too, although I'm not sure if he understands why I'm laughing.

Kate glances between TJ and me.

"TJ's cat is named after the Norse god Loki. He's as much of a troublemaker as his namesake."

"Loki's a good kitty," Deacon says, then squirms in my arms for me to put him down.

"How much did your daddy pay you to say that?" I ask him.

He gives me a blank look before hugging Asgard.

"Will Charlie be okay around your adorable cat?" Kate asks TJ.

"Don't listen to my knuckleheaded brother. Loki is a great cat, and Charlie will be fine around him. So does that mean you're coming back for dinner?"

"I'd like that. Thank you."

"All right, then. We'll see you later." He dips the brim of his cowboy hat at her and rounds up Deacon and Asgard.

I drive Kate to the bakery and tell her I'll drop by the house in a few hours to help her. "And I know someone who supplies large dumpsters. I can arrange for him to drop one off so we can start tossing what you don't want to keep."

"That would be great." She gives me a quick kiss on the cheek, the sexual tension from earlier lingering at the edges.

Not quite the kiss I was hoping for.

But before my body can respond and pull her closer to me, she's out of the truck and walking to her rental car.

Tonight, my body says. *You'd better be planning to kiss her tonight.*

12

KATE

The moment I step into the house, I hear a muffled thud coming from the living room. Soon after, Charlie enters the foyer and gives an excited bark. I fuss with him for a few minutes as I tell him about the ranch. He listens intently, interjecting a bark into the conversation every so often.

The box with the letters from Charlotte and John is on the kitchen table where I left it this morning. As I make lunch, my gaze keeps drifting to it, and an urge builds to read another letter. Just one.

That's all.

Maybe I can find out what happened to him since his name didn't ring any bells for Tilly and Meg.

I grab my plate and stroll to the table. The green linoleum flooring is cool against my bare feet.

I sit on the chair and remove the next letter from the box. It's addressed to Charlotte:

My dearest Charlotte,

Every time I think of the Chevy Bel Air, I'm reminded of the time we made love in it by Stinson Beach. It's one of my fondest memories of our time there before I was shipped off. The way your dark hair shone in the glow of the sunset. The way it brushed against your bare breasts. The way you said my name in the heat of the moment. Those are the memories that keep me going during this war. Those are the memories that keep me warm at night.

I just know that one day soon we'll be driving down the coast together and reliving that day. Only this time I won't be leaving you. This time I'll be with you forever.

Like with the other letters, he continues with stories about his friends on the front with him. He avoids talking about the horrors of the war, and I suspect that's for Charlotte's benefit. Unlike nowadays, with our 24-7 news on TV and the videos and photos on social media, Charlotte was oblivious to the truth.

I take a bite of my sandwich and read another letter from her. Like before, she shares a fond memory from that trip to the beach.

And let's just say my great-aunt was more adventurous than I realized—especially when it came to the Chevrolet Bel Air's back seat.

I fold the letters away, head upstairs to my room, and change into my dusty yoga pants and a clean tank top. Then I sort through Charlotte's room, which mostly contains junk she stockpiled over the years. Unfortunately, there are no hidden treasures or journals to give me further insight into the woman.

Well, that's disappointing.

I do find some old photos of the two us, taken while she was visiting my family, and some drawings I sent her during the first year or two after that. Charlotte had stashed them in an album with a few other mementos from that trip.

The doorbell rings as I make my way downstairs. I open the front door, but it's not Noah like I was expecting. "Hi, can I help you?" I ask the older man.

"Are you Kate? Noah sent me with the dumpster."

"Wow, that's fast."

"That's what happens when you owe Noah a favor. He's worse than a gangster who wants to be paid now or else you'll lose a limb."

I feel the blood drain from my face, making me look even more like Elvira. Add fangs and the look would be complete.

He barks a laugh. "I was kidding ya. At least I was about the gangster part. I did owe him a favor, otherwise you'd be waiting until next week for the unit." He hands me a clipboard with a form attached. "You just need to fill this out first."

"Thank you. You're a lifesaver." I take the form and fill it in, then hand it back to him.

"Where do you want me to put it?"

I tell him, and five minutes later I'm the proud (temporary) owner of a large metal container in my driveway. He's about to pull away when Noah arrives in his truck.

While I wait for Noah to come inside, I dump a load of clothes into the washing machine. These will be donated to the Golden Falls homeless shelter. Yesterday I phoned my parents' house and talked to a woman who does the laundry there. She walked me through how to use the washing machine and dryer.

The woman deserves a raise.

And a medal.

"Noah here, reporting for duty," he says behind me as I

push the start button. The bright side? The machine doesn't explode like a nuclear warhead.

I turn to him. "Thanks for arranging for the unit. We might as well begin tossing the piles I've identified as trash into it. That will give me more room."

"Sounds good. Where do you want me to start?"

I take him to the attic. My limp is more pronounced now than it was at the ranch, but Noah doesn't say anything. I mentally thank him.

I flip on the light. The single bare bulb creates shadows in the dimly lit room. "Those piles are for the garbage bin." I point to the stack of old papers, broken appliances, and clothes that had made for some very happy, chubby moths.

Then we get to work. Taking everything downstairs. Bit by bit.

"Does the name John Turnbull sound familiar to you?" I ask Noah as we walk up the attic stairs for what feels like the thousandth time in the past hour.

He thinks about it for a moment. "Can't say it does. Why?"

"I've been reading love letters that he and Charlotte wrote to each other while he was serving in the military during the Korean War. The Chevy Bel Air used to belong to him. According to the letters, they created some pretty steamy memories in the back seat."

Noah laughs, the deep sound igniting something low in my belly. "You mean Charlotte and this John Turnbull fucked in the back seat?"

My face heats at the crass way he says it. "Yes, that's one way to put it."

That only makes him laugh harder. "I take it you're not one for dirty talk during sex, Princess."

"We're not talking about my sex life, thank you."

I pause at the top of the stairs, needing a moment to recover from the growing ache in my leg. It's not used to all this up and down on the stairs.

"You okay?" Noah asks. Concern replaces the laughter in his voice—which for some reason warms me to my bones, even though it shouldn't make a difference.

I nod. "I'll be fine. My leg just needs to get used to working out on the stairs. But it will be better for it. Stronger. Faster. Able to leap tall buildings in a single bound."

His lips twitch as he fights a laugh. "What do you usually do when your leg hurts?"

"Soak in the bathtub. But I'm fine now, so let's get back to this." I gesture to the pile that still needs to be tossed into the bin.

"I can do this while you're in the bath. There's no point making things worse by pushing too hard."

"I'm fine, Noah. I'm not an invalid." My tone holds a huffiness that isn't normally there. My grandmothers taught me that pouting isn't becoming.

Of course they also taught me that manual labor wasn't becoming either—a sentiment that most of my friends share— so there's always that.

"Never said you were. But we're almost finished here, and I'm assuming you'll want to shower before we head back to the ranch." He lightly brushes his thumb against my cheek, causing my heart rate to spike.

"You have a bit of dust here." His voice is low and gritty, and the warmth from a few minutes ago flares to something hotter.

My lips part slightly of their own accord. But just as I think he's going to kiss me, he returns to the remaining stack of papers.

I will my pulse to return to normal before I have a heart attack or do something equally embarrassing—like spontaneously combust from his touch.

My leg sides with Noah, and the ache intensifies. Well, that just sucks.

"All right," I say, doing my best to sound upbeat. "If you're looking for me, I'll be in the bathtub."

While waiting for it to fill, I swallow a couple of pain meds from the medicine cabinet. The soothing aroma of clary sage wafts in the steam blanketing the room. I readjust my ponytail into a messy bun and slip into the water.

I groan. Not the Oh-God-I'm-dying-here kind of groan. This is more along the lines of an orgasm-associated sound.

Just minus the good stuff.

I sink lower into the water, once again thanking Charlotte for installing the large tub. The woman really was an angel (excuse the pun).

Leaning back against a folded towel, I close my eyes. But instead of thinking about Charlotte and John's letters, my mind wanders upstairs to Noah. Yes, I'll admit I might have sneaked a peek at the way his muscles bunched under his T-shirt when he hoisted up stacks of paper.

And I might have appreciated the way his muscles moved when he flung said paper into the bin outside.

As the pain eases, I feel a relaxed smile slide onto my face. Noah-therapy. Now if only I could bottle it for whenever my leg is acting up. That would be the ultimate medicine. Plus, it has no side effects.

Well, almost no side effects. The thought of Noah is causing my girlie parts to ache in a whole different way.

Don't think about him. Don't think about him. Don't think about him.

That's about as effective as telling great-aunt Margie not to ogle the hot lifeguards at the country club.

A tap at the door jerks me from my thoughts.

"Are you okay in there?" Noah says through the door.

Without thinking, I grab the face cloth and attempt to cover myself with it—momentarily ignoring that the bathroom door is locked. Unless Noah plans to smash the door down, he can't get in.

"Yes, I'm fine," I say over the nature sounds playing through my Bluetooth speaker. "I'm almost finished."

"Okay. I'll wait for you downstairs."

"I won't be long."

I push myself up and carefully climb over the edge. The ache in my leg is still there but has downgraded to a version I can live with.

I style my hair and change into my favorite Louis Vuitton outfit. It's a vintage-pink sleeveless princess dress that falls just above my knees. A narrow white belt completes the look.

Noah is in the living room, playing with Charlie, when I enter.

"I'm ready to go."

He turns around. "Wow, you really clean up well."

I give him a little curtsy. "I'll take that as a compliment."

The corners of his mouth tilt up. "That's good, because it was intended to be one. Are you ready to meet Asgard and Maui?" he asks Charlie, who barks and wags his tail.

On the way out, I remove his leash from the antique table by the door. He happily follows Noah outside. Noah opens the rear door to the truck, and Charlie jumps onto the back seat. Then he scampers between the two front seats to make himself comfortable on the passenger side.

"He's used to sitting up front," I explain to Noah.

"Fair enough." He opens the passenger door for me and a doggy smile greets me.

Noah's hands rest on my waist, and my whole body heats up. Oblivious to my body's reaction, he helps me onto the passenger seat, and my temperature climbs a couple of degrees more. At this rate, I won't need my cardigan even if the evening air cools. I'll still be feeling flustered.

Charlie climbs onto my lap and parks his front paws on the armrest beneath the window. I fasten my seat belt.

Noah turns over the engine and pulls away from the house. "Are you okay if I have a shower once we get to the ranch? I'm sure Violet and Sophie are dying to ask you all kinds of questions about your life in Beverly Hills." His mouth shifts into a cocky smile. "Or you can join me in the shower. That would be fun, too."

My girlie parts second that opinion.

"I'm sure it would be fun." The words slip from my mouth unabashed—mostly because it's probably true. "But for now I'll have to pass. I just fixed my hair and makeup."

What the heck was I thinking? Now he'll believe the option is open for later on.

Judging from his laugh, Noah is thinking the same thing.

"Have you ever had sex in the shower?" He asks the question as if it's nothing more than small talk, but the smile playing at the corner of his mouth is hard to miss.

"Haven't we already established that we aren't talking about my sex life?" I try to keep my tone on this side of scandalized, but it's hard to do that when his question has me intrigued.

Shower sex sounds like something Charlotte would have done with her mysterious fiancé. It was never anything that Mathew and I ever did.

Maybe we should have.

Maybe then he wouldn't have cheated on me with my best friend...or any other woman.

He's a player, a voice in my head points out. *He always was, always will be. You were just too busy ignoring the truth to see it.*

And in time, he'll probably cheat on Tiffany, too.

"I'm sorry, Princess," Noah says on a laugh. "But I can't help myself."

The rest of our conversation is much tamer. He tells me about his day. And I tell him about the letters between Charlotte and her mystery man, and how neither Meg nor Tilly knew him or remembered Charlotte talking about him.

"Do you think he died during the war?" he asks.

"There's a good chance that's what happened. That, or he changed his mind about being with Charlotte and disappeared. But either way, I'm learning more about my great-aunt than I knew before. I still haven't figured out why she never fell in love with anyone else. Maybe she believed John was her soul mate."

"Do you believe in soul mates?"

"Definitely not. Which is a good thing, given that the last man I fell in love with—and only man I've ever been in love with—ended up cheating on me. With my best friend. I'd like to think that he wasn't my only chance for love. I'd also like to believe that the next one will be faithful."

Because if he isn't, I'm becoming a nun.

It's not too late to become a nun if you've already had sex, is it?

"What happened to the girl he cheated on you with? Are you two still friends?" If his expression is anything to go by, there's a good chance he's hoping the answer to that will be no.

"Yes, because I forgave her. I guess you can thank the near-death situation for that. The day I discovered her in bed with my boyfriend, I escaped his house with the goal of getting away for a few days. I didn't exactly want to talk to anyone about it. It was both humiliating and a humongous kick in the butt to my self-esteem. I needed to figure out my game plan. Instead, I was on the highway when a delivery truck lost control and I ended up in a near-fatal accident. What about you? Do you believe in soul mates?"

His face reddens, his hands tighten on the steering wheel, and I think his teeth might have just been ground to a fine powder. "Wait a second! That's the car accident that resulted in your injured leg? Your boyfriend cheats on you with your best friend, he gets laid, and you almost died?"

"Er, yeah, that's one way to put it. So about that soul mate stuff...."

"And you just forgave them because you were in the accident and almost died? An accident you wouldn't have been in if you hadn't caught him cheating on you?"

"Well, it's not so much that I forgave Tiffany as I let it go because we travel in the same circles. It was easier that way. And don't get too far ahead of yourself in thinking I forgave my ex. If his man parts spontaneously fall off, that's because I cursed him a few thousand times while I was recovering for that to happen." I smirk at Noah. He doesn't see it, his attention still on the road. "I thought that would be fair enough revenge. But you also have to remember that all Mathew did was cheat on me. He wasn't the one who caused the accident. It was just dumb luck that I was in the wrong place at the wrong time."

For a second, it looks as if Noah is going to argue that, but I guess he must have realized I'm right. I'm used to that response. Troy and Drew and my stepbrothers all had the same reaction when they found out what happened.

But I do plead the fifth when it comes to how a cement truck accidentally dumped its contents into Mathew's sports car a few months after the accident. The top had been down on the convertible at the time. I had nothing to do with it....But I have a suspicion I know who the guilty party is.

"Anyway, that's all in the past," I remind Noah. "But my question still stands. Do you believe in soul mates?"

"Nope. Not at all."

"And you've never been in love?"

His anger on my behalf abates, to be replaced by some other raw emotion that has nothing to do with me. He rubs the back of his neck but doesn't say anything.

Interesting.

"So you have been in love? What happened?" *Please tell me*

you're nothing like my ex-boyfriend, and you were perfectly capable of keeping your man parts zipped up.

"Pretty much the same as what happened to you. But how about we compare notes later?" He nods toward the ranch house that has come into view.

"Okay, but I'm holding you to that, cowboy."

And so is Charlie, if his bark is anything to go by.

We arrive at the ranch house a few minutes later, and Noah parks in the large curved driveway in front of it. He helps Charlie and me down, and we walk up the porch steps to the front door. Noah opens it and gestures for us to enter. Voices can be heard from another room, along with the sound of a child imitating a car engine. "*Vroom. Vroom.*"

A second later, Deacon rolls through a doorway, sitting on a toy car powered by his feet. "*Vroom. Vroom.*"

"Hey, little buddy," Noah says, "hope you're obeying the speed limit. Otherwise your uncle Austin might give you a ticket."

"*Vroom. Vroom,*" is Deacon's reply.

"I already tried that warning," a deep male voice says, and a good-looking man with short brown hair, scruff, and hot-looking glasses enters the foyer. Like Noah, he's wearing jeans and a dark T-shirt. "Hi, you must be Kate Snow." He holds out his hand to me and I shake it.

"Kate, this is Austin Brooks, the town sheriff."

"Ah yes, I've met your grandmother. She's really sweet."

"She did mention that she'd met you, but the jury is still out on the sweet part." His affectionate tone implies he believes the opposite.

A grin appears on his face. "So I hear I'm the one you plan to murder."

13

KATE

"**V**room. *Vroom*," Deacon says as he drives around us in the foyer.

Noah laughs at Austin's comment. "Since you didn't pick me to be the one you killed, that leaves me with fire-truck or marry. So which one is it, Princess? Did you want to fire-truck me or marry me?"

I look Austin squarely in the face. "I've changed my mind. You get to live. Noah is the one I'm going to do away with." I smile sweetly at Noah, and this time it's Austin who cracks up.

Noah scowls at him.

"Since Noah's the one who is no longer with us," Austin says, "why don't I take you into the kitchen and introduce you to everyone?" He offers me his arm and I take it.

Charlie trots merrily beside me, with Noah trailing us. We enter the huge, modern kitchen, which is a direct contrast to Charlotte's.

Originally, when TJ invited me to join them for dinner, I was under the impression it would only be Noah's two brothers, Sophie, and TJ's wife, Violet.

I didn't expect to meet the town's sheriff...or a man who

looks strangely familiar, but I can't figure out why. Like the three brothers and Austin, he's also from the pages of Hot Hunks.

Seriously, what is in this town's water?

"Really?" Noah says, sounding mildly irritated. "Ryan, too?"

The man frowns. "Happy to see you as well, Noah."

Austin smacks him on the back. "Meg and Tilly were at it again."

"Again?" I ask.

The frown vanishes, replaced by a knowing grin. "Marry"—Ryan glances at Deacon, then back at Austin—"fire truck, and heaven?"

"Are you telling me that Tilly and Meg have been asking all the woman in town which of you three they want to marry, fire truck, and do away with? Like some unofficial poll?"

The three women in the kitchen—two of whom I'm guessing are Sophie and Violet—start laughing.

"Because Noah, Austin, and Ryan are still single," the blonde woman explains, "Meg and Tilly have decided to find them wives."

"But I don't live in Copper Creek," I point out. "And as soon as I'm finished cleaning out Charlotte's house, I'm returning to Beverly Hills. They both know that." They must have already polled every other woman in town and, out of desperation, added me to the mix.

"I suspect they're hoping you'll stay," she says.

"So you must be the vet," I say to Ryan, remembering the third option in Tilly's game.

"That's right."

I kneel next to Charlie. "You see this nice man? This is who you'll have to visit if you get into another disagreement with a duck and he wins."

Charlie tilts his head to the side and gives Ryan his infamous doggy grin.

Ryan crouches and scratches him behind his ears. I stand.

"Anyway, this is Sophie." Noah gestures to the gorgeous blonde who is holding two wine bottles in her hands. She's wearing a white lace sundress, cowboy boots, and a wide leather belt with a horse's head engraved on it.

Standing next to TJ is a beautiful brunette who must be Violet. Her loose, knee length, off-the-shoulder dress has a bohemian look to it and is set off with a leather belt that isn't quite as wide as Sophie's. Unlike Sophie, Violet is wearing sandals.

TJ has his arm around her waist, and you can see the love in his eyes as he smiles at her. The same expression is reflected back at him.

"You've met my brother TJ," Noah says, continuing with the introductions. "That's his wife, Violet."

The pair say hi to me, their smiles warm and welcoming. There's something different about their smiles compared to the ones I've witnessed over the years at events I've attended back home, but I can't place what it is.

"I'd like to say that Deacon has told me all about you," Violet says. "But it's Charlie he hasn't stopped talking about."

I chuckle. "That's doesn't surprise me. Charlie has that effect on kids."

"And this is Aubrey." Noah points to a pretty, dark-haired woman standing with Violet and TJ. "She's the other brilliant veterinarian at the clinic." Aubrey says hi.

"Would you like a glass of wine or something?" Sophie asks. "But just a warning, they won't be anywhere near as good as what you're used to."

"I'd love a glass of white wine. Thanks. And don't worry, I'm not a wine connoisseur." Not even close.

She hands me a glass of wine.

"*Vroom. Vroom,*" Deacon says, wheeling himself between his parents and me.

"You have a beautiful home," I say to Violet.

"Thank you."

"Mommy," Deacon says, looking up at Violet. "What does hooked up mean?"

For a second, Violet's mouth drops open, and the room goes oddly quiet. Noah stiffens next to me.

"Where did you hear that phrase?" Violet carefully asks her son, her expression now composed.

"Uncle Noah hooked up with a lady at the library when I met Charlie."

I fight back the urge to laugh. Just barely.

At hearing his name, Charlie walks over to Deacon, tail wagging, and waits for the little boy to pat him. Which he does —but it's not enough to distract him from his question.

He continues watching his mother expectantly.

"Well, um," Violet begins, then throws Noah a death glare. "It's when two people...go out for coffee together."

Deacon nods, but it's clear this isn't the end of it. He's thinking.

I take a sip of my wine.

"Is that how you got the baby in your tummy? You and Daddy hooked up?"

I choke on my wine.

That has more to do with the last part than the part everyone else is reacting to.

Aubrey and Sophie hug Violet, congratulating her. The guys do the same with TJ, giving him man-hugs, and then hug Violet with more vigor.

It takes several minutes for the excitement to die down. Deacon has long since grown bored waiting for a reply to his question and is now playing with the three dogs.

"Congratulations," I tell Violet and TJ the second I have a chance. Violet's back is to him and his hand rests protectively on her belly.

Soon after, we have dinner, which is a lot of fun. Everyone shares funny stories about their day. This surprises me because I'm a complete stranger. But then it's not like they have to worry about their stories being shared on social media or in the tabloids.

They don't have to worry about being stabbed in the back.

And because of their openness, I don't feel so guarded when I tell them about my latest stable-cleaning adventures.

"I'm sure to his little mouse family, his scampering around Scoundrel's stall was a riot," I say, "but I wasn't so impressed." I look at Noah. "I'm just surprised you didn't hear me screaming while you were here at the ranch."

"Maybe you need to get a barn cat," he suggests.

"Can you rent them?" I ask in earnest.

"You want to rent a cat?"

You'd think from his tone that I'd just asked him to go shopping at Saks Fifth Avenue. Naked.

"Sure why not? I'm only here for another week. As it is, I have to find Lady and Scoundrel new homes. I don't need to add a barn cat to that list, too." Because I'm assuming the kitty won't want to return to Beverly Hills with me. I don't have a barn there...nor do I have any mice.

"I don't know about Beverly Hills, but I don't think it works that way here. You adopt cats. You don't rent them."

That's probably true for back home, too.

"So I guess Wilbur and his family have nothing to worry about then." I pop the tasty green bean into my mouth.

A slight frown forms on Noah's brow. "Wilbur?"

"Yes, I named the mouse Wilbur."

"Can I meet Wilbur?" Deacon asks. Then he turns his mom and firmly states, "Green beans are yucky."

AFTER DINNER, I'M TALKING TO AUBREY AND RYAN WHEN NOAH approaches our group. Turns out the reason that Ryan looked familiar is because he used to be a Calvin Klein model while in vet school.

"Did you want to go for a walk outside for a bit?" Noah asks me as Ryan poses a question to Aubrey.

"Sure. Let me get Charlie."

I turn to find him busy playing with Deacon and Maui. Asgard is watching over everyone. I decide to leave Charlie to his fun.

"Looks like it's just you and me," I tell Noah.

"What size shoes do you wear?"

Okay, that's a strange question.

I tell him.

"You're the same size as Sophie—which is what she guessed." He leads me to the foyer and pulls out a pair of cowgirl boots from the closet. "She said you can borrow these. You'll probably prefer walking in them instead of what you're currently wearing. Especially where I'm planning to take you." He looks pointedly at my cream ballet flats.

"Where are you planning to take me?"

"You'll see, Miss I Don't Like Surprises. I promise you, you'll like it."

"All right. I'm in." I can be adventurous. Like Charlotte.

It's not like Tiffany, our friends, or my stepmother are going to see me wearing the boots.

Just like they'll never see me wearing Charlotte's rubber boots.

A few minutes later, I'm ready to go. "Hey, look at me, I'm a cowgirl." Honestly? Forget what Lucinda and my friends think. I need to get a pair of boots like these. They look cute with my dress. Like Beverly Hills meets country.

Maybe I can start a new fashion trend.

We step outside and I'm immediately thankful that I brought my cardigan. The night air is cool, especially for this California girl.

It's dusk, so we can still see the scenery around us—the wild grass blowing in the breeze, the wooden fence, the occasional grouping of trees—but just barely.

We've been walking for a couple of minutes in silence when he finally speaks. "The woman Deacon mentioned before dinner? I didn't hook up with her at the library."

"You don't need to explain her to me, Noah. You're a good-looking guy who is single, not a monk. You are allowed to have sex, and no one has the right to judge you, and that includes me."

He nods, seemingly happy with my assessment of the situation. "It was a one-time thing, and it happened over a month ago. Despite what you've heard, I'm not a player. At least not anymore."

"So do you want to hook up with her again?" Or maybe they already have.

"Not at all. I prefer to keep things simple when it comes to my love life."

I laugh. I can't help it. "Do you actually have a love life, or is that your code for getting laid?"

He grins but keeps walking. "Good point."

"So are you going to tell me how you ended up also being a member of the I've-Been-Cheated-On club?"

"It was while I was in Seattle. I fell in love with her, and I thought she was in love with me. Turns out I was just the guy she was fucking while waiting for the man she really wanted to propose to her. I was the entertainment. He was the wealth she craved."

Ouch.

I know exactly the type he's talking about.

I reach for his hand and give it a consoling squeeze. "I'm so sorry, Noah, that you got dragged into that mess."

He threads his fingers with mine. "I've never admitted that to anyone before. Not even my brothers know about her."

"What happened after you discovered the truth?"

"I told her to never contact me again. Then I swore I'd never repeat that mistake."

"Good plan."

We stop at a wooden fence. It's gotten darker since we began walking, and I have no idea where we are now. I can make out shapes in the low twilight lighting, but that's about it. I'm not familiar with the area like Noah is.

Noah starts to climb the fence.

"Where are you going?" I ask.

"To the other side." He jumps down. "Your turn."

I'm about to protest but then change my mind. Charlotte would have hightailed over the fence, no questions asked.

But I'm not Charlotte.

I stare at the fence as though it might turn into a fire-breathing dragon when I touch it.

"Is it because of your leg?" Noah asks.

"Is what because of my leg?"

"Your reluctance to climb the fence. Don't worry, I'll help you down."

"No, it's not because of my leg. But hey, if I can clean out a stable, I can do this. Right?"

"Right."

I place my foot onto the lower beam. "Okay, I'm coming over."

Climbing a wooden fence isn't all that difficult. It's getting to the other side and jumping down that's tougher—especially when you're wearing a Louis Vuitton dress.

I swing my leg over the top beam.

But I misjudge where my foot is in relation to the wood, and the next thing I know, I'm falling....

14

NOAH

One minute Kate is climbing over the fence; the next she trips over the top beam and releases a startled shriek.

I attempt to catch her. All I succeed in doing is slowing her descent when she crashes into me.

We land in a tangled heap on the ground, with Kate straddling me, the air knocked from my lungs.

Neither of us moves, our gazes locked. Kate's breath is coming in fast, and mine has done a complete turnaround. Each inhalation is perfectly synchronized with hers.

There's a loud pounding in my chest like my heart has taken up the drums and is using my ribs as an instrument. I wouldn't be surprised if Kate can hear it in the near-quiet of twilight.

She moves her hips slightly but makes no attempt to climb off me. Her core brushes against my hardening length. There's no missing the impact she's having on my body.

She leans down, placing her hands on the ground on either side of my head. "I want to kiss you, Noah." Her voice is a breathy whisper.

"I want that, too."

"I know that I shouldn't because I'm only here for another week. And I'm not the kind of woman who goes 'round kissing men—"

"Princess."

"Yes?"

"Just shut up and kiss me already."

I don't need to tell her twice. She lowers her mouth to mine.

The first touch of her lips is sweet and tentative. It's the gentle brushing of flesh against flesh. My body shivers unexpectedly at the sensation.

Not wanting the kiss to end at just this, I cup the back of her head, tangling my fingers in her hair. This time the kiss is less sweet, less tentative. It's possessive, dominating, sublime.

In the distance, a dog or a coyote or a wolf howls, but other than that, I block out everything that isn't this strong and sexy woman straddling me.

I don't know how long we've been kissing when she pulls away. Not long enough, if you want my opinion.

"Wow," is the only coherent sentence I can say—which is telling, given it wasn't even a proper sentence. But since my breath is coming in rapid pants, I'd say that even one word is pretty spectacular.

She rests her forehead against mine, her breath not much slower. "Wow is about right. I figured you'd be good. I just didn't figure you'd be *that* good."

I chuckle. "Right now, Kate, I think you're my new favorite person. You're doing a lot for my ego."

"Something tells me your ego wasn't at stake."

"You'd be surprised. What you see on the outside isn't necessarily what's on the inside."

She moves off me and pushes herself to her feet. I do the same.

"Why do I have a feeling that has nothing to do with the woman who broke your heart?"

"Because you're smart."

She snorts a laugh. "Too bad you're the only one who sees me that way."

"You have a college degree. How can people not think you're smart? I thought you have to be smart to get in."

"For the most part, that's true. There are other ways to get into college that have nothing to do with your brainpower. But that's not what I meant. I have a degree in art history. When you live in a family of overachieving men who have law degrees, medical degrees, and MBAs, my degree is considered cute. Nothing you take seriously.

"Even my cousin who works with my uncle on his...with his construction company has a college degree in structural engineering. His educational background has never been looked down on."

"Well, I don't care what your family says, I still think you're smart."

She smiles brightly at me. "Thank you. And whether you go to college or not has nothing to do with being smart. Not everyone wants to attend college or should go there. That doesn't mean they're not smart." She reaches up and gently kisses me. "What did you mean by what's on the outside isn't necessarily what's on the inside? I get the general premise behind the saying, but what does it mean to *you*, Noah?"

I take hold of her hand and we begin walking again. "I told you that Charlotte helped me with my reading. There's more to it than that. I guess people would now call what I struggled with a learning disability. But no one knew about those things when I was a kid. Or at least they didn't know about them in Copper Creek.

"I struggled with reading so much that my grandfather would put me down in his own way. He'd make me feel like an idiot and worthless. The only future I had to look forward to was as a ranch hand. I wanted more than that—especially since I hated cattle. I didn't want to spend the rest of my life stuck on the ranch."

"So you left and became the incredible man that you are…"

I laugh. "That's not what I was going to—"

She stops me before I can say anything more, her fingers against my lips. "I would. I mean, sure you drive me crazy whenever you call me Princess. But you're sweet and considerate and extremely talented. You care about other people, and they care about you in return. Your friends and family love you."

If there's more to be said, she doesn't get a chance to say it. My mouth finds hers again.

Have I met anyone like Kate before? Never.

She's nothing like Samantha.

Yes, they're both gorgeous and come from a different world than I'll ever exist in: a world that revolves around wealth.

But that's where the similarities end. Kate has a heart like no one else. A heart that some douchebag took a huge chunk out of when he cheated on her—with her best friend, no less. Kate won't admit it out loud, and maybe she hasn't even admitted it to herself yet, but his stupidity left a mark.

The way Kate kisses leaves me believing that not only was he a douchebag, he was a major dumbass, too.

She looks up at the sky. "Wow, I can't believe how bright the stars are."

"This is nothing compared to in another hour or so."

"You're lucky. It's so beautiful out here."

"I loved Seattle and the ocean, but you're right. It is beautiful here. I guess I never appreciated it until I had to return."

"Had to?"

I'd rather go back to kissing Kate, but something about her makes me want to open up to her more. She might be a princess who has expensive tastes and who doesn't actually work for a living like the rest of us, but she isn't spoiled in the way my ex was. Samantha would have sent someone to pack up the house and clean Scoundrel and Lady's stable.

Kate is doing both without a single complaint.

"My grandfather figured out a way to force me to return after I refused to talk to him for years," I explain. "If my brothers wanted to keep the ranch, I had to return to Copper Creek upon his death and help run it. While I might have disliked him for what he did to me growing up, I couldn't turn my back on my brothers just to spite him."

"So you returned home. Are you sorry that you did?"

I shake my head. "Not at all. My brothers are here, and I have some pretty great friends here, too. And unlike before, I'm involved with running the ranch. Before I left and experienced big city life, I didn't want to be stuck in a small town. But now I couldn't imagine living anywhere else. I guess it took me living somewhere else to appreciate this town and the ranch."

"That makes sense. And you do have some pretty great friends. I really like them."

"They seem to like you, too....So what about you? What are your friends like in Beverly Hills?" I hope the rest of them are better than her best friend. What kind of friend sleeps with her best friend's boyfriend?

"They're a lot like me. They like to shop on Rodeo Drive. They like to party, which I don't do anymore." A raw emotion flickers on her face but it's gone so quickly, I probably just imagined it.

"Why not?"

"My leg. It's not a huge fan of dancing. And since partying mostly involved dancing for us, I had to step away from it."

"Do you miss it?"

She thinks about it for several seconds. "Not really. We used to drink a lot when my friends and I partied. I don't miss that. And I don't miss the drugs."

I stop. "You used to do drugs?" She doesn't seem the type.

She shakes her head. "I never did, but it was around. I wasn't even interested in trying them. Some of my friends couldn't say the same. They associated partying with drugs.

"I was given addictive painkillers after the accident, while I was in a coma. But I refused them once I was able to. It was tough at first, but I didn't want to risk a long-term addiction."

"You were in a coma?"

"Yep, for two weeks after the accident that injured my leg. That's why as bad as my ex-boyfriend's betrayal was, it's nothing compared to recovering from the accident."

Kate shares about her friends, but the more she tells me about them, the more I don't like them. While Kate seems to be blind to their flaws, they sound like a bunch of stuck-up, privileged bitches who care mostly about themselves.

They sound like Samantha's kinfolk—once I saw her for who she really was.

The only friend who sounded like a decent person was Kate's cousin, who died of leukemia when they were kids. Kate becomes animated when she talks about her.

We return to where we climbed the fence, and I help her over. This time she succeeds without any issues, and we start walking toward the house.

At one point she pauses and points to the sky. "Oh, look, a shooting star."

Her excitement at seeing it makes me grin. She's like Deacon when he learns I'm taking him out for ice cream.

"Did you make a wish?" she asks.

"I don't think wishing on a shooting star actually works."

"Oh, hush. Of course it does. It's in all the fairy tales, so it must be true." Her tone contains a hint of her big, gorgeous smile.

"Have any of your previous shooting-star wishes come true?" I ask.

"This is the first one I've ever seen."

"Really?"

"Yes, really."

I turn to her. "So what did you wish for?"

"I can't tell you. It won't come true if I do."

"Fair enough."

"But I can give you a hint."

I laugh. "Okay. Give me a hint, and I'll see if I can guess. My guessing won't disrupt the magic will it?"

"Not at all. All right, here goes. I would love to do what I was doing in the field fifteen minutes ago."

I was expecting a complicated riddle I had no hopes of solving—riddles aren't my thing. I'd be a real idiot not to figure out this one.

I lower my head to hers. The first contact is the brushing of lips. She releases a stuttering sigh.

"Is that what you were wishing for?" I ask.

"Definitely something in that category."

The next contact is far from teasing. It's deep, exploring.

And her stuttering sigh is upgraded to a soft, needy moan. Her arms find their way around my neck.

I place one hand on her lower back, pulling her to me. The other hand has a will of its own and slides up her rib cage. My fingers trace across one of her tits. This is met by another soft moan. I gently cup my hand against her breast, sweeping my thumb across the nipple hidden beneath her dress and bra.

Kate arches, pressing her breast farther into my palm.

Oh, Christ, I want her so badly. But not out here. Not like this.

Her hand drifts to my chest and remains there as we kiss, her thumb brushing against my T-shirt. My skin hums beneath it, hums and craves something more.

We continue kissing, sweet and exploring, deep and demanding.

Eventually—and reluctantly—I pull away. My body is so turned-on, I'm afraid of what I'll do if we don't stop kissing soon. "We should head back before my brothers send a search party for us."

Kate places her hand against my cheek. "Thank you."

"For what?"

"For everything. For that kiss. It was exactly what I needed."

That gets a dopey smile from me, even though she can't see it. "Anytime. All you have to do is ask."

Deacon is already tucked into bed by the time we return to the house. No one says anything about us being gone for so long, but from my brothers' amused looks and the questioning ones from Violet and Sophie, it doesn't take much to guess what they're thinking.

Except, they're wrong.

Unfortunately, the evidence is kind of damning. Kate's usually smooth hair, with the hint of a wave, has taken on an I've-just-been-freshly-fucked style.

She and I spend the next two hours talking and laughing with my brothers and our friends. And for the first time since meeting Kate, I'm seeing a different side of her. She's more relaxed—like she's actually having fun.

By the time we leave, Sophie, Violet, and Aubrey have convinced her to join them for their next girls' night out. Kate is practically glowing after that.

I drive her and Charlie home and walk her to the front door.

She lets Charlie in, then smiling softly, turns to me. "Thank you for the incredible night, Noah. I can't remember the last time I've had so much fun. Your brothers and friends are great."

"They like you a lot, too." I run my thumb along her lower lip, starving for a taste of her again.

But it's getting late, and I have to get up early if I plan to spend the day here, helping her clean out the house after my morning chores.

Which won't happen if I kiss her the way I want to.

So I just brush my lips against hers and pull away before my willpower falls down a well.

"I'll see you tomorrow," I tell her. "I'll be over as soon as I can get away from the ranch."

Disappointment plays briefly in her eyes, but it's gone as quickly as it came. She smiles. "I'll see you then."

With that, she disappears into the house.

And I drive home to have a long, cold shower.

15

KATE

"Kate, sweetheart," my stepmother says the next morning via Skype. Her hair and makeup are perfectly in place. Like it is every time we Skype.

I, on the other hand, am far less put-together. My yoga pants, which she can't see, are dusty. My hair is up in a messy ponytail and I have a minimal amount of makeup on: light foundation, lip gloss, mascara. Anything more will be ridiculous for what I have planned today.

"How are things going?" Pity is her go-to tone for this session. Either because of how I look or because I'm in a small town without the amenities of Beverly Hills or a combination of the two.

"So far, so good." If we don't count the part where I'm still cleaning the stable every morning. But there are definitely worse things I could be doing.

Have I ridden Lady or Scoundrel yet? Not on your life.

Or my life—which I happen to value.

"How much longer before you return to Beverly Hills? Everyone misses you. Your friends miss you."

These would be the same friends who have texted me every

day with pictures of the latest purses, shoes, or outfits they've bought.

Or updated me on the current gossip.

Or told me about the newest and hottest club they went to last night.

"I'm not sure. I'm getting there, but Charlotte had a lot of stuff in the house that I have to deal with before I can put it on the market." And there's still the issue of finding Lady and Scoundrel new homes.

Loving homes, not the glue factory as one of my stepbrothers suggested.

"But as soon as I know, I'll call you," I tell her.

Lucinda then shares about the tea party she's organizing, renovations she's thinking of doing to one of the guest houses, the shocking gossip she just heard this morning about one of her neighbors.

None of what she's saying I pay much attention to. I'm too busy reminiscing about Noah's kisses last night. My body lights up like a rogue firework just thinking about them.

"Kate, are you listening to me?"

My stepmother's annoyed voice snaps me from my thoughts about Noah's earthquake-worthy kisses.

"Sorry, I missed that. What were you saying?"

She explains once again about the problem she's having with the caterer. This time I do a better job focusing and responding.

"I should let you go now," I eventually tell her. "If I don't finish packing up the house, I'll never get to return home." That earns me another pitying look as if I've just mentioned that I'm suffering from a terminal disease.

I end the session. Charlie lifts his head with an *Is-she-gone-yet?* expression. He's been snoozing next to me on the couch since I sat.

"Are you planning on sleeping all day while I work?"

He barks and lays his head back down, enjoying the morning sun shining through the living room window.

I giggle. "You silly dog. All right, you catch up on your beauty sleep for the both of us, and I'll get to work."

Several hours later, I'm in the living room, packing away antiques to be shipped to Beverly Hills. The front door opens and Noah calls out, "Hey, Kate. I'm here with the cavalry."

"I'm in here."

Noah walks into the room a moment later, followed by seven people I hadn't expected to see.

"Hi?" I say to Noah's brothers, Violet, Sophie, Aubrey, Ryan, and Austin. All of them are wearing casual clothing: shorts, jeans, T-shirts.

"We've come to help you," Violet explains.

TJ wraps his arm around his wife's waist from behind. "No, the rest of us have come to help Kate. You're putting your feet up and supervising."

Violet rolls her eyes, then turns to kiss him. "Will you worry less if I do that?"

He kisses the end of her nose. "Damn straight."

"All right, I'll supervise."

"And by supervise, she doesn't mean you'll be spending the day kissing her while the rest of us work." Jake slaps his brother on the back.

All eight of them look at me expectantly, waiting for me to tell them what needs to be done. Once I get over my initial shock, I thank everyone for helping me and assign each person a task.

And this includes Violet, who is to keep Charlie company while the rest of us work. He moves next to her and plunks his head on her lap.

TJ laughs. "That's one way to keep you in place." He gives his wife one more quick kiss, then gets to work.

We work hard for the next several hours, stopping for lunch

once the pizza Violet ordered arrives.

Everyone grabs a slice and heads outside to the sorry-looking patio. The men pop open their beers. Violet was busy making virgin Strawberry Daiquiris while we were working—the only thing that TJ and Charlie would let her do. Sophie fills the glasses, and I hand them out to the girls.

We each find a spot to sit. There are only two chairs, which are for Violet and TJ. The rest of us get comfy on the low-rise stone step surrounding the patio, separating it from the sad-looking garden.

Noah sits next to me. "Hey, how are you doing?"

He doesn't have to say it; I know what he's referring to.

"I'm doing fine. Thank you so much for this." I nod at his friends.

"They offered to help when they found out what you and I were doing today."

I bite into my pizza slice and moan at the mouth-watering taste.

Noah gives me a funny look.

"What?"

"Do you usually eat pizza like you're about to have an orgasm?"

Everyone else is laughing over something TJ said, so they don't hear his question.

But that still doesn't stop my face from heating up.

"No, but I've never had pizza like this one. It's so good." I take another bite, close my eyes, and repeat the sound.

A little louder this time.

I open my eyes in time to catch Noah staring at my lips, his own slightly parted. His breath is coming in a beat faster than before.

Someone coughs, and I drag my gaze from his mouth to see who it is...to find everyone watching us.

Oh, shoot.

Just how loud was I?

"Good pizza, huh?" Austin says with a laugh, and my face heats high enough to incinerate my slice.

"It's very good pizza," I mumble and stuff some more of it into my mouth. This time I keep the sounds more PG rated.

Despite my mortification, I enjoy the teasing that comes from the group. It's not just me who's the target of their playful banter and joking around. Everyone gets their own share of teasing.

IT'S LATE AFTERNOON BY THE TIME WE CALL IT A DAY.

"Thanks for helping me," I tell them. I hug Violet, Sophie, and Aubrey. Genuine hugs, not the fake ones common in my social circle back home.

After everyone leaves, Noah says, "There's still some stuff I want to finish before I go home."

"Okay. I'll be in the kitchen if you're looking for me."

By the time Noah has completed the last of his tasks, the kitchen is packed up, other than the few items I'll still need over the next few days.

I'm leaning against the counter, vaguely aware that I'm rubbing my injured leg when Noah enters the room.

"You know what helps TJ when his bum knee acts up?"

"TJ has a bum knee?"

"Yep, from when he was active on the rodeo circuit. It abruptly ended what was once a promising career."

"So what's this magical secret you speak highly of?"

"You'll see. Do you have a swimsuit...or are you comfortable skinny-dipping?" He steps closer to me. "Although if my vote counts for anything, I'm all for skinny-dipping."

I laugh, doing my best to ignore the panic scampering through me. "I'm sure you would be."

"I take it that's a no on skinny-dipping?"

"I'd say you're right."

"So what about a swimsuit?"

I shift on my feet and decide this would be a good time to drink a glass of water.

Or a bottle of wine.

I remove a glass from the cupboard and fill it with water from the tap.

Then proceed to gulp it down.

The last drop falls onto my tongue, but before I have a chance to refill the glass, it's removed from my hand.

Noah puts it on the counter. "Spill it, Kate. Why are you freaked out about me seeing you naked or in a swimsuit?"

I cringe. "I have scars from the accident."

He shrugs. "I can imagine you do, but what does that have to do with anything?"

"No, I mean they're bad scars. They're so bad, in fact, my stepmother booked an appointment with a plastic surgeon for me."

His forehead crinkles with several deep lines. "What difference does it make if you have scars? It doesn't change who you are."

My voice wavers through the three stages of being caught with your hand in the cookie jar before dinner. Panic. Frustration. Resignation. "It makes me unattractive. Undesirable. Less than perfect."

"Says who?"

I don't answer and reach for the empty glass. Maybe I can fill it with wine instead of water this time.

Sounds like a plan to me.

Noah stretches his arm back and grabs the neck of his T-shirt. He smoothly pulls the fabric over his head, revealing mouth-watering abs and a thick, jagged scar at his side. It travels several inches toward his belly button.

"Does this scar make me unattractive? Undesirable? Less than perfect?" he asks. "All right, you can skip the less-than-perfect one. I've never been perfect and I never will be, scar or no scar."

I trace my finger along it. "How did you get this?"

"You're avoiding the question."

My mouth slides up to one side. "So are you." At his mirror image of my smile, I sigh. "Okay, you win. No, it doesn't make you undesirable. But you can hardly compare our situations. That's like comparing apples to margaritas. You have one scar. I can't say the same."

"How about you show me your scars, and I'll be the judge."

"What here? Now?"

"Sure why not?"

"Because...because you'll see my panties." Said panties grow damp at the thought of that.

The cocky smile is back on his face. "And they're hideous granny panties?"

"Well, no." I don't think I've ever owned a pair like that. My stepmother has frequently emphasized the importance of wearing pretty underwear...even when no one will see it. "But even if they were, it wouldn't make a difference."

"Did you bring a swimsuit with you?"

I nod. I have no idea why I brought it. Maybe it was out of habit from traveling to all those tropical locales with my family over the years.

"So put it on, and show me the scars you're so freaked out about. I can guarantee they aren't as bad as you think."

I deliberate for a few seconds the pros and cons of doing as he asked. But then, what difference does it make? I'm not in Copper Creek for much longer. It's not like I'll have to witness month after month of him cringing every time he sees me.

"Okay. I'll be right back." I go upstairs to my room and quickly change into my red bikini and matching cover-up that ties at the waist.

I let out a hard breath. *I can do this. I can do this. I can do this. This is Noah we're talking about. He's sweet and funny. He's been hurt in the past by his grandfather's words. He would never hurt me. At least not intentionally.*

I return to the kitchen. Noah is busy on his phone when I enter.

Sensing me, he puts the phone on the counter behind him and looks in my direction. He swallows. Hard.

Maybe he's having second thoughts.

Maybe he's not sure if he can take it.

I can do this.

Without looking at him, I untie the cord holding the cover-up closed, pull the fabric away from my shoulders, and let it fall to the floor.

It's only then that I look up.

Noah is staring at me, but the expected repulsion on his face is absent.

What is there?

Lust.

Hot. Body-trembling. Lust.

His gaze sweeps over me and the heat in his eyes intensifies—igniting a fire deep in my belly.

This isn't what I was expecting.

Or maybe he hasn't really seen the scars.

Maybe he's just taken by my breasts.

He slowly approaches me and drops to his knee. Part of me wants to snatch up my robe from the floor and cover the scars.

Another part of me is curious about his reaction. It tells me to stay put.

That's the voice I listen to.

He lifts his hand and gently rests it on the worst of the scars.

It's long and thick with short deep lines intercepting it for the entire length. Think Frankenstein.

There are also shorter, equally noticeable scars on my thighs from shattered glass and serrated metal edges that bit into my skin during the accident.

He moves closer to a scar that covers a portion of my upper thigh and lightly kisses it.

He then takes his time kissing each scar, making sure none are left wanting.

Unlike my stepmother who—in her trying-to-be-helpful way—leaves me feeling like an ugly stepsister, Noah makes me feel the opposite.

He makes me feel beautiful. Worthy.

Wanted.

Oh God, and do I ever want him.

I thread my fingers through the soft strands of his hair. He looks up at me, searching my own heated gaze.

He stands, and before I realize what he's doing, he has me on the counter, his hard body pressed between my legs.

He shifts closer to me so his thick length is pressed against my core. "Do you feel that?"

I nod, not trusting my voice.

"Does it feel like I find you undesirable?"

Nope. Quite the contrary.

I shake my head.

"Trust me, Kate, there's not a single part of you I find undesirable." He kisses my shoulder. "There's not a single part of you I don't want to kiss or taste."

A tiny moan escapes me, and I move my hands to his chest just so I can touch him.

His mouth continues exploring, moving up my neck to my ear. "I desperately want to be inside you. I want to prove to you that you're more than perfect for me."

He nibbles my earlobe and I groan out, "I want that, too."

16

KATE

I can't remember the last time I've had sex. It was with Mathew. That much I remember.

But none of it matters in this instant.

The only thing that's important is my body wants Noah—and it would seem the feeling is mutual.

Noah pulls away from my earlobe. It groans in protest at being abandoned.

He searches my eyes for something. "What are you saying, Kate?"

"That I want you to...I want you to fuck me, Noah." My face heats but I don't care. Speaking dirty feels forbidden and exciting.

Like something I should have tried a long time ago.

Noah's shocked expression transforms into a new level of lust—and every body part tingles in anticipation.

"Even though your leg is sore?"

"I'm sure it will survive. Maybe an orgasm is exactly what it needs to dull the pain."

He leans closer again, his woodsy scent teasing me, his light beard brushing against my cheek. "I'm all for testing that theo-

139

ry." His husky voice leaves my girlie parts doing a happy hula dance.

He scoops me up in his arms and walks toward the staircase.

I grin at him. "Is this because you're being chivalrous or because you think I'll be too slow on the stairs?"

"Have you considered I could be a romantic?"

At the impish gleam in his eyes, I laugh. "I'm going with option two. You're too horny to wait for me to make it upstairs."

He winks at me, and I laugh again.

In my room, he lowers my feet to the floor. Then his mouth is on mine, and my hands are exploring his chest, his shoulders, his back, his abs.

My hands move to his belt, and I make quick work of unbuckling it.

Just not as quick as Noah is at untying my bikini top. The two red triangles flop to the carpet. He cups my breasts in his big, strong hands. My nipples tighten.

"It's like Easter and Halloween and Christmas all rolled into one," he says.

"You're comparing me to holidays?"

"The best kind. The kind with chocolate."

I unzip his jeans and slip my hand through the opening. "Trick or treat," I say with a grin, marveling at his thickness.

"I'm definitely hoping for a treat." Before I can respond, he has me on the bed and is shucking off his jeans and briefs.

Oh. My.

He's more than ready for action.

"I don't suppose you have any condoms in there." He points to the bedside table.

I shake my head, disappointment slouching inside me. "I wasn't expecting to have sex while in Copper Creek. And I'm assuming if Charlotte had any, they disintegrated several decades ago."

He removes his wallet from his jeans pocket and pulls out a foil package. "Fortunately, I have two."

I gasp. "Only two? There go my plans for a night filled with passion." A grin dances at the edges of my mouth.

This results in an answering grin on his face. "I'll remember that for next time."

"Please do. You wouldn't want to disappoint me, now would you?"

He doesn't reply. He just tosses the condom onto the bed next to the pillow, his eyes dark with want.

"I know it's been a while for me," I say, "but I do remember you need to put that on first."

"True, if I was planning to enter you right now. But you promised me a treat, and that's what I plan to get first."

He climbs onto the bed and straddles my legs. He then unties the sides of my bikini bottom and tosses it to the floor. He leans down, his cock brushing against my stomach, and he captures my mouth in an all-consuming kiss.

By the time his tongue has finished ravishing mine, my entire body is a melted puddle of goo. If that's how it responds to his kiss, I'm in serious trouble when it comes to something more.

I reach for him, but he pulls back before I have a chance to make contact.

I'm about to protest, but he grabs hold of my legs and pulls them apart, stilling all words on my lips.

A moment of self-consciousness drops in for a visit, and my mind inventories in annoying detail each of my scars.

"Hey, where are you going?" Noah's voice is gritty with lust, rough with frustration.

I prop myself on my elbows. "What do you mean? I'm right here?" I wave at him.

He lifts an eyebrow, the frustration still there, but now it's a bedfellow to amusement.

"That's not what I meant. You're tensing up. Whatever you're thinking right now, you're wrong." He kisses the scars, one at a time. "Stop overanalyzing things, relax, and let me taste you." He kisses my leg again, only this time a lot closer to my core.

"Sorry. I promise to do better..." I barely get the last part out. He separates my sex and kisses one side and then the other.

And just like that, my body returns to its previously relaxed state.

His tongue continues to tease me, flicking against my clit. Laving me with attention. Until I'm writhing and moaning softly on the bed.

His hand moves to my hip in an attempt to keep me still.

Good luck with that.

His thumb takes over the job of his tongue, which plunges deep inside me. "Oh God," I groan. This is met by a chuckle from Noah.

He keeps pushing me to the brink until I have nowhere left to go—except to tumble off the cliff. My insides clamp down on his tongue. By the time I've finished my free fall, I'm completely wrung out.

The best way to go.

Noah travels up my body, planting soft kisses near my belly button. On my rib cage. Between my breasts.

On my mouth.

He deepens the kiss, awakening my body once more.

Needing to touch him, I wrap my fingers around his cock. It fills my hand with its velvety softness.

Noah groans out a word that could be "Christ." I pump my hand along his hard length. A low growl pushes from his lungs, leaving me feeling more empowered than I have in a while.

I love the sound of it, the feel of it against my mouth as he continues kissing me.

My thumb traces around the head, spreading the moisture beading on the tip.

This time I can definitely make out what Noah says and I giggle. I'm getting to him. But then I think I got to him the moment I practically begged him to be inside me.

Noah pulls back, grabs the package from the bed, and a moment later is covered and ready to go.

He aligns himself with my entrance and slowly pushes himself in. My body rejoices at the feel of him. Welcomes him. Hugs him tight.

Once he's fully seated, he pauses, his ragged breath warm against my shoulder.

I wrap my legs around his hips and groan as a delicious new sensation hits me down low.

Noah begins moving inside me, slow and rhythmically at first, then increasing with speed and roughness. The heat that had dropped to a gentle boil after he had eaten me out is now at the level of a volcano about to explode.

I won't last much longer.

I moan something to that effect. He keeps going until my muscles tighten hard around him and I cry out. If I thought I'd seen the stars last time, that was nothing compared to now.

Noah grunts out his release a moment later and collapses on me. I welcome his weight pressing down on me as we fight to regain our breaths.

Once it's returned to a level that doesn't sound like we've just sprinted the last mile of a marathon, Noah removes himself from me.

I'm too spent to figure out what comes next. A not-so-drowsy voice in my head reminds me of a conversation Noah and I had before. He doesn't do repeat business. When it comes to sex with a woman, it's a one-time thing for him.

I momentarily wrap myself in disappointment, then shove it aside. So what if it was just a one-time thing? I'm only in

Copper Creek for another week at the most. I've had my fun. Now I can focus one hundred and ten percent on the job.

My body busts out laughing. *Good luck with that goal.*

Noah returns to the bed and pulls me to him. I settle my head on his chest and listen to the relaxing beat of his heart. Why does this have to feel so right when I know it shouldn't?

"You said your stepmother booked plastic surgery for the scars?" He doesn't say it in a tone that implies that it's a good idea. His question is more out of curiosity.

"She did, but I canceled it. I decided to keep them to remind me what happens when I trust someone with my heart."

"Couldn't you have gotten a tattoo instead?"

"I don't like needles."

He laughs. "Can't say I blame you there."

"Are you saying I should have the surgery?"

He tenderly strokes my cheek with his thumb. "I told you the scars don't bother me. They're a part of you, and I happen to think every part of you is great. But you come from a world that embraces looking perfect. I bet there are more plastic surgeons per capita there than in most other places."

I giggle. "You're probably right about that. I'm sure my stepmother has them on speed dial for the moment she spots her first crow's foot."

"How's your leg doing now?"

"It's better. Maybe sex is the cure after all. Must be all those endorphins. In that case, I should add daily sex to my therapy plan. Forget painkillers—sex is where it's at."

His sexy one-sided grin is back. "Well, I volunteer my services while you're staying in Copper Creek."

"That's very noble of you."

"Isn't it? Like you said before, it's a sacrifice I'm willing to make."

"Even with your no-more-than-once-with-a-woman rule?"

"I think I can make an exception." He flips me over and shows me exactly how big a sacrifice he's willing to make.

And I, for one, am truly grateful that he's so giving.

Now if only I could bottle his sacrifice and take it back home with me to Beverly Hills.

That would be something.

17

NOAH

The sun is just above the horizon as I step out of Charlotte's house the next morning. Kate was still asleep when I left her bed.

I hadn't meant to spend the night. But after I took her for the second time, I didn't have the will or the energy to leave.

As I shut the front door behind me, the distant sound of an engine alerts me to the new arrival. Kate never mentioned she was expecting anyone, especially before six a.m.

From the porch I watch the black SUV pull up in front of the house and park. Then a guy my age, wearing jeans, a long-sleeved T-shirt, and black work boots climbs out and strides to the porch steps.

As soon as he spots me, a scowl appears on his face. "Who the fuck are you?"

I fold my arms across my chest. "The same can be asked about *you*."

"I'm Troy, Kate's cousin. Now, are you going to tell me who the fuck you are?"

Since I don't know how much Kate has told him, I go with the simple answer. "Noah."

He looks me over. Unlike his clothing, mine are messy and wrinkled—casualties of packing up Charlotte's home yesterday and being left in a pile on the floor while I was getting to know Kate better.

"So you're the person she hired to look after the two horses?" he asks. "Aren't you here a little early for that?"

"I run a ranch. This isn't early." I still don't move to let him past. "But the question is, why are *you* here so early? If you're her cousin, then you'd know she isn't an early morning person."

His scowl deepens. "Who are you to say when I can see my cousin? You're just the hired stable hand." He stomps up the steps, his pissed-off gaze never leaving my face.

"Because she's sleeping. So unless she's expecting you, I'd suggest you come back later." If we were both bulls, we'd be charging each other, battling for domination.

His eyes narrow. "If you're the stable hand, how is it you know that she's sleeping? And why are you on my cousin's porch and not dealing with the horses?"

Good questions. Neither of which I have an answer for without revealing the truth about last night.

Before I'm able to bullshit my way out of things, he points at the door like I'm five years old and he's my father. "Get inside."

I snort a laugh. "I don't have to do what you say. Besides, I have better things to do."

"You have a choice. We either go inside and have Kate confirm who you are...or I call the police and have you charged for trespassing."

What is it with this family and their desire to have me arrested?

I roll my eyes. "Fine." I open the door and enter the foyer.

Sure, I could have just let him contact Austin or one of the deputies. But that would be even more awkward for Kate.

"So are you planning to wake her up?" I ask. "Or are we just shooting the breeze over coffee?" I don't bother to keep the sarcasm out of my tone.

"Wake me for what?" Kate says, coming down the stairs, voice still rough with sleep. She's gripping the railing, her limp more pronounced than normal.

Shit, is that because of the sex last night?

"My leg is always stiff first thing in the morning," she says, seeing my expression. "It will be better once I've finished my morning yoga practice." That explains her outfit: the clean pair of black leggings and a light-pink tank top that hugs the curves I'm intimately familiar with.

Her gaze then falls on her cousin, and she grins. "Troy, what on earth are you doing here?"

He waits for her to reach the bottom of the stairs and scoops her up in a big hug. She laughs and hugs him back.

Once he's finished hugging her, he lowers her to her feet. "You're looking good, cuz. The mountain air agrees with you."

She beams at him. "Thank you. Now are you going to tell me why you're here?"

"Sure, right after you explain the cowboy." He gestures in my general direction.

"Troy, this is my friend Noah. Noah, Troy."

We nod at each other, testosterone boiling under the surface.

"So, are you going to tell me why you're here," she asks, "or is it a state secret?"

"You haven't exactly answered my question."

"Sure I have. I told you Noah is my friend."

"Who was sneaking out of your house before six a.m."

Her eyebrows pop up on her forehead. "Are you interrogating me about my sex life?"

The scowl on his face when he first arrived is nothing compared to what he levels at me now. "Are you telling me you had a one-night stand with a cowboy?"

"Let me see if I've got this straight," she replies. "Is it that I had a one-night stand that's the problem or that I had sex with a cowboy?"

"Or all of the above," I add.

Kate laughs. Troy scowls some more.

"Look," Kate says to her cousin, "you know more than anyone how lonely I've been ever since the accident. Noah is the first guy who hasn't made me feel like a leper."

"That's because he wanted to get into your pants," he growls out.

"Have you thought that maybe I was the one who wanted to get into *his* pants? Happy now? And just so you know, that last one was a rhetorical question."

My guess, based on his expression? That's a no. He's not happy.

"So a deal is a deal," she says. "Why are you here?"

"I figured you could use some help with packing up. That, and I had an idea, but I wanted to check out the house first."

"What idea?"

Troy turns to me even though I'm not the one who just asked the question. "Don't you need to be somewhere?"

"If he wants to hang around to hear this, I'm okay with that," Kate says. "I can make us breakfast, and you can see for yourself that Noah is a nice guy, and he can discover that you aren't always a jerk."

His eyes widen. "Are you telling me that after being here for only a week, you can cook now?"

"Well, not exactly. But I do know where there's an amazing bakery in town and I bought some croissants there yesterday." She looks at me. "Are you okay with that, or do you need to leave?"

"I'm good with that."

Kate doesn't wait to find out if her cousin is okay with her plan. She walks toward the kitchen. Troy and I remove our boots and follow her.

She starts the coffeemaker and looks through the fridge. "I have some eggs. I can make some scrambled eggs if you want."

I catch the panicked expression Troy sends my way, and he shakes his head. Kate doesn't notice.

"I make a mean scrambled egg," I tell them. "If you want, I can cook them while Troy tells you about his idea."

"I'm good with that plan," he says, sounding somewhat relieved, "but I really do need to inspect a few things first before I explain my idea. Do you mind if I check them out while Noah makes the eggs?" he asks Kate.

"Go ahead."

He heads out of the kitchen and I gather the ingredients I'll need.

Kate removes a croissant from a paper bag. "Sorry about Troy. He's not usually like that."

"That's okay. I get it. He's protective of you."

"He is. All of my family is. But that doesn't excuse his behavior. And you really didn't have to stay. I know this is kind of awkward—"

I don't give her a chance to finish the sentence. My mouth crashes against hers, and my body hums in satisfaction. Yes, normally the reason I bail is because I don't like dealing with the awkward morning after, when the woman hints that she wants you to call her.

But that isn't a problem with Kate and me. She won't be here much longer. She's not expecting me to call her.

I pull away and wink at her. "Was that awkward?"

"Give me a second while I regain my breath long enough to talk," she says with a grin. "I know I'm not going to be around much longer, but I'm really hoping we can have a repeat of last night before I go. I know you're not into having sex more than once with the same woman, but I'm hoping you can make an exception."

I move to trap her body against the counter and run my lips against her jaw. Her light floral scent teases me, and I have the sudden urge to lift her onto the counter and show her just how much I fucking want her again. "I'll have to get back to you on that." I chuckle against her ear.

"We could call it my prize for cleaning Lady and Scoundrel's stable," she murmurs.

"And what about Troy?"

"He's not the one cleaning the stable, so he doesn't get a prize."

"That's not what I meant. I'm hardly going to be fucking you with him around."

She lets out a hard breath. "I'm sure we'll figure out something."

I kiss her briefly, then start making the food. She doesn't have a lot of ingredients, so the eggs will be pretty basic.

"Where did you learn to cook like that?" she asks.

"I can follow a recipe, which is about the extent of my cooking skills. Before Violet and Sophie moved in with us, my brothers and I took turns cooking. We weren't bad, but Violet and Sophie are much better at it. They've kind of taken over the kitchen."

"Can I help?"

I show her how to crack an egg and dump the contents into the bowl. She attempts to duplicate my results. With the first try, she doesn't hit the bowl hard enough and her efforts don't even leave a dent.

The next time she hits the egg too hard against the edge of the bowl. Half the egg white and yolk and a few eggshell bits end up in the bowl; the rest slops down the side onto the counter.

It takes several attempts for her to get it right. Add to that the laughing and joking around while I'm making the eggs, it's no wonder it takes so long to finish cooking them.

We've barely finished making the scrambled eggs by the time Troy returns to the kitchen.

"All right," Troy says after we've been eating for a few minutes. "I've had a chance to survey the property to see what kind of work is needed. As you know, Kate, Dad's show has finished filming for the season. The new schedule doesn't start until mid-August."

"What show is that?" I ask even though I'm not a big TV watcher.

He tells me the name, but it still means nothing to me. "It's a home renovation reality show. I'm part of the construction crew that works on the houses the show features."

"Please tell me you're not thinking of bringing the show here. My family hasn't exactly had good experiences with reality shows."

"What kind of experience have they had with them?" Kate asks.

"Bad ones. TJ was one of the contestants on *Cowboy Most Wanted*." No thanks to me. At the time when I entered him—without his permission—I thought it would help promote the ranch.

All it did was promote shirtless photos of him.

Kate's and Troy's expressions are blank. Neither of them has any idea what I'm talking about.

"What's *Cowboy Most Wanted*?" Troy asks. "Some agricultural reality show?"

"It's like *The Bachelor* and *The Bachelorette*."

He shakes his head. "Can't say I've ever heard of them. I don't watch reality shows."

"I've heard of them," Kate says. "But I've never watched them. My friends are into them big-time."

"You're not missing anything." I eat another forkful of my eggs.

Kate tears a piece off her croissant. "So what does Uncle Jacob's show have to do with Charlotte's house? The last I heard, he wasn't planning to expand it to outside the LA area."

"He isn't," Troy says. "What I'm proposing is that you and I renovate this house. It will give me a chance to showcase my skills. And you will end up with a house that will be more appealing to potential buyers."

"Yes, but I'm not a contractor. That's all you. Sure, I know how to put pillows and blankets together to make something more aesthetically pleasing, but I don't know the first thing about renovating."

"True or false. You've been coming up with ideas on how the place would look if someone knocked down the wall between the kitchen and the living room." He takes a bite of his eggs, waiting for Kate's answer.

She shrugs but doesn't look surprised by his comment. "Okay, I might have thought of a few ideas that would look good."

"True or false. You already have a Pinterest board for this house, and you already know what style you would go for if you were to decorate it."

She squirms on her chair. "What? Are you hacking my Pinterest account now?"

He laughs. "No, but I know you that well. I'm not saying you have to be involved with the physical labor. Christ knows that's not your thing—"

"Hey, guess who's been cleaning the stable every day while I've been here?" She points to herself. "*Me.*"

"Well, you might find the physical aspect involved with the renovations a lot more fun than cleaning stables."

"It can't be much worse, that's for sure. But what you're saying is that I won't get to go home in a week. I'll have to stay here for longer than that." She doesn't sound too enthusiastic about the idea.

"It's not like you have anything pressing at home waiting for you. I already checked with your stepmother. Your schedule is free for the next three months." He picks up his phone and taps on the screen.

Kate opens her mouth to say something.

"And I quote," he says, looking at his phone and interrupting whatever she was going to say. " 'And then I can go home and find another project to keep me busy.' Does that text sound familiar? And when I asked you if you had any idea what that was going to be, your reply was that you had no clue."

"And your point is?"

"I know you've been restless ever since the accident, Kate. You've been looking for something to pour your heart into. Even before that, it was like there was something missing but you couldn't figure out what it was.

"This project could be it. Stay here in Copper Creek for the next three months and help me in whatever capacity you want. You tell me what you're envisioning for each of the rooms. I'll tell you what is feasible and what isn't. If in the end it turns out that you get little or no satisfaction from doing this project, then at least you can cross home design off the list of what you're passionate about."

Kate's lips twitch up to one side. "How long have you been rehearsing that speech?"

Troy laughs. "I'm right, though, aren't I?"

When she doesn't answer, he powers on. "I'm not saying you have to live here permanently. I'm saying give me three months. We finish this project, have my father come out to see what I'm capable of—what *we're* capable of—and then you move back to Beverly Hills and you never have to return to Copper Creek again. The house will sell quickly, and you can wipe your hands clean of the town."

"But what about my friends?"

I can't be certain, but an emotion like anger or frustration flickers on his face. "Your friends aren't going anywhere. They'll still be there when you return." He rolls his eyes, which Kate misses because she's busy scanning the kitchen.

It's my gaze that catches his, and I read his message perfectly clear. He wants me to convince her to stay...because he has the same low opinion of her friends that I have.

And I haven't even met them.

"But you don't even have a crew," she tells him. "How are you planning to renovate this house if you don't know any tradesmen?"

"I can help there," I say. "I know skilled tradesmen who come highly recommended. And they'll know others, too. If you need general laborers, I'm sure you'll have no problems finding some in the area. I know a few names there as well. Plus, I did some work on construction sites before I ended up in Seattle. If you're okay with hiring me only part-time, I'd be happy to help out." And the money would go a long way toward restoring Charlotte's Bel Air.

It would be a win-win for us all.

Only Kate doesn't seem too convinced about that.

18

KATE

Both men wait for my answer while the theme music to *Jeopardy* plays in my head.

The problem is, I don't know what I want to do. Troy is right. I have been restless for a while—even since before the accident. But how is being stuck in the middle of nowhere, with no high-end stores in sight, the solution?

I glance between the two men and mentally list the pros and cons of Troy's plan.

Pros

1. He's right. I love interior design. I love the thrill of finding the right items that perfectly showcase a room's theme.

2. He's also right about the Pinterest boards. Yes, plural. I have one for each room. I'm thinking contemporary western, but with lots of white to contrast with the rustic elements.

But let's not mention that to Troy for now.

3. It could possibly equate to more sex with Noah. That would be a definite perk.

4. I really do have nothing planned for the next three months (so I'm available to do this).

5. More incredible sex with Noah.

Cons

1. Being stuck in a small town for three months.

2. No shopping on Rodeo Drive the entire time.

3. I'm not around to help Victoria with planning her wedding...which is okay, given that I'm not in the wedding party.

4. Three months of cleaning the stable...unless I can find someone to help me.

The teen that Roxy suggested had unfortunately experienced a run-in with a skateboard and is out of commission for a few more weeks.

"Okay, if I agree to this," I say to Troy, "you have to do something for me in return."

He nods. "All right, you've got yourself a deal."

"You don't want to know what it is first?"

"Sure, what is it?"

"You're going to clean Lady and Scoundrel's stable. Every. Single. Day. Come rain or come shine."

He shrugs, not at all surprised by my request. He already saw it coming.

"Make that two demands you agree to."

He sighs, an okay-lay-it-to-me sound. "You will play nice with Noah. Like I said before, he's my friend." Who I'm hoping to have more sex with if I'm going to be stuck in Copper Creek for three months.

"Sure, no problem. Any other demands?"

I look over at Noah. "Is there anything you can think of?"

There's an unmistakable twitching at the corner of his mouth. "Nope, sounds like you have it all covered."

Reaching across the table, I hold my hand out to Troy. "All right, you've got yourself a deal."

God, I really hope I'm not going to regret this.

"So when do we get started?" I ask.

"How about after breakfast? You and I need to discuss your

vision for the place, then figure out exactly what needs to be done to meet it."

I shake my head. "You're going to be cleaning the stable first after breakfast, stable boy. But don't worry, I'll show you how to do it before I start my morning yoga practice." I'm practically dancing with glee at how I'll no longer have to deal with the horse poop.

Noah pushes away from the table. "And on that note, I need to return to my ranch since I have morning chores to do."

"I'll walk you out," I tell him. Then to Troy I say, "I'll be back in a minute—then I can give you a tour of the stable and show you what you'll need to do. You aren't by any chance afraid of horses, are you?"

"Not particularly. Should I be?"

"Not when it comes to Lady and Scoundrel. They're real sweethearts."

Troy nods as if to say, "If you say so," and I walk with Noah to the front door. He stops to pull on his boots, and we step outside onto the porch.

"So you think Lady and Scoundrel are sweethearts?" Noah asks, a cocky grin on his face.

I grin back at him. "I'm still alive to be able to make the comment, so yes, they are."

"And so now that you're staying in Copper Creek for the next three months, when are you planning to ride those two sweethearts?"

"Ride them?"

"Yes, ride them. As in put saddles on their backs and take them out for some exercise on one of the local trails."

I feel my eyes widen. "I can't do that."

"Why not? You're already capable of putting their halters on and leading them to and from the pasture."

"But that's different. That doesn't involve me actually getting on the back of one of them."

"Are you afraid of heights?"

"No, but I don't know the first thing about riding a horse."

"Well, Princess, you're in luck. I *do* know the first thing about riding horses. And I happen to be free later this afternoon. So how about I give you the first lesson then? You can ride Lady, and I'll take Scoundrel."

"I don't know...."

"You remind me a lot of Charlotte. I wouldn't be surprised if her love of horses is in your blood. I bet you're an amazing rider, you just don't realize it yet."

I snort a laugh. "You're really grasping for straws there."

He shrugs in that sexy way of his. "You won't know unless you try it."

"You promise Lady won't let me die if I attempt to ride her?"

"I can't promise you that. But I will promise that she won't *try* to kill you."

I smack him on the chest. "You're not doing a very good job reassuring me, cowboy. I hope Charlotte did a better job with her students than you're doing."

He laughs, the sound low and husky, then leans in, his breath brushing against my cheek. "If you give it a try, you'll get to decide the when, the where, and the positions we'll be fucking in for the next week." His beard softly scrapes against my jaw.

At his words and the feel of his beard, my legs quiver and heat rushes to my core.

He's really not playing fair.

"Okay," I say, my voice barely more than a needy whisper.

His hand moves to my hip and continues until it's flat against the curve of one butt cheek. He pulls me to him, leaving zero space between us. His woodsy scent wraps around me.

At the memory of what it felt like to have him inside me last night, my entire body heats up like a firecracker.

"See you later, Princess." He slaps me on my butt. But

instead of the action igniting indignation in me, my body becomes even more turned-on.

Before I can find my voice to respond, he's jogging toward his truck.

Leaving me to wonder what the heck I just agreed to.

19

KATE

Troy and I spend the next few hours discussing my vision for the house. Troy tells me what is doable and gives me an estimate of the costs.

"One thing you need to consider is what the home-buying market for this region can handle when it comes to the cost of the house," Troy explains after I tell him I want the window in the attic to be replaced with something bigger, to let in more light. "If you add too many expensive additions, you might end up with a house that won't sell quickly, or you'll be forced to take a loss on it because you had to reduce the price in order move it."

"It's not like I paid for the house. It was given to me. And it's not like I can't afford to put money into it so that it makes a nice home for a family."

"Are you sure?"

"Yes. It doesn't mean I'll go overboard with everything. That's where you might need to rein me in."

By the time Noah shows up later in the afternoon, Troy has a good idea of what I'm looking to do with the property.

"While you're learning how not to fall off the horse," he

161

says, "I'll play around with my computer program to formalize the plans. Then we can move forward from there."

Noah hands him a piece of paper. "Here's the list of the various tradesmen I know in the area. They've either worked on the ranch at some point, or I personally know them."

While they discuss the list, I go upstairs to change into a pair of designer jeans and a shell-pink, short-sleeved top. Unlike Noah, I don't exactly look like I'm about to ride a horse. No one will confuse me for being a cowgirl.

We head to the stable, where he removes the two halters from the wall and hands me the one for Lady. We then walk to the pasture. My body trembles the entire time. Out of excitement? Possibly. Nervousness? More likely.

Lady and Scoundrel spot us and plod over. Lady nudges Noah from behind with her head.

"Is she flirting with you?" My tone holds a note of mocked exasperation. "Is there any female who doesn't flirt with you?"

A devilish grin appears on his face. "Jealous?"

"Ha! You wish." To Lady I say, "Don't worry, I'm not trying to steal him from you." She snickers—or whatever the sound is that horses make when they're amused.

While Noah is putting the halter on Scoundrel, I do the same to Lady. "We're not returning you to the stable yet. Noah has convinced me to actually climb on your back so we can go sightseeing. That sounds like fun, doesn't it?" I stroke her nose.

Once their halters are on, Noah and I walk toward the gate, the horses sandwiching us from either side.

"Do you think she'll mind that I'm a rookie when it comes to riding horses?" I ask Noah.

"I doubt either of them will care. They're both used to newbies riding them. Until a few years ago, Charlotte was teaching riding lessons with them."

Does that make me feel better? Slightly.

At the stable, Noah shows me how to saddle Lady;

then he does the same for Scoundrel. He gets me to tighten the cinch around her belly and gives me a brief lesson on mounting her, getting her to start walking, steering her, and most important of all...convincing her to stop.

He takes one of the riding hats Charlotte kept in the stable and pops it on my head. I give him my best pouty face. "How come you get to wear a cowboy hat and I don't?"

Never mind the part where I don't have a cowboy hat.

Or is it a cowgirl hat when a female wears it?

"Because I've been riding since pretty much the day I was born. I don't need to protect my head like you do."

"So your head won't crack open if you fall off the horse?" I flash him my best Sure-it-won't expression.

He laughs, the sound low and sexy, and my girlie parts sigh. "Sure it will, but the odds of that happening are a lot lower because I know what I'm doing."

"You're really not helping me build my confidence," I half-heartedly grumble.

"It's also because the horses will only be walking—trotting at the very most."

Noah double-checks Lady's saddle to ensure it's still tight. "Remember, with riding, it's all about the legs. The inner thighs are what will keep you on the horse."

"I thought that's what the saddle handle is for."

"You mean the horn?"

"Horn? Like a car horn? I get to honk it if another horse is in the way?"

He chuckles. "Not that kind of horn. This one doesn't make any sound. Its purpose also isn't to keep you from falling off. That's what your legs are for. It's not only the horse who gets exercise when you ride." He looks me over. "But tell me if your leg starts hurting."

I nod, even though that's the last thing I plan to do. My

injury has defined me enough as it is. I'm not letting it take this from me, too.

"There's a trail down to the river the horses are familiar with. Do you want to go there?" Noah asks.

"That would be great. I haven't had a chance to see anything beyond the house and the drive into town."

What I've witnessed is impressive enough, especially with the mountains in the background. I'm beginning to understand why Charlotte chose to live here.

But the mountains still don't make up for the lack of Rodeo Drive.

I study Lady and the saddle. "So, how do I get up onto her?"

"Put your left foot in the stirrup and hold on to the saddle, then pull yourself up. I'll help you if you want."

"Yes, I want."

I lift my sneaker-covered foot and place it in the stirrup. Noah settles his hands on my hips. There might be a layer of denim between his skin and mine, but it doesn't stop the hum buzzing through my body at his touch.

"You ready?" he asks.

"As ready as I'll ever be."

"On the count of three. One. Two. Three."

I pull myself up with the saddle while Noah lifts me. I swing my right leg over Lady's back and adjust myself on the seat.

I swallow. "Damn, that's a long way down."

But not as far as it would be if I was riding Scoundrel.

"It's not as high up as you think," is Noah's not-so-helpful comment.

"Easy for you to say, you're on the ground."

He chuckles. *Jerk.* A hot, delicious, panty-dropping jerk, but a jerk all the same.

He mounts Scoundrel. "Lady is used to following Scoundrel, so you pretty much just have to keep her from eating the grass while we're moving." He explains how to do that, and then we're off.

Noah leads the way, frequently checking over his shoulder to make sure I'm okay. I give him the thumbs up every time I catch him doing that. Otherwise, I'm preoccupied with appreciating the view. And I don't mean Noah's rear end, although that's mighty fine, too.

I'm talking about the colorful wild flowers growing along the edge of the dirt trail. The leafy trees and the bushes. The pine trees. The birds chattering high in the branches. The blue sky above us. The mountain range.

I close my eyes for a moment, soaking in the warm sunlight on my face and enjoying the fresh pine scent. In my head, Tiffany is lecturing me about the dangers of developing premature wrinkles because I'm not wearing a sunhat.

Pushing away her voice, I open my eyes and duck before a low branch can slap me in the face.

Fortunately, Noah doesn't witness it.

Note to self: No more closing your eyes while on horseback.

We continue until we arrive at the slow-moving river, and we follow alongside it for a while. The farther we travel, the more confident I grow riding Lady.

Eventually, we stop our horses by a grassy cove.

Noah attempts to help me down—but my foot gets tangled in the stirrup. He places his hands on my waist to steady me. It's not enough to save me, and I crash into him.

Noah steps back, somehow keeping us upright.

"So much for nailing that landing. But thanks for the great reflexes." I pat his nice, hard biceps on both arms.

"Happy to oblige ya, ma'am."

"Ooh, is that your sexy cowboy talk coming out?" I ask on a laugh.

"Possibly. Is it making you horny?"

"Possibly."

"We might have to do something about that."

"You might be right."

One of the horses snorts, reminding us they're still here.

Noah releases me, takes hold of both horses' reins and leads them to the water. Once they're happily drinking, he walks toward me, leaving them to enjoy their break. "By the way, congratulations."

"For what?"

His mouth quirks to one side. "On surviving your first ride."

My mouth is a mirror image of his. "I haven't made it to Charlotte's yet. I'll only consider it a success once my feet are firmly planted on the ground outside her stable."

There's still a chance I'll die on the way back.

Lady whinnies as if to agree.

Not exactly reassuring.

He laughs. "Okay. Congratulations on your half success. What do you think of riding so far?"

I can't help the smile that grows on my face. "I'll admit, you were right. I'm enjoying it."

I mentally high-five Charlotte's memory and limp to the water's edge.

But the limp is for a different reason this time—and it's more pronounced.

"You okay?" Noah asks.

"I think I discovered muscles I didn't know I had." *Hello, inner thighs. Sorry for ignoring you all this time.*

If they're achy now, I'm not looking forward to tomorrow, when I'll be walking around like I'm still riding a horse.

"Sorry about that."

I wave off his words. "That's okay. I'm positive I'll survive." I glance behind me, at the trail we came down. It seems to be the only one leading to this small stretch of land, which is otherwise secluded. "Is the trail leading from Charlotte's property the only one that can access this area?"

"That's right."

I walk to the river's edge. "How deep is the water?"

"It depends on the time of year and where you're standing. It's deeper farther out."

I remove my sneakers and socks. Noah doesn't say anything, but I can feel the weight of his gaze on my back.

I grab the hem of my top and pull it up over my head. I fold the fabric, place it on the grassy bank just behind me, and unzip my jeans.

"Is there any reason why you're removing your clothes?" Noah asks. He's not laughing, but it's lurking beneath his tone.

"I've never stayed in a small town before. I've also never skinny-dipped before." I shimmy the denim down my legs. "I just figured now that I've crossed the first one off the list, I might as well work on item number two."

I remove my jeans from around my ankles, fold them, and place them with the top on the grass.

I glance over my shoulder to see if Noah is still watching me.

He is, a predatory gleam in his eyes, but he's no longer where I left him standing. He's walking toward me. Butt. Naked.

His lean, muscled body is as spectacular as I remember it from last night.

"You do realize the basic premise behind skinny-dipping is the lack of clothing? And that includes your underwear," Noah points out.

I laugh, unhooking my bra in the back. "Thanks for the clarification." I toss it onto the ground, not paying attention to where it lands. My gaze remains locked on Noah's face.

I hook my thumbs under the lace waistband of my panties and slide the fabric down my legs. I barely have enough time to toss them to the grass before Noah's warm arms wrap around my waist from behind.

I shriek and giggle at the same time.

"How are you with cold water?" he asks, advancing into the river.

"How cold are we talking about?"

"Cold enough that you're going to want me to warm you up afterward." His hand shifts up to cover one breast, clarifying exactly what he means by warming me up.

"I'll hold you to that," I say at the same time he pinches my nipple, and it comes out as a moan.

He shifts his hold on me, so that he's carrying me in both arms, and keeps striding deeper and deeper and deeper into the river. My feet disappear into the water and I gasp.

Damn, that's cold.

He keeps going.

And then the moment I was bracing for, the moment I was partly hoping wouldn't happen does: Noah drops me into the water.

Double damn, that's cold.

By the time I find my footing, I'm already fully submerged.

I push myself up to the surface to find one wet and grinning Noah. Water runs down the sides of his face.

I shove wet strands of hair out of my eyes. "Oh God, you jerk," I say, only half meaning it.

I lunge at him. He catches me and lifts me up. My legs automatically wrap around his waist. His arms tighten around me.

The water might be cold but I'm suddenly not.

And neither is he, if his heated gaze is any indication.

I lower my head to his, and our mouths meet.

If I had been sitting on the fence as to whether I should say yes to Troy's plan and be stuck in Copper Creek for the next three months, this kiss would have sealed the deal.

Our tongues dance and glide and make promises we have every intention of keeping. I'm so focused on that and the man holding me—my bare breasts pressed against his chest—that at first, I don't register the polite coughing from somewhere near us on the water.

It's only when the cough becomes a little louder and more insistent that I'm jerked back to the here and now, and I notice the not-so-distant laughter of kids downstream.

Both Noah and I turn our heads to discover two older men in a canoe. Both are wearing matching dark-green baseball caps, tan short-sleeved shirts, royal-blue neckties, and badges on their sleeves.

Holy fruitcake.

"We're…um…sorry to interrupt," one of them says. "But in a few minutes, a troop of boy scouts is going to come paddling this way. And well…"

"Oh, shit," Noah mutters. I drop my head to his shoulder, doing my best to hide my heated face.

"So if you don't mind," the other man says.

"If you can give us some privacy," Noah says, "we'll be out of here before they get here."

"Thanks for being understanding."

"Not a problem." Noah lowers me to my feet.

I don't even check if both men are looking the other way. I hightail it back to shore with Noah right behind me.

20

NOAH

I prop up the hood of the Thunderbird. It's been two weeks since Kate and I first had sex. Two weeks since her cousin—who is fortunately staying at the hotel in town—showed up in Copper Creek.

It's also the first time in over two weeks that I've had a chance to work on my car. Kate is with Violet, Sophie, and Aubrey in Golden Falls, having a girls' day out. Troy drove to Billings to order supplies from the home renovation store there. Which means I have the day off from working on the house.

"So what exactly is going on between you and Kate?" Jake asks behind me. The crunch of his boots against the gravel outside the barn gave away his approach long before he asked the question.

"Hi to you, too." I grab the oil rag from the tool bench and turn around while wiping my hands. "Is there any particular reason you're asking me this? Or are you going all estrogen on me and need your daily gossip fix?"

"Real cute. I'm just curious. You can't fault me for that. You've made it clear to TJ and me that you're not interested in

170

dating. And history certainly supports that. Yet you're spending all your free time with her—which I might add, most people would consider that dating."

"I'm helping her and her cousin with the renovations. You know that." Surprisingly, Kate has actually been doing some of the physical labor.

And let me tell you, Kate in a tight tank top while swinging a sledgehammer is both scary and a turn-on.

"Didn't they hire some men to do that?"

"They employed four men to work full-time on the house, but given their deadline, they need all the extra help they can get. Besides, it's not like I'm working there full-time. The ranch is still my first priority." Which he knows.

He also knows that I'm getting paid, and the money will be going toward restoring the Chevy Bel Air.

"So nothing's going on between you and Kate?"

"We're just friends." Who fuck.

"That's too bad. She's good for you—any idiot can see that. You know there's nothing wrong with having more in your life than just the ranch. I should know."

Before he and Sophie finally ended up on the same page about how they felt for each other, the ranch was his life. He didn't even have a hobby until several months ago—when he took up leather crafting.

I toss the oil rag onto the bench. "Thanks for the advice, but Kate and I are just having fun. She's only here for a few months, and in the meantime, we're working hard—the whole team is working hard—so she can return to Beverly Hills and put Charlotte's house on the market."

"You lived in LA for a short time, didn't you?"

"Yes, before I moved to Seattle." I grab a wrench from the toolbox.

"Would you consider moving back there?"

"What? Seattle or LA?"

"LA."

I shake my head. "The place didn't appeal to me. I might have craved living in a big city when I left here after high school, but that desire has long since gone. I prefer small-town life."

"Even if you fall in love and the woman lives in a big city?"

It takes a second for his meaning to sink in and I burst out laughing. "Your falling in love with Sophie has fried some of your brain cells, bro. One, I'm not in love. I'm as far from being in love as you can get. Kate and I are just having fun. That's all. Two, she and I come from very different worlds. She'd probably have an allergic reaction if she even tried to wear clothes with nondesigner labels."

With the exception of when she was wearing Charlotte's clothes to clean the stable. And even then, she no doubt spends an hour in the shower afterward, scrubbing off any remaining molecules of regular-people clothing.

"The woman can't stand living in a small town," I remind him.

"Yet she's here for the next two and a half months."

"That's because her cousin is very persuasive and because she knows there's a ticking clock. She's not expecting to live here for the rest of her life."

I could tell him about my misadventures with dating a woman whose world revolved around expensive clothing, bags, shoes, and cars, but I don't feel like getting into that right now. Or at all.

Even though Samantha and Kate are like night and day in many respects, that is the one thing they both agree on: money is everything.

Jake's phone pings. My guess is, based on the goofy expression on his face, Sophie sent the text.

"You up for Joe's tonight?" he asks.

I'm about to tell him I'll pass, but I'm cut off before the words can make it past the gate.

"Kate will be there."

21

KATE

"What do you think?" I ask Sophie, Aubrey, and Violet. We're in Golden Falls for the day, at a store that sells western clothing and boots.

And in case you're wondering, there isn't a single designer label here.

What's even more surprising is that I don't shudder at the thought.

Or rather, I don't shudder as much as I would have several weeks ago.

The three women study my feet, which are currently in a pair of cute cowgirl boots with intricate floral designs stitched into the leather.

"I love those," Sophie says. "How do they fit?"

I walk up and down the space between where they're sitting on the bench and the display of boots on the wall. "They feel good."

"You'll need to wear them in for a bit before you can spend long periods in them," Violet warns.

Aubrey nods. "That's right. And you know the best way to do that?"

I shake my head.

"Go dancing." She turns to the other two. "What do you think? We can take her to Joe's tonight and teach her how to line dance."

"That's a great idea. We can invite the guys, including Troy and Ryan." Sophie turns to Violet. "Is Austin off tonight?"

Violet shrugs. "I have no idea what my brother's schedule is, but I can ask him." She types on her phone and a moment later gets a pinged reply.

She rolls her eyes. "My brother asked me if I should be dancing, given my delicate condition."

"Ask him what century he's from," Aubrey says on a laugh.

Violet types another message. This is answered soon after. "He said the century that appreciates pregnant women are delicate creatures who shouldn't go dancing."

She starts typing on the screen, but a tune from her phone interrupts her.

Sophie and Aubrey both snicker. "Looks like someone's in trouble now," Aubrey says in a mock singsong voice.

I look between the three of them, wondering what she's talking about.

"Austin squealed to TJ about Violet's plans to go dancing," Sophie clarifies for those of us sitting in the balcony seats.

"I swear, this is going to be one super long pregnancy if those two keep this up," Violet grumbles and accepts the call.

"For someone who breeds horses for a living," Aubrey says loud enough so TJ can hear her, "you'd think he would be a little less freaked out about you carrying his child."

"I think it's sweet," I say, trying not to sigh dreamily. "So far the only luck I've had with boyfriends is him cheating on me with my best friend. And I'd hardly call that lucky."

Violet jumps up from her seat, still talking to her husband. The next thing I know, she's hugging me. "I can totally relate to that....No, not you, Snuggle Bear. I'm bonding here with Kate and telling her the only difference is my boyfriend at the time was also married. He forgot to mention that little tidbit." She looks at me when she says it.

I cringe. "Ouch, that *is* bad."

"But fortunately, Snuggle Bear is nothing like that. Isn't that right, Snuggle Bear?"

Aubrey and Sophie burst out laughing.

Violet listens to whatever TJ is saying. "Well, let's see, if you're hoping to save your masculinity, because we both know Aubrey and Sophie are dying to tell everyone in Copper Creek my new name for you, then I would stop acting like I'm too fragile to do anything....Yes, I know I don't normally call you Snuggle Bear, but I can always start."

"How are you doing with those boots?" the woman who was helping me a few minutes ago asks. This is the same woman who thought I was from another planet when I listed the high-end designers who make cowgirl boots that I wanted to try on.

It was Sophie who had to translate to the woman for me.

In the end, I decided it wouldn't kill me to shop for the same brands that Sophie, Violet, and Aubrey wear.

Turns out, even though the boots aren't by a designer, they are comfortable and fashionable.

"I'm going to take them. Thank you." I remove them from my feet and return them to the box. The woman takes it from me and walks to the cash register.

Violet ends the call. "That worked. At least for now. We just have to tell the rest of the guys, and we're all set for tonight."

"I texted Jake and he told Noah," Sophie says. "They're both in."

I'd be lying if I said that hearing Noah's name doesn't cause my skin to tingle—as if it's remembering his every touch.

"And I invited Ryan," Aubrey says.

"I'll text Troy once he returns from Billings," I tell them, even though I'm not sure he'd be interested. Western music isn't his thing.

It's not mine either, but I'm happy for the chance to hang out with Noah and his friends—and to see how the other side parties.

"What are you planning to wear tonight, Kate?" Aubrey asks.

"I have no idea. I don't exactly have anything with me that would work in a western bar."

"Are you looking to get some clothes for tonight?" Violet asks as I walk over to the display of cowgirl hats.

I try on a plain black one. "That's not a bad idea." It will be like when people buy those tacky T-shirts while visiting a new city or a foreign country. "I might as well. Like they say, when in Rome, dress like the Romans."

"Didn't they wear togas?"

Aubrey laughs. "You could wrap a sheet around yourself. I'm sure you'd be a big hit with the guys at Joe's....That hat looks great on you, by the way."

"Thank you. I think I'll get it." Another quaint little souvenir of my time in Montana.

I pay for my boots and hat, and we head to another store.

We're looking through the racks of clothes there when Sophie calls me over. "I found you the perfect outfit. The guys at the bar will go crazy over it. Of course they'll have to get past Noah, Ryan, and Austin first. And Austin scares the shit out of most guys."

She hands me the clothing...what little there is of it. The spaghetti-strap tank top is tan, crocheted, and ends several inches above my belly button. The long fringe around the hem makes up the rest of the top. I love it. It's sexy and reminds me of what I used to wear during my party days.

But it's what Sophie picked out to cover my legs that has me mentally running in the other direction.

"I can't wear those." I point to the denim shorts that reveal a lot more than they cover—even though I would have worn similar ones before the accident.

"Sure you can. From what I can tell, you've got great legs. Why not flaunt them?"

"Except I don't have great legs. I look like a ghost, for one thing."

Sophie, Aubrey, and Violet aren't highly tanned, but at least what tans they do have prevent them from looking like someone who hasn't moved onto the afterlife yet.

"It's May in Montana, when most of us are still sporting our winter tans. You don't look that much paler than us."

"It's not just that. My leg is badly scarred from the car accident I was in last year. It looks hideous." Yes, that's one of the adjectives a guy used after seeing the scars a few months ago. I was by the pool at the country club when he said it.

"I bet it doesn't look as bad as you think it does," Sophie says. "Was your leg burned?"

"No, but glass and jagged pieces of metal ripped up the skin."

She cringes. "Oh, God. That sounds painful."

"Maybe I can wear something else with the top."

"Your jeans will go with it. But you should try on the shorts and see what you think."

"All right." I guess there's no harm in trying them on.

I disappear into the fitting room.

I change into the outfit, then check out my reflection and grimace. The top is adorable. But while the shorts aren't super short, all of my scars are on display.

"Kate?" Sophie says from the other side of the door. "Are you going to show us?"

Us?

I hesitantly unlock the door and open it. Sophie, Violet, and Aubrey are waiting for me when I emerge from the cubicle. I tentatively step out, prepared to meet their horrified expressions.

"Ohmygod," Sophie says, grinning. "You wear that outfit tonight, and you'll knock Noah on his ass. It looks amazing on you, Kate."

"But what about my scars?" I ask, doing my best to cover them with my hand, which is pretty useless, given the extent of them.

"Your scars are fine. They don't bother Noah, right?"

I almost burst out laughing. They don't bother him because we've been sleeping together.

Well, not technically sleeping, but he has seen them and he still kisses them every time he goes down on me.

"No. He's fine with them."

The three women exchange knowing glances—after I've just confirmed what they've suspected all along. Noah and I are more than friends while I'm in Copper Creek.

"No, it's not like that. We're just friends. Well, I guess now I'm his boss. Actually, more like the cousin of the boss." Which sounds better in my head, because now I'm not having sex with one of my employees.

All three look like they believe that as much as they would believe it if I had announced I'm the Easter Bunny.

Which is crazy when you consider it. Noah has a reputation of never having sex with the same woman twice. Why would Sophie, Aubrey, and Violet think things would be any different with me?

Even if they are.

"In that case," Aubrey says, "you can also dance with Austin and Ryan. They're both great dancers."

"And if any other guy can get past those three," Sophie says, "you'll be so busy dancing, we might not see you for the entire evening."

"Just because Noah is fine with these scars doesn't mean

other men will be." Maybe if I wasn't so pale, the scars wouldn't be so noticeable.

"Kate, those scars don't change who you are," Violet says. "You're sweet and funny and intelligent. The scars won't chase guys away. The men around these parts are more put off by women who are high-maintenance than they are by scars."

By high-maintenance, she's referring to me. She's just too nice to say it out loud.

I check out my reflection again and nod. "You're right. And I'm buying both the shorts and the top." Especially since they'll look adorable with my new boots and hat.

The girls cheer my decision. Warmth fills me at their encouragement and support...which is an odd way to feel, given I go shopping all the time with my friends back home.

A voice in the recesses of my head points out that their idea of being supportive isn't quite the same as it is for Violet, Sophie, and Aubrey. I ignore the voice.

"Now I just hope I don't look too foolish attempting to line dance."

"Nobody's going to care," Aubrey says. "But if you want, once these two bail on us to go home to their sweethearts, you can come over to my house. I'll teach you some moves so you don't feel completely out of place tonight."

"You would do that for me?"

"Of course. It'll be fun. I'll even help you get ready so you look a little less—"

"High-maintenance?" I fill in, grinning.

"Yes, that. I can even teach you how to flirt cowgirl style. I mean, given that you and Noah aren't dating."

I choose to ignore the smirk in her tone and the fact that she's calling me out on being a liar. "That's even a thing?"

Sophie giggles. "So that's what I did wrong all those years I was single."

Aubrey lets out a snorted laugh. "No, your problem was you couldn't talk to guys you were interested in without getting all tongue-tied. The inability to flirt was the least of your problems."

I look at Sophie for confirmation.

She nods. "She's right. Just ask Ryan tonight. The poor man needed a translator to figure out what I was saying to him."

"But you don't have trouble talking to Jake."

"He's almost the only one she didn't have trouble talking to back then," Violet says. "But that's also because they were best friends."

I smile. "And now he's going to be your husband."

Sophie's answering smile has the same dreamy expression I've seen on Violet.

I pay for my clothes, and we head over to a nearby café for lunch.

"The secret to flirting cowgirl style is letting the guy notice that *you've* noticed him checking you out," Aubrey explains after we order our food. "Give him a flirty, confident smile to show him you like what you see while you openly check him out."

Violet and Sophie look like they're trying not to burst out laughing.

"Oh, sure you two laugh now"—she flashes them what appears to be a fake scowl—"but I know what I'm doing."

The door to the cafe opens and a man enters. He's good-looking, not much older than us, wearing jeans, a checkered green shirt, and cowboy boots. He heads for the counter.

I'm not the only one who notices him.

Aubrey pushes her chair away from the table and stands. "Watch and learn, ladies. Then your homework assignment today is to practice on your husband, fiancé, and boyfriend."

She messes up her hair slightly, the brown waves falling just above her breasts. She's wearing a fitted dark-green T-shirt with the vet clinic's logo—small and white—above her right boob. Paired with the slim-fitting jeans and her cowgirl boots, she exudes a confident brand of sexiness.

One my friends back home would approve of...if they could get past what Aubrey is wearing.

With a subtle, teasing smile on her face, she sashays to the counter as if she has all the time in the world.

"Wow, she's really good." My voice is an awed whisper.

"She is," Violet says, her tone not so much awed as it is on the shocked side of things.

"Did you know she could do that?" she asks Sophie.

The equally stunned blonde shakes her head. "I've never seen her flirt like that before."

Aubrey brushes her hair out of her eyes, gaining the cowboy's attention.

His gaze sweeps down her body and he smiles approvingly. Aubrey leans back slightly, making a show of checking out his butt.

"Are you taking notes, Kate?" Sophie asks.

"How does she make it look so easy?" I mentally follow along with her actions as if I'm the one doing them. Flirting was never my thing. Luckily for me, it isn't an essential skill I need for landing a boyfriend.

But maybe it's a necessary skill for keeping said boyfriend.

Aubrey tosses her hair over her shoulder while giving her cowboy a smoldering look.

"Seriously," Violet says, "where did she learn to do all of that? And why haven't I seen her do it at Joe's? I can't remember the last time I've seen her flirt."

"Me neither," Sophie responds.

The cowboy leans closer to Aubrey as if he's about to share a secret.

The waitress delivers our order and asks if we would like anything else. We tell her we're good for now.

Smiling sweetly, Aubrey runs her fingers down the cowboy's arm.

And then kicks him in the shin.

"What the hell?" he cries out.

Sophie winces. "Ouch, that's gonna hurt."

"Yep, that's more like the Aubrey we know and love," Violet says as Aubrey flounces back to our table.

I pick up my water. "I assume the last bit isn't part of the whole cowgirl-flirting concept she was talking about."

"Yeah, I recommend you avoid that last move. Noah probably won't appreciate it."

I don't have a chance to tell them again that nothing's going on between Noah and me—depending on your definition of "nothing's going on." Aubrey drops to her seat.

"What a dumbass," she grumbles. She grabs her vegetarian burger and sinks her teeth into it like she's imagining sinking them into the cowboy's arm.

"What the heck happened up there?" Violet asks.

We have to wait for Aubrey to finish chewing before we get an answer. "He asked me out on a date."

I blink. "And that's a bad thing?" As far as I can tell, Aubrey doesn't have a boyfriend, either in Copper Creek or anywhere else.

"Very much a bad thing. Boyfriends are nothing but trouble." She glances at her two friends. "Present company's boyfriends excluded. You two landed the only two decent boyfriends out there. The rest were abducted by aliens."

I chuckle. I can't help it. "I have to agree with Aubrey on that one. Although I think my brothers and cousins aren't too bad, but I might be biased there."

"Too bad your brothers and cousins don't live in Copper

Creek." She takes another bite of her burger. "Plus, the jerk made a douchebag comment right after he asked me out."

The cowboy collects his order and leaves without giving Aubrey a second glance.

We finish our food and head back to Copper Creek...to begin my transformation for tonight.

22

KATE

I wait in the middle of Aubrey's living room while she searches for a song on her iPhone. Her coffee table is now against the wall after we moved it there to give us more space.

I'm wearing the outfit I bought earlier, including my boots. Aubrey figured it would be easier to practice in them than in the dress I was wearing while shopping.

She turns on the music and stands next to me. A sexy male voice starts singing through the Bluetooth speakers.

"The best thing to do is follow what the people in front of you are doing," she says. "Once you've danced to the song a few times, it becomes second nature."

She demonstrates the moves for the first verse. Fortunately, I'm a quick learner—thanks to years of dance class. We go through the sequences a handful of times together. By the end of the song, I've mastered several basic steps.

"Not every song will involve a line dance. Usually you can tell which ones they are because everyone rushes to the dance floor whenever the song begins. There are other styles of dance too, depending on who you end up with. Some men are like talentless octopi. You want to avoid them. Don't worry, I'll warn you which ones they are if they come near us.

"You can't go wrong with any of the Daniels brothers. Although talking from past experience, you'll never get Jake and TJ away from Sophie's and Violet's sides. Austin and Ryan are also great dancers. So is Chase Scottsdale. But alas, he's been so busy lately with a new start-up business, he's rarely at Joe's these days.

"That's about it when it comes to the men in town who are both great dancers and decent guys. But based on what you're wearing tonight, I'd be surprised if Noah lets anyone near you who doesn't belong to our circle of friends."

I groan. "As if my overly protective male relatives aren't bad enough, now I have an overly protective male friend." Whom I kiss. And have sex with.

Aubrey snorts a laugh. "I've known Noah my entire life. Yes, he's protective of his friends and family and anyone he cares about, but it's different with you. *He's* different with you."

"It doesn't matter. He and I both know that anything between us has an expiry date."

Her mouth moves into a Cheshire-cat grin. "Ha! I knew it. So there *is* something going on between you two. And don't even try to deny it. You're fooling no one. The main thing is you both know it's short term, so there won't be any hurt feelings in the end." She starts a new song.

After Aubrey teaches me some more dance steps, she restyles my hair into messy waves. My usual high-maintenance, Beverly-Hills appearance has gone into hiding. Now, I resemble a fun-loving sexy cowgirl.

She nods her approval.

Unable to resist, I get Aubrey to take my photo and I send it to Troy.

Me: Going line dancing tonight.

> Me: I'm going to Joe's with Noah and his
> friends if you want to join us.

Aubrey and I drive to Joe's in my car. We park next to TJ's truck and enter the bar.

The bar looks exactly like I imagined it would: Peanut shells underfoot. Dim lights. Loud country music. Several pool tables in one room—players hunched over them, sticks in hand.

The complete opposite of the nightclub scene back home.

Aubrey grabs hold of my wrist and practically drags me across the room. Several men check us out as we make our way to the table where our friends—minus Noah and Ryan—are waiting for us.

"Kate?" TJ asks as we approach, clearly unsure if it's me—or someone who vaguely resembles the woman he has met.

I smile. "That's right."

"Wow. You look so different."

Both Jake and Austin agree with him.

"I'm assuming that's a good thing?" I say, thankful that no one back home can see me now.

What does it matter if they see you in an outfit that is as far from Neiman Marcus or Saks Fifth Avenue as you can get? a voice in my head asks. *When was the last time any of your friends asked you to go dancing with them?*

Sophie and Violet hug me, even though I just saw them a few hours ago.

"You look amazing," Sophie says.

"You really do," Violet adds.

The music changes to a song Aubrey and I practiced dancing to earlier.

She grabs my arm before I'm able to thank Sophie and Violet. "Okay, let's show them how a Beverly Hills cowgirl dances. And Austin, you're coming with us." To me she explains, "There's a benefit to being friends with the sheriff.

Once the scumbags see us dancing with him, they'll think twice about hitting on us."

"Wow, way to go, Aubrey, making me feel used," he says with a laugh.

She backhands him on the chest. "Oh, quit your complaining, big boy. You know I won't be crimping your style. The badge bunnies will still find you irresistible."

And with that, she drags me onto the dance floor with Austin trailing behind us.

We get into formation and move with the music.

Aubrey's right about one thing—Austin is a great dancer.

I follow what everyone does, only messing up a few times in the beginning. My limp is hard to miss, but no one seems to care. Everyone is too busy having a good time to notice.

We stay on the dance floor for several more songs, then return to the group to get drinks.

Troy, Noah, and Ryan are there when we arrive.

I hug my cousin. "Hey, you made it. I wasn't sure if this would be your scene."

"Since when is it yours?"

"There's a first for everything." I release him.

"I'm impressed," Ryan says to me. "Nice dance moves. Have you done that before?"

"Aubrey's a great teacher."

Noah remains speechless for a second, then wraps a hand around the back of my neck and crashes his mouth against mine.

For our first kiss in front of his brothers and friends and my cousin.

And there goes my claim that nothing's going on between us. Sophie and Violet won't believe me after this.

That's my last thought as his kiss consumes me, making me hotter than when I was kicking up my heels on the dance floor. My arms go around his neck, and his other hand rests on my lower back, pushing its way through the fringe of my top.

I'm vaguely aware of the music as his tongue dances with mine.

By the time we finally pull apart, the last strains of the song are playing.

"Hi, I'm happy to see you, too." My voice is so soft, I'm not sure if he even hears me.

"Love the outfit. The shorts look great."

Even though he doesn't say the words, I know that he's referring to the scars and my newfound self-confidence.

"Thanks!" I reach up and kiss him. It's not the same consuming kiss he just gave me. It's just the brushing of lips, but it still has my pulsing racing like a horse in the Kentucky Derby.

A new song begins. One I recognize from this afternoon at Aubrey's. She's already dragging Austin and Ryan onto the dance floor with her.

I grab Noah's hand. "C'mon, Cowboy. You're going to prove that you can live up to the reputation Aubrey told me about."

"What reputation is that?"

"The one where you're a great dancer."

We take our positions next to our friends on the dance floor. Noah effortlessly performs the moves, his body having long since memorized them. The pride on his face as I replicate the dance steps stirs an emotion I haven't experienced in a while. Not since my first steps after the accident.

The song switches to one I don't recognize. It's not a line dance—that much I can tell.

Noah leads me through the dance moves. My years of ballroom dancing at private school pay off. I might not know the steps, but I do know how to let a man lead, and I quickly figure them out.

The song is upbeat, and we're twirling around the floor like nobody's business. Aubrey's dancing with Ryan, Violet with TJ, and Sophie with Jake. Austin and Troy are talking to some women near the bar.

We dance for several more songs; then the music changes to a slow dance. Noah pulls me close so our bodies are touching. My arms go around his neck and I sway along with him.

He brushes his lips against my jaw. "I want to spend the night with you tonight." The scraping of his beard excites my girlie parts, and they're defenseless against his husky voice.

"Okay," I say on little more than a whisper. Noah has never spent the night before. Usually we have sex and he returns to the ranch—other than that first night when he ran into Troy in the morning.

We all stay at Joe's for two more hours. Violet and TJ are the first to leave.

"So what's the verdict?" Aubrey asks me as we drive to her house. Noah is planning to meet me at Charlotte's since I need to drop Aubrey off first. "Did you have fun tonight?"

"I loved it."

"Enough to want to do it again before you leave Copper Creek?"

"Absolutely. It's been awhile since I last had that much fun." And even back in my party days, it was nothing like tonight.

Noah's truck is in the driveway when I arrive at Charlotte's house. I enter through the front door, but he's not in the furniture-less living room or the kitchen.

The sound of running water pulls my attention upstairs. I find Noah in my bathroom, filling the claw-foot tub. Steam raises in the air, lightly scented with lavender.

"I figured you might want to soak in the tub first." He steps closer to me and caresses my leg where the scars are the worst. "How's your leg doing?"

"It's actually doing really well." Especially given all the dancing tonight.

Noah undoes the button on my denim shorts. "I really approve of these. I hope I get to see you in them more often." He unzips them, apparently more eager to see me out of them than in them.

"They're not exactly practical for working on a renovation site."

"They would look hot, though, with nothing more than a bra, steel-toed boots, and a tool belt." He slowly runs the tip of his tongue along his lower lip. "It would be my new favorite fantasy." His voice gets huskier with each word.

"What was your old favorite fantasy?"

"You in cowboy boots, a hat, and these shorts. But since I already got to live that fantasy, I needed to come up with something new."

His fingers slip under the hem of the crocheted top, dragging it up my body. He pulls the top over my head and drops it onto the tile floor.

My nude strapless bra joins the pile a second later, and he kisses the top of each breast. "I've been waiting too long to taste these babies again."

I have to agree with him there.

He pops a nipple into his mouth and sucks hard. My legs? They're threatening to give out from the hot, wet sensation against the hard peak.

I grab the side of the tub to steady myself...and am reminded that the water is still running. The tub is close to overflowing.

I stretch toward the taps and turn one off—only for Noah to

protest. I'd inadvertently reached too far, pulling my nipple from his mouth.

"Sorry. I didn't want the bathroom to flood." I quickly turn off the other tap.

"Good plan." He goes back to sucking on me.

Luckily for the other taut bud, Noah considers its needs, too. He pinches and rolls it between his finger and thumb. My breaths are noisy like I'm running a marathon; only this one will end in the promised land.

The land of mind-numbing orgasms I know and love. The land where Noah is the king.

I thread my fingers in the silky strands of his hair. They gently wrap around my fingers and I tug on them hard.

He groans against my nipple, taking me to another level.

Once he's ensured that each peak is thoroughly worshiped, he kneels in front of me and peels my shorts and nude lacy panties down my legs. His fingertips lightly trace against my skin. I shiver at his touch.

I step out of the final pieces of clothing and he slowly pushes himself to his feet, planting kisses on his way up—on my legs, my stomach, my chest.

Except I'm naked and he isn't, and I don't see the fairness in that.

"Are you joining me in the water?" I ask, reaching for the hem of his T-shirt.

"Would you like me to?"

"Of course. It's part of my water-therapy session. Doctor's orders."

"Well, in that case..." He grabs the back of his collar and yanks the T-shirt over his head.

Getting a little impatient for him to be rid of his clothes, I happily help him by undoing his jeans and removing them.

He climbs into the tub first and settles in. I join him, easing my way into the glorious heat.

Noah grabs my hand, tugging me toward him. I shift to sit between his bent legs, so that I'm resting against his chest. Bubbles cover the top of my breasts.

Now, I know what you're thinking happens next. That we have wild bath-time sex, which results in water spilling over the sides and our moans echoing against the tiles.

Sorry to disappoint.

I rest my head on his shoulder and we just talk. Talk about the renovation. Talk about my life in Beverly Hills. Talk about Noah's time in Seattle and how much he admired his boss—the man who taught him everything about restoring cars.

By the time we're finished talking, the water has cooled off, and we're more than ready to warm up.

23

NOAH

A few days after the evening at Joe's Bar, Kate and I lean against the kitchen island that will eventually be replaced. Troy and the crew have left for the day.

"Where are you planning to sleep now that the major renovations are getting started?" Oddly enough, it's not a question I've asked her before now. But Charlotte's house is old, which means it's not safe to sleep here during the renovations, no thanks to potential contaminants such as asbestos and lead paint.

"I'm renting a room at the hotel. I talked to Megan the other day, and she said they had vacancies."

"You don't need to do that. You're more than welcome to stay at the ranch."

"I can't impose like that. The hotel will be fine."

"You're not imposing. Besides, your staying at the ranch will save my ass."

"And why's that?"

"Because if Violet and Sophie ever find out you're staying at the hotel and I knew about it, that would be the end of me." I chuckle. "You're their friend—and they would love to have you

194

closer to them so they can grill you about all the dark secrets they're positive I've shared with you."

Her eyebrows lift. "Have you shared any dark secrets with me?"

"I don't have any. And you know everything there is to know about me. More so than my family and friends. They don't know about my ex-girlfriend."

Surprise clouds her face for a second before it's replaced by her stunning smile. One of my favorite smiles—along with her post-sex one.

"Will I be staying with you or in the guest room?" she asks.

Forget what they tell you about how there's no such thing as a dumb question. There is, and that one is a prime example. "In my room, of course."

"Won't it be a little confusing for Deacon? Or do you usually bring women home to sleep in your room?"

Hell, no. Even before Deacon moved into the ranch house, I had a policy that prevented the women I planned to fuck from coming home with me. We always went to their place. It was my number one rule.

"Well, no..." I tell her, unsure what that has to do with anything.

"His mom and dad are married, so it makes sense that they are in the same room. And Sophie and Jake are getting married soon, so that's fine, too. But you and I are only together while I'm in Copper Creek."

I get what she's saying, but I really don't believe it'll make a difference. It's not like our sharing a room will turn Deacon into a hooligan.

"You can stay in the guest room if it makes you feel better." I turn around and pull her against me. "But don't think for a second that you're off-limits while we're living together. Except you'll have to come to my room because the guest room is next to Deacon's."

"I can do that. But are you really sure your brothers will be okay with me staying at the ranch?"

"If you want, I can ask them."

She nods.

I send both TJ and Violet texts to double-check with them. I know whatever they say will be echoed by Jake and Sophie.

We don't have to wait long for their replies. The text has barely left my phone before I get a pinged answer from Violet.

I show Kate the phone and she laughs at her friend's message.

> Violet: Of course she's staying here, dumbass. Where did you expect her to stay?

TJ's text comes soon after.

> TJ: I take it you've had your question answered. You're lucky you didn't ask her in person. She might have cuffed your head for being an idiot.

"And if you had any doubts about if Violet considers you a friend…" I say after Kate reads the message.

We go upstairs, and I help her pack her suitcases.

I hold up a pair of red lacy panties and a matching bra from her suitcase. "I want to see you in my room tonight wearing these and only these. But if you want to add a tool belt, I'll be supportive of that fantasy, too." I wink at her.

"I'll keep that in mind." She laughs and removes the dresses from the closet that look like they belong from another century. She slips them into garment bags and puts them on the bed.

"You're bringing those with us?"

"Sure. They were important to Charlotte. I've decided to keep them, at least for now. Or until I can figure out what to do with them." From the same closet, she pulls out the box holding the letters between Charlotte and her mystery man. That, too, goes on the bed.

"Did you ever figure out what happened to John?" I ask her, nodding at the engraved wooden box.

"Sadly, no. Their letters to each other suddenly stopped. The question is, how did she get back the ones she sent him? Maybe it's one of those mysteries I'll never solve."

Have I read the letters? No. Kate's just talked about them. All we know is that Charlotte and John were engaged while he was serving in the Korean War, they were in love, and they'd had wild sex in the Bel Air before John was deployed.

"It's just sad that I'll never get to learn more about him," Kate says. "From what I could tell, he was the love of her life, and she never fell in love again. Or I'm assuming she never fell in love again. According to Tilly and Meg, Charlotte did date, but she never had any long-term relationships."

"You mean she was a player?"

Kate backhands my chest. "Women aren't players. They're testing their options."

"So I'm just an option you're testing?" I laugh at her flushed response.

We load the truck, and Charlie jumps onto the rear seat of the cab once we're finished.

"You do realize I'm driving my car there," Kate tells him.

He barks, climbs onto the front passenger seat, and makes himself comfortable.

"Oh, like that is it?" she says on a laugh, and we return to the ranch in our respective vehicles.

Deacon is outside playing with Maui when we arrive. Jake and TJ are watching the pair, as is Asgard.

As soon as I step down from the truck, Deacon comes hurtling toward me, with Maui hot on his cowboy-booted heels. He flings himself into my arms, and I scoop up the giggling boy.

Charlie visits with his new buddies.

"Hi, Uncle Noah." Deacon parks both hands on my cheeks, squishing them together to give me a fish face.

"Hey, little man," I attempt to say, which makes him giggle harder. He then waves at Kate as she approaches us. "Hi, Auntie Kate."

He started calling her that a few days ago; none of us have bothered to correct him.

I lower him to the ground. "Are you okay if Kate stays here for a few weeks while we work on her house? She'll be staying in the bedroom next to yours."

He grins at Kate, revealing a mouth full of baby teeth. "Are you going to read me bedtime stories?"

"Don't your mommy and daddy usually do that?" I ask him, mostly because I know they do.

"Yes. But now Auntie Kate can tell me them, too."

She crouches to his level. "I can certainly do that. I love reading bedtime stories." She tickles him and he flings himself at her, almost knocking her onto her ass.

Once Deacon peels himself off her, she asks, "Are you going to read to Charlie? He loves it when you do that."

Deacon can't read yet, but he loves to point to the different pictures in his books and tell Charlie what they are.

"You guys want to help us bring Kate's stuff into the house?" I call out to my brothers, who look amused at the interaction between Kate and TJ's son.

"Sure."

"Why not?"

They push away from the fence and grab her stuff from the truck to take upstairs.

Kate, Deacon, and the dogs follow us.

In her room, Deacon clambers onto Kate's bed, pulling himself up with the covers and making a mess of them. Then he plunks himself in the middle of the pillows.

Maui barks and jumps his front paws onto the bedding. That makes Deacon giggle, and he scrambles over to him.

And now the bedding is a bigger mess.

Charlie tries to put his paws onto the bed, but he doesn't come close to Maui's level of success. So he barks at the injustice of being too short.

"Maui, down," Jake says, nudging the one-year-old black Lab off the bed. Maui flashes his puppy-dog eyes that worked a lot better on Jake when Maui was a young puppy. The same puppy-dog eyes that still have Sophie giving in to his wishes.

"Deacon, you're not supposed to be on Kate's bed," TJ reprimands, a heavy dose of eye rolling in his tone. There's also a spark of amusement because none of us were much better when we were Deacon's age.

Actually, when I think about it, we were a helluva lot worse. Deacon hasn't tried scaling the living room curtains.

Yep, guilty as charged.

He scoops up his son and lowers him to the floor. Deacon quickly distracts himself by playing with the dogs.

"That's okay," Kate says, doing her best not to laugh. "It'll be messy when I sleep tonight."

My brothers herd the dogs and Deacon from the room.

"We'll leave you two to unpack," Jake says. "But remember the rules: No shutting the door when you have a girl in your room."

I flip him the finger. Fortunately, Deacon isn't around to see it.

Laughing his head off, Jake departs the room. I close the door behind him, ignoring his dumbass rule.

Kate's busy emptying one suitcase and putting the contents into the dresser drawers. I grab her from behind and pull her against me, allowing my hands easy access to her breasts.

One hand moves under her tank top, and I palm her tit and the lacy fabric covering it.

She moans, the sound quieter than back at Charlotte's house, so not to be heard by everyone else in *this* house.

My other hand slips from her waist to between her legs. She's wearing my favorite pair of shorts—and not just because I know the courage it took for her to wear them the first time.

I press my fingertips against the seam, knowing the exact spot to apply pressure to get the reaction I want.

"Oh, God. You're not playing fair," she half moans, half whispers.

"Never said I was going to play fair. I just want to give you a taste of what you can expect later."

I roughly turn her around and kiss her long and deep until I can feel her trembling against me.

My kiss becomes more tender, and my heart stirs in my chest. I attempt to ignore it but it's no use. It's official: I'm starting to fall for the woman in my arms.

The woman who has no use for small-town life.

Doesn't that fuck all?

The phone rings from Kate's purse. She ignores it and we continue kissing.

It stops ringing.

A minute later it starts ringing again.

Once more, Kate ignores it as our kisses go back to being deeper, more consuming.

The phone stops ringing only to start again several seconds later.

Kate groans.

"You should probably answer that."

She nods, breath ragged.

Then she pulls away and removes the still-ringing phone from her purse. She looks at the screen and groans even louder this time.

24

———

KATE

I accept my stepmother's call and step away from Noah. "Hi, Lucinda." I'm vaguely aware of him walking out of the bedroom to give me some privacy.

"I was in Neiman Marcus today shopping for a dress for myself," she says, without missing a beat, "and I found the perfect cocktail dress for you for the tea party. It's a blue-and-white floral A-line dress that is sleeveless and the hem falls to just below the knees. It's absolutely gorgeous."

"It sounds really pretty." I prefer pinks over blues, but the dress does sound nice.

"I thought you would say that. So I went ahead and bought it. I didn't want to risk it being gone by the time you return."

I thank her because it is *her* party after all, and I want to make sure I look good for it. It's important to her. Besides, Lucinda has good taste when it comes to dresses.

She then explains about some of the issues she's been dealing with when it comes to the caterer and the award-winning cake decorator, the latter who will be creating the centerpiece for the tea party. This is followed by her

201

mentioning the prestigious home design magazine that will be featuring the party in an upcoming issue.

And this is why I groaned when I saw who was calling. I knew it wouldn't be a quick call. They haven't been lately whenever Lucinda phones me. But at least she has been calling me. The same can't be said about my friends, especially Tiffany.

Although according to Tiffany, she has an excuse. She's been busy planning her own surprise, but she can't tell me what it is yet.

"Anyway, he has confirmed that he will be returning to the States in August and will be happy to be your date," Lucinda tells me, which is when I realize that I haven't been paying attention to her for the past few minutes.

"Date? What are you talking about?"

"You need a date for the party. But it can't be just anyone. You need to prove to the world that you've moved on after what happened."

Something about her tone sets off warning bells in my head, but I don't know why.

"I can do that without a date." I'm assuming she's referring to the accident. Except why would I need a date to prove to everyone that I've moved on from it?

But this is Lucinda, so I'm sure in her mind it makes perfect sense.

"It's already been arranged," she says.

"Arranged with whom?"

"Cameron Vansteen." There's no missing the slight irritation in her tone because it's obvious I haven't been listening to at least part of her one-sided conversation.

Cameron has been living in Norway for the past several months, working on some start-up venture there—and getting it on with a member of the royal family.

But you didn't hear that last part from me.

"His good looks make him the perfect choice," Lucinda says.

I bite my lip to keep from laughing out loud. She has managed to make him sound like a piece of steak.

"I still don't know why I need a date, but fine, I'll go with him." It's not like it will be a real *date* date. Cameron will be more like a paid escort, only he won't get paid in the traditional sense.

For him, the party represents a networking opportunity. That's the only reason he agreed to be my date.

"WHAT'S THE WORST DATE YOU'VE EVER BEEN ON AFTER THE AGE of twenty?" Violet asks, stirring the sauce on the stove. Sophie and I are peeling and cutting the vegetables.

We've been working on dinner for the past thirty minutes. That in and of itself is a blast. We like to talk.

About everything.

Okay, maybe not everything. We don't go into intimate details about our relationships—a.k.a. no bedroom talk. What we do in the bedroom stays in the bedroom.

"That would have to be the guy who ended up being my boyfriend after college," Sophie says, expertly dicing the carrots. A skill I've yet to master.

"Was it a first date?" I ask.

She nods. "Our mutual friends introduced us. We saw a movie and went out for pizza. Which would have been fine, but the waiter was a guy I had been crushing on in college. I hadn't seen him in a while, but apparently the crush still hadn't resolved itself."

Violet laughs and we both look at her. "Sorry, but I have a feeling I know where this is going."

"I think you do," Sophie says. "The waiter asked me what I would like to order. Back then, I couldn't talk to guys I crushed on. The words came out in whatever order they felt like, and I'd sound like a complete idiot."

"And that's your worst date? You couldn't order your meal?" That doesn't sound too bad. "You could at least talk to your date, right?"

"That's only because I wasn't attracted to him, which was why our relationship didn't go anywhere in the end. But having problems talking to the waiter wasn't the worst part. That would be when out of frustration, I dropped my head in my hands and knocked over my water glass. The waiter jumped back, trying to avoid water splashing on him.

"He stepped on the hem of a girl's prom gown right behind him and she went flying forward. Into the waitress who was about to serve a table their pizza. The pizza slid off the pan and landed on a little old lady's head. Unfortunately, she was wearing a wig, and it and the pizza landed on the floor."

Violet and I exchange glances, then burst out laughing.

"Okay, you win," I say, eyes filling with tears at the image now in my head. "That's got to be the most embarrassing date ever. I can't top that."

Violet snickers. "Me neither."

"That doesn't matter." Sophie points her knife between us. "You both owe me a story to make me feel somewhat less mortified."

Violet turns the heat off under the saucepan. "All right. I went on a date with a guy in college who was a complete bore. All he did was talk about himself the entire time. In third person. He'd say things like, 'Peter was starting quarterback in high school, but decided to focus on his law degree in college' or 'Peter has been nominated for some boring award you wouldn't care less about.' All right the last one wasn't completely true. The award had a name, but I didn't care enough to remember it."

"Oh God, the guy sounds creepy," I say.

"I know, right? But it turns out I wasn't on a date with Peter. It was his friend. He wanted to make sure I wasn't some crazy weirdo before his friend, Peter, went out with me."

This time it's Sophie and I who are laughing hard.

"I assume you never went out with the real Peter after that?" Sophie barely gets out.

"Definitely not. I still have no clue who he was. I never met him. It was his weird friend who asked me out on his behalf."

That sets us both off laughing again...no thanks to the wine Sophie and I have been drinking.

Once she and I finally stop giggling, both women turn to me, expectantly. "Seriously, I can't top either of those stories. The worst I've had to deal with is a few boring guys who loved to boast about their daddies' money. That, and the blind date that almost got me arrested."

Both women gape at me. Sophie gestures for me to keep talking. "I vote you tell us about the blind date."

Violet agrees.

I share with them about how the guy had stolen a Ferrari before picking me up for our date, how our date had ended with the cops chasing us, and how my date and I were hauled down to the police station.

Violet grabs an empty vase from the cupboard. "And the winner of the worst date *ever* is Kate." She hands me the vase while she and Sophie crack up.

Grinning, I press my hand to my chest. "Oh, this is such an unexpected honor. I didn't even prepare an acceptance speech."

That has them doubling over with laughter.

Dinner is pretty much a duplicate of girls' cooking time, minus the worst dating tales. There's plenty of laughter and sharing of funny stories. Deacon also entertains us with his own antics, with Maui and Charlie as his assistants.

Afterward, once we've finished cleaning the dishes and the table, everyone goes off to do their own couple-or-family-related things.

"Let's go for a walk," Noah says in my ear so Charlie can't hear.

"All right." Because it's late June, it's warm enough to go outside without a jacket.

I slip on my boots, which I wear practically all the time now.

Holding hands, Noah and I walk our usual route to the barn. Crickets chirp from the long wild grass, accompanied by birds in the nearby trees.

Neither of us talks much as we walk. That's nothing new. There's something comforting about being with the man you like while blanketed by the sounds and scents of nature.

And let's not forget the tantalizing scent that's all Noah.

We stop at the tack room so he can grab some clean horse blankets, then head down the trail to the river.

We end up at a small sandy cove that I've never been to until now. Noah stretches a blanket out on the sand near the water's edge and folds the other one into a long makeshift pillow. Not far from us, a tire swing dangles from a large cotton-wood tree.

"You guys have a tire swing?" I point at it even though he already knows it's there.

"My grandfather hung it there when my brothers and I were kids. He thought it would keep us out of trouble. In his mind, it was better if we drowned in the river than to do something stupid around the dangerous ranch equipment or risk getting trampled by a herd of stampeding cattle." He sits on the blanket and pats the spot next to him.

I join him. The view surrounding us is like nothing I've ever seen before, with the low slope of the Bitterroot mountain range on the other side of the river. I can only imagine how gorgeous this place will be when the leaves change color in the fall.

"But no one drowned, right?" I ask.

"That's right. I guess the old man wasn't that big a fool when he came up with the idea. And he was probably right about the ranch. My brothers and I were your typical boys, always looking for adventure, never thinking of the risks first." He rests his hand on my lower back, his thumb lightly stroking against my tank top.

The familiar hum that always visits whenever he touches me lingers beneath the surface. The move is sweet and intimate, tender and exhilarating. It's never felt this way with any other man...and that scares me.

I'm not talking about a serial-killer-is-chasing-me-with-a-chainsaw scared. It's more like when you eat the most amazing dessert and you know you'll never have anything like it again.

But what Noah and I have also comes with a ticking clock, counting down the seconds before I return to LA.

So enjoy what time you have left together, a voice in my head says. *Don't worry about what could happen tomorrow, or next week, or in three months from now.*

"Did you and your brothers hang out here a lot when you were kids?"

"Yes. We used to come here every day in the summer with our friends, including Violet and Austin. This was the place where we used to dream up our craziest schemes."

I nudge him with my shoulder. "Like what?"

"Like when I was ten years old and we thought it would be a brilliant idea to sneak some hot sauce into Mrs. Eversteen's chili during the county fair cook-off. She was our math teacher and no one liked her. She was a cranky old bitch even at the best of times."

He smirks in that sexy way of his that always leaves my body tingling.

"So what happened?"

"Austin decided that he would be in charge of the mission. He was the oldest of the five of us, so that made sense. Violet and I were supposed to distract Mrs. E while Austin dumped the hot sauce into the chili. Everyone else was assigned lookout duty.

"Turns out that Violet and I sucked at being a distraction. It didn't help that Mrs. E was determined to win—and hell if a couple of kids were going to keep her from doing that. She had won the category for the past three years, and there was no stopping her from winning again.

"She discovered what Austin was up to, which wasn't hard to figure out since he was caught dumping the entire contents of the bottle into the pot."

"Oh, no!" I press my fingers against my mouth to suppress the laugh that has no intention of being held back. I giggle.

Noah grins at me. "Oh no, is right. It didn't take much to figure out who his accomplices were. Her husband was the town sheriff at the time, and he decided that we needed to be taught a lesson. He had his wife dish out five bowls of chili and we all had to finish it."

"Surely the law isn't allowed to punish kids that way."

Noah shrugs. "I have no idea. All I know is that our parents were also at the county fair and they agreed with his punishment. I don't think they realized how much hot sauce Austin had poured into the pot. I swear fire came out of our ears as we ate it, but we did our best not to let Mrs. E know just how much it burned."

A laugh erupts from my lungs at that image.

"And you know the best part?"

I shake my head.

"Austin went on to become a winner in the county fair cook-off years later. Except his specialty is barbecue sauce. He's been unbeatable."

That makes me laugh even harder. "I'm sorry I missed all of that."

"Me too. You know why?"

"No, why?"

He leans closer, his mouth a breath-width from mine. "If you had lived in Copper Creek as a kid, you would have been that girl whose pigtails I would've pulled."

Then his lips are on mine.

His kiss isn't demanding. It's sweet and tender. Unassuming.

He gently tugs on my lower lip with his teeth.

I moan softly and part my lips to let him in.

25

NOAH

I wake up the next morning with Kate's sexy ass pressed against my overly eager morning wood.

And it feels good.

I'm not talking about how I'm hoping I won't have to deal with my hard-on the old-fashioned way: with my fist.

I'm talking about the idea of simply waking up with Kate in my arms. We've done it a few other times, and it never gets old.

I kiss her naked shoulder...just because I can.

At my touch, she stirs and mumbles, "Five more minutes."

"Hey, sleepyhead. I need to get up soon. You can stay in bed if you want. I'll shut the door and no one will know you're in here." They'll assume she's in her own room.

She twists around in my arms and smiles at me. "That's okay, I should head over to the house. I'm going to be a nice cousin and go back to cleaning Lady and Scoundrel's stable so that Troy doesn't have to. He's busier than I am with the renovations."

I move slightly and my still-eager cock brushes against Kate's leg. I moan.

A hand wraps around it. Not my hand, like it normally would be once I hit the shower. It's a warm, soft hand.

"Let me help you with your little dilemma," she says and I groan.

"Never say *little* when you've got a man's cock in your hand. Both might take great offense to it."

"I'll take your advice under advisement."

"You do that." I roll over her and drag the tip of my tongue along the shell of her ear. "I've got a few minutes before I have to get up. How about I help you with your need for me to be inside you?" I trace my lips against her jaw.

"Now that you mention it, I wouldn't mind an orgasm or two before I have to get back to work. It'll remind me of what I have to look forward to tonight."

"Sounds like a plan." I shift my body down with the goal of worshiping her gorgeous tits.

Which is why I barely register the click of my bedroom door.

"Hi, Uncle Noah." Deacon's voice is like a bucket of icy water dumped on your head. No hard cock can survive it.

Kate gasps and frantically grabs for the sheet.

I turn around to face the little boy, doing my best to keep from pulling the sheet off her and to cover her body with my own. He's standing near the foot of the bed.

"Hey Deacon, is there something I can help you with?" I aim for a casual tone, as if there isn't a naked woman in my bed.

"Play with me."

"Sorry, little buddy. I have to get to work now. Did you want to help me clean out the stable?"

Deacon screws up his nose. "The stable stinks. Horses go poop there."

"True enough."

Because this situation isn't mortifying enough for Kate, TJ

and Violet walk into my bedroom, having heard their son's voice.

"Oh, my," Violet says, quickly covering Deacon's eyes with her hand.

"Deacon, what did we say about going into Uncle Jake's and Uncle Noah's rooms without permission first?" TJ asks.

"You only said Uncle Jake's room." The little boy has a brilliant future as a lawyer.

"Right, but I meant Uncle Noah's room, too. It was just implied."

Deacon makes the sound I'm familiar with. I used it quite a few times growing up. It's the one that says you know the other person is bullshitting you.

"Okay...we'll give you some privacy now." Violet steers their son from the room, her hand still covering his eyes.

"Sorry about that," TJ says. "We had no idea he was up here. Mornin', Kate."

She murmurs an embarrassed-sounding "Hey," and he leaves the room, shutting the door behind him.

I collapse back on the bed, succeeding in dragging the sheet off her. "Why we never installed locks on the bedroom doors when we took over the ranch is beyond me."

"Do you think he saw anything?" She whispers it as if he's still standing in the room and she doesn't want him to overhear.

"Nothing that will scar him for life."

She seems to relax slightly at that.

"Well, I guess there's no hiding now that we're having sex." That gets me backhanded in the chest. "What?"

"We can't let it happen again."

Uh oh. That doesn't sound good. "What can't we let happen again?" I hope she isn't referring to the sex.

"I can't stay overnight in your room anymore. I'll have to return to mine once we're finished." She releases a long, frustrated breath.

Good. At least I'm not the only one disappointed with that solution.

"Or I can install a lock on the door."

"You can do that, but it'll probably be less confusing for Deacon if I sleep in my room."

"Even though he knows you slept here last night?"

She nods in the way women do when they believe they're right, end of story.

"All right," I say on an exhale. But I can't completely complain, even though I want to. At least she hasn't instituted a sex ban on us. Living with her for the next six weeks with no option of having sex would leave me with the worst case of blue balls known to man.

Kate gives me a quick kiss. "I should get up now. You've got work to do, and I have a stable to clean and two horses to say hi to."

I kiss her back. "Okay. I'll see you in a few hours. Are we still on for your riding lesson?"

"Yes." She climbs out of bed, slips into her clothes, and casually walks from the room as though Deacon hadn't just been in here while she was naked. But I know her. On the inside, she's anything but casual.

I follow suit and get out of bed, adding *Buy lock from hardware store* to my mental to-do list.

26

NOAH

It's been well over two months since Troy showed up in Copper Creek and convinced Kate to renovate Charlotte's house. Along the way, they've had a number of setbacks: the wiring wasn't up to code; the chimney and the various vents in the roof also needed to be brought up to today's standard; there was an issue with the plumbing; the skylights in the attic were leaking; the support beams in the living room went the wrong way, and the roof needed to be retiled.

I don't even want to consider the money Kate has poured into the place.

"I can't believe how great the house looks so far," I say, surveying the open-concept living room. Troy was right about Kate having an eye for design.

"It definitely looks better without the wallpaper," she says.

Amen to that.

The tacky, pain-in-the-ass-to-remove paper has been stripped from the walls, which have since been repainted white. The god-awful green linoleum kitchen floor has been replaced with medium brown tiles that now match the hardwood floor in the living room.

Troy and Kate also added decorative wooden beams in the ceiling. Wooden beams that were once part of the old barn.

Troy enters the room. "You guys ready to leave yet?" He hands me an envelope with my name on it.

"What's this?"

"I have no idea. I found it in the guest room upstairs. It had fallen behind the drawers."

Kate looks at the envelope. "That's definitely Charlotte's handwriting."

Curious what's inside, I rip it open and remove what looks like a letter.

Dear Noah,

If you're reading this, it's because I'm dead and my lawyer has given you this letter at my request.

I know you love the old Chevy Bel Air and you were hoping I'd sell it to you so you could perform your magic. I hope you can understand why I couldn't do that while I was still alive. I have some very fond memories of the car from my time with the man who was my soul mate. I'm sure you don't want to know what those memories are, but I assure you that I was once a young woman with the same sexual urges you have. Yes, I am aware of how popular you are with the young ladies in Copper Creek.

I knew that once I gave you the car, I

would lose an important part of me. You see, my dear John and I were to be married. But, unfortunately, he was sent to Korea to fight in the war. He was supposed to return to Copper Creek soon, and we would finally be husband and wife. The war had different plans for us, and John died a week before he was due to return home.

There was no other man for me after that. He was my one-and-only. That doesn't mean I didn't date other men. I just never fell in love with any of them, and I never told anyone about the one man who changed my life for the better. The man who took me away from a life I didn't really belong to. I hope one day you will understand that kind of love. I hope one day you'll find a woman who will cherish your heart the way John cherished mine. You deserve that, Noah. Never doubt it.

I never told you, but I've always considered you to be my grandson. I enjoyed spending all those days when you were younger, helping you learn to read. I enjoyed every minute you spent with me, talking about your schoolwork, your family, your friends. I never got to know my own great-nephews and great-nieces, with the exception of one great-niece. I blame that on my unwillingness to return to LA and my family's dislike of staying anywhere other than a big city or a five-star resort. I hope you have a chance one day to meet Kate. I *have no doubt that she's the same sweet and beautiful girl as when I visited her in California. She has my spunk and determination. I think you would like her very much.*

Now that I've moved on to join my one true love in heaven, the car is yours. It is my hope that after you restore it to its former glory, you will create your own memories in it, much like John and I created all those years ago.

Love,

Charlotte

AT LEAST KATE AND I NOW HAVE CLOSURE AS TO WHAT HAPPENED to John, and why Charlotte chose to never marry after he died.

Sniffing and grinning at the same time, Kate wipes the tears from her face.

"Is everything okay?" Troy asks.

Kate nods. "Everything's fine." She kisses me on the cheek. "I'm just sorry I won't be around to see the car after you've finished restoring it."

I'm sorry she won't be the one with whom I'll be creating those memories that Charlotte hinted at.

My gut stirs as if plagued by a heavy dose of sour milk. The idea of having sex in the car with anyone but Kate doesn't feel right.

That's because you're falling for her, dumbass.

Never mind falling. I'm already there.

Unfortunately, it will never work out between us. Copper Creek is my home. Kate lives in Beverly Hills. We're from two different worlds.

"Are you talking about the Chevrolet Bel Air Charlotte left Noah in her will?" Troy asks.

"Yes," Kate replies.

"Vintage cars are huge in LA," Troy tells me. "I have a friend who collects them. I bet he'd be interested in buying it from you once you've finished restoring it."

I shake my head. "It's not for sale." Charlotte wouldn't have wanted me to sell it. And I don't want that either.

Kate checks her phone. "We should get going if we're going to meet up with everyone at The Barn."

The Barn? It's exactly as the name suggests. Except it's been a long time since animals stepped inside it. Now it's a place where the artisans in the county sell their products during the warmer months.

Sophie and Violet told Kate about it and she wanted to check it out, to see if there's anything that would work in Charlotte's house.

TJ's truck pulls up to The Barn shortly after the three of us arrive. Jake, Sophie, Violet, and Deacon are with him.

"I didn't realize I was supposed to bring a date," Troy says, spotting the occupants of TJ's vehicle.

Kate laughs. "Maybe you'll get lucky and meet someone here."

I smack him on the back. "And if not here, there's always the county fair afterward." Which is the other reason for today's visit to The Barn. Because Kate is returning to Beverly Hills in ten days—after her uncle inspects the house—Sophie and Violet wanted to make sure that she experiences another aspect of small-town life before she leaves.

Troy doesn't have a chance to respond. Sophie and Violet rush over and hug Kate.

"You look great," Sophie says to her. And she does. She's wearing a white sundress covered in large pink roses and her cowgirl boots and hat.

The dress isn't from a high-end designer. The mom of one of the kids Kate has been working with made it for her.

Kate beams, and my heart does its own quick two-step dance. Like it always does when she smiles that way.

Inside The Barn, we wander around, inspecting the assortment of western-themed decor.

Kate picks up a square, rustic piece of wood with a cartoonish squirrel painted on it. She shows it to Violet. "This would be perfect in the nursery." She points to the selection of similar artwork, but with different woodland animals painted on them.

Kate has been decorating the baby's room for Violet and TJ's upcoming family member.

"Oh, that's adorable," Sophie says, and Violet agrees.

"Are you sure you want to return to Beverly Hills?" Sophie asks Kate. "Noah, how about you kidnap her? And then when Jake and I eventually have a baby, she can decorate that nursery, too." She grins at Kate even though she knows Kate has no intention of staying in Copper Creek.

I park my hand on Kate's lower back. "I would, but I think Austin might have something to say about that." Her relatives, too.

Kate laughs. "You're probably right about that."

TJ picks up the six wooden pictures, and Kate continues with her search. By the time we're ready to leave, she has found several different items for the house. I swear I can't remember the last time I've seen her this excited.

Troy and I load up my truck; then we all head to the county fair.

As soon as we arrive, Deacon bounces up and down like a puppy on a pogo stick. "Daddy, I want to see the petting zoo."

TJ lifts him onto his shoulders, and we weave through the crowds toward it. I hold Kate's hand the entire way. It feels natural. Being here with her feels natural.

Which is completely screwed up because this isn't Kate's world. It's mine.

As we walk, Sophie points out the things we should check out after we see the animals. She, Violet, and Kate chat and laugh together the entire way there. Kate's excitement at the sights around us—the farmer market booths, the stages with the various country music acts, the magician entertaining the kids, the jugglers, face painters—is hard to miss.

Someone Troy seems to know stops him to talk, and Troy tells us he'll meet us at the petting zoo in a few minutes.

Once we get there, TJ lowers Deacon to the ground. The small corral houses the usual assortment of animals: lambs, goats, piglets, rabbits, chickens, a giant tortoise.

Deacon grabs hold of Kate's hand and drags her off to introduce her to all the animals.

"I don't know about you," Violet says, watching the duo, "but he's going to miss Kate."

"I know the feeling," I say under my breath, not meaning for anyone to overhear me.

"I knew it!" Even without looking at Violet, I can tell she's grinning.

I turn my head to her. "Knew what?"

"That you're in love with her."

I roll my eyes, mostly to distract her from the truth. "That's quite the leap from me missing her once she returns home."

"Not really. You two are great together. And I don't just mean because you make a great-looking couple—which you do. It's obvious to anyone who has seen you two together that you've become close friends. And as we know, friends make the best couples." She nods at Sophie and Jake who are visiting the piglets.

She's also referring to TJ and herself. TJ and Austin might be best friends, but Violet and TJ have also been friends for as long as I can remember.

"None of that matters," I say. "In case you're forgetting, she's returning to Beverly Hills in less than two weeks. She even has a date lined up for once she gets back."

"She told you that?"

"I overheard her talking to her stepmother on the phone about it."

Violet groans. "It's not a real date. Her stepmother organized some big event, and because she doesn't want Kate to be dateless for it, she set her up with someone they know. Kate's not interested in him at all. He's only going with her because he wants to schmooze with a couple of the party guests for business purposes....Have you told Kate how you feel about her?"

"Why would I do that?"

The goat Deacon and Kate are visiting sneezes, and Deacon giggles uncontrollably. Kate grins at him—and for a moment, an image of her grinning at our own little boy almost knocks me on my ass.

Violet flashes me a look that can only be translated to mean one thing: she thinks I'm an idiot. "Because then she would know how you feel."

"And then what? Kate doesn't belong in Copper Creek. She belongs in Beverly Hills."

"She belongs where there's a guy who is in love with her and with friends who think she's amazing and who don't want her to leave."

"She has friends back home."

"I don't know about that. From what she's told Sophie, Aubrey, and me, her friends don't sound like very good friends."

So it's not just me and Troy who feel that way.

"Have you told her that?" I ask.

"The last thing Kate needs is for me to criticize the women who she thinks are her friends. But I've met people like them when I worked in LA. She deserves better."

"It doesn't matter. She needs to return to Beverly Hills. Copper Creek can't offer her what she wants."

Violet's eyebrow rises. "And what exactly is that?"

"A project she can get excited about. That's the only reason she agreed to stay in Copper Creek—to do the renovations. She wanted something to keep her busy for a few months. She wasn't looking to stay here permanently."

"Are you sure about that? Maybe she just needs another reason to stay here. Maybe that reason is you, Noah."

27

KATE

I adjust the super-chunky throw artfully arranged at the end of the bed in the attic.

"You know, that's the fifth time you've done that in the past two minutes," Troy says behind me. I didn't even hear him come up the stairs. "It looks great. The room looks great."

For some reason, the idea that my uncle will be seeing the house soon has my insides in enough knots that it will take a lifetime to untie them.

The room has come a long way since the bat incident. It now feels airy—thanks to the white walls and the white ceiling and the pale hardwood floor. The addition of the new light fixture, skylights, and the bigger window helps, too. We even added a rustic wooden beam that stretches along the center of the ceiling, from the window to the door.

The room isn't as wide as before, but the storage space we added under the sloped ceiling, on both sides of the room, makes up for the lost wasted space with something more practical.

I even found what resembles small barn doors, which I painted white, to use for the cupboard doors.

It's the perfect space for a teenage girl or a guest room.

"So what's going to happen between you and Noah after today?" Troy asks.

"What's the sudden interest in my relationship?"

"It's obvious you like him."

"I do. A lot. But that doesn't matter. I'm returning to my life tomorrow. What Noah and I had was just a fun summer fling." And in time, my heart will agree with me there.

"And then what?"

Good question. I'm not sure what I'm going to do next now that I've finished this project.

"I guess help Lucinda with the final details for her tea party, and then there's Victoria's wedding later this week." The wedding that I've heard so much about from Tiffany.

The wedding that's the talk of the town—and not just because of the humongous age difference between the bride and the groom.

The wedding that I've been excluded from, other than as a guest.

It's also the wedding I need to buy a new dress for once I return to Beverly Hills.

The thought of finally being able to shop on Rodeo Drive again makes my insides do a series of backflips that would impress even the stingiest of Russian judges.

"I guess my question shouldn't be about Noah, then. It should be about Cameron Vansteen. What's going on between you two?"

"Nothing. Lucinda asked him to be my date for the tea party. But that's all for show. You know, so I won't be dateless for her big event." I study the blanket for a second and adjust it once more.

"So you haven't heard?"

I straighten. "Heard what?"

"He's also your date for your friend's wedding. Philip told

me Lucinda arranged it with Cameron." Philip is one of my stepbrothers.

I shrug. It must be a recent development, because Tiffany never mentioned it to me. And given how involved she is with the wedding planning, she would know that he's now my date.

"She knows I don't have any time to arrange for a date when I return, so I guess since he's already helping me out with her tea party, why not ask him to be my date for the wedding, too?"

"Or maybe she's hoping that wedding bells aren't too far off in the distance for you as well. Philip mentioned that she's getting a little stressed that you're already twenty-eight years old and still single."

I laugh. "I'm practically a spinster." I check the clock on the wall. "We should go downstairs. Your father will be here soon." He's driving in from Billings Airport.

Or rather, his assistant is driving him from the airport.

Downstairs, I give the place one final check. "Your father's going to be so proud of what you've accomplished," I tell Troy.

"We'll see. But remember, I was the one who brought *your* vision to life. This is as much about what you've accomplished as it is about what I've done."

The front doorbell rings its upbeat sound—a point missed by my body. My heart rate speeds up, my palms grow yucky, and my throat tightens to the size of a stepped-on drinking straw.

I have no idea why.

This is about Troy proving to his father what he's capable of on his own, without his father always looking over his shoulder. It has nothing to do with me.

"Showtime," Troy says and rolls his eyes.

Before I can ask what that's about, he opens the front door. Uncle Jacob and his assistant step into the house.

"Hi, Kate." My uncle hugs me and introduces me to Mark, his latest assistant. "I'd ask you how you're doing, but I'm excited to see what you two have been up to while in this godforsaken town."

Nope, my uncle hasn't changed much. He's very much a Beverly-Hills-is-the-only-place-that-matters kind of person—like the majority of my family. Even before his show became the success it now is, he was wealthy. The show's success only increased his wealth tenfold.

Troy and I show him around, explaining what we did, the problems we faced, and the solutions Troy used to deal with them. During my years in private school and then in college, I had countless exams—both oral and written—but not once did I feel as nervous as I do now.

You shouldn't be nervous, I remind myself. *You smashed down a wall dividing the kitchen and living room. And you were kickass when you did it.*

Noah even said so himself.

Sure, my manicure is a mess from the physical labor I did to help out—and from cleaning the stable. But it's nothing my wonderful manicurist back home can't deal with. I've already got an appointment with her for the day after tomorrow.

Which is a good thing, because Lucinda will freak if she sees my hands looking like this, since everything about the tea party has to be perfect.

My attempt to distract myself from my unexplained nervousness fails. It doesn't help that Uncle Jacob has adopted the expression of a stone statue, not once giving away what he's thinking.

And we're not talking a happy Cupid statue—at least that would be a bit more reassuring.

He has the look of a statue who's been pooped on by one too many pigeons.

"I wouldn't have put the beam across the ceiling that way," he says, pointing to the beam in question.

I catch Troy rolling his eyes.

"Where did you get the wood from?"

He nods as I explain where it came from and how Troy and I prepared it. He then tells me how *he* would do it.

I'm not a hundred percent positive, but I swear Troy groans softly beside me.

And so continues the fun.

Every time Troy or I explain how we did something, my uncle tells us how he would have done it. Some of his suggestions are good, and I lock them away for future use. Others leave me mentally shaking my head.

On the bright side, he did agree with how Troy approached a few problems we had to deal with. So there's always that.

I chalk it all up to a learning experience.

An hour and a half later, our tour comes to a close.

"By any chance are you interested in joining my team?" Uncle Jacob asks me. He couldn't have surprised me more if he had transformed into a giant butterfly with googly eyes.

I look over at Troy. This was supposed to be about him proving himself to his father. It was never about me being part of the team.

My cousin gives me a slight nod of encouragement. Too slight to be noticed by his father, but not missed by me.

"It's not something I had considered, but I might be interested."

"Evie is leaving the show because she's pregnant and wants to focus on her family." Evie is the designer on the show. At one point, the tabloids had made it look like she and my uncle were involved—when they weren't.

My uncle is happily married to my aunt.

"You're pretty, Kate," he says. "You would make the perfect replacement for her."

I bite my lip to keep from saying what's on the tip of my tongue. It shouldn't be about my looks. It should be about what I bring to the team with my design know-how.

But I know better than to say that, because he's partly correct. Appearance is everything when it comes to television and you're a female trying to become established in your career.

But despite that, I do a little happy dance on the inside. Not because I want to be on TV. But because now I have a chance to turn something I love doing into a career.

I have a purpose—the thing that has been absent for a while now.

"Thank you, Uncle Jacob. I would love to do that."

"We have a team meeting at nine a.m. on Tuesday. I'll introduce you to everyone then." He holds out his hand to me like I'm a business associate...which I guess I am now.

After I shake it, he turns to Mark. "Tell Patricia that we have Evie's replacement, and she can call off the search for someone to fill the spot."

His assistant nods, removes his phone from the pocket of his trousers, and hurries outside to presumably make the call.

Because my uncle has to catch a flight to New York City for a TV interview, he and Mark leave shortly after Mark returns.

Once they're gone, I let out a hard breath, unsure what to do with myself. My gaze travels around the first floor, taking in everything I've accomplished. I have no idea if Charlotte would have appreciated the changes I made, but I love how it turned out.

Now I just have to hope someone else falls in love with the house and wants to buy the property.

Troy gives me a big hug, then playfully messes my hair up. "Welcome to the team, cuz."

"Wow, I wasn't expecting that."

He smiles. "You've earned it."

There's something slightly off about his smile, but before I have a chance to question it, my phone rings from the kitchen table.

Thinking it's Noah, I rush over to it as fast as my leg allows.

It's not him. It's Tiffany.

I accept the call.

"Please tell me you're returning tomorrow night, and please tell me you haven't gained any weight while in Montana." The words rush out faster than a float in the Rose Bowl Parade speeding down a steep slope after the brakes fail.

"That's right, and no I haven't."

Tiffany lets out a noticeably relieved breath. "That's good. One of Victoria's bridesmaids is sick, and you're the only person who is her size."

28

KATE

Standing in Charlotte's kitchen, I glance briefly at my phone, checking that it hasn't sprouted wings and is exhaling tiny puffs of flames. It hasn't, which means I'm not hallucinating.

I return the phone to my ear. "What exactly are you trying to tell me?" I ask Tiffany.

"She needs you to be her bridesmaid."

That's what I was afraid she was going to say. "I can't be her bridesmaid. I haven't had any bridesmaid training." The girls who are in the wedding party have been doing practically everything together—according to Tiffany's regular updates to me. And the rehearsal was last week.

I'd be like the cheerleader who has been skipping out on practice.

And that can't be good.

"Don't worry, you'll be fine," Tiffany tells me. "I'll walk you through everything ahead of time. There's nothing to it really."

"Victoria already has five other bridesmaids. Surely no one will notice if she's missing one."

"Her fiancé's grandsons are the groomsmen. And there are

six of them. It wouldn't be right to tell one of them that they've been demoted."

"I'm sure they'll understand. It's not like they're going to get angry at the bridesmaid for being sick."

"You're Victoria's friend. Surely you can understand how important this is to her."

Troy is watching me with great interest, a slight frown on his face. I lift my shoulders in a *What-can-you do?* shrug, even though he has no idea what's going on.

The front door opens and Noah enters the house. My heart starts beating loudly—a songbird flapping its wings against the bars of its gilded cage, eager to fly to him. Tiffany's words are lost on me over the pulse pounding in my ears.

But I'm sure whatever she's saying isn't all that important.

I walk over to him, throw my arms around his neck, and gaze into his gorgeous brown eyes. Every part of me in contact with his hard body hums with need.

His arms go around my waist, his own gaze locked on mine.

"Aaand that's my cue to leave," Troy says, walking past us. A moment later, the front door clicks shut behind him.

Tiffany is still talking, oblivious that I'm no longer listening to her. "Give me a second," I tell Noah, then lift the phone back to my ear. "I have to go now. I'll see you in two days."

"But what about Victoria's wedding? She needs you to be her bridesmaid."

"Okay, I'll do it," I murmur, not really paying attention to her anymore. I end the call.

"Hi," I say, softly, to Noah.

"Hey. Is your uncle still here?"

I shake my head. "He left a few minutes ago."

And that's about the extent of our conversation before his lips are on mine. Our tongues worship each other with their own sensual dance.

The kiss doesn't last long, but it's enough to leave us breathless when we pull apart.

"I thought instead of having dinner at the ranch tonight," Noah says, "we can eat here. Just the two of us. I brought food with me."

"I'd like that." If it means I don't have to share him with anyone. "And I've got some big news to tell you."

He grins my favorite smile—the one when he's thinking about sex and me. "I still need to shower, so how about you join me and tell me there?"

"I like where this is headed." I'm leaving tomorrow morning, so I need to make the most of my last moments with him. And that includes all the sexy times we can handle.

He goes out to his truck and returns with several brown paper bags filled with food. He also has his sports bag. We put the food in the fridge and head upstairs.

In the bathroom, I turn the shower on and adjust the temperature. By the time I swivel around, Noah is standing in front of me, naked and already at half-mast. My body vibrates with anticipation.

Even if I was staying permanently in Copper Creek, I'd never grow tired of seeing him like this. I spend a brief moment memorizing everything about him. His sexy, self-assured smile. His strong body that is gifted at making me feel needed and desired. The way his gaze is taking me in like I mean the world to him.

It isn't long before I've shimmied out of my clothes and I'm standing in the bathroom naked.

Noah cups my breasts with his large hands and brushes the already taut nipples, making them even harder. "So what's the big news you have to tell me?"

"My uncle offered me a job with his team. His designer Evie Gladstone is leaving the show and I will be her replacement.

I'm going to be on TV. It's like a dream come true." I sound like a babbling idiot but I don't care.

"I didn't realize you're interested in being on TV."

"I'll admit that part isn't my dream. But being a designer is. Being recognized for what I love doing definitely is. I just didn't realize that until I was working on this house."

"So I guess congratulations are in order." His languid smile brings a rush of heat low in my belly. It's only by sheer determination on my part that I don't melt to the floor.

He takes my hand and leads me into the large walk-in shower. The new white tiles gleam back at us.

Hot water rains on us, forming tantalizing streams down Noah's muscled chest, abs, legs—and everything in between.

He reaches around me to grab the body wash from the wire rack in the corner, pours some in his hand, and starts cleaning my parts that are eager for his touch. My shoulders, my arms, my breasts. Pretty much everywhere.

That gets a needy gasp out of me.

Not to be left out of the feast, I pour some sugar-and-vanilla-scented liquid into my hands and follow the identical path he took, lathering him with the same erotic touch.

We continue our journey, exploring each other's bodies, reacquainting ourselves with familiar sounds. Gasps. Moans. Groans.

Our mouths reunite as our hands home in on the parts yet to be worshiped. My soapy hand wraps around his cock. His slippery fingers find the sensitive bundle of nerves between my legs.

"Oh God, Noah."

We keep teasing each other, pushing one another closer to euphoria. My legs and body quiver with need.

His fingers move away from my core. Before I can moan in protest, his cock is covered, both hands are around my waist, and he lifts me. My legs automatically go around his hips. He readjusts himself so his tip is against my entrance; then he thrusts deep inside me, possessing me, consuming me.

Reminding me what I'll be missing once I return to Beverly Hills.

He anchors me against the wall and takes me to new heights. Higher and higher and higher we climb until there's nowhere left to go. My heat clamps down on his length, and I light up like New Years Eve fireworks.

Noah follows me seconds later as he grunts out his release.

For a long moment, we cling to each other, unwilling to let go just yet. My forehead is on his shoulder, his arms wrapped tightly around me. We both know this won't be the last time we make love tonight. We want to make the most of our final hours together while we still can.

Eventually, the cooling water reminds us that shower time is over. We quickly rinse off and get dressed: Noah in jeans and a white T-shirt, me in a floral sundress.

In the kitchen, we gather the food from the fridge and the few dishes that haven't been packed away. He spreads out a blanket on the grass in the backyard and we sit.

"Mmm," I groan around a mouthful of food. "This is so good."

What's so good? The quiche. They say real men don't eat quiche. Well, they're wrong. Because Noah likes it, and you can't get any more real or male than him.

He also included a baguette from Good Creations, specialty cheese from Cora Ridge Creamery, an assortment of cut meats, berries, and a bottle of white wine.

No one can ever claim Noah isn't romantic.

We spend the time eating and talking. Talking about the little things that have nothing to do with us as a couple, that have nothing to do with my returning to Beverly Hills. And we also avoid the topic of how we'll never see each other again after tomorrow morning, when I leave for the airport.

Denial? Currently my best friend.

We laugh and we flirt. And yes, more kissing is involved as we walk hand in hand around the property after we've finished eating. We visit with Lady and Scoundrel.

We fuss over them both. Noah has his own horse back at the ranch, but since we've been a couple, he's been riding Scoundrel while teaching me how to ride Lady.

"I'm going to miss you two," I tell them. "Cleaning your stable? Not so much. But don't worry. I'm sure I'll find you a new home soon."

Both horses nicker and whiny.

The sun is setting as we drive to the ranch. Noah is in his truck; I'm in my rental car.

We spend the rest of the evening pretending today isn't our last day together. Anyone who sees me has no idea that my heart is moping around in my chest, even though I am excited to return home and start my new career. They see the smiling, laughing, happy Kate. They don't see the Kate who's wondering if she's making a mistake.

"Read me a story." Looking hopeful, Deacon hands Noah and me a picture book the moment we step into the foyer after taking Charlie for a walk around the ranch.

Laughing, Noah picks him up. "What do you say, Kate? Should we read him a story?"

"And Charlie, too," Deacon adds.

"Of course, he wouldn't miss it for the world," I say, grinning.

Noah carries him upstairs, and we take him to his bedroom. We settle him on his bed, with me on one side, Noah on the other, and Deacon and Charlie sandwiched in the middle.

Noah begins reading the story out loud. His words come slower than for most adults his age, but not by much. I know he struggled with dyslexia growing up, which made things harder for him than they were for his brothers. But despite that and what his grandfather believed, he still turned out great.

Charlie listens to us, his head on Deacon's thigh. Deacon's hand is on Charlie's fur, right next to Noah's much larger hand. This is how it normally is when we read to Deacon.

We finish the story and tuck him in bed.

"I'm going to miss you," I tell him.

Deacon tilts his head to the side. "Where are you going?"

"Charlie and I are going home to California."

"When are you coming back?"

Smiling softly, I shake my head. "We're not. Charlie will be helping other kids learn to read."

Deacon's lips move into a pout that is enough to break my heart. "Can't you stay? You can live in Uncle Noah's room. Or my room." He scrambles out of bed.

"Hey, buddy, where do you think you're off to?" Noah asks.

Deacon doesn't say anything. He just rummages through his toy box. A minute later, he pulls out whatever it is he's looking for with a triumphant grin on his face.

He climbs onto his bed and hands me the treasure: a small plastic dinosaur. His favorite toy dinosaur. "This is so you don't get homesick."

"I won't get homesick, because I'm going home."

He adamantly shakes his head. "No, *this* is your home."

"Say good-bye to Kate," Noah says. "It's time for you to go to sleep."

Deacon bounces up onto his knees and throws his arms around my neck. "Bye-bye, Auntie Kate." I hug him back; then he hugs Charlie.

TJ and Violet are coming down the hallway as we step out of Deacon's room.

I send Charlie downstairs to join Maui and Asgard, and Noah and I go to Noah's room.

As soon as the door clicks shut behind us and Noah has secured the lock, his mouth is on mine.

During the past three months, he and I have kissed thousands of times. Yes, his kisses are that addictive.

But something about *this* kiss is different.

And I have no idea why.

29

NOAH

Tell her that I love her or forever keep silent? The question pays me a visit like the ghosts of Christmas past, present, and future. It's the same question that has played in my head since Violet told me I need to tell Kate how I feel about her.

Easy for her to say. Things worked out fine for TJ and Violet. Same for Jake and Sophie.

But my situation is different.

Or is it?

Violet wasn't living in Copper Creek when she and TJ fell in love. She was in town while the TV crew was shooting his segment for *Cowboy Most Wanted*.

If the truth hadn't come out about how they felt for each other, Violet and Deacon would be still living in LA, and TJ would be one cranky bastard.

Kate slips her hands under the hem of my T-shirt and my heart rate picks up, igniting the volcano that has been temporarily dormant since the shower back at Charlotte's.

Only now it promises that the next time it erupts, the destruction will be all consuming. But more importantly, there will be nowhere to go but forward—for better or for worse.

Her touch is enough to wipe away all additional thoughts, other than the one about how much I crave to feel her under me, to feel her heat wrap around me.

To feel my soul splinter into thousands of breathtaking stars.

I reach back, tug the T-shirt over my head, and toss it to the side.

Kate's dress and my jeans are removed shortly after.

The warm glow of the sunset streaming through my bedroom window caresses her nearly naked body. I drop to my knees and plant a kiss next to her belly button. An image of kissing her stomach, swollen with my seed, flashes in my head. It leaves me numb with a raw desire, one I've never experienced before.

Not even with my ex-girlfriend who I had once loved. What I felt for her was a joke compared to what I feel for Kate.

I slip my fingers under the lace waistband of her panties and reverently peel them down her legs. My fingers burn a path as they travel along her soft, pale skin.

At her ankles, I lift up one foot, remove the silky fabric from around it, then lower the foot and repeat on the other side. Except this time I keep hold of her ankle. I have other plans for that foot.

I place it on my shoulder, opening her up to me. Kate's eyes are filled with a liquid heat like no other and her body trembles. She leans back against the door, unable to stand up on her own any longer.

I flick my tongue against her clit, tasting her like I've longed to do ever since the last time I ate her out. I can't get enough of her. Even the smoothest whiskey can't compare.

She moans the sweetest sound, encouraging me to keep going.

I push two fingers inside her and pump them in time to the swirling of my tongue around her mound, driving her closer to the place I want her.

Not the place where I take her a minute later, as she clenches hard around my fingers. But to the place where I can touch and caress her soul. Where I can show her without any doubt how I feel about her.

My name tumbles from her lips in a satisfied moan. Before she has a chance to recover and say anything else, I unfold myself to full height, scoop her up in my arms, and carry her to my bed.

I gently lower her to the mattress, remove a foil square from my bedside drawer and place it next to her on the bed, then join her. We resume kissing, each kiss less frantic than they've been during the past few days. We're taking our time when our time together is quickly ticking away.

Kate's hand finds my length, and I almost cry out from her touch. I'm so hard, it's verging on painful. I need her, and I need her now.

I quickly deal with the protection and position myself between her legs. Her sex is hot and slick with desire. Christ, I'm not going to last much longer.

She wraps her legs around my waist, and I ease my way into her warmth. My brain almost short-circuits at how amazing it feels.

Tell her you love her, my heart implores.

Don't be an idiot, my brain tells it, with the few remaining cells that aren't drunk with need.

I ignore both and move in and out of her, slowly at first. Showing her with actions for now rather than with words.

They will come soon enough.

But my self-control can only last so long, and before I know it, the movements upgrade to something faster, something desperate. The volcano low in my gut pulsates with molten lava, heating me from within. I groan, barely able to restrain the sound.

Kate cries out and her soft heat squeezes me with everything it's got, down to my balls. The pressure in my lower back intensifies.

It takes only three rapid thrusts on my part before the volcano erupts and spills everything inside her. My sperm. My white-hot desire for her. My love.

I grunt out my release.

Once I've recovered enough for my brain to somewhat function again, I remove myself and deal with the condom.

Kate is where I left her when I return. Her gaze is still a little dazed, her hair looks freshly fucked, and her skin has a sexy flush to it.

She's the most beautiful sight I've ever seen.

I sit down next to her, my pulse thumping loud in my ear. *Tell her*, my heart demands. *Don't be the fool who lets her get away because you weren't man enough to admit your feelings to her.*

Releasing a long breath, I brush a strand of hair out of her face. She turns her head slightly and our eyes lock.

"I know the timing isn't the best," I tell her. "And I know I shouldn't feel this way but I do." That's right, love has reduced me to a rambling idiot.

But oddly, I don't care.

"I'm in love with you, Kate."

She pushes herself to sit. Even before she speaks, I know what she's going to say. Her apologetic eyes are saying it for her.

The love I feel for her is completely one-sided.

She parts her lips to speak, but I'm faster than her words. I place my finger against her mouth. "I don't expect you to feel the same way as me. And I'm not expecting you to say you love me in return. But you're leaving tomorrow, and I just wanted to put it out there. Now that I've done that, how about we forget for now that I said it? Let's enjoy our final night together."

She nods, and relief rushes through me that we're not going to talk about this.

I'd rather my last memories of Kate not be of her pitying me because she doesn't feel the same way about me that I feel for her.

Tomorrow I can lick my wounds in peace.

Maybe throw myself into restoring Charlotte's car.

Or take up origami.

30

KATE

Two days later, I'm standing outside the Catholic Church, doing my best to ignore how the other bridesmaids and I are dressed like the blue cotton candy Deacon ate at the county fair a few weeks ago.

Doing my best not to think about Noah and the chunk of my heart I left in Montana.

When he told me that he was in love with me, I'd never been happier. I was about to tell him that I loved him, too, but then I'd felt a twinge of pain in my bad leg, reminding me of what happened the last time I gave my heart to a man.

Mathew didn't treat it like the valuable gift that it was. To him, it was something to be mocked and not respected.

So what did I do after Noah and I made love? I left the next morning like the coward that I am.

My other reason for leaving had to with finally having a career doing something I'm excited about. Sure, Noah and I could try to have a long-distance relationship, but that's not what I want.

I want to live in the same city as the man I love and not have to worry about scheduling in time to see each other. Sure, other couples do it all the time...but they generally only have to drive across town.

They don't have to fly across two states to see each other.

Victoria glances down at her Givenchy wedding gown. She's always been gorgeous, but this dress makes her look like royalty.

And her entourage of bridesmaids would agree. They're all fluttering around her, spilling saccharine words at how wonderful she looks.

But while their words might be true, something about them is as genuine as imitation sugar.

"Kate, don't you think that Victoria looks like an angel?" Tiffany asks me.

"Absolutely, her groom is a lucky man." I walk over to where everyone is fawning over Victoria. A couple of birds sing sweetly in a nearby tree, not at all bothered by the high afternoon heat.

From the moment I joined Victoria and her bridesmaids at her parents' mansion this morning, I'd been made to feel like an outsider.

I don't think they meant to do it intentionally. They were just being themselves. I just didn't notice it until now—until after I got to know people in Copper Creek.

"Could you please stop doing that?" Victoria says, tone as sharp as a rusty pitchfork. To my surprise, it's directed at me.

"Doing what?"

"Limping."

Scattered titters from the flock of bridesmaids set me slightly on edge. I do my best to ignore them. "I can't help that I limp."

"Sure you can. Just don't do it. It's as simple as that."

One bridesmaid tosses me a sympathetic look and mouths *Bridezilla.*

The corners of my mouth twitch despite my attempts to fight off a grin. Victoria spots this with eagle-eyed clarity and directs her scowl to the flock of bridesmaids. The one in question flashes her an innocent expression, and it's all I can do not to laugh.

Tiffany pushes her way through the flock to join me.

"She doesn't seriously expect my limp to vanish just because she commanded it to be so, does she?" I ask my best friend, my voice low so Victoria can't hear me.

"She just doesn't want you to upstage her on her big day."

"How would my limping possibly upstage her? I could understand it if I somehow managed to knock over one of the wedding cakes. But that would be me making a scene, not upstaging her."

And then it hits me like two tons of horse manure. "She didn't originally ask me to be a bridesmaid because I limp. True or false?"

Tiffany squirms.

Oh.

Wow, she must have really been desperate to have me fill in for the other bridesmaid.

What did the woman have? A common cold that made her look like Rudolf—and no matter what she did, her nose would be bright red for the wedding?

"Well, I'll do my best not to limp."

Tiffany gives me a small smile. "That's all we're asking."

We?

The wedding planner steps outside like a May storm cloud with a clipboard. "All right, ladies. The handsome groom is eager to get started. Places, everyone."

The flock squawks and rushes into position. Once we're ready, the wedding planner says through her headset, "The bird is ready to roost. I repeat. The bird is ready to roost." I barely keep from laughing out loud.

She opens the door, the music starts, and one by one, we're directed to walk down the aisle.

Once upon a time, I loved to be the center of attention like most of my friends. We thrived on it. But now nerves pummel me like a tsunami at the thought of making a fool of myself and upsetting Victoria.

And right on cue, my leg stiffens. It doesn't help that I have to wear stilettos like the rest of the bridesmaids. I used to live in shoes like that before the accident. But ever since then, I've had to avoid them because they're too difficult for me to walk in. My balance is off-kilter in them because of my limp.

I tried telling Victoria that; she didn't care. Her wedding. Her rules.

No, no, no.

Not now, I tell my leg. *You can freak out all you want after this. But not now.*

It doesn't listen. My limp becomes more pronounced than normal, my balance less stable.

Instead of focusing on everyone watching me—which they would be doing either way, because, hello, we are at a wedding—I ignore the whispers and pretend that it's Noah waiting for me at the altar.

Can you blame me? It's that or be reminded of whom Victoria is marrying. Couldn't she have married someone closer to her age? Like the groomsmen?

Or one of their fathers?

Imaginary Noah flashes me his cocky smile and the tension in my body starts to drain.

I focus on him and the music and ignore the voice in the back of my head reminding me of Noah's words before we made love for the final time.

He was talking about being in love with the Copper Creek Kate, not Beverly Hills Kate.

I'm definitely the latter. The thrill I got while shopping on

Rodeo Drive yesterday and while relaxing in the spa confirms it.

This is where I belong.

You belong in Copper Creek with Noah and your friends, the voice in my head says.

I mentally hum the wedding march to drown out the voice and switch to thoughts about meeting my uncle's team for the first time.

At least that's something to look forward to.

SEVERAL HOURS LATER—WHICH FEELS MORE LIKE A LIFETIME than two hundred and forty-five minutes—the wedding ceremony, the wedding photos, the dinner, and the speeches are a thing of the past.

Hallelujah.

I'm about to sneak out of the country club reception hall and reply to Violet's text, when someone lightly grabs my arm.

"Hello, stranger," my date says.

Yes, even though I was a bridesmaid, which has meant being stuck at the head table until a short time ago, Cameron Vansteen still agreed to be my date. His family is friends with the groom's family, so he was going to be here anyway.

And I'm the date designated to keep his mother from setting him up with the woman he has no intention of going out with. Neither of us views this as a real date.

I grin at him. "I hope your mom wasn't too busy trying to set you up with your future wife in my absence."

He kisses me on both cheeks, then shifts closer to my ear. "I don't suppose you're interested in kissing me just to get her off my back for a bit?"

I shake my head. "Sorry, these lips have gone into hibernation for a while."

"Because of that dick you were dating?"

I assume he's talking about Mathew since no one knows about Noah, so I just laugh. "You don't mince words, do you?"

"I don't have patience for cheaters. Especially when the guy's girlfriend is in a coma and he's screwing around with her best friend."

I cringe at the truth in that, then smile. "Strange to say, I'm oddly touched by your sentiment."

The song that was playing ends and a slow song begins.

"I don't suppose my pseudo-girlfriend, who won't let me kiss her, would like to dance?"

My smile widens. "Given your opinion of my ex-boyfriend, that's the least I can do. But only if you don't mind me dancing without my shoes on. I can barely walk in them. There's no way I can dance in them."

"You've got yourself a deal." He waits for me to remove my stilettos and slip them under the head table; then he leads me to the dance floor. My arms go around his neck, his go around my waist.

"You do realize that after tonight and your stepmother's party next week, the socialites' tongues will be wagging and claiming we're an item?"

"Given that their tongues have been wagging ever since news leaked that my boyfriend cheated on me," I say, hips swaying while I pretend I don't miss being in Noah's arms. "You're not far off there."

"Are you okay with that?"

"Not really. But there's not much I can do about it." That's the one thing my world and small-town life have in common. It's probably one of the very few things they have in common.

A mischievous gleam appears in his eyes, which reminds

me a lot of Noah. My heart squeezes like a sorrowful accordion pushing out the last of the air.

"So what do you say we have some fun with it?" Cameron asks.

That's enough to temporarily appease my heart, and I'm sure my expression matches his. I've only been back for a few days, but other than the shopping trip on Rodeo Drive, I'm already bored. My new job can't start soon enough. "What do you have in mind?"

"This."

That's the only warning I get before he dips me. Then he pulls me up hard against his body. The gleam in his eyes tells me it's all an act, mostly for his mom's sake.

I laugh, once again attempting to block memories of Noah. I'm not too successful. Dancing with Cameron reminds me of when Noah and I danced at Joe's. This is fun...but dancing with Noah, his brothers, and their friends was infinitely better.

Cameron continues to entertain me on the dance floor until the song comes to an end. The bouquet toss is announced and all the single women rush to the dance floor. I chuckle at the half-panicked expression on at least a dozen or so men's faces.

A soft, dainty hand wraps around my wrist. "Come on, dear. You're still single. At least for now." Cameron's mother winks at her son. "You have to get out there. It's tradition."

For a petite woman, his mother is surprisingly strong. And since I don't want to make a scene, I let her drag me onto the dance floor. But not before I look over my shoulder and roll my eyes for his benefit.

He mouths an apology on her behalf.

All the eager-to-get-married women crowd at the front of the group. I wouldn't be surprised if someone doesn't get maimed by an errant elbow. I remain in the back.

My phone buzzes in my clutch. Normally I would ignore it, but since I'm not actually planning to catch the bouquet—and there's no way Victoria can throw this far—I check to see who texted.

SOPHIE: How are things back at home? We miss you here!

"Is everyone ready?" Victoria calls out.

This is met by a chorus of yesses as I type my reply.

"Three...two...one." Victoria's countdown results in some exuberant *I've got it*s and *Mine*s. I keep typing about how I miss everyone in Copper Creek. Because I do.

Someone shrieks. I assume it's from whoever caught the bouquet.

And then out of nowhere, I'm clobbered on the top of my head, and the bouquet drops onto my bent arms.

I look up from my phone, slightly dazed at what just happened. Dozens of disappointed faces stare back at me.

"Sorry," I say to the nearest of them and attempt to hand the bouquet to one girl.

She declines it. "It doesn't work that way. Now you're the one who's getting married next."

From the corner of my eye, I spot Cameron's mother, who is rubbing her hands together in glee.

31

KATE

Tuesday morning, I attempt to squeeze my way out of the crowded elevator in the building where my uncle's company is located.

"Excuse me," I say to the large man in a suit talking on his phone. He's been arguing with the person on the other end ever since he stepped into the elevator.

He doesn't budge.

I tap him on the back. "Excuse me." Still no response.

The woman next to him steps to the side to let me through just as the doors are closing. I practically hurl myself through the opening...

And collide with a college-aged girl carrying a cardboard tray with Starbucks coffees.

Which are very hot.

And which I'm now wearing.

"Ohmigod, I'm so sorry," she gushes, eyes wide.

"No, it was my fault." Ignoring the burning liquid for a moment, I grab some money from my purse and hand it to her. "That should be enough to replace them. Could you tell me where the ladies' room is?"

With her gaze still focused on my coffee-stained silk top, she points down the hallway. A fancy etched-glass door stands behind her, the doorway to my uncle's company.

"Interesting look, cuz," Troy says, approaching us from the direction she was just pointing. "I know you're family, but you might have wanted to put a little more effort into your outfit."

Coffee girl's eyes widen some more and her face reddens, but I have a feeling that has nothing to do my newly stained outfit and everything to do with Troy.

I smirk at him. "You know me, always trying to put my best foot forward."

"Come on, let's get you cleaned up," he says to me, then turns to Coffee Girl. "Grab one of my spare shirts in my desk and bring it to the restroom."

Before either of us can say anything, he's pushing me in the direction he came from. We duck into the ladies' room.

"You do realize this isn't the men's room, right?" I say to him as we walk over to the sink. "And what's with you and Coffee Girl?"

Yes, I'm full of questions this morning.

He grabs a bunch of paper towels from the dispenser and hands them to me. "Coffee Girl?"

I dab the stain with the towels. "Yes, the girl who was carrying coffee until I decided to repurpose my top." I release a hard sigh. "This isn't going to come out, is it?"

He shrugs. "Beats me. I don't make it a habit of getting coffee dumped on me."

"Okay, let's get back to Coffee Girl. She obviously likes you."

He lifts his shoulders in a shrug. "Not interested. She's too young. Plus, I've got some other things in the works, so I'm definitely not interested."

That gets my attention. "Do I know her? The thing that's in the works?"

"It's not that kind of thing."

"So what is it?"

"Nothing you need to know about for now."

The door opens and Coffee Girl enters, carrying a folded white shirt. She passes it to Troy, who takes it and practically dismisses her with a "Tell my father that Kate and I will be there in a minute."

"Okay," is all she says, face still flushed, before scurrying out of the room.

My phone vibrates in my purse. I remove it and check the screen.

"Are you and lover boy still talking to each other?" Troy asks, sounding somewhat surprised.

With a cry of faked outrage, I press the phone to my chest, hiding the screen against my wet top. "Hey, why are you reading my personal texts?"

"I take it that's a yes, then."

I shrug. "He's my friend." Who I've talked to every night on the phone before going to bed.

Troy's eyebrow quirks up. "Are you sure that's all he is?"

I study Noah's text. Anything to avoid eye contact with Troy. "Absolutely."

"Why am I having a hard time believing that?"

Some more shrugging on my part.

"He's in love with you, isn't he?"

My gaze shoots up to his. "Why would you think that?"

"Because I had a feeling that he was. What about you? Do you love him?"

I fidget with the top and pull it away from my chest. "I'm here, so obviously not."

That results in a grunt from Troy. "You do realize I've known you all your life? I can always tell when you're lying." Okay, he's got me there. "Here, change out of your top and put this one on." He shoves the shirt at me. "I'll wait for you in the hallway."

Once he's left the room, I quickly re-read the text.

Noah: How is your first day at work going?

Me: Great so far.

Fortunately, this isn't FaceTime or Skype, so he has no idea just how great my morning has been so far.

Me: Have my first team meeting soon. Talk to you later!

I miss you.

There's no time to dwell on those three words. I remove the stained top, replace it with Troy's shirt, and hurry out of the ladies' room to join Troy, who is busy typing on his phone.

At the click of the door behind me, he glances up and a smile dances at the corners of his mouth. "Nice shirt."

The shirt in question is several sizes too big for me in all directions.

Not quite the first impression I was hoping to make.

"I don't suppose you have a narrow women's belt in your desk drawer?" I ask.

He shakes his head. "Sorry." He doesn't look too sorry. More like still amused.

He takes hold of my upper arm. "All right, you don't want to be late for your first day on the job."

By the time we step into the conference room a minute later, there are only three empty seats available. And none of them are next to each other.

I take the chair next to Evie Gladstone. Troy takes the seat across from me.

I'm about to introduce myself to Evie, but my uncle strides into the room, halting my plans. "Let's get started," he says before even taking a seat.

He glances around the table. "What happened to the coffee?"

"There was an incident with it," an older woman sitting next to Uncle Jacob's chair says. "Jeanette went out to get some more. She should be here shortly."

"Fair enough." He then addresses the group. "First, I've got two announcements to make. As many of you know, Evie is leaving us. For the rest of you who actually work hard and avoid the water-cooler gossip..." His pause is met with an amused chuckle from the group. "That was my first announcement. Second, I'd like to introduce you to my niece, Kate Snow. She will be Evie's replacement."

He nods at me.

"Hi," I say, "I'm really looking forward to working with all of you."

Uncle Jacob leans back in his chair, folded hands on his flat stomach. "How about you introduce yourselves and tell Kate your role here, and then we'll discuss some other changes we're doing to the show just to spice things up this season."

One by one the team members introduce themselves. They're all smiles and jokes and everyone makes me feel welcome.

"I'm Rebecca, the show's home designer," the woman with short red hair says.

"I didn't realize there's more than one designer on the show." I assumed that Evie was it.

"There is only one," she clarifies. "Me. I hate the idea of being on camera, so that's where Evie came in...and now you. I work on the designs, and then Evie was the TV personality."

"It worked out better than I ever expected," my uncle says, beaming like he has found the pot of gold under the rainbow. "Rebecca is an amazing designer. I couldn't imagine ever having to replace her. And I know you'll do a great job too, Kate, showcasing her work like Evie did for the past six seasons."

Disappointment eddies in my stomach in an endless spiral,

and I feel my mouth stretch into a smile that is as plastic as the lids on the Starbucks coffees. "Sounds great."

And now I see why my uncle hired me for Evie's job. I'm a better actress than I realized.

I release a mental sigh.

32

KATE

"**H**ey, beautiful," Cameron says, wrapping his arms around my waist from behind.

I startle. Until he had done that, I'd been staring at my parents' fountain in the middle of the extensive patio, not paying much attention to the guests milling around, chatting, laughing, gossiping.

"Sorry, didn't mean to freak you out."

I laugh softly. "Don't worry. I'm sure my heart will recover."

Maybe from him startling me—I'm not so sure about from everything else.

A distinctive clicking sound warns me that we're not so alone—if you exclude the hundred or so guests not currently paying attention to us.

A camera lens is pointing in our direction. When the owner, a woman I don't recognize, realizes the moment she thought she was capturing is over, she lowers her camera, smiles at me, and walks off.

She doesn't get too far before she is approached by Cameron's mom, who is all smiles.

Cameron's arms drop away from my waist. "Uh, oh. Why do I have a feeling my mother is up to no good again?"

I turn to him. He's also dressed up for the occasion, in a gray Armani suit and a red-striped tie, the knot slightly relaxed. "Do you know who that woman is?"

"She's some up-and-coming celebrity photographer. Lucinda must have invited her. She's definitely not paparazzi."

"That makes sense. Lucinda said a magazine will be featuring the party in an upcoming issue. But that wouldn't explain why the photographer was shooting photos of *us*."

"She probably thought she was capturing a romantic moment between us to include with whatever article she's writing. If you want, I'll make sure our photos aren't part of it."

"Yes, please." Even though there's a zero percent chance of Noah seeing the pictures, I don't want to risk someone else showing them to him. It's bad enough I didn't return the sentiment when he told me that he loves me—even though a large part of me wanted to tell him the truth. I don't want him thinking I hooked up with another man as soon as I left Copper Creek.

Cameron glances at where his mother is now standing with Lucinda. They both look over at us and beam. "I don't know about you, but I could use a drink."

"Do you think if we disappear with a bottle of wine anyone would notice? Maybe then you can tell me all about the scandalous affair you were having with a member of the royal family." I grin at him so he knows that I'm kidding...about the last part.

The escaping-with-a-bottle-of-wine part sounds good to me after the week I've had since returning home.

A waiter carrying a tray of champagne flutes approaches us at the same moment as Troy. "Mrs. Snow will be making an announcement shortly. Would you care for some champagne?"

The three of us each accept a glass from him before he walks off to the next group of guests.

"Do you have any idea what this big announcement is?" Troy asks me, then nods his greeting to Cameron.

"I have no idea what it could be," I tell him. "But it must be pretty big if she's toasting the news."

Tiffany is with a group of our friends not far from where Lucinda and Cameron's mother are standing. The women with Tiffany remind me of a buzzing beehive. Smiling. Giggling. Yapping excitedly. Tiffany's back is to me, so I can't see what she's doing, but the attention seems to be focused on her.

None of this is too surprising.

What is surprising is that I'm only noticing it now, even though, when I think about it, it has been this way ever since my accident. Once upon a time I used to be an active member of the hive, but now I feel like I've been discarded, the piece of honeycomb nobody wants.

The opposite of how everyone in Copper Creek treated me.

And not for the first time since leaving the small town, a piece of me aches for what I left behind.

For whom I left behind.

The clinking of metal against glass reaches my ears and I turn my attention to my stepmother. Cameron's mother is smiling next to her, a spoon in one hand, the champagne flute in the other.

"Thank you, everyone, for joining me today," Lucinda says through the microphone she's now holding. "I have a very special announcement to make." She directs her smile at me and raises her glass slightly, enough to be noticed by me and only by me.

"Is she planning to announce that I'm now nothing more than the face for the real designer on your father's show?" I say to Troy, voice low so no one else can hear me. I keep my focus trained on Lucinda but I can feel him shift next to me.

"I'm sorry you got blindsided by that," he says. "I should have told you, but you were so excited when Dad offered you the position, I didn't have the heart. I couldn't remember the last time you'd been that excited in the past year...other than when you were in Copper Creek, renovating your great-aunt's home."

"One of my dreams for the past few years, ever since I began hosting my annual tea party," Lucinda says, "is to be able to announce a very special engagement." She pauses long enough to glance over at Cameron's mother.

"Fuck," Cameron says under his breath. "I hope she isn't about to announce that you and I are engaged."

My head spins to him so fast that I'm surprised I don't have whiplash. "What are you talking about?"

"The photographer. She's recently done engagement photos for several celebrities."

"And you think that's why she was taking our photo when you had your arm around me? That's crazy. We aren't engaged. Heck, we aren't even really dating."

"As everyone knows," Lucinda says, "Tiffany Cartwright is like a daughter to me. Which is why I'm delighted to announce her engagement to Mathew Underwood."

A thunder of applause breaks out around me...but all I can think about is how I feel nothing. Not even a smidgeon of regret that it's not me up there by his side.

It's also clear from my friends' expressions, I'm the only one who didn't know about the engagement.

Mathew joins Tiffany and kisses her. It's a sweet kiss. Nothing like the kiss Noah gave me after he told me that he loved me, even though I didn't tell him what he wanted to hear.

My knees grow weak just thinking about it.

I love him. Why couldn't I have just pulled up my big-girl panties and admitted that to him when I had the chance?

Yes, Mathew hurt me, but that doesn't mean Noah will end

up doing the same. Mathew is a jerk. Noah isn't—he's an amazing, loving man, something Mathew doesn't know how to be.

"You still love that douchebag?" Cameron asks, volume low, tone incredulous. "Even after he hurt you, you still love him?"

Huh? Did I just say out loud that I love Noah? Only I didn't say his name. I just said "I love him."

Troy chuckles. "I can guarantee that's *not* who she's talking about."

I can tell the moment Cameron puts things together. His eyes gain a thoughtful expression. "When you joked about your lips going into hibernation, it was because of the man you've fallen in love with?"

I nod and sit down hard on the edge of the fountain, my knees now weak for a different reason.

Cameron looks between Troy and me, a confused crease between his eyes. "But I thought you were in some small hick town for the past few months."

I nod again, still in a daze.

"She fell in love with a cowboy there," Troy says, filling in the pieces for him.

"And the dirtbag didn't feel the same way about her?"

I shake my head. "No, he told me that he loved me. I was the idiot who was too scared to stick around. Loving him meant giving up my friends here"—Troy snorts at that part—"and the things I love about Beverly Hills." Except that had all been a lie —a lie I'd told myself to make leaving Copper Creek easier. It had been an excuse, not reality.

"You really gave him up for those plastic, privileged women?" Troy asks.

"Yes, because apparently I'm not much better than they are."

Troy and Cameron join me on the fountain's edge.

"Kate," Troy says, "you've never been like them. You're a sweet and funny and smart woman. Yes, before Copper Creek, the idea of wearing anything that wasn't by a designer label would have been unthinkable to you. But you stopped caring about all of that stuff once you started falling in love with the place."

He's right. I did stop caring about all of that.

I started to care about other things, more important things.

Genuine friends.

Lady and Scoundrel.

An amazing man who fell in love with me.

I cringe. "It's too late now. I didn't tell Noah that I love him when he told me he loved me."

"So what, you think he fell out of love with you in a week?" Cameron asks, sounding somewhat skeptical. "Trust me, if that's true, then he never loved you like he claimed he did. It's not that easy to fall out of love." Something about his tone makes me think that he speaks from experience.

"So what should I do about it?"

"What does your heart tell you to do?"

I smile. "It's telling me to go back to Copper Creek and tell him that I love him. And hope he gives me a second chance."

"And if he doesn't. I still have the job opening for a fake girlfriend."

I laugh. "I'll keep it in mind."

"What about your new job?" Troy asks.

"I think you and I both know that's not the job for me. I loved working with you when we were renovating Charlotte's house. I loved doing the hands-on designing and getting messy." I shrug. "Being the voice for someone else's designs just isn't me."

He gives my shoulder a friendly nudge. "I was hoping you'd say that. I've already told my father that I'm leaving his company and creating my own. I have several renovation jobs lined up in Copper Creek and the neighboring towns. When I said, before the meeting last week, that I had some things in the works, that's what I was talking about.

"So if you're planning to permanently move back to Copper Creek, I would be interested in forming a home design and renovation company with you. As partners."

I blink. Twice. Then smile. "Are you serious? I would love to do that." Because the one thing I've learned during the past three months is that Troy and I make a great team.

I scramble to my feet. "I guess I'd better let the realtor know that Charlotte's house is off the market." And make sure no one sells Lady and Scoundrel.

Because they're *my* horses, and I'm not ready to give them up either.

"Are you planning to tell Noah now too?" Troy asks.

I think for a second, then shake my head. "No, I have a better idea." I remove my phone from my clutch and hit speed dial.

Sophie barely has time to say hi before I launch into an enthusiastic, "I need your help with something."

# 33

NOAH

I enter the kitchen, my hair still damp from my recent shower. Jake is leaning against the island, typing on his phone.

And wearing a business suit.

"Where is everyone?" I ask. For five p.m., the room is oddly quiet. Usually Sophie and Violet are busying cooking dinner. "And why are you wearing a suit?"

I can't remember the last time he wore one...other than for Halloween last year. Sophie was dressed as his sexy assistant.

He stops typing and pushes away from the counter. "We're going out and they're meeting us there."

"Where are we supposedly going?"

"The new homeowner moved into Charlotte's house the other day—"

"Holy shit, that was fast. I didn't think it would sell *that* quickly. And how come this is the first I've heard that it's sold?"

"I guess that's because you've been too busy moping around since Kate left. You've missed all the latest gossip."

I grunt. "I haven't been moping. I've been super productive, in case you haven't noticed. And since when were you so tuned-in to the gossip? Did you trade in your balls for ovaries and I didn't know about it?"

He just laughs at that. "Anyway, the owner is having a housewarming party today and we're going to it."

"By we, you're talking about you and Sophie, right?" I say, even though I know that's not exactly the "we" he's referring to. But I can always hope, especially since I'm not in the mood to be in Charlotte's house if Kate isn't there.

"No, I mean you, me, TJ, the girls, Deacon, and two dozen or so other people. So go get changed into your costume so we can head out already."

"I'd rather stay home, pop open a beer, and work on the Bel Air."

"You mean like what you've been doing for the past two weeks since Kate left? Tell you what, we'll drop in on the party for a few minutes. If you still want to go home after that, then fine. Go home and wallow if you must."

"Ha! You should talk. I remember you doing the same when things went south for you and Sophie. Maybe, bro, I learned from the best." I slap him on his back. "Okay, let's get this over with so that I can come home and mope in peace."

"Costume?"

"Sadly, it's at the dry cleaners, so I'll have to go without it." It's not, but I'm too lazy to change when I have no intention of staying at the party for more than a few minutes.

A short time later, we're in my truck, heading toward Charlotte's house. The early signs of dusk creep toward us over the valley.

"Have you talked to Kate since she returned home?" The corners of Jake's mouth twitch briefly. A commiserating smile.

"A few times." More like every day, which is how I know her best friend is now engaged to Kate's ex-boyfriend.

"And you're still in love with her?"

I glare at him as if his suggestion is ridiculous.

That cracks him up. "Don't even try to deny it, Noah. It's obvious you love her."

"Doesn't matter. Can you see me living in Beverly Hills? I would never fit in there. Copper Creek is my home."

"You might have a point there. But does that mean you're admitting that you're in love with her?"

"Will it make you happy if I do?"

"Only if it makes *you* happy."

I laugh but don't answer him. He already knows the truth. He doesn't need me confirming it.

I pull into Charlotte's driveway and park my truck behind a long stream of vehicles. The windows on the lower level of the house are lit up—illuminating two individuals in costumes standing on the porch, making out. One is dressed as Thor, the other Sif, a goddess from Norse mythology.

TJ and Violet.

I open the driver's door. "All right. Let's get this over with."

Jake snickers. "Good thing you're not going as a jolly old elf."

I flip him the bird, which only makes him laugh harder.

TJ and Violet unlock their lips as we approach. Violet types on her phone, then smiles brightly at me. "Why don't you go in and enjoy the party?"

My stomach ties itself into a knot of epic proportions, knowing that Kate won't be inside. *You need to move on*, I remind myself. *She belongs in Beverly Hills, not here.*

I open the door and head inside. Roxy's soulful singing voice comes from the living room, where she's entertaining guests with a song from an old-time movie. Deacon is dancing in front of her and stealing the show.

I make my way to the kitchen to grab a beer. A handful of people are milling around in there, but most are in the living room, watching the dynamic duo.

None of the guests hold any interest for me—other than the

black-haired woman wearing a familiar red dress from a histor-ical romance. My breath comes to a sudden halt.

"Kate?" I'm hallucinating. That must be it.

My hallucination nods.

And I keep gaping at her.

She steps closer to me. *Christ*, my hallucination is as beau-tiful as the real deal.

"Hi, Noah." My name comes out as a wisp of a sound, barely loud enough to be heard.

She cups her hand against my cheek. On instinct, I lean into it.

"I've missed you so much," she tells me.

"Not that I'm not thrilled to see you, but what are you doing here? I thought you were back in California." I keep my voice low so no one, other than Kate, can hear me over Roxy's singing.

"The day you told me you loved me? I didn't say anything because I was scared. And stupid. But I love you, Noah." The last part comes out as a hushed whisper and at first, I'm positive I've misheard her.

But her eyes tell a different story.

I've gone two weeks without touching her. Two weeks of thinking I'd never get to see her again. And now I can't go another two seconds without my mouth against hers.

Applause breaks out, but I can't tell if it's for us or for Roxie and Deacon.

I only know that it's enough to end the kiss. Unfortunately.

Kate pulls away and grins at what is definitely *our* audience. "Can we go somewhere to talk in private?"

I thread my fingers through hers, still not believing that she's back in Copper Creek, afraid to let her go in case she disappears. I follow her upstairs to the attic.

She flicks on the light, gestures for me to continue up the stairs, and locks the door behind her.

My mouth curls up to one side. "You planning on kidnapping me?"

"Nope—just want to make sure no one interrupts us."

I keep walking up the stairs and enter a room that's nothing like the one I chased the bat from three months ago. Now the walls and slanted ceilings are white, with built-in, floor-level cupboards along the walls on both sides of the bed.

The queen-sized bed—with off-white bedding—is missing a headboard. Instead, the window is behind it and the floor-length, off-white curtains are currently closed.

She's also added several potted ferns and a wicker laundry basket since I last saw the place.

"This is incredible." It's like our own private sanctuary. Something I appreciate with the party going on downstairs.

She smiles, an adorable blush coloring her cheeks. "Thank you."

And then I sober. "Congratulations on selling the house. You must be relieved." She said that she loves me, but that doesn't really mean a whole lot...unless she's expecting to have a long-distance relationship, which I'm not interested in doing. I want to be able to wake up *every* morning with her in my arms —and not just on alternating weekends or whenever she can get away from LA.

"I didn't technically sell the house. I took it off the market. I'm moving here. This is now my home. Copper Creek is now my home."

"But what about your new job with your uncle's company? And in case you haven't noticed, Copper Creek isn't Beverly Hills."

"You're right. It isn't. It's so much better. The man I love lives here. I've got two horses that I missed. And I have some amazing friends here, too. Turns out, my friends back home weren't really the friends I thought they were. It took the friends I made here for me to realize it."

I gently kiss her, happy that she's finally figured that out.

"But what about the job with your uncle? I thought you were excited about it." *Shut up, Noah. You don't want her to return to Beverly Hills. You want her to stay here.*

"I decided not to accept the position. Turns out, it wasn't what I was expecting. Plus, my heart was still here. No job can make up for what I would have lost by not telling you how I feel about you." She rests her hand over my heart.

At her touch, my already erratic heartbeat kicks up a notch.

"And because I decided to make Copper Creek my home," she says, "a new opportunity came up. And this one I have no intention of turning down."

"What opportunity?"

"Troy and I are going to start our own home-design and renovation company in the area. He's incredibly talented, but his talents were going to waste with his father's show."

I gently press my lips to hers. "Christ, Kate. I love you so much. I never thought I'd get to say that to you again."

And that's as far as the talking goes.

Our mouths and our tongues and our hands go on to prove how right those words are. I don't know how I survived the past two weeks—or maybe I didn't. Because right now? I'm the poor sap who got lost in the desert and is now drinking the water he missed out on.

But not just any water.

The finest water around—the one no other could possibly live up to.

Now I get why Kate locked the door, because if someone were to come up, I'd have to push them out the window. Nothing is taking me away from her for the next thirty-or-so minutes.

My hands move to palm her breasts and I frown

I look down at the red dress. "How exactly am I supposed to cop a feel when you're locked up tight?" I might be clueless about women's clothing from centuries ago, but I do know this: men back then were screwed.

These days, some guys struggle with undoing bras. They fumble like a drunk football player trying to receive a pass. In the old days, no one stood a chance of getting a woman out of her clothing with a simple flick of the wrist.

Her breasts were hidden behind a fortress wall.

Kate laughs the sound I've missed so much. "Apparently my great-aunt loved her costumes to be authentic, including the undergarments. Sophie had to help me with the corset."

I scowl some more. "So I can't get you out of it until all the guests leave?" Maybe I can encourage them to leave *now*.

"Unless you want to spend thirty minutes getting me back into my clothes before we go downstairs, the breast groping will have to wait a little longer."

My gaze travels down her length. "Are your breasts the only things locked up tight?"

She grins at me. "Everything else is free game."

Thank Christ for that small miracle.

I give her one more deep, breathtaking kiss as I encourage her to lie back on the bed.

My mouth moves away from hers. "So how about I see what exactly you have under the skirt? But just so you know, I don't have any condoms with me. I wasn't expecting you to be here."

Her grin returns, bigger and brighter than before. "I thought you might say that. There's some under the pillow."

I push myself off the bed, retrieve the string of condoms, and lightly run my hands up the outside of her legs. They tremble at my touch.

I know the feeling. My body is shaking in anticipation of what it will feel like to make love to her again. To hear those noises she makes when she's getting close and when her body falls apart.

To show her how much she means to me.

My hands continue pushing the satin fabric of her dress and the thick cotton of her slip up her bare legs.

Even though the rest of her outfit resembles clothing from an era long since passed, I'm pretty sure the black lace panties with a little red bow didn't exist back then.

I grin up at her. "Nice touch."

"I thought you'd approve."

I remove them and pop the scrap of fabric into my pocket. "I'll just save them as a souvenir."

I then take my time, making up for the two weeks we were apart. Worshiping her, eating her out until she resembles a limp noodle, satisfaction stamped on her gorgeous flushed face.

Once her eyes are less dazed and she's grinning at me, I remove my jeans and briefs, roll on a condom, position myself, and thrust inside her.

Her soft heat instantly welcomes me, and I groan at how amazing she feels. I slowly move inside her, filling her, stretching her, savoring her. No other woman has made me feel the way I do when I'm with Kate.

She's my one and only—my soul mate.

We don't rush to get to the peak. If all the partiers are gone by the time we're finished, I won't be disappointed. Hell, if she and I never leave this room, I'm good with that, too.

She wraps her legs around my hips and my movements become desperate. My balls tighten, and her heat begins to clamp down on me.

She cries out her release, along with a few *Oh, God*s and my name. The pressure low in my gut grows more intense and I can't hold back any longer. I grunt my own release, my love for her filling every part of her, marking her. Claiming her.

Once I've regained my breath, I remove myself from her and deal with the condom, then I pull on my clothes and lie down beside her. She has already straightened her dress and shifts happily into my arms.

"We should go down soon before everyone starts to wonder where we've disappeared to," she says, the satisfied flush still on her face.

I grin. "I wouldn't be surprised if they've already guessed what we've been up to."

"You're probably right."

I adjust my position so I'm looking down at her. "Are you okay with that?"

"Why wouldn't I be?"

I tenderly kiss her. "Good to know. And would you be okay if I refer to you as my girlfriend?"

She settles her hand on my face, her palm brushing against my beard. "I wouldn't have it any other way."

And then we're kissing again—because I've waited long enough for Kate to come back into my life.

Her guests can wait a little longer to see her again.

EPILOGUE
KATE

Eight Months Later

"**W**here are we going?" I ask Noah as he leads me toward the small barn on the ranch, where he performs his car-restoration magic.

"You'll see soon enough."

He completed the Thunderbird last fall. It's gorgeous. And fun to drive around town in. I haven't seen the Chevy Bel Air. He's still working on it, and I'm not even allowed a sneak peek until it's finished.

I expect us to keep walking along the path that leads to the river. It's where we hang out when the weather is warm. But instead of heading down the fork in the path toward the river, Noah walks me to the closed barn doors.

"Are you ready?" he asks.

"Ready for what?"

"This." He slides open the door, revealing the Bel Air.

Unlike the last time I saw it, the car is no longer rusty and sad looking. Now it's freshly painted, shiny, proud.

"Wow, it's gorgeous." I enter the barn and look inside at the car. The last time I saw the interior, it was dirty white and in need of repairs and new parts. It's still white, only now the upholstery is free of holes, bright and clean. It actually resembles the color it's supposed to be.

The car's exterior was originally Neptune green (a.k.a. mint green), but we both agreed that wasn't very manly. It's now red.

I'm positive Charlotte and John would approve.

Noah nods at the Bel Air. "You ready for a test drive?"

"As if you have to ask." I open the passenger side and lower myself onto the seat. The car even smells new.

Noah climbs into the driver's side and turns over the engine. The sound isn't as smooth as his truck or my car. He didn't upgrade the engine to a modern-day equivalent—although he did soup it up a bit. He wanted to keep things as authentic as possible.

He carefully pulls out of the barn and slowly drives along the wide gravel path leading to the driveway. Once we're on the road, he presses his foot on the accelerator.

And I'm grinning like crazy.

A year ago, when I first saw the car rusting in Charlotte's yard, I never expected to one day be riding in it. But back then, I never expected to make Copper Creek my permanent home either.

Noah steers us down a road that eventually leads to a steady incline. Surprisingly, the car doesn't complain.

At the top of the hill, he pulls into a gravel parking lot that I recognize. It's the beginning of a hiking route we've used several dozen times. The view is amazing from up here. The trees below and in the area are now in full bloom. The river curves through the valley, still high from the melting snow in the mountains.

The sun is low in the sky. In another half an hour or so it will be sunset.

Noah climbs out of the car and opens my door. He then leads me to the front of the vehicle and we lean against the hood, looking out at the valley in front of us.

"I'll never grow tired of the view here," I say.

"Me either. I loved Seattle, but it's nothing like Copper Creek."

I laugh. "Including the winter." I won't lie. Winters in Montana aren't my favorite part about living here, especially when it comes to my leg. Winters in Beverly Hills are so much better.

But I survived last winter.

How? Snuggling up to Noah. In bed. In front of the fire. In the bath. On the couch.

My favorite way to spend the cold winter months.

"Yes," he says, "but at least here there's something that makes winters worth it."

"What's that?"

He shifts away from the hood and pulls me to him. His arms go around my waist and he leans in so his breath brushes my ear. "Being with you. Making love to you. But do you know what would make them even better?"

"What's that?"

He drops to one knee.

This isn't the first time he's done that, but usually he's removing my clothing and undergarments when he kneels in front of me.

This time he's got a different expression on his face. It's not filled with heat—although that's there too. This time hope is the predominant emotion.

My vision suddenly grows blurry.

"That you'll spend them as my wife," he says. "That you'll spend the falls and the springs and the summers as my wife, too. Because you're the reason I love living in Copper Creek. You're the reason I have a smile on my face every time I see you. And even when we're not together, I have one on my face from thinking about you."

He opens his hand, revealing a beautiful diamond ring. "Kate, will you marry me?"

Those tears that clouded my vision? They're now rolling down my face. I nod. "I would love to marry you, Noah." I can't imagine a man who I would rather be with.

Noah stands and barely manages to slide the ring on my finger before my arms are around his neck and we're kissing.

The moment couldn't be more perfect as the sun gets ready to set. It reminds me of Charlotte's letters to John. The only difference is, the day they first made love in the Chevy Bel Air, they were overlooking the Pacific Ocean. We're overlooking a different slice of heaven, but I don't doubt the outcome will be the same.

I slip my fingers under the hem of his T-shirt and push the fabric up his body, exposing his delicious abs. He grabs the collar and yanks the material over his head.

Once that's done, we go back to kissing, my fingers wrapped in the soft strands of his hair.

"I think we should christen the Bel Air," Noah murmurs against my lips.

"I think you're right. It would only be fitting."

Fortunately, this isn't a popular hangout for the teens in town. We don't have to worry about someone stumbling across us at this time of day. The hikers have all gone home now. We're completely alone.

Well, mostly alone—if you don't count the wildlife.

We make our way to the rear passenger door, items of clothing coming off as we continue kissing. We climb into the back seat while helping each other remove the remaining pieces of clothing. But unlike before, the movement isn't rushed. We savor the moment—savor what we feel for each other.

Sex in the back seat of a car isn't normally as romantic as it might sound. It's synonymous with being forbidden, dirty. Fun. But as I sink onto Noah's hard length, I can't think of anything more romantic than making love to my fiancé in the vintage car he restored with his own hands...with the sun setting behind me.

It truly is magical.

MISTLETOE WISHES

A COPPER CREEK NOVELLA

Mistletoe Wishes was originally part of the *Holiday Heart-On* charity anthology. The steamy, laugh-out-loud short story has been expanded to novella length and is now dual POV.

BLURB

What happens under the mistletoe doesn't always stay under the mistletoe...

A year ago, I left my hometown to start a new life due to a broken heart. No, not the kind that comes from a derailed love life. An infection stole my heart's will to keep beating.

And now I'm back in Copper Creek to help my father with the town's fun-raiser Christmas charity event. What I'm not here to do is spend time with hot firefighter Gavin Ross. Gavin has been my best friend since second grade. He's also the man who I've ghosted for the past year.

Because how can I face the man whose late girlfriend's heart now beats inside me? The man who I've been secretly in love with...forever?

1
___

ALLY

I enter the building that's been like a second home since I was a little girl. If your second home has a pole in the middle of the room. Not a stripper pole—though that would be cool.

A firefighter pole.

Ryan is talking to Sierra, one of my best friends growing up. They're standing at the reception desk, both dressed in their volunteer firefighter gear of a dark blue T-shirt and pants.

He looks at me over her shoulder. "Hey, Ally."

Sierra whirls around, her blond ponytail whipping around her head, a huge smile on her face. She rushes over and hugs me. "I was positive you were lying when you said you were coming back for Christmas."

I return the hug, squeezing her tighter than I could a year ago. "I don't lie."

She snorts out a laugh and steps away. "Right. So it wasn't a lie the previous five times you said you were coming for a visit but then backed out at the last moment?"

"Exactly." I give her a curt nod which ends in a smile.

Ryan flashes me a devilish grin, and an *uh-oh* warning shimmies up my spine. "Does Gavin know you're in town?"

"Nope. I'm here to visit Dad. Is he around?"

"He's in his office."

"Are you going to be here for the festival?" Sierra's smile is even wider than Ryan's.

I nod, confused by the question. She already knows the answer because we've been talking weekly on the phone for the past year—ever since I moved away from Copper Creek. "Of course. Dad told me the proceeds are going to the Go Red for Women program. And given that I'm the poster child for the importance of a healthy heart—"

"*Meow!*" The hearty sound and the solid body rubbing against my leg have me glancing down.

"Phoenix!" I scoop up the adorable, cuddly ginger cat.

He purrs loudly, his large body vibrating in my arms.

Sierra scratches him behind the ear. "He's missed you."

"I've missed him, too. I've missed all of you." I hadn't realized how much I would miss everyone when I moved to Billings, Montana.

"Including Gavin?" Amusement crinkles the corners of Ryan's eyes, and his observant gaze has me squirming. No wonder the former Calvin Klein model turned veterinarian is so good with animals. Nothing gets past him.

I look down at Phoenix, letting my hair curtain my face and hide just how much I've missed Gavin, my best friend. The guy I grew up with. The guy I fell in love with. The guy who'd been in love with someone else until a year ago.

When she died in a car accident.

"Yes, including Gavin." I kiss Phoenix's head.

"I have some great news," Sierra says. "Mrs. Jenkins is retiring from teaching soon. And I happen to know the school is still looking for her replacement. You should apply. I know they would love to have you back. And since the teacher you were subbing for in Billings has returned from her maternity leave, you can move back to Copper Creek." Sierra grins. Problem solved. In her mind.

"Mrs. Jenkins is retiring?" I ask, avoiding the reason I can't move back here. "Isn't she like two hundred years old?" She's also the sweetest woman to walk the earth. "The school won't be the same without her."

"It won't. But please tell me you'll apply for her position. I mean, unless you want to stay in the city." Sierra flashes me her puppy-dog eyes that no mere mortal can resist.

I laugh and put Phoenix on the ground. "Okay, I'll apply for the job if it makes you happy." I'm sure I won't be the only candidate applying for it, so it's not like I'm breaking my no-moving-back-to-Copper-Creek rule.

"It does. Sooo, does that mean you don't have a big-city boyfriend waiting for you to return? Nothing new since we last talked?"

"Nope, no new boyfriends in the past seven days." It's been a few years since I last had a boyfriend.

Sierra's gaze drops to my chest. It's only then I realize my fingers are rubbing the long, ugly scar over my sternum and hidden under my sweater. Ryan also hasn't failed to notice what my hand is doing.

Oops.

I switch to plucking stray cat hairs from my sweater. "I should go see Dad before he wonders what happened to me."

I hurriedly enter his office to find him typing on his computer. Scattered on his desk are bits of paper with scribbled notes, some of which are probably at least a week old. "Hey, Dad."

He looks up, and a big, relieved smile stretches across his face. "Ally." My name is a reverent whisper on his lips.

He stands and gives me a hug that would squish me if I were a slug. "God, I've missed you, Noodle."

Laughing, I return his exuberant hug. "I can see that. I've missed you, too."

He takes a step back. "You're looking good. Are you still remembering to take your immunosuppressive drugs?"

"Absolutely."

"No infections I should know about? You're eating okay?"

"Check. And check. Don't worry, Dad. My new heart and I are doing great."

I might be thirty-three years old, but Dad seems to forget—as his daily texts can attest. In his eyes, I'm still twelve.

Losing Mom when I was in preschool probably has something to do with that, too. Her death turned him into a superhero, if being overly protective is a superpower.

I kiss him on the cheek. "I'm all good. And I'm happy to be back in Copper Creek for Christmas."

"Does Gavin know you're here?" It's obvious from the way he asks the question that he knows the answer.

I wince. "I haven't spoken to him since the accident. So that would be a no."

"That's because you've been ghosting him."

"I haven't been ghosting him." *I've totally been ghosting him.* "I've just been...busy—"

Gavin walks into Dad's office before I can finish my sentence.

Shirtless.

His muscled abs and chest glistening with drops of water.

And *holy all things yummy on a stick*, my mouth goes dry, and my heart—his old girlfriend's heart—trips over itself.

Right, his *girlfriend's* heart. That's why the organ is reacting that way. Because I'm not in love with him anymore. *Nope. No siree.* But Madison's heart is clearly still in love with the man.

Madison was a brilliant ER physician. She saved sooooo many people's lives. I've saved no one. Not even a tiny bit. I don't deserve a man like Gavin. Madison should still be alive so her heart can beat for him—in her own chest.

Gavin's warm brown eyes shift in my direction. Excitement flickers in them. But just as I'm beginning to think everything's okay between us, the excitement extinguishes like a candle in a blizzard.

His gaze darts back to my father. "Ryan said you wanted to talk to me, Chief."

Loud laughter spills in through the open door, and Gavin rolls his eyes.

"Why are they laughing?" And why do I have a feeling it has something to do with me?

And the part where Gavin is shirtless.

"They're laughing because I'd just stepped out of the shower when Ryan told me the Chief needed to see me. He told me it was important and there was no time to dally."

"The fact that Ryan said 'dally' didn't set off any alarms?" Dad tries to fight off a grin.

Gavin shrugs. "Sure, in retrospect."

While my heart is recovering from seeing the man who used to be my best friend, my eyes drink him in. Drink in the man who doesn't have an ugly-ass scar on his chest. An ugly-ass scar capable of repelling the opposite gender.

"So I take it you didn't need to see me?" Gavin asks Dad without giving me a second glance.

I guess I have no one to blame but myself for that.

Gavin had texted and phoned me numerous times over the first two months after the accident. I never replied to any of them.

Listened to his voice messages a million times?

Absolutely.

Read his texts over and over until I had them memorized? Definitely.

I open my mouth to apologize for ghosting him, but before the words come out, a little whirlwind in the form of seven-year-old Presley comes charging into the office.

"Ally!" She hurls her body at me.

2

ALLY

I catch Presley in my arms and give her a big hug. "Hey, Sweet Pea."

She returns the hug, giggling. "You have to see all the pictures I've made while watching your *Art with Ally* YouTube videos. Mommy says my bedroom looks like an art gallery." She turns to Gavin. "Isn't that right, Uncle Gavin?" She doesn't even bat a cute little eyelash that he's shirtless in my father's office.

Gavin chuckles that low, sexy rumble of a laugh I've never grown tired of hearing. "That's right. It's impossible to tell what color your walls actually are, because they're covered in your beautiful pictures."

"I can't wait to see your artwork," I tell Presley.

"It was Uncle Gavin who told me all about your YouTube videos." She bounces on her toes. "They're so amazing. You're so amazing."

"Thank you. I'm glad you like them."

Presley turns back to Gavin. "Mommy told me to tell you she won't be able to help with your booth. She's covering another nurse's shift at the clinic. But Ally can help you instead."

289

Gavin's eyebrows lift. "Your mom told you that Ally can help me with my booth?"

"No, silly. I just figured Ally can help you since she's here."

"I think that's a great idea," Dad says.

No, it isn't. It's a bad, *bad* idea. "Dad, I'm here to help you with *your* booth."

"That's not necessary anymore. Tabitha King has offered to help me."

"The Chief and Miss King are dating. Miss King has been all gooey eyes since they started going out." Presley makes a goofy cross-eyed expression, and a giggle-snort tumbles past my lips.

"How come I didn't know about your dating life?" As far as I knew, Dad had never dated after Mom died. She was his one and only—or so he'd once told me.

Dad just shrugs. "Well, since I've already got a wonderful assistant, you're free to help Gavin with his booth."

My traitorous heart does a happy dance. *Madison's traitorous heart.* Mine gave up its will to live last year after a viral infection resulted in severe myocarditis.

"What is your booth?" I ask Gavin. If it's a kissing booth and he's shirtless for it, he'll strike gold when it comes to bringing in money for the fun-raiser.

"He's selling his wooden carvings." Presley's mouth curves into a big, proud grin.

Okay, that idea works, too.

"I would love to help you. If you want my help." I mean, I did ghost him for the past year. I wouldn't be surprised if he tells me to go hug a tree with a grumpy cougar in it.

"Sure, I could probably use your help." The enthusiasm in his tone is flatter than a deflated inflatable Santa.

"Great. Perfect." I stretch my lips into a reasonable facsimile of a smile.

Presley and I climb into Gavin's truck a few minutes later,

and he drives to his parents' house to drop her off. The house I had practically grown up in when I was a kid. It hasn't changed much over the years. The interior is a mishmash of several styles—country, modern, florals, and plaids—but it's cozy and smells the same as it did back then. Like banana bread and hot chocolate.

"Ally!" His mom throws her arms around me as soon as I walk through the front door.

Then she hurls what feels like a billion questions at me. How's my job? Have I met anyone special yet? What restaurants do I recommend in Billings? What are my friends there like? How's the nightlife?

"Okay, Mom," Gavin says after I've answered about a dozen of the questions. "That's enough of your interrogations." He flashes her one of his grins that always has my heart stumbling over itself. This time is no exception. "We've got to get going. Ally can answer the rest of your questions later."

"Well, you'd better drop by before you leave for the big city," she tells me, her smile warm and bright. "I can't wait to hear more about it. I've missed you, Ally." She gives me another of her big motherly hugs.

"I've missed you, too." Caroline has always been like a second mother to me. "And I will definitely see you again before I go back home."

"Bye, Presley," I call out. She disappeared into the living room shortly after we arrived—while Caroline was asking me all the questions. Her giggles and the background music from whatever TV show she's watching spill into the hallway.

"Bye, Ally!" she replies in a singsong voice, her pitch a near shout.

Gavin opens the front door and walks out without a word to me. I make a move to follow him, but his mother grabs my hand and gives it a squeeze. "He's missed you. I don't know what happened between you two, but I hope you both can fix it."

Her words surprise me. *What happened between us?* Was it that obvious?

I don't have a reply for that. She doesn't need to hear how I've always been in love with her son, but he doesn't see me that way. So I just smile and promise her he and I are good.

Sure, we're not like we used to be, but we can still be friends.

Maybe.

Possibly.

Okay, I have some major work ahead of me if I want us to be friends. Casual friends. Not best friends. I can't expect him to want that after I turned my back on him. Besides, it's not like I live in Copper Creek anymore.

Guilt wiggles its way inside me at how I was responsible for the death of our friendship. But I needed a new start after everything that happened. With his girlfriend. With her heart. With *my* heart.

I don't mean that it failed due to the viral infection and needed to be replaced. It had already been dinged before that because I'd been in love with Gavin, but he'd never felt that way about me.

Oh, well. That's all in the past.

I nudge the guilt aside with my shoulder and follow Gavin to his truck.

A chorus of "Deck the Halls" comes from the house next door, where a group of carolers is singing. I hum along and climb into the passenger seat, then click my seat belt into place, the song now playing in my head.

Gavin doesn't say anything. He just starts the engine and pulls out of the driveway.

At least when Presley was with us, she talked nonstop on the way to his parents' house. Gavin and I didn't have to make conversation. Silence now fills the interior of the truck. It's nothing like the comfortable silence that easily stretched between us in the past. That silence was a big hug, a warm smile, a fuzzy blanket. This silence is…an echoing emptiness felt in the bones.

"Sooo, what's new in your life?" I watch his expression for some sort of reaction.

He shrugs, his gaze on the road. Not even a teensy, tiny flicker of a smile crosses his face. "Nothing really."

He doesn't ask me a question or give any hints that he wants to talk to me, so I turn my attention to the colorfully lit homes and trees lining the street. God, I really love this time of year. It's so magical.

It doesn't take long before I realize he's driving to his house. I don't bother to question it. I sit back and enjoy the ride through the small town that still feels like home.

After fifteen minutes of driving in silence—the Christmas music from his playlist the only sound in the truck—Gavin parks on the street in front of his house.

The rustic two-story home glows in the golden lights decorating the exterior. The place is cozy, the perfect size for a small family—the family I'd envisioned him one day having with Madison.

We jump down from the truck, and I start to walk to his front door.

"We're actually going around back," he tells me and heads to the gate at the side of his house. I trail after him along the path that hasn't been shoveled since the last snowfall. Luckily, only an inch or two of snow covers it.

We step into his large backyard, the snow much deeper here, and that's when I see the shed that wasn't there before.

Or rather, the quaint little wooden structure that looks more like a small cottage than your typical garden shed. An intricately carved sign with the words *Gavin's Workshop* hangs on the door.

"This place is new," I say. "I love it."

"Thanks. I needed somewhere to store my carvings and decided to build a workshop."

He unlocks the door, and we step inside. Gavin flips on the light, illuminating an interior that resembles an old-fashioned painting of Santa's workshop. A work counter sits in the middle of the room with an unfinished project on it. The rest of the space is filled with carvings, the larger ones on the floor and the smaller ones arranged on the bookshelves. Most of the designs are of woodland critters and mythical creatures, like dragons and gnomes.

"Wow, you've been busy." I walk over to inspect his work.

"I've had a lot of free time."

Madison wasn't one to sit around and read a book or watch TV. That meant when they were together, when their schedules coincided, they were always on the go.

And when he wasn't busy with Madison, he was hanging out with me.

Until the accident that changed all our lives, he hadn't had much time for his carvings.

"They're gorgeous." I crouch and inspect a wolf pup about a foot tall. The details are incredible, especially the fur. I stand, open my purse, and remove the palm-sized wooden gnome Gavin carved for me three years ago. "He comes everywhere with me."

Surprise widens Gavin's eyes. "You still have it?"

"Of course. He's my lucky gnome." I'd had him on me when I found out I was getting a new heart. Only I hadn't realized at the time it was Madison's heart.

I run my thumb over the gnome's features and return him to my purse.

"So you're not seeing anyone?" Gavin's tone is Switzerland. He might as well be asking if I want milk with my dinner.

"I've been too busy to worry about dating. Plus this way, I don't have to worry about catching something nasty because my immunosuppressive drugs put me at risk for all kinds of infections." The words come out light and breezy. But the loneliness of not having a special someone in my life is a ten-ton wooden gnome on my chest.

"Are you okay?" A frown pinches Gavin's brow, his gaze focused on my chest.

I glance down. My hand is rubbing at the spot where my scar is, like it's an old penny that needs polishing.

I drop my hand away. "Yeah, I'm fine."

"So what are you doing in the city that has you so busy?"

Trying to find myself after everything that happened a year ago. "This and that. What about you? Are you seeing anyone?" *Ugh. Why the hell did I just ask him that?* I don't want to know if he's found someone new. If he's fallen in love again.

Gavin shakes his head and picks up a cute little dragon from his collection. Sadness hangs off him like a well-worn T-shirt.

He must still be mourning Madison. He's not ready to move on with his life yet.

"Have you thought of doing a live demonstration tomorrow during the festival?" I ask, eager to change the topic. "It would be a great way to get attention for your booth. Especially if you do it shirtless." I grin, thinking of the shirtless Gavin in Dad's office, his chest glistening with water droplets. "That's bound to get plenty of women who are into hot firefighters checking out your booth."

"You think I'm hot?" Gavin's mouth curves to one side with that damn sexy smile of his. Luckily for me, he's not currently shirtless; otherwise, I might have gone up in flames.

Also luckily for me, he's a firefighter. He has an extinguisher in his workshop.

"I've always thought you were hot," I say under my breath.

I kneel and pretend to study the large comical face carved into a tree stump. The laughing expression on its gnomish face is no doubt directed at me.

"I have to be somewhere in a few minutes," Gavin tells me. "And you're coming with me."

I push to my feet. "Where do you have to be?"

"You'll see." He reaches behind his head and grabs the neck of his T-shirt. He yanks it over his head in that way only guys can do and tosses it onto the counter. He removes a T-shirt from a small stack of folded red T-shirts on a wooden chair and pulls it on.

He grabs another one. "Here, put this on." He tosses it at me, and I catch it. "I'll meet you outside."

And he leaves.

Alrighty then.

3

GAVIN

I pace along the snowy path I haven't had a chance to clear yet. If I'd known I would be bringing Ally to my house, I would've shoveled it last night.

Ally.

I can't believe she's back in Copper Creek. It's been a year since I've last seen her. A year since my best friend made it clear she no longer wanted to be part of my life. Losing Madison was bad enough—she was a great physician and a caring person—but her death was nothing compared to Ally shutting me out.

She'd had fucking heart surgery. With scalpels and the heart on ice and an anesthesiologist. Not the tweezers-and-a-buzzing-red-nose-when-you-screw-up kind of surgery. Yet, not once did she tell me how she was doing. All my updates came from her father and Sierra.

Before that, Ally would've told me everything that was going on in her life—even when she went away to college.

Her classes.

Her friends.

The exams she struggled with and those she aced.

Her practicums.

Her dates.

All of it she shared with me. Okay, I hadn't been interested in the details of her dating life. Hearing about it had almost killed me, especially when she'd dated that one guy. What was his name?

Todd? Troy? Trevor?

Turd Breath? Yep, that was his name. Or at least the name I referred to him as...in my head.

He was the one Sierra had told me was *The One*.

Can't say I was too disappointed when Turd Breath got a job across the country. He'd decided he wanted to spread his oats and didn't see Ally as part of his future.

Dumb asshole.

I kick a patch of snow on the side of the path.

She had come home that Christmas heartbroken. I was the one who put the smile back on her face. I'd planned to tell her then how I felt about her—that I'd been in love with her forever. But she'd dramatically flopped back on her bed, declared she never wanted to date again, and would remain single for the rest of her life.

I might be a firefighter who has braved burning buildings, but telling Ally how I felt about her? Yeah, I wasn't that brave.

I didn't want to risk our friendship.

Even after she moved back to Copper Creek to teach at the elementary school, I'd been too chicken to tell her the truth.

Then I met Madison. Our relationship had been simple and easy...until it wasn't.

"That's bound to get plenty of women who are into hot fire-fighters checking out your booth."

Ally thought I was hot?

In all the years I've known her, not once has she given any indication she saw me that way.

You're reading too much into what she said.

The workshop door opens, and Ally steps into the cold evening air. The red T-shirt she's changed into peeks out between the opening of her coat, and she's holding the sweater she was wearing.

The light breeze ruffles strands of her chocolate-brown hair around her face. I lift my hand to tuck them behind her ear, but common sense bites me in the ass, and I let my hand drop to my side.

I could kick Ryan for his stunt back at the station—for sending me into the chief's office when he knew damn well Ally was there. He knew how hurt I'd been after she ghosted me.

Yeah, a few beers might have been involved when I divulged that to him.

Ally closes the door behind her. I reach for the doorknob to lock it, and my body accidentally brushes hers. Our skin doesn't touch, but that doesn't stop a flicker of heat from dancing along my arm.

It spreads throughout my body, making a beeline for my groin. That much hasn't changed in all these years—other than when I was in a relationship with Madison. My body had the decency then to respect what she and I had. But clearly, it's chosen to ignore how Ally's cold shoulder gutted me.

Traitor.

I lock the door and head for my truck, not daring to say anything. Pretty much like on the way over. The hurt from the past year still bubbles inside me, but another emotion fizzes alongside it. Hope?

I squish it underfoot as I approach the driver's door. Only fools hold on to hope like a child clinging to a favorite stuffed bear—or in my case—a stuffed dragon.

I climb into my truck, fasten the seat belt, and turn over the engine.

Ally pulls herself into the passenger seat and clicks her seat belt into position.

You can't keep trying to pretend she's not sitting there like you did on the way to Mom and Dad's. Things are already awkward enough.

"What are your plans now that your teaching contract is finished?" I ask, genuinely curious.

Her father and Sierra occasionally dropped hints over the past year as to what Ally has been up to, which is how I know her last position has ended.

A soft laugh eases past her lips. "Which one told you? My dad or Sierra?"

"I can't remember." *Sierra.* "It was one of those things they said in passing...to everyone in the room."

More like the empty room.

Sierra cornered me a month ago and updated me on Ally's job situation. She'd been excited, hoping maybe Ally would finally be coming home. To stay.

I shrugged it off at the time—the hurt still kicking me in the ass—and pretended it didn't make a difference to me.

I don't think Sierra bought the act. She always was too astute for my own good.

"So, what are your plans?" I ask again since Ally still hasn't answered the question.

I shift my gaze from the road in time to catch her chewing her bottom lip. She turns her head to look out the side window. "I don't know. I haven't been offered any temporary or permanent positions yet. I'll have to wait to see what happens after the holidays."

I don't bother to tell her Mrs. Jenkins is retiring. Sierra and her father would've already told Ally that.

She'll apply for the position if she wants to move back to town. It's not my job to convince her to stay—even though part of me wishes she would.

A part of me that isn't still hurting.

4

ALLY

Gavin kills his truck's engine. Outside the window, snowflakes twirl in the air and land on the wintery landscape.

Ahead of us, in the town square, is a log cabin I recognize from growing up in Copper Creek. Santa's Workshop. White Christmas lights twinkle on the pine trees, workshop eaves, and the various concession-stand huts.

Gavin takes my hand and leads me to one of them. An unexpected tingling spreads through my arm from where his hand touches mine. *Well, that's new.*

Noah grins at me from the other side of the counter. Instead of his usual cowboy hat, a white mop cap is perched on his head. "Hey, Ally. I heard you were back in town."

I smile at the man who used to be one of Gavin's and my classmates. "Why are you wearing that silly hat?"

Noah's grin stretches wider. "Because I lost a bet with my wife."

"What bet?"

Kate appears at the stand's window, her brown hair twisted into two braids under her own mop cap. She and Noah are

301

wearing the same red T-shirts Gavin and I have on. Fortunately, the one Gavin gave me is my size. It must have been meant for his sister.

"I thought he should dress the part if we're volunteering to do a couple of shifts in Roxie's concession stand for the fun-raiser. And since the stand is called Mrs. Claus's Treats, it only makes sense that we all—including Noah—wear the hats." Kate wraps her arms around her husband's waist and kisses him on the cheek. "And you have to admit, he looks cute."

Noah grunts but still manages to give her an adoring smile.

Gavin chuckles. "We'll have two gingerbread hot chocolates. With extra whipped cream and caramel sauce swirled on top." My favorite. "Thanks." He pays for them.

Kate hands us the drinks once they're ready. "Aren't you performing at the seniors center soon?" she asks Gavin.

"That's the plan. We're heading there now."

"Performing?" I divide a glance between Kate and Gavin and sip the hot chocolate. God, it's just as good as I remember.

Kate leans forward, elbows on the counter. "As part of the fun-raiser, the seniors have hired various individuals in town to drop by today and tomorrow to entertain them for a few minutes. And Gavin here signed up to do it."

"What about you, Ally?" Noah nods at me. "I seem to remember whenever you and Gavin sang together at our school talent shows, you two always won."

Kate's eyes widen. "You used to sing together in your school talent shows? How come no one told me this?"

I lift my shoulders in a nonchalant shrug. "Because that was so long ago." Way, way, *waaaay* before she moved to Copper Creek from Beverly Hills. "Gavin and I haven't sung together in forever." Or at least it feels that way.

Gavin and I say goodbye to Kate and Noah and walk over to Santa's Village. Ten or so young kids are braving the cold to line up and see Santa (aka my father). The door to the hut opens and Santa steps out. He places his hands on his pillow-stuffed stomach. "Ho, ho, ho."

This results in the little kids cheering and bouncing.

One of the adults with them turns and spots Gavin and me. Mrs. Price. Our fourth-grade teacher. "Ally! You're back. I've missed seeing your cheeky face around town."

Gavin chuckles next to me again, and I give his arm a tiny jab with my elbow.

Mrs. Price smiles at us, her wrinkled cheeks pink from the cold. "When are you moving back to Copper Creek? Your father mentioned your teaching contract in the Billings school has finished."

"I don't know if I am. I don't have a job here." Or anywhere.

"Mrs. Jenkins is retiring. You could take over her spot. You're an excellent teacher. Principal Standover would be an idiot not to rehire you. Of course, this is assuming you won't break some poor man's heart in Billings by moving here."

I laugh because that's one thing I don't need to worry about. Being intimate with a man means letting him see my Bride-of-Frankenstein scar, and I have no interest in doing that. "I definitely won't be breaking anybody's heart. I'll drop off my résumé on Monday." I guess, what could it hurt?

I loved being a teacher at that school. And I do miss Copper Creek.

"Perfect. I'll tell Principal Standover to expect it." She returns to her grandkids, and Gavin and I continue walking toward the seniors center while sipping our hot chocolate.

"How have things been going?" Gavin asks me, apparently over whatever was bugging him while we were driving to his house.

"Not bad. I haven't had any side effects from my drugs."

"That's good, but that's not what I'm talking about. I've missed you, Ally." He shoulder-bumps me. "I've missed saddling up the horses and riding with you. And I've missed you lacing up skates and playing hockey against me."

I snicker. "I am a pretty awesome hockey player." By awesome, I mean I suck. "I've missed you, too."

I look up at the lights decorating the birch tree in front of us, not letting Gavin see in my eyes just how much I've missed him...and how my heart still gallops every time I hear his deep voice. "How's Clover doing?"

"The horse has been pretty cranky with you gone."

Amusement tugs on my lips. "Cranky? Right. I don't think that horse has a cranky bone in her body."

"Okay, you might be right about that."

We enter the seniors center, sign in at the reception desk, and head to the large multi-purpose room. The inside of the room and the Christmas tree have been decorated with a rustic, ski-resort aesthetic.

The fresh pine scent tugs back memories of Dad, Gavin, and me searching the local mountains every Christmas for the perfect tree. Trees that were usually far from perfect. Trees that left Gavin laughing so hard, he got a stitch in his side. Every time.

Trees that look nothing like the one in the corner of the room.

Gavin leads me over to a table with a group of people whom I've known most of my life.

Andrew beams at us. "There he is. And he's brought Ally to sing with him."

"Oh, no. I'm just here to watch." The words rush from me in a whirl.

He taps his fingers on the table with no particular rhythm. "Sorry, that just won't do. You have such a beautiful singing voice, Ally. We'll even double the amount of our donation if you sing with Gavin. We all remember how great you two were together at the school talent shows."

The group at the table starts chanting, "*Du-et. Du-et. Du-et.*" Everyone else in the room peers in our direction and joins in on the chant.

"Looks like you don't have a choice." Gavin's heart-melting brown eyes are lit with amusement that make it impossible to say no.

"I guess not." Because heck if I'll be the one responsible for the fun-raiser bringing in less money.

"Do you remember 'Please Come Home for Christmas'?" Gavin asks me as we walk to where the guitar is kept next to the piano.

"I do." It was the song we sang during our senior year talent show. We won.

I remove my winter coat and put both it and Gavin's jacket on the piano bench while he makes sure the guitar is in tune.

I carry the stool into the center of the room, and Gavin sits on it. Then we sing the classic ballad, the lyrics flowing easily, as if the talent show was just yesterday.

It's only when we get to the line about being with the one you love that I glance at Gavin.

Our gazes lock, the air between us humming with electricity. And I get lost. Lost in his eyes. I can't tear my gaze from him, and he doesn't seem to be able to look away either. We continue singing, and every emotion vibrating in me pours into the lyrics.

The final notes of the guitar fade, and the room breaks into applause.

Gavin's and my gaze remain locked for another beat, then I turn to the audience and curtsy, my heart still *thump-thumpity-thumping* in my chest.

Andrew points at the ceiling. "You're under the mistletoe. Now you're supposed to make a wish."

Laughter breaks out around the room. "That's a shooting

star you make a wish on," Rita says. "You're supposed to kiss under the mistletoe."

"No, it's definitely make a wish. But just so they have all their bases covered, Gavin and Ally should do both under the mistletoe—kiss *and* make a wish."

Rita laughs again, the sound paper thin and raspy. "Not a bad idea."

Now everyone is chanting once more. Except this time they're chanting, "*Kiss the girl. Kiss the girl.*"

Heat rushes to my face and the *thump-thumpity-thumping* in my chest picks up speed.

"We should probably kiss to appease this bunch. Otherwise, we'll never hear the end of it." Gavin's low, grumbly-rough voice sends desire quivering up my spine.

"Right. Good idea." *Bad idea. Really, really bad idea.* But there's no way I can admit to him why that's a bad idea. So I glance up at the mistletoe and throw out a wish, just in case there's some tiny truth in what Andrew said: *I wish I had a normal life, with a job I love, a man who loves me, a family...and a cat.*

Gavin leans the guitar against the stool. "Ready?"

"Yes." As ready as I'll ever be. *It's just a quick kiss to appease the group. Nothing more. It will be over before I know it.*

Gavin's lips press lightly against mine, and my thoughts from a second ago vanish in a cloud of sparkly dust. I'd be lying if I claim I've never wondered what it would feel like to kiss him. I always figured it would feel...good. And it does.

But until now, I'd never believed such a simple kiss could leave my body trembling for more.

And just like that, my lips part and my tongue welcomes Gavin's. He shifts his head and deepens the kiss.

His hand slides to the nape of my neck, and his fingers tangle with my hair. His other hand moves to my lower spine, and he pulls me to him.

Our tongues glide together, moving in a sensual dance, tasting, consuming, igniting a flicker of heat low in my belly. It's been a long time since I've let a man touch me this way. A long time since my body has felt this alive.

And it's with Gavin.

The man I've dreamed about kissing for as long as I can remember.

Hoots and whistles break into my fog-filled consciousness, reminding me where we are, and I jerk away from him, breath ragged.

I'm not the only one who appears breathless. Gavin stares at me as though he's never seen me before.

I glance around at the grinning faces. "I-I should go," I tell no one in particular.

"I'll drive you home." Gavin bends to pick up the guitar.

"No, that—that won't be necessary. My car's at the station." Which is right down the block. "I'll—I'll see you tomorrow for the festival."

And then I bail, grabbing my coat on the way out.

5

GAVIN

Ally disappears out the rec room door, and the lightness floating in me from our kiss sags like a hot air balloon snagging on a tree.

That kiss. I can't remember the last time it felt that good to kiss a woman. Madison was a great kisser and things were hot between the sheets, but that kiss...the one with Ally...there is no other comparison.

"Well, that was seriously hot," one of the elderly women says. Her crinkly voice is loud enough for everyone in the room to hear. "I think those two young'uns just melted the Christmas ornaments."

Chuckles ripple through the room.

"I'm surprised the tree didn't combust into flames." The laughter in Mrs. Markstrom's voice rings like sleigh bells in the frosty night air.

Andrews's booming laugh accompanies it. "Good thing our Gavin is a firefighter."

Beaming at me, the other seniors nod. All are oblivious to the turmoil brewing in me—a turmoil wilder than the blizzard

308

that made Rudolph the red-nosed reindeer famous. All are oblivious to how that kiss stirred my body to life.

A kiss from a woman who ran out of here like her house was on fire. I thought from the way her body melted into mine it meant Ally also enjoyed the kiss. So why bolt?

Was I the only one who enjoyed it?

That's...if you don't count our audience, who clearly appreciated the show.

I huff out a breath, hiding my frustration over the situation.

I need to talk to Ally and find out how she really feels about what happened. I need to know she doesn't regret the kiss.

Yes, because her running out of here doesn't scream regret.

"I'll see you all soon," I tell the group. If I hurry, I should be able to catch up with her.

And then we can talk. Really talk. About the kiss. About why she disappeared from my life without even a single text to let me know she was doing okay.

I hurry out of the room...and almost collide with Jake Daniels—Noah's brother.

The part owner of Pine Meadow Ranch is about my height, but his broader shoulders are blocking my view of the exit.

"Hey, just the man I was hoping to run into," Jake says. Something about his voice has an apology for not stopping to talk to him stalling on my lips. "Jim Alastair called. His daughter is being released from the hospital tomorrow morning and is dying to see the Christmas lights on their house and front tree."

I inwardly groan. And...that's why I won't be chasing after Ally to talk to her. "But he doesn't have them up yet because he and Nicole"—his wife— "have been in Helena with her for the past few weeks," I say, filling in the rest of what Jake was about to tell me.

"That's right. He's donating to the fun-raiser if we can do

them for him. TJ's also gonna help, so it should only take an hour or so."

"Sure, I can help." It's the least I could do for Presley's best friend, who recently had surgery. I'll go over to talk to Ally once I'm finished helping with the lights.

We walk toward the entrance to the building. "By the way, was that Ally I saw rushing out of here a few minutes ago?" Jake asks. "I didn't realize she was back in town."

"She's just down for the holidays. Then she's heading back to Billings." I'm assuming she's returning there. She didn't really say what her plans are—other than she's applying for Mrs. Jenkins's old job.

"That's too bad. While we were in high school, I thought you two would end up together."

I shake my head. "Nope. We were just friends."

Jake makes a noise that could be a choked laugh or a grunt. "You were never just friends, Gavin. Everyone knew that...other than the people you two dated. TJ, Noah, and I would have bets on which boyfriend or girlfriend would finally figure things out so you and Ally could be together. But they were as clueless as you two."

Bets? They actually bet on us? "Don't know what you're talking about. It wasn't that way with her."

Jake definitely choke-laughs this time. "Right. If you say so."

I don't bother to respond. There's no point until I've spoken with her and see where things stand with us.

Jake and I arrive at the Alastair's home at the same time as his brother TJ. The three of us park our trucks on the street in front of a house that looks like something from a fairy tale. Even more so once it's decorated with the lights Jim puts up every year.

It's dark out, but at least the snow has stopped falling, and it's no longer windy. It's not the best situation for putting up the lights, but it could be a lot worse.

"I'll get the key from the neighbor," Jake says as TJ walks toward us. "Jim already told her I'd be coming over."

He returns a few minutes later with the key. "Everything we'll need is in the garage," he explains, heading up the snowy path to the house. "Give me a moment, and I'll open the garage door."

TJ and I are chatting when the door starts to slowly lift. The light from inside the garage stretches across the snow-covered driveway, pointing out it's not only the lights that need to be put up before the family returns tomorrow. We'll also need to shovel the snow.

Jake is scratching the back of his neck and staring inside four large plastic containers as we approach. I peer inside them to see what has him frowning.

The Christmas lights are in the containers, but they're a huge tangled mess.

Oh, shit.

An hour? More like it's going to take us several hours to untangle and hang the lights.

Several hours before I can talk to Ally.

6

ALLY

"Ally," a crinkly woman's voice says behind me as I step onto the sidewalk in front of the seniors center. My heart is racing from the kiss I still feel on my lips.

I swivel to discover Gladys McLinn beaming up at me. Her nose and cheeks are red from the cold, and the breeze ruffles white curls peeking from under her green woolen hat. She shuffles forward, her puffy coat swamping her petite frame, the hem brushing the top of her boots.

"Just the person I was hoping to see," she says, her smile not dimming. "Are you participating in the fun-raiser?"

"I am." *Just don't ask me what I've done so far to help out.* The last thing I want to discuss is the kiss. Or that Gavin and I were singing together for the seniors. Though I wouldn't be surprised if she's heard about it all by tomorrow morning.

I wouldn't be surprised if the entire town knows about it by then.

"Oh good!" she declares. "It's my turn to host tomorrow's book club, but I haven't had a chance to bake anything for it. I would love it if you could help me bake a pie and a couple of batches of cookies. Tonight. We can have mulled wine and catch up on what you've been up to while we work." She flashes me a hopeful grin.

"I would love to help you!"

Gladys has always been like a grandmother to me, especially after her husband passed away twenty years ago. They'd never had kids, so I became their unofficial granddaughter.

"Did you drive here?" she asks.

I nod. "My car is at the fire hall."

She points to the small light-blue car sitting in the seniors center parking lot. "Mine's over there. I just need to make a quick stop at the grocery store. How about I meet you at my house in say, ten minutes?"

"Sounds good." I escort her to her vehicle, then take my time walking to where I'm parked, careful not to slip on the sidewalk and land on my ass.

The cool night air feels good on my kiss-heated cheeks.

God, that kiss. That turn-me-inside-out-and-upside-down kiss. It had only lasted a moment, a blink of an eye, a tiny taste of what it would be like to make out with him.

No, no, no, no. Don't think about kissing Gavin. It was a one-time thing that happened because the seniors offered to increase the amount of money they were donating if I sang with him.

Hopefully, it raised a lot of money, given how they cheered when we kissed, even if that hadn't been part of the deal.

I drive the short distance to Gladys's house, which is located on a side street lined with other cozy, gingerbread-style homes. Multicolored Christmas lights twinkle along the eaves and in the snow-dusted apple tree on her front lawn.

I park behind her car on the road, walk up the path to her front door, and ring the doorbell. A second later, tiny barks answer from the other side.

"Sit, Buttercup," Gladys says behind the closed door. "Ally's here to help make treats for book club."

The door opens, and Gladys lets me into the warm house. If Gavin's shed resembles Santa's workshop, Gladys's house makes me think of Santa's home. The place is an array of reds and greens and gold, with wreaths, pillows, snow globes, ornaments, pine branches filling every available nook and cranny.

The rich scent of baking gingerbread cookies fills the air. The place feels like a second home, especially at this time of year.

Buttercup, a fluffy white-and-gray mixed-breed, gives another small bark. Her butt is still parked on the floor, but her tail is wagging like crazy.

"I've just put a batch of cookies in the oven," Gladys tells me as I crouch to give Buttercup some loving. The little sweetheart laps up the attention, immediately jumping to all four paws and peers up at me with my favorite doggy grin.

Smiling at the fluffball, I scratch her behind the ear. "Yes, I've missed you, too, Buttercup."

I push to my feet and follow Gladys into the kitchen, where we get to work on making the cranberry pear pie.

"I think the fun-raiser is such a great idea," she says as she rolls out the dough. I'm busy slicing the pears. "The girls and I came up with all kinds of ideas for hiring the volunteer participants. We even tried to convince Gavin and the male volunteer firefighters to do *The Full Monty* dance." She snickers.

I choke out a laugh. "I bet Sierra was all for that." She would have paid for front-row tickets.

"Why, yes, she was." Gladys chuckles. "But, alas, the guys weren't as enthusiastic about the idea."

I grin, imagining just how well that suggestion had gone with my father. "I bet they weren't. That's too bad. I'm sure it would have raised a lot of money for the cause." I would have paid money to see Gavin remove his clothes...even if it was only his shirt.

AFTER WE FINISH WITH THE COOKIES, GLADYS AND I WATCH *Rudolf the Red-Nosed Reindeer* on TV, like we did when I was little. It's after 11:30 p.m. by the time I return home.

I lie in my old childhood bed, unable to sleep, and stare at the stars through the open curtains. Dad's home is on an acreage, which means no light pollution to obscure the stars. The night is both beautiful and clear.

But it could be stormy and scary for all I'm concerned. I can't stop thinking about the kiss and the way Gavin stared at me while we were singing the last part of "Please Come Home for Christmas." My thoughts had slipped to the kiss a few times while helping Gladys with the cookies, but she had kept me otherwise preoccupied. Now that I'm home, in bed, the memory of his lips against mine won't leave me alone.

My hand fumbles around in the bedding, searching... searching...searching. My fingers glance across the smooth surface of the screen, and I grab the phone.

I open to my texts, and my thumbs hover over the keyboard. I type:

Sooo, about that earth-shattering kiss...

Delete. Delete. Delete.

I drop my phone back on the bed. And that pretty much sums up the next thirty minutes. Every time I try to text Gavin and ask him about the kiss, I remember it was all a show.

The way Gavin looked at me?

Nothing more than my imagination. A mirage.

Giving up on sleep for a bit, I disappear into the steamy romance I started yesterday. *One More Chance*. Maybe Simone and Lucas will have better luck at love than I seem to be having.

GAVIN'S LIPS MOVE OVER MINE AS HIS FINGERS TRAVEL ALONG MY naked body. Down, down, down. My clit begs him to keep going. To release the pressure that's been building for the past few minutes. God, I want him so badly. So completely.

His gaze goes to my chest. "Madison," he breathes.

I look at what he's staring at and groan. The scar. That's why he said his dead girlfriend's name.

A muffled noise from downstairs sinks into my consciousness, shakes me out of my nightmare, and I slowly open my eyes. It takes a second for the cause of the dream to sink in.

The kiss.

Jiminy Cricket. Gavin hadn't been staring at me during the final lyrics of "Please Come Home for Christmas" because he realized he loves me or anything like that.

It was because of Madison.

He was singing to her.

To her heart.

Tears leak from the corners of my eyes and soak into my pillow. I squeeze my eyes shut, banishing the tears. I'm being an idiot. Of course he hasn't stopped loving her. How could I expect otherwise?

I push myself up to sit and take a deep breath. Gavin and I will never be. It's time I finally get over him and move on—no matter how hard that will be.

Swallowing down the tear-studded knot in my throat, I

glance over at the bedside table for my phone. It's not there. Right, it was in my bed last night. It takes me a moment to find it buried under the covers. I turn it on...only to discover the battery is dead.

Oops. I was going to charge it last night, but then I fell asleep before I could crawl out of bed to plug it into the wall.

I get up and search for the charger in my suitcase. I pull out a lacy pair of purple panties and a bra. I'd forgotten I'd stuffed them in there at Courtney's insistence. My friend in Billings had dragged me to the lingerie store a few months ago, telling me I needed to buy some pretty underwear for when I was ready to let a man love me.

I shove them back in the suitcase, locate the charger, and plug my phone into the wall. I get dressed in my jeans and the red T-shirt Gavin gave me last night, pull on my elf hat, and join Dad for breakfast.

"Mornin', Noodle. Have a good night?"

I kiss him on the cheek. "I should be asking you the same. Soooo, is Tabitha going to be my stepmom?" I flash him a teasing grin. "It's about time you found someone who makes you happy."

"I was going to say the same to you. I don't remember the last time you had a boyfriend."

I grab a glass from the cupboard, fill it with water from the tap, and carry it to the table. "I don't tell you every time I have a boyfriend."

"Fair enough. So when was the last time you had one?"

I open my pill container and remove the three medications I take daily to prevent my body from rejecting Madison's heart. "I don't remember the exact date." This time I flash him the grin that always leaves him exasperated.

"You're evading the question."

I swallow the pills with the water. "I know. And I'm doing a great job at it."

"Noodle," he draws out my nickname in a way that does nothing more than make me laugh.

"Okay, it's been a while, but it's all good. I don't need a man to make me happy."

"You're right. You don't. But it wouldn't hurt to have that special someone in your life like your mother was for me."

"Except Mom died twenty-six years ago, and you've only recently started dating."

Dad puts a plate filled with egg-white-only scrambled eggs on the table. "And that's because you were—and still are—the most important thing in my life after we lost your mother. You were my number one priority."

I open my mouth. He raises his hand. "Please don't try to use the same excuse on me about why you're not dating. Anyway, I am happy. Tabitha is a wonderful woman. She lost her husband several years ago. She's only recently been able to let someone new into her heart. And she's been worth the wait."

"I'll keep that under consideration," I say and fill my plate with the heart-smart breakfast Dad prepared.

7

GAVIN

I check my phone for the fifth time since getting up this morning. Still nothing from Ally.

I went to her father's house last night after I finished putting up the Christmas lights for the Alastairs. It was after 11:00 p.m. by the time I arrived. I knocked on the door, but no one answered. The house had been dark, so either she was already asleep or wasn't home.

I'd driven back to my house and done what I hadn't had a chance to do while helping with the lights—think about the kiss.

After thirty minutes of wondering what it had meant to Ally, my heart wringing with all sorts of possibilities, I sent her a text.

> Me: So, about that kiss…

> Me: I think we need to talk.

I then paced in my living room, but the small space hadn't done much for the uncertainly that snap-crackled and popped

319

under the surface. Knowing there was only one thing that would help, I headed to my workshop and began working on a new project.

Usually, wood-carving relaxes me and distracts me from whatever stress is knocking on my door like an incessant woodpecker.

This time, not so much—especially when Ally still hadn't responded to my text thirty minutes later.

And when I woke up this morning and there was still no reply from her, I knew I had my answer.

She regretted the kiss.

What I felt for her—the love and the aching need to be with her—was completely, utterly one-sided.

I finish loading the wooden carvings for the festival into my truck and drive to my sister's house.

"Love the elf hat," Becca says, grinning at me from the doorway in that teasing way of hers. "Women will be clambering over you—it's sooo sexy." She makes a cross-eyed expression and then rolls her eyes. "Of course, they'll be all over you," she mutters. "I swear no woman can resist you."

Except for the woman I want.

Ally obviously has no problem resisting me.

I snort a self-deprecating laugh. "I wouldn't go that far."

Becca smirks. "You were always considered a hot commodity in high school."

"Again, that's a bit of an exaggeration."

"Not from where I stood. Oh God, if I had heard one more giggling girl proclaim they were in love with you, I would've screamed."

I shrug. "What can I say? Small school. Small pickings."

She chuckles. "True, but you were still one of the few guys that girls drooled over."

"Sounds pleasant," I drawl. "What were they? Saint Bernards?"

She chuckles once more. "Saint Bernards are probably more loyal."

I choke out a laugh. I don't doubt that, and that's not a slight on those girls.

Becca turns and calls into the house, "Presley, are you ready? Uncle Gavin is here."

Footsteps thunder down the staircase.

"Coming!" Presley charges in a blur of pink past her mother, a backpack looped over one shoulder. "See you later, Mommy!"

Becca grabs her daughter's shoulders and gives her a quick kiss on the cheek. "Be good for your uncle. He looks tired."

"Okay, Mommy," Presley says over her shoulder, already racing to my truck.

Becca's mouth curls to one side again. "Late night, huh?" The smirk falls away, replaced with a hopeful gleam in her eyes. "I didn't realize you were seeing anyone."

"I'm not." Haven't been interested in anyone since Madison died—other than Ally. But that's nothing new when it comes to the woman I grew up with. "April is returning from the hospital today, so TJ, Jake, and I were putting up the Christmas lights on her home. It was a late night."

And staying up late to see if Ally responded to my text didn't help.

Becca's face morphs into her oh-that-was-so-sweet-of-you expression. "Presley is excited to see her best friend again. She misses her." Becca heaves out a soft sigh. "I was just hoping you were ready to open your heart to someone new."

Yeah, I know.

This isn't the first time my sister has hinted at this. She has always been a romantic.

I check the time on my phone. "I'll be late if I don't get going. See you later." Before she tries to get in another word, I hightail it off her porch, and Presley and I head to the festival grounds in the center of town.

Numerous other vendors are already setting up their displays in the large, heated tent by the time we arrive at my assigned booth. I help Presley onto the seat at our table. She opens her backpack and removes a thick stack of paper and a box of crayons. While I start setting up the displays of carvings, she gets to work on her artwork.

And I do my best not to think about the kiss between Ally and me yesterday.

Christ, why did my sister have to agree to work a shift at the clinic? Today of all days. Now I'll be stuck working with Ally— the woman who ghosted me for the past year. The woman who once again has my heart in her pretty fist and doesn't seem to want it.

8

ALLY

I park my car on a side street and walk to the tent where the booths are set up. I blow out white puffs of air, something that would have been a challenge a year ago...if I hadn't been in the hospital, attached to life-support, wondering if I would even live to see Christmas.

Presley is at Gavin's booth when I arrive. She's sitting at a table and busy drawing.

She looks up as I approach and grins. "Hi, Ally. I wanted to help out, too." She picks up her paper and shows me the crayon picture of a smiling heart with arms and legs. "It's to remind women that a healthy heart is a happy heart."

"It's perfect. And what a great idea."

"I'm making lots of them to hand out to everyone who comes to the booth." Next to Presley is a big stack of blank paper, weighed down with one of Gavin's carved gnomes. On the other side of her is a much shorter stack with happy hearts drawn on the pages.

Gavin is busy setting up his display. He turns around and nods at me. "Hey." But that seems to be the extent of his conversation with me. He goes back to removing the various wooden carvings from large cardboard boxes and placing them on the shelves and on the ground.

I walk over to him. "How can I help?" My arm accidentally brushes his. Even though I'm wearing a cute puffy ski jacket, the brief touch has my heart happy for the wrong reason, as if our skin had actually touched.

It's the same reaction that happened last night outside of his workshop when our arms touched.

I chew on my lower lip and will my heart to get a grip. Whatever happened between Gavin and me yesterday at the senior center was nothing.

"Hi, Gavin!" a woman singsongs, her generous boobs bouncing as she sashays over to us. She's wearing the same red T-shirt all the festival participants have on, but she's made some adjustments to the neckline. Whereas my neckline covers my long ugly scar, hers scoops down to flaunt her assets. Fluffy red tinsel has been attached to the low neckline, which further draws attention to her skin.

I pull my jacket tighter around me, hiding the scar that no one can see.

She smiles at me, the curve of her mouth wide. "And you must be his girlfriend, Madison. I'm so thrilled to finally meet you," she gushes, her tone all candy canes and chocolate kisses. "You saved my mother's life last year when she was having a heart attack. Thanks to you, she's alive to enjoy another Christmas."

Her comment is a punch to the solar plexus. "I'm happy to hear that about your mother, but I'm not Madison." *I'm just the woman who has a YouTube channel for kids. I'm not making a difference. Not like Madison did as an ER physician.*

I smile, but it feels fake and shallow and not quite so perky.

The woman looks at Gavin.

"Madison was in a car accident last year and died," he explains.

The woman gasps, her hand going to her heart. "I'm so sorry, Gavin. Your girlfriend was a wonderful woman."

Deciding I don't really want to stick around to hear about the virtues of the woman I'll never live up to, whose heart I don't deserve, I join Presley at her table.

People start arriving at the festival after that. Gavin has to leave to take the empty boxes to his truck. Presley and I throw ourselves into the job, with me talking to people about Gavin's work and Presley handing out her drawings. Gavin returns a short time later carrying hot chocolates for the three of us.

"People can't stop talking about your carvings," I tell him. "I sold six of them while you were gone. And your pictures, Presley. Everyone loves those, too."

She beams at me and gets to work on a new one.

"You're adding a cat to the pictures now?" I ask as she draws what I hope is a cat and not a different animal.

"It's a kitten. This one is for Mommy. I'm trying to convince her to get us a kitten. Cats fill our hearts with love and joy, and that makes our hearts happy."

"And a happy heart is a healthy heart," I say, sensing where she's going with this.

"Exactly. Do you have a cat?"

"Unfortunately, I don't. I would love to get one, but I'm not supposed to change kitty litter because of the drugs I take for my heart. So that means no kitty for me."

Presley's bottom lip pushes out. "Oh, that's sad."

I nod, my heart tugging at that reality. "Very sad."

Her face brightens. "So if you move back to Copper Creek, you can see Phoenix whenever you want."

"That would definitely be a perk of moving back here."

A group of people arrives at the booth, preventing us from talking further.

"Hi, you're Ally Fontaine, aren't you?" a woman I don't recognize asks.

"That's right."

"It's because of what happened to you that I signed my organ donor card earlier this year. After I heard that a donor's heart saved your life, I realize just how important it is to sign the card. I won't need my organs once I've died, but someone else might be able to use them. So thank you! If I hadn't heard about what happened to you, I would have never thought to sign it."

I smile at her. "Thank you for telling me that. It means a lot to me."

The woman and her friends end up buying a number of Gavin's larger carvings. At the rate his creations are selling, I wouldn't be surprised if he raises a huge amount of money for the Go Red for Women fun-raiser.

Gavin joins me by the display shelf once there's finally a brief lull in the crowds. "How come you didn't respond to my text this morning?"

"Sorry, I didn't see it. I forgot to charge my phone and the battery was dead when I got up. And then I forgot to grab my phone before coming here." I wince, knowing why he'd texted me. It was to tell me the kiss was a mistake and we should forget it happened.

Not a problem. I can do that. Eventually. Once my lips quit tingling from the kiss he gave me last night.

"So the kiss yesterday..." he says. Behind him, Presley is busy with her artwork.

"Don't worry about it. It didn't mean anything. It can't mean anything."

He frowns. "Why not?"

I sigh, the sound exasperated because isn't it obvious why not? "Because I have the heart of the woman you loved." I point to my chest for extra emphasis.

"What does that have to do with the kiss?"

Seriously? Do I have to spell it out? "Because you loved her. Because I'm not her." Not even close.

Gavin looks at me as though I just kicked him in the nuts. "Last year I lost two people I care about. Losing you hurt the most."

I ignore what he said. All the reasons men will reject me if given a chance to get close to me bubble under the surface. "And I have an ugly-ass scar on my chest. An ugly-ass scar that is a reminder of how you lost your girlfriend."

His frown returns. "Do you really think your scar would bother me? It just means you're still alive. That you're a fighter." Anger simmers in his tone, but he keeps his voice low so no one else can hear him.

I huff, "I'm not a fighter." The volume of my voice matches his. "I'm scared. Scared my body will suddenly reject Madison's heart. Scared I'll never be worthy of the sacrifice she made so I could live—"

"Madison didn't make a sacrifice so you could live." The anger in his tone is now at a full boil. "She died because her car hit black ice and lost control."

I recoil as if his voice burned me.

"Excuse me," a man says, thankfully interrupting us. He smiles pleasantly at the two of us, clearly clueless that we were arguing. "I have a question about one of your larger carvings."

I spot Ryan approaching Presley's table.

Gavin goes to help the white-bearded man.

"Hey, I need to go. Something came up," I tell Ryan, my heart thumping with a silent plea for him to say yes. "Can you help Gavin out for the next hour?"

9

______

ALLY

"Sure, go ahead. It's the least I can do to help out with the cause," Ryan says.

"Thanks. I owe you one." I leave the festival and keep walking with no destination in mind. I'd been so busy with Gavin's booth, I hadn't realized it was already dark. Christmas lights twinkle on the buildings and trees, easing the sting from Gavin's and my argument.

I end up at a playground where he and I spent a lot of time together as kids, building snowmen, having snowball fights, creating snow angels on the field.

We would sit on the swing and share our secrets that no one else knew about. It was our special place. The place where I told him about my crush on Mark Sanderson during our sophomore year. And where Gavin told me Mark was a douchebag.

It was where I shared I wanted to be an elementary school-teacher. He told me I could be anything I wanted because I was so smart.

I sit on a swing and relive the happy memories I have of hanging out with Gavin on the playground. Gavin teaching me

328

to kick the soccer ball into the goal. Our co-ed soccer team winning games. Gavin telling me I'm a talented artist. Gavin telling me I'm beautiful and amazing and any guy would be lucky to have me as a girlfriend.

"What are you doing out here?"

I startle at Sierra's voice and glance over my shoulder. "Damn, I always suspected you had ninja blood."

She chuckles and walks to the other swing. "Wouldn't that be great? I thought you were helping Gavin at the festival."

"I was. But Ryan showed up and took over for me." Close enough.

"Sooo, I was visiting my grandmother this afternoon."

I cringe, knowing what's coming next. I wouldn't be surprised to find a string of texts from her when I get home because of the rumor now flying around the center.

"What's this about you and Gavin kissing?"

"It was nothing. Nothing more than peer pressure."

A laugh erupts past Sierra's lips. "Right. Since when did a group of senior citizens chanting count as peer pressure? At least give it a few more decades before you call it that."

"It isn't what you're thinking. We just kissed to make the seniors happy."

"That's not how my grandmother tells it." Sierra sits on the swing. Other than the occasional car driving past and the faint Christmas music coming from the festival, the place is quiet.

"How did she tell it?" I ask, my words sitting on a mental cringe.

"That it's clear you have it bad for each other."

I snort out a laugh. "Your grandmother has quite the imagination." *When it comes to Gavin.*

"Really? I'm not blind, Ally. Even in high school, I knew you were in love with Gavin. But then he started dating that cheerleader. After that you were dating Tim Rutherford. You've never both been single at the same time. And then you stayed away after the transplant. But now neither of you is dating anyone, and you both live in the same town."

"Well, technically, I live several hours away in Billings. Not exactly the same town."

She gives me the evil eye. "I thought you were planning to apply for Mrs. Jenkins's job?"

"I'm still thinking about it. I love Billings." It's a beautiful place with so much to see and do. A different kind of *so much to see and do* compared to Copper Creek.

"You used to love living here. But I do know what you mean. The nightlife and shopping are definitely better in the city."

I laugh. "You have that right."

"Nice deflection, by the way."

The corner of my mouth twitches. "No idea what you're talking about."

"*We* were talking about Gavin. And how much you love him. And how you two can finally be together."

Last year I lost two people I care about. Losing you hurt the most.

I flick his words aside like they're a pesky gnat. He was just talking about our friendship. It doesn't mean he loves me like I love him.

"Gavin deserves someone as great as Madison. She was perfect for him and he loved her. He doesn't need to be with someone who's a constant reminder his girlfriend is dead. I'm still alive because she isn't."

"You're right. You're alive because she's dead. But you didn't kill Madison. You were at the top of the heart transplant list—and Madison requested her organs be donated. If it hadn't been you, someone else would have ended up with her heart. Your condition was rapidly deteriorating. You might not have even survived long enough to receive someone else's heart."

"I know. But it doesn't change things. Madison was this

amazing ER doctor who saved lives. I teach art to kids with YouTube videos."

"You're also an excellent teacher. And you make a bigger difference than you realize. And most importantly, you have a great heart. I don't mean Madison's heart. That's nothing more than a muscle that pumps blood through your body. I'm talking about the very things that make you *you*, Ally." Sierra stands. "And just so you know, Gavin was upset when you didn't return home after the surgery. Not that he would admit it. Yes, he was mourning the loss of Madison, but when it came to you, it went deeper than the loss of a girlfriend."

I stare at Sierra for a second, absorbing everything she just told me. But in the end, it doesn't change anything. Yes, he and I kissed. And it was an incredible kiss that no other man's kiss will ever come close to comparing to. But it hadn't been real. Not in the sense I wish it were.

Do you really think your scar would bother me? It just means you're still alive. That you're a fighter."

What Gavin didn't say was that he loves me. What he told me was something a friend would say.

"I have to go babysit my tiny terror of a niece for a few hours. And make sure she eats lots of chocolate before my brother and sister-in-law get home." Sierra grins, an adoring yet impish gleam in her eyes, and leaves me on the swings.

She's a few yards away when I call out, "What time is it?"

"Time for you to tell him you love him."

Yeah, that's not happening.

"Also, it's five forty-five," she adds.

I watch her receding figure disappear down the street, then I walk over to a smooth patch of snow and lie on it. I stare up at the stars and create a snow angel.

"I'm always going to have your back, Ally." That's what Gavin told me when we were fourteen and I had a hideous zit at the end of my nose. On picture day. I wanted to hide my head in a

paper bag for the photo...and for the rest of my life—or until the zit vanished—whichever came first. *"No matter what the douchebags say, you're pretty. And no matter what those witches say"*—he cocks his head toward the three girls who'd made fun of the zit—*"you'll be beautiful long after their meanness turns them into ugly old toads. Your face could be all scarred, and you'd still be a hundred times prettier than them."*

That might be so, but that doesn't change anything. Those were the words spoken by a best friend. They weren't the words from a man who has yet to see the scars on my chest.

Who has yet to see the things that would once again remind him of everything he lost.

Gavin thought I was a fighter?

I guess he doesn't know me as well as he thought.

I'm not a fighter. I'm a woman who is scared of rejection. But unlike the immunosuppressants I take to prevent my body from rejecting Madison's heart, there's nothing to protect me from Gavin's rejection.

To protect my heart from breaking.

10

GAVIN

"**M**y wife has a thing for gnomes," the man tells me, holding the large wooden whimsical statue. His white beard resembles that of a gnome. "She's goin' to love this one. It's nothing like any she owns."

His eyes shine with love—like they have every time he has mentioned her in the past five minutes while checking out the wooden carvings.

I glance at the table where I left Ally and Presley. Ally is no longer there, and Ryan is now standing beside my niece.

I scan the area but can't find Ally. Maybe she went to get us some hot chocolate. She must have asked Ryan to watch the table and Presley while she's gone.

My heart still feels like a popsicle stick has been hammered into it after Ally told me the kiss didn't mean anything. That it can't mean anything.

She doesn't love me.

Why am I even surprised? If she loved me, she wouldn't have ghosted me for the past year. Christ, if she cared for me like she used to, she wouldn't have ghosted me, period.

But the rest of what she said before the man pulled me

333

away to ask questions about my carvings doesn't make sense. What does Madison's heart have to do with Ally and me—other than Ally is alive because of the tragic accident that claimed my late girlfriend's life?

And why would she think I'd care about the scar on her chest? It's just a scar. God knows I've got several on my body. Scars that Ally knows about. She was there for some of them—like the one on my shoulder from when I jumped out of a tree, didn't land on my two feet, and rolled onto a sharp branch. It sliced one helluva trail through my skin.

Ally and I were nine years old when it happened.

She held my hand while the doctor tended to the wound, and once it healed, told me it made me look like a brave warrior who had slayed a terrifying dragon and lived to tell the tale.

Hell, what does the scar on her chest even have to do with the kiss? The kiss she couldn't get away fast enough from once it was over—as if a dragon was chasing her and threatened to crispy-fry her.

"I hope your wife enjoys the gnome," I tell the man and ring up his order.

I thank him for buying the carving and check the time as he strolls away from the booth. The festival closes in less than thirty minutes, and then I'll drop Presley off with Mom.

I join Ryan and Presley at the table. She's explaining to him the concept behind the heart drawings.

"I could use one of those for my clinic," he tells her. "But can you draw it with some cats and dogs on it, as well?"

"Yes!" Presley grabs a new piece of paper. "Do you also want some bunnies and hedgehogs?"

Ryan's mouth stretches into a wide grin. "Absolutely. The more animals the merrier."

She gets to work on her new masterpiece.

"What happened to Ally?" I ask him, as Presley draws a large heart in the middle of the page.

"She said something came up and asked if I would cover the rest of her shift for her."

"Any idea what that might have been?" Was she upset because I let my frustration at how she responded to our kiss get the best of me? I couldn't help it when she thought she wasn't worthy of Madison's heart. Yes, Madison was a kick-ass ER physician who saved lives, but she wasn't perfect. And if there was anyone who deserved her heart, it was Ally.

Ally is the one who makes kids smile when they're having a bad day—who can make anyone smile when their day is crappy. There's just something about her that glows. Glows like a firefly deep in the forbidden forest, guiding people to a happier place.

Ryan shrugs. "Sorry, no clue."

A boy from Presley's class approaches the table and checks out the art project she's drawing. "That's really good." He places his elbows on the table, perches his chin on his hands, and grins at her. "You're such a talented artist."

"A little too early to be flirting with my niece, don't you think?" I mutter low enough so Steven can't hear.

"Something tells me she could be fifty and still be too young, in your opinion, for a man to flirt with her," Ryan says, amusement shaping his words into a chuckle.

I cross my arms, narrowing my eyes at the little punk. "You might be right about that."

The kid doesn't even notice me watching him. He continues chatting to her about her drawing.

"So what's going on between you and Ally?" Ryan's tone is nonchalant, as if he's asking if I like sugar in my coffee. But something about his voice has me turning to him...in time to catch the subtle uptick of one side of his mouth.

"Nothing," I reply just as casually. What are the chances that a dragon will pop out of a fantasy novel and incinerate me so I can avoid answering his question?

"Nothing?" A dark eyebrow jerks up. "From what I heard this morning when Gertrude Wishmill brought her dog in, you and Ally kissed last night. Gertrude couldn't stop talking about it." He flashes another smirk at me. "I could have told her that Sir Fluff-Meister had an incurable disease that would cause purple smoke to blow out of his ass, and she wouldn't have heard me. You and Ally have become quite the hot topic."

"Welcome to the joy of living in a small town."

"You're deflecting."

"I'm not deflecting." *I'm totally deflecting.* "There's nothing to say. The folks at the center promised to increase their contribution to the fun-raiser if we sang together. And then they started chanting for me to kiss Ally."

Ryan barks out a laugh. "And because of that, you two kissed? Well, damn, if I'd known that was all it would take, I would've offered to donate to your favorite charity when I first noticed you two were into each other."

I huff or grunt. Definitely a grunt. "We're not into each other."

"You are. And don't try to claim otherwise. I can spot a liar a mile away. You have it bad for her. So when are you going to admit it to yourself and her?"

I peer past him to see how Presley is doing. She's busy talking to Steven, a grin stretched across her face. "It's not that way between Ally and me," I tell Ryan, my attention still on my niece.

He makes a noise that borders on a harrumph. "That's exactly how it is between you two."

"If it were—which it isn't," I hurriedly interject, "it doesn't make a difference. Ally doesn't live in Copper Creek. It was bad enough to date Madison when she was living in Golden Falls. It would be even worse with Ally. In case you're forgetting, Billings is much farther away." But if she gave me a chance, I would make it work. One way or another.

What I hadn't told him or anyone else in town was even if Madison hadn't died, our relationship had been nearing an expiration date.

We hadn't wanted the same things. Her career goals hadn't included me in her life.

"I have an ugly-ass scar on my chest. An ugly-ass scar that is a reminder of how you lost your girlfriend."

Ally's words repeat in my head on an endless loop. Does she think I'm still mourning Madison's death—that I'm not ready to move on?

Or does she really not want to be the woman I move on with?

11

ALLY

I gently rock to and fro on the swing, my feet planted on the ground. The festival booths will be closing up soon. Only the food stands will stay open for a few more hours.

I've been out here for a while, contemplating how much I've missed Gavin over the past year. That I'm happy to have him back in my life—even if it's not in the way I wish it were.

I rub the spot on my chest where my scar haunts me. If the donor had been anyone but Madison, I wouldn't be dealing with guilt heavier than Santa's sleigh. Plus, reindeer.

Okay, that's not true.

A family would have lost a loved one. Someone's life would have been cut shorter than it should've been. That part would have been the same regardless of whose heart I ended up with. Guilt would have still plagued me, but...I would have also felt immense gratitude. Gratitude that the person signed the organ donor card, making it possible for me to be here today and tomorrow and for the rest of my days—which will hopefully be many, many more to come.

I push to my feet. I should probably head back to Dad's.

Make some popcorn and hot chocolate and watch a Christmas movie. The perfect end to the night.

Tomorrow...tomorrow I can start thinking about the next stage of my life.

I'll make the most of the heart beating in my chest—make the most of the gift of life granted me. Maybe I can do something with my art and teaching skills that will raise more money for the Go Red for Women program. I could also use them to build awareness about being an organ donor.

And I'll apply for the teaching position at Copper Creek Elementary School and see what happens.

I walk along the sidewalk to where I parked my car. The houses on both sides of the street are brightly lit, casting a colorful glow on the snowy front yards and the path.

A man is walking toward me, a navy beanie on his head, his hands shoved in the pockets of his winter coat. It's not until he steps into the light of the nearby lamppost that I recognize him.

I wave at Ryan. "Thank you for covering the rest of my shift."

A knowing smile tilts the corners of his lips, only I have no idea what he's grinning about. "Did you get to do whatever it was you needed to rush off for?"

"I did, thanks." That's not a lie. I needed to get some air, which I got at the playground.

"Gavin missed you while you've been living in Billings." Ryan pauses as if deliberating his next words. "He cares a lot more for you than you realize, Ally. And in the same way I suspect you care for him."

A strained chuckle falls from between my lips, carried on a cloud of puffy white air. "I highly doubt that." *Oops*. I didn't mean to admit that much.

His smile widens. "Maybe it's time that you two talk and really tell each other how you feel."

I snort out a laugh. "Are you sure you're a vet? Or is this how you normally talk to your patients?"

He shrugs, his smile dropping away. "Talk to Gavin. Let him know how you feel. Love isn't easy. But neither is pretending it doesn't exist. Don't you think you owe yourself more than that?" He gives a small nod, the corners of his mouth sliding up again. "I have to get going. But just think about it, Ally."

"Okay," I reply, even though I have no intention of doing that. No intention of leaving myself raw and exposed, only to feel the sting of rejection.

I'd rather hug a cougar. Or a jellyfish.

I hurry back to my car and drive to Dad's.

Gavin's earlier words leak into my thoughts once again. *Last year I lost two people I care about. Losing you hurt the most, Ally.*

I park on one side of the driveway and climb out of my car. The house is dark, other than the living room light, which is on a timer. Dad won't be home until later. It's just me and Madison's heart and my ugly scar.

I remove the popcorn popper from the bottom cabinet in the kitchen and pour the kernels into the top. I flip on the switch. A loud whirling noise fills the kitchen, and I get to work on the hot chocolate.

But as much as I try to concentrate on the task, Ryan's and Sierra's and Gavin's words keep replaying in my head.

"He cares a lot more for you than you realize, Ally. And in the same way I suspect you care for him."

I stir the chocolate powder into the milk warming on the stove.

"Gavin was upset when you didn't return home after the surgery. Yes, he was mourning the loss of Madison, but when it came to you, it went deeper than the loss of a girlfriend."

"Do you really think your scar would bother me? It just means you're still alive. That you're a fighter."

As if those memories are not enough, I replay the kiss from

last night. Even now, my body tingles from just thinking about it. Is it possible Gavin feels the same way I do?

Could he ever love me the way I love him?

The popcorn has finished popping, so I turn off the popper and pour some hot chocolate into my mug. But instead of sitting on the couch to watch a movie, I grab the red-and-green plaid throw from the back of the recliner, pull it over my shoulders, and go outside onto the deck.

I lean against the wooden railing, my hands wrapped around the hot mug. The sky is clear, the stars twinkling in the crisp air.

"I know you still love him," I call out to the heavens in case Madison happens to be listening. "And he will always love you. But maybe it's time I pull up my big girl panties and take a chance on love. Maybe it's finally time I see if Gavin could love me the same way I love him."

I release a long breath, all my fears and insecurities riding on it. *I can do this.* Gavin thinks I'm a fighter. Then that's what I need to be. I need to fight for the man I love. What's the worst that can happen? He doesn't feel the same way about me? It won't shatter the heart that's beating in my chest...it will just feel like it is.

I go back inside and head for my old bedroom, abandoning the popcorn on the coffee table and my plans to watch a movie. I need to do something that will make a statement—that will chop down the tangled, thorny bushes I've grown around my heart since the surgery.

What to do? What to do? What to do?

My gaze falls to my suitcase. It's where I left it on the floor, still packed as if ready for a quick getaway. The first thing I can do is unpack it.

I unzip the bag and start putting away my clothes. I pick up a sweater, revealing the brand-new purple lace bra and matching panties underneath it. I hadn't planned to bring them to Copper Creek but had shoved them into my suitcase at the last moment.

I finger the lace of the bra, and an idea skips its way in. I know what I need to do.

I ignore the rest of the unpacking. I'll finish it once I've talked to Gavin. I shower, put on the lacy underwear, and take a second to study the scar that has kept me from being intimate with anyone. The scar symbolizing I am a survivor.

I pull on my favorite red dress. The boat neckline hides the scar. I don't bother zipping it up in the back.

I finish getting ready, leaving my hair loose, making my eyes look sultry. Then I slip on a pair of red stilettos, download Bon Jovi's "Please Come Home for Christmas" onto my phone, and drive to Gavin's house. *Please be there. Please be there.*

He isn't.

Of course not. That would be too simple.

I drive into town and past the fire hall. Gavin's truck is in the parking lot. *Perfect.*

I park my car and enter the building through the main entrance. The place is dark other than the light coming from the garage where the two fire trucks are located. I step inside and spot Gavin. He's the only person here. Everyone else will be on call, and it's too late for my father to be at work.

I walk over to the bench near the fire pole, turn on the song I downloaded, and place the phone on the bench.

Gavin turns around, but I don't give him a chance to speak. I remove my coat, doing my best imitation of an erotic dancer... which I have zero experience at.

I toss the coat to the side. It lands on Phoenix, who was walking into the garage at the wrong moment. He lets out a loud meow from under it.

"Oops. Sorry." I pick up my coat, plonk it next to him, and continue with my dance.

I move to the pole and sway my hips to the slow melody of

the song, channeling the YouTube pole-dancing videos Sierra and I watched years ago for a giggle while drinking margaritas.

I grab the pole, my feet planted on either side of it, and do a chair sit. I pivot my knees to the side and pull myself to stand.

And *damn on a popsicle stick*, pole dancing is a lot harder than I realized.

I slowly peel the front of my dress down, exposing my bra and scar. I look up at Gavin from beneath fake eyelashes. The fake lashes Sierra and I bought for Halloween a few years ago.

Gavin doesn't say anything. He just stares at me, his mouth open, eyes dark.

Confidence flickers and smolders in me, and a shy smile grows on my face. I reach behind me and unzip the dress the rest of the way. It drops to the floor, leaving me in nothing more than my bra and panties and stilettos.

I nudge the dress to the side with my foot, and my eyes move up Gavin's body and his jeans. *Hmm.* Shouldn't he be wearing his uniform if he's on shift?

I grab the pole again and wrap my leg around the cold metal. My hips gyrate and undulate in time to Bon Jovi's singing. My gaze catches Gavin's, and the heat in his eyes sends a shiver shimmering up my spine.

A small sound—half whimper, half giggle—pushes past my lips. I nibble my lower lip, fighting to contain my laugh.

Gavin steps forward.

Still holding on to the pole, I pirouette and do a firefighter spin. Then I cartwheel my legs. The landing would've been easier if I wasn't wearing stilettos.

I lose my footing and find myself being pulled against Gavin's hard body. His arms circle my waist, mine go around his neck. Instinctively, we sway to the song, our eyes lost in each other's...and then we're kissing. Our lips and tongues move together in time to the sweet melody.

An alarm goes off, the loud noise startling me. I freeze as Gavin mutters, "Fuck."

Before my brain can clue into what's happening, Gavin grabs one of the firefighter jackets from the wall and wraps it over my shoulders, covering me up as the first firefighter slides down the pole.

I watch in horror as one by one, three other men follow him. *Oh, damn.*

"Hey, Ally," Ryan says, spotting me. "Don't let us interrupt." His mouth tilts into a grin.

"Don't worry, they were just leaving," Gavin tells me. "We were having a quick meeting, but these dumbasses like to practice using the pole whenever they can."

Meeting? Dad never mentioned that. He told me he would be late. I assumed he meant he had a date with Tabitha.

Gavin cups my face with his hand. "Let's get out of here."

12

ALLY

I quickly put my clothes back on, and Gavin and I return to his house, each driving our own vehicles.

I park my car behind his truck and climb out. Gavin takes my hand, and we go inside his house. We barely have our shoes off before he pulls me into his arms. His scent, all rugged and spicy hotness, wraps around me. I lean into him, craving his touch, craving to kiss him once more.

I briefly register how his home hasn't changed much since I was last here. It's still simply decorated with neutral light colors and splashes of greens and blues. A Christmas tree stands in the corner of the living room, the lights the same ones I helped him pick out last year.

The large watercolor print with two dragons—one black, the other white—hangs above the couch. The picture was a gift from me a few years ago.

He still has it. Despite everything that happened between us. Despite the past year. He still has it.

My gaze flicks back to him.

"I love you, Ally. I've been in love with you for as long as I can remember, but there never seemed to be a good time to tell you how I felt." Gavin's eyes search the depths of mine.

"I love you, too. I just didn't think you felt the same way about me. So I never said anything."

He traces his thumb along my bottom lip, and I draw in a quick breath, so soft, it's barely audible.

"I want to kiss you again," he tells me, "but there are a few things we need to clear up first." He leads me to the couch, and we sit.

A nervous tension knots in my muscles. This—us—is so new, and I'm not sure what to do. *Do what you two used to do when you were best friends and hung out together all the time.*

I sink into him, my legs curled to the side. The familiarity of our old friendship, of this, loosens the knots. Our fingers remain woven together.

"First," Gavin says, "I'm not interested in you because Madison's heart is in you. Nor do I have some sort of warped belief that being with you is the same as being with her. She's not who I want, Ally. You are."

I let out a relieved breath and smile. Even without me saying it, without me admitting it to myself, he understood one of my concerns. My fear.

"I loved Madison, but I wasn't in love with her at the time of the accident. Not the way I used to be. Our relationship had been falling apart for a while, but we'd been too stubborn to acknowledge it. We were already dealing with the challenge of her living an hour away from Copper Creek because of her job. I was looking to settle down and have a family. Madison wasn't."

"She wasn't?" Madison and I hadn't talked about any of this. There were a lot of things we never talked about.

"On top of that, she wanted to move to a major city and do a cardiac fellowship. Ironically." Gavin places his hand over my heart, and my heartbeat accelerates. "Yes, I was devastated when she died. She had been a part of my life for the past three years. She was my friend. But when you ghosted me, that hurt more than Madison's death. Because it was like you had died, too."

His voice and his face are so full of pain, it almost steals my breath. And it would have if not for the love shining in his eyes. Love directed at me.

I lightly kiss him, the gentle press of my lips against his. "I'm so sorry. I never meant to hurt you. I was dealing with so much guilt that she died and I was the one who survived. I felt like I didn't deserve her heart and I didn't deserve you as a friend. I was so afraid that every time you saw me, you would no longer see me, your friend, but you would only see Madison, the love you lost."

Gavin plants a soft kiss on my forehead, on the tip of my nose, on my lips. "You're the love I lost, but I've found you again."

His mouth is on mine once more. And we're kissing—kissing and easing away the pain, loneliness, regret that have plagued us for the past year. Kissing until his earlier words seep into my fog-filled brain.

I pull back slightly. "I'm applying on Monday for Mrs. Jenkins's old job. But what if I don't get it? I don't want to give up teaching."

He smiles, confidence in me shining on his face like the star on top of the tree. "You'll get it."

"But what if I don't?" Because that's still a possibility.

"Then we'll figure something out. I'm not expecting you to give up a career you love so we can be together. But we'll worry about it once we know what will happen with the job opening."

I nod. "Okay." Another thought worms its way in—one that is also important to our future together. "You said you want a family. But I can't give you that. I want to. I really wish I could.

But my immunosuppressive drugs are contraindicated in pregnancy."

"How about adoption? Are you okay with that?"

I grin, falling in love with Gavin even more than before. "I'm definitely fine with adoption."

"And we'll get a cat." His warm breath brushes my lips. "I volunteer to do the kitty litter."

I laugh softly. "Thank you."

"I was thinking...since you'll get the teaching job no problem, I'm hoping you'll move in with me. We have a lot of lost time to make up for, and then we can get our cat sooner."

"I'm definitely all for that idea. Maybe we should consummate this plan." My fingers slide under the hem of his T-shirt, brushing the soft skin covering his hard muscles. "I want to make love to you, Gavin."

His eyes darken, desire swimming in them. "Here or in the bed?"

"I plan to make love to you in every room of the house at some point, so we might as well start here."

He sucks in a sharp breath, eyes light with excitement. "I'm good with that."

"I thought you might be." I shift my body to straddle his hips and help him shed his T-shirt. I drape it over the back of the couch. "Do you have any condoms down here? I'll talk to my doctor about going on the pill, but given my insecurities with the scar"—I touch the spot where it stretches down my sternum—"I didn't need to be on any protection. I was too afraid to be intimate with anyone." *Until you.*

Heat and tenderness and understanding burn in his eyes. And he stands, scooping me up in his arms.

My arms loop round his neck, my legs circle his hips, and he carries me upstairs to his bedroom. His bed covers are still messy from when he got up this morning. He prefers them that way when he goes to bed at night.

I grin at them. In all the years I've known him that part of him has never changed.

He lowers my feet to the floor. Our hands get busy, stripping clothes off the other person. The movements aren't frantic and desperate. They're slow and deliberate. Mouths, fingers, and tongues explore valleys and ridges and sensitive spots.

Gavin reaches around me and loosens my bra. It drops to the ground to join the rest of my clothing. He kisses my scar with so much love and reverence, my knees grow weak, and I have to sit on the bed.

God, this man. This sweet and amazing man.

Gavin joins me, and I scoot to the middle of the mattress. He trails his fingers down my stomach to my panties, and his thumb traces over the seam of my sex beneath the cotton. I whimper, needing his touch more than I need oxygen. Needing Gavin more than I need air.

He strokes me until I'm almost coming apart, hooks his thumbs in the waistband of my panties, and slides them along my legs. He discards them over the side, props my feet on the bed, and spreads my knees open.

He kisses the inside of one knee...and then the inside of the other. Flames flicker and swirl with silent promises where his lips brush my skin. The flames continue down my thigh, dancing and twirling, as he kisses his way to my core. Each press of his lips, each taste of his tongue, is more heady and delicious than the last.

My body is on fire—on fire for him—and I've never felt more content.

His fingers part my lips, and he kisses each side of my seam with great hunger and zeal. His tongue swipes my mound, spreading the wetness around. And with each swirl, each kiss, each lick, I glide closer to the point of no return.

And then there is no turning back. A flash of white heat fills my lower belly and spreads to every cell, every synapse. I moan, unable to hold back any longer—I've waited too long for this moment. Next time...next time we can go slower.

"I need you inside me. Now." My voice is smoky-rough, desire trembling in each syllable. The expression on Gavin's face warns me he also won't last much longer.

He retrieves a condom from a box in the drawer of his bedside table and strips out of his boxer briefs. His cock springs free, so full, so ready, and I run the tip of my tongue along my bottom lip, imagining other ways I want to eventually please him.

I wrap my fingers around his hard length and slowly pump my fist, enjoying the silkiness of him in my palm.

The crinkle of a metallic wrapper has me looking up. Gavin removes the condom and rolls the protection on. He positions his tip at my entrance and slowly pushes in.

A hiss of air escapes him. "So goddamn perfect," he murmurs. His eyes lock on mine. "So goddamn perfect."

Gavin doesn't rush as he thrusts inside me. He takes his time, watching me as I eventually come again. My soft heat convulses around him, sending another wave of satisfaction through me, and I cry out my release. "Oh. God. Gaaaavin."

He continues thrusting inside me, faster and harder and faster until he groans, his release spilling from him.

It takes us a minute before we're able to speak coherent sentences once more, Gavin breathing heavily into the crook of my neck.

He leaves for a moment to dispose of the condom, climbs back onto the bed, and pulls me to him. Our limbs tangle, and I rest my head on Gavin's chest. His heart beats loud and strong, and mine meets it beat-by-beat.

Gavin strokes the curve of my spine, and we talk. Talk about the past year we were apart.

Talk about the future.

Our future. Together.

EPILOGUE
GAVIN

Five Months Later

I stand in the hallway of the elementary school I attended two decades ago. Brightly painted artwork decorates the walls—pictures of horses and dogs, trees and wild animals. I read the names on each project and recognize many of them. I was here just last month, talking about fire safety.

The end-of-day buzzer rings. *Five. Four. Three. Two. One.* The classroom door opens, and a stream of second graders pours out of the room, giggling and calling out to each other.

I wait for the last of the stragglers to leave the room, then silently slip inside. My heart beats in anticipation at seeing my favorite elementary school teacher.

Ally is standing at her desk in front of the window, looking at the open book in her hand. Sunlight glints off the golden-brown strands in her hair and caresses her sun-kissed skin. Christ, she's gorgeous.

"It's hard to believe that the first time we met was in this classroom," I say, walking toward her.

She looks up from the book. The beautiful sunny day is nothing compared to the smile and love on her face. And it's all directed at me.

I nod at the table where we once sat. Okay, maybe it's not the same table, but it is in the same spot. And like back then, four wooden chairs are seated around it.

"I was assigned to sit next to you," I say, remembering that moment like it was yesterday. "So I sat down, and you smiled at me. You were missing one of your front teeth, and just like that, I was a goner."

I put my hands on her hips, my fingers caressing her curves. "I knew then that you would always be mine."

Ally laughs, the soft sound teasing. "You did, did you?"

"Absolutely. And I was right, wasn't I?" It might have taken us a long time to get to the point where I could say she was mine, with plenty of ups and downs that I wouldn't wish on anyone. But we're here now, and there's no place I would rather be.

I pull her to me...and kiss my best friend, my lover, the woman who will one day be my wife.

And fall even deeper in love with her.

TURN THE PAGE FOR AN EXCERPT
FROM DECIDEDLY WITH WISHES

Visit your favorite Copper Creek characters in *Decidedly with Wishes*. The hero and heroine visit Copper Creek, where the professional hockey player hero grew up.

CHAPTER 1
NALA

To-Do List #543

1. Take flower girl dress to children's hospital for Sarina to try on.
2. Order more pink organza and gold thread.
3. Flirt with new mailroom guy so he'll deliver the daily mail to me first.

Few greater joys exist in life than when you see a child smile.

"You look like a princess, sweet cheeks," I told Sarina, my best friend's six-year-old daughter. She gave me a wide, toothy smile that had my heart floating in my chest like the balloons in the movie *Up*.

The sleeveless dress I'd designed for her was ice blue, with appliquéd gold floral patterns on the bodice and skirt. Impressed?

Sure, it took forever to sew, but it was worth it.

The tulle underskirt gave the dress the fullness of Cinderella's gown, only instead of brushing the floor, the hem swung midcalf. I'd even hand-stitched gold thread and beads onto the Velcro straps on Sarina's ankle-foot braces. Cinderella's fairy godmother and those mice couldn't have done much better.

Sarina had been born with spina bifida and needed her crutches and braces for walking. But that didn't mean she deserved anything less than the finest of princess dresses.

I glanced at Amelia, who was leaning against the counter in the occupational therapy clinic at the children's hospital, to see what she thought. Around us was an array of equipment in primary colors: seats, soft steps constructed from the same material as gym mats, scooters and swings that the children lie on, stomach down.

Amelia and I had been best friends since high school. We'd gone through so much together over the years, both highs and lows. There was nothing I wouldn't do for her and her daughter. Which was why I was there, at the clinic where Amelia worked full time.

She beamed lovingly at her daughter. "Auntie Nala's right. You do look like a princess."

"Like Cinderella?" Sarina's hopeful smile lit up the room.

"Exactly like Cinderella," I said.

The little girl loved her Disney princesses, but Cinderella was her favorite. Both were blonde.

But if Sarina was Cinderella, her redheaded mother was Ariel from *The Little Mermaid*—something Sarina had pointed out numerous times.

"What do you say to Auntie Nala?" Amelia asked.

Sarina crutched the short distance to me and hugged my leg. "Thank you, Auntie Nala."

I crouched to her level and returned the hug. "You're welcome, sweetheart." I pushed myself to my feet. "I should get back to work before my grandmother misses me."

My grandmother was the CEO of Ayanna, a high-end fashion house that had been dressing some of the most famous women for more than five decades.

She'd been in her twenties when she created the company, which had started as nothing more than her kitchen table. Despite the odds stacked against her, she'd been determined to make it a huge success. Back then, it was challenging enough for a woman to break into the fashion industry and make a name for herself—even more so when you were a Black woman.

Bibi hadn't given "two shakes of a goat's ballocks" about either of those limitations.

"You aren't going to watch me play wheelchair hockey?" Sarina inquired.

I exaggerated a gasp, hand pressed to my chest. "You're playing hockey in the dress?"

Sarina giggled. "No, silly. I'm gonna change first."

"Well, that's a relief. There's not enough magic in the dress to help you win the game." I stroked the top of her head. "Not that you need any help in that department. You're the best wheelchair hockey player I know."

She grinned; then her expression became as serious as a chocolate-coated Bundt cake. "Don't you want to meet the San Francisco Rock players?"

"While I would love to meet them," I said, not caring one way or another if I did, "I really do have to get back to work."

As executive assistant to the company's CEO (and future CEO), it was my job to make sure the ship sailed smoothly. Which meant I was lucky to escape for as long as I had.

"Have you shown your grandmother Sarina's dress?" Amelia asked me.

"Not yet."

"But you're still planning to show it to her and tell her about the fashion line you want to create?" Disbelief and a heavy dose of eye-rolling laced her tone.

For good reason.

"I plan to talk to her about it this afternoon," I told Amelia and crouched to Sarina's level again. "How about I walk you and your mom to the gym? I can't stay and watch, though."

She grinned and nodded, and I helped her out of her dress and into her shorts and hockey jersey.

When we entered the gym a few minutes later, kids ranging from ages five to nine years old were hanging out on the other side of the room, waiting for the game to begin. The air was thick with excitement.

"I need to go now." I hugged Sarina goodbye. "Your mommy will send me a video of you playing, okay?"

"Okay, Auntie Nala. I love you."

I grinned the smile reserved for my favorite girl. "I love you, too." Then I watched as she and her mother walked toward the awaiting kids and their parents.

The opening notes of the song I'd programmed on my phone for Bibi played in my purse.

I removed it and accepted the call. "Hi, Bibi," I said at the same time as I turned around and walked into a brick wall. A brick wall I could've sworn wasn't there a moment ago. "Ugh!"

I ricocheted back a step, almost losing my footing, thanks to my heels. And I would have if the tall, blond wall hadn't grabbed my arm first, steadying me. My bare skin tingled at his touch.

His skin was that light-golden tan that came from being out in the sun for short periods of time—paler than the summer tan surfers often wore. His eyes were the deep blue of the sky just after sunrise, the perfect accompaniment to his crisp, pine-forest scent. And for a second, I was lost in them both.

He released my arm, much to the limb's dismay, as my grandmother asked if I was returning soon. Marketing needed me to discuss a photo layout with them.

"Sorry about that," the man, who looked vaguely familiar, said.

I covered the phone receiver with my palm. "No, that was completely my fault."

Was he one of the models we had used?

Maybe.

Even though Ayanna's target market was women, having a hot guy in the fashion layouts never hurt sales.

And you had to agree that this man was definitely the type women could easily imagine as their date if they wore one of our dresses.

His lips curved into a soft smile, and my heart thumped unexpectedly in my chest.

"Hey, Lawson." Another tall, good-looking man walked past us, pulling my attention away from the blond wall. "Are you playing with us or just here to pick up pretty women?"

That was when I noticed both men were wearing San Francisco Rock jerseys. They must've been the hockey players Sarina had told me about.

Lawson glowered at his teammate. "Lay off it, Mathews."

"Maybe she'll be your date for your cousin's wedding." The other dark-haired man chuckled at his teammate's expense.

My grandmother mentioned something else in my ear.

Smiling politely, I nodded at Lawson. To Bibi, I said, "I'm heading to the office now."

"Perfect. I'll see you shortly." And with that, she ended the call as I walked toward the exit.

My heels clicked against the concrete steps and echoed in the empty stairwell. My mind whirled a mile a minute as I went over my mental checklist of things I needed to do after speaking with my grandmother.

And then I revisited a different mental checklist as I prepared for the presentation she didn't know about.

I stopped at my office first and jotted a few items in the notebook I kept on my desk. The pink pages with floral edging happily accepted my new list of things I needed to accomplish prior to leaving for the day.

Okay, it's now or never, I told myself as I tucked my portfolio under my arm.

Bibi's office door was open when I arrived. Judy, her assistant, glanced up from her computer. "Hi, Nala. She's ready for you."

"Thanks, Judy. Oh, in case I don't have a chance to tell you before you leave, give Owen my congratulations on his kindergarten graduation tonight."

She smiled warmly. "I'll be sure to tell him that."

I lifted my chin, and with a slow cleansing exhale, I cleared my brain of everything not related to the presentation I was about to make.

I've got this.

It wasn't like I was a woman who was new to the industry, hoping for a chance to prove herself. I'd been creating dresses since I was seven years old, when my parents gave me a toy sewing machine. From the first moment I put needle to fabric, I'd experienced the exhilaration of creating something with my own hands.

Sure, the sewing machine hadn't been all that great. The stitches unraveled faster than a pelican took flight if I was unlucky. They lasted a little longer if good fortune was shining on me.

But that hadn't stopped me from sewing dresses for all my dolls and stuffed animals.

A month later, Bibi gave me my first real sewing machine—and there was no stopping me after that.

I stepped into her office.

She was standing by the high-rise window overlooking the bay, her attention on the contents of the portfolio resting on her forearm. The late afternoon sun lit her face, softening the deep lines I knew so well.

"Hi, Bibi." I walked over to her and kissed her vanilla-and-lavender-scented cheek. Her skin was a shade darker than my golden-bronze tone, and her hair under her hunter-green turban was short and gray. Other than that, we shared a number of the same features, especially our brown eyes.

She closed the leather portfolio before I had a chance to see what she'd been looking at. "Hello, Honeybee. How was your little outing?"

"It was great. Sarina and Amelia asked me to say hi to you."

Bibi smiled warmly at their names. Then the corners of her mouth tilted down, furrows forming between her brows. "I still can't believe that little girl's father wanted nothing to do with her because she was born with spina bifida."

Bibi frequently said that, though it never changed anything. And I doubted it would've made a difference even if Sarina hadn't been born with the spinal defect. He hadn't been interested in being a father, period.

Where was he now?

In an urn on his grandmother's mantel. Amelia had long since moved on, doing her best to give Sarina all the love and support a single mother could.

"You said you wanted to discuss something with me." Bibi stepped away from the window and set the closed portfolio on the corner of her neatly organized desk.

"Yes. I would like to create a line of dresses for girls. They would be classic, fairy-tale-style dresses for girls of all ages, up to and including teenagers, and would still keep with the company's vision."

"There are several companies who already do that. We've always focused on women in their late twenties and older. It doesn't make sense to diversify beyond that."

"I know, but these dresses aren't your typical dresses. They're designed specifically for girls with certain physical disabilities, and for girls who experience difficulty with their fine motor control, such as fastening buttons. They'll be easier to put on and do up. They won't irritate those individuals who are sensitive to something as simple as the way a label or seam might rub against their skin. They'll accommodate whatever aid the girl needs to be mobile, whether that be leg braces, crutches, or a wheelchair. And they'll make the girl feel like a princess—someone who doesn't have to settle for less.

"She can go to birthday parties or the prom or to the theatre with her family, and she'll know that she looks as beautiful as her non-disabled counterpart." I presented Bibi with my design portfolio.

She leafed through the pages, stopping long enough to study the sketches and to read the features of each dress.

"They're gorgeous designs, Nala, which comes as no surprise. But we're dealing with such a niche market, it wouldn't be viable."

Was that news to me?

Not at all.

It was precisely what the banks had told me when I approached them. While some were impressed with my background—a degree in fashion design and an MFA in Fashion

Marketing & Brand Management, both from the San Francisco Academy of Art—all had said the same thing: go talk to my grandmother.

She was my only hope.

"I understand the line won't bring in a lot of money. And we wouldn't produce the number of dresses we normally do with our other lines. That means the dresses would only be available online."

I had given the last point a lot of thought. As great as it would've been to have them available in select shops, it wasn't feasible. Most stores wouldn't be interested in carrying them because it was such a niche market.

Bibi continued flipping through the pages, reading my business and marketing plans.

The sinking sensation in my gut?

Definitely not a good sign.

After the minutes stretched into what felt like a lifetime, she handed the portfolio back to me. "I really don't think it will work. However"—she drew the word out with her dramatic flair, giving me a tiny ray of hope—"I will consider giving it a trial run on one condition."

"Anything." I said it a little too hastily, but this line of dresses had been a dream of mine for the past two years.

Bibi opened the lower drawer of the desk, riffled through the files, and removed a folded piece of paper. She passed it to me. "Do you recognize this?"

I opened the page and could've sworn my eyes widened to rival an owl's. "Where did you get this?" My gaze rescanned the bucket list I'd written in college.

Or rather, a black-and-white photocopy of the list. The original version had color illustrations sketched in the side margins.

"You have my permission to create the line of dresses, with you as the head designer. We can see what happens and evaluate in a year or two to decide if it will remain part of the company's portfolio."

I was about to fling my arms around her and tell her a million thank-yous—but she beat me to the punchline.

"However." The word punctured the air like a honey-covered bullet. "Before I grant you permission, you need to complete everything on that list." She nodded at the piece of paper in my hands. "And you've got three months to do it."

I stared at her, unblinking, positive I'd misheard her.

Bibi wasn't the kind of woman who made jokes, but maybe that was part of her early New Year's resolution. Her *very* early New Year's resolution, given it was six months and six days until the new year.

So, I did what anyone would do in this situation—I laughed.

Only Bibi didn't laugh with me.

All right—let's step back for a second and discuss my bucket list.

Did it contain death-defying feats such as skydiving?

Thank the Lord, no.

Item #1: Ride a horse (a real one, not a carousel horse).

Item #2: Go on a hayride.

So far it didn't sound too tough, right?

And it wasn't...if you didn't count the part where I didn't know anyone who owned a horse.

But it got better.

Or worse, depending on your perspective.

Item #3: Learn to make a beautiful cake (like a wedding cake).

Why did I put the previous point on the list? I had no idea. It might've been because one of my college roommates had been newly engaged, and we'd been flipping through her wedding magazines, discussing our dream weddings.

That was before the fiasco with the man who would later be my fiancé...and then ex-fiancé.

Item #4: Kiss in front of the Eiffel Tower.

A little problematic given I didn't have any plans to fly to Paris anytime within the next three months.

Item #5: A date with a hot hockey player.

Yep, no idea why that had made the list either. I hadn't known any hockey players at the time (and still didn't). And it wasn't as though the San Francisco Academy of Art had a collegiate hockey team.

But my friends had been hockey fans, and I guess the vodka coolers we'd been drinking had given me all kinds of ideas.

Hence item #6: Find a husband.

My gaze shifted from the list in my hand to my grandmother's smiling face—a smiling face with satisfaction clearly painted on it.

"And just so you know," she said, "he can't be a fake husband. So no pretending you got married. It has to be true love."

I hadn't thought my grandmother was going senile, but now I was having second thoughts. "You really expect me to fall in love and get married in less than three months?"

"Absolutely not. To fall in love requires you actually getting out and meeting men. Since you spend most of your time either here or in your apartment making dresses, I can guarantee there are no men in your life right now."

I inwardly huffed at that.

ACKNOWLEDGMENTS

First, I want to say a big thank you to everyone who has eagerly been awaiting Noah's story. I hoped you enjoyed reading it from both Noah's and Kate's point of views as much as I enjoyed writing it.

As always, Hang Le did a wonderful job designing the cover. Originally, she had picked a guy for it, but he looked too similar to the models in the first two covers. I decided because *Fix Me Up, Cowboy* is so different to those books, Kate needed to be on the cover. Hang found some sexy cowgirl images but they just weren't right. And then she found the picture that was perfect for the cover. She preformed her editing magic and voila.

I also want to thank my editor Bev Rosenbaum, as well as Hope and Jessica from Flat Earth Editing for the copyediting and proofreading. All three individuals helped make this book sparkle. Even though Bev's feedback resulted in me rewriting over half the book, her suggestions were right on. I especially owe Jessica a huge amount of gratitude. My experience with horses goes back to when I took weekly riding lessons as a kid in England, but English-style riding is very different to western. The equipment is different, too. Jessica is the one who makes sure I get the horse-related terminology correct for western-style riding.

Naturally, I can't forget Brenda St. John Brown who shared her own brilliant wisdom when it came to this book. She also talked me off the ledge when I wasn't sure about something. If you haven't already checked out her books, please do. They are so good!

The inspiration for Kate's dog Charlie came from another friend. Melanie and I first met almost two decades ago when our first-born sons ended up in NICU. She has a Cavalier King Charles Spaniel who is absolutely adorable. I wanted to write a story with the breed in it after falling in love with her dog. I looked it up and discovered they make great reading therapy dogs. And just like that, Charlie came into the world.

A huge thank you goes out to all my readers and fans of my books. I love each and every one of you. I couldn't imagine doing any other job. But what makes it especially wonderful is all the sweet and supportive comments you guys send me, whether it's on social media or via email.

And finally, I would like to thank my cheerleaders who have been there for me since the very beginning: my husband Ralph, our three teens, and our cat, Callie. My youngest teen was the inspiration behind Kate's love for interior design. Anja loves to spend her time on Pinterest, planning out her future house. She's got a great eye for it.

ABOUT THE AUTHOR

Born in Brighton England, Stina Lindenblatt has lived in a number of countries, including England, the U.S., Finland, and Canada. This would explain her mixed up accent. She has a kinesiology degree and a MSc in sports biological sciences.

In addition to writing fiction, she loves photography, and currently lives in Calgary, Canada, with her husband and three kids.

For news about her books and to sign up for her newsletter, check out her website at stinalindenblattauthor.com.

* 9 7 8 1 9 9 0 1 7 7 5 6 9 *